# Someone on the island
# is "acting out,"
# with murderous intent . . .

A jigger of tranquility is all Em Johnson wants, but now that her beloved Tiki Goddess Bar has been chosen as the location for *Trouble in Paradise*, TV's hot new reality show, life is anything but tranquil. When a member of the camera crew is found dead in her kitchen—stabbed to death with Chef Kimo's sashimi knife—the scene on the sleepy North Shore of Kauai goes from eccentrically crazy to downright dangerous. Suspects lurk behind every paper drink umbrella.

It's not enough that Chef Kimo is the number one suspect or that the life's-a-party Hula Maidens nearly burn down the place while dancing the hula with flaming coconuts. Em still has to deal with her Uncle Louie's wedding to the Black Widow—until his fiancée's Mercedes plunges into the Pacific. Roland Sharpe, handsome Hawaiian fire-dancing detective, warns the locals not to interfere, but Em and the madcap Maidens can't help themselves and soon wind up knee deep in danger again. Can the irrepressible troupe solve *three* murders before the champagne goes flat?

# The Tiki Goddess Series

Mai Tai One On

Two To Mango

Three To Get Lei'd

Too Hot Four Hula (2014)

# Three to Get Lei'd

Book 3: The Tiki Goddess Mysteries

by

## Jill Marie Landis

Bell Bridge Books

This is a work of fiction. Names, characters, places and incidents are either the products of the author's imagination or are used fictitiously. Any resemblance to actual persons (living or dead), events or locations is entirely coincidental.

Bell Bridge Books
PO BOX 300921
Memphis, TN 38130
Print ISBN: 978-1-61194-288-0

Bell Bridge Books is an Imprint of BelleBooks, Inc.

We at BelleBooks enjoy hearing from readers.
Visit our websites – www.BelleBooks.com and www.BellBridgeBooks.com.

10 9 8 7 6 5 4 3 2

Cover design: Debra Dixon
Interior design: Hank Smith
Photo credits:
Tiki (manipulated) © Annsunnyday | Dreamstime.com
Shrimp © Burlesck | Dreamstime.com
Knife (manipulated) © Dio5050 | Dreamstime.com
Drink (manipulated) © Dancingalligator | Dreamstime.com

:Lgtl:01:

Dear Readers,

Aloha from the land of palm trees, gentle breezes, rainbows, sunshine, Mai Tais, murder, mayhem, and the Hula Maidens.

The Hawaiian words used here and in the other *Tiki Goddess Mysteries* should be self-explanatory. Since there are only twelve letters in the Hawaiian alphabet, words often look alike but have many different meanings. Hawaiian words are not pluralized, so where I have written *leis, muumuus,* and have added an "s" for clarity, *kala mai,* pardon.

Slang phrases such as*: for reals, oh shoots, lots of stuffs,* and *choke* (meaning crowded . . . "It's choke in the ballroom.") might be mistaken for typos, but they aren't. "Lucky you live Kauai!" is also a local saying.

Though the Hula Maidens and the rest of the cast of characters, including David Letterman—the taste-testing parrot—spend lots of time with cocktails in hand, this is a work of fiction. Please drink responsibly and always, always have a designated driver, a taxi waiting, or have someone phone a friend for you when you have no business behind the wheel.

For more recipes, tips on island style living, tiki lore, and updates about what adventures await the Hula Maidens, please stop by and visit www.thetikigoddess.com

Until next time, Tiki On!

—*Jill Marie Landis*

"Life is full of ups and downs, honey. We have to celebrate every minute before we drain our last tiki mug."

—*Uncle Louie*

# 1

### Cue the Maidens!

*IS A JIGGER of tranquility really too much to ask for?*

Standing behind a twelve-foot koa wood bar, Em Johnson, manager of the Tiki Goddess on Kauai's North Shore, started prepping for the day ahead. After filling the ice bin, she sliced fruit for the sectional dish that held lime, pineapple, lemon slices, and maraschino cherries for the tropical concoctions tourists ordered in droves.

Across the room, Pat Boggs, better known as "Sarge," struggled to wrangle an incorrigible group of geriatric hula dancers into some semblance of order. The senior dancers, a.k.a the Hula Maidens, had stubbornly conned their way into becoming the featured act at the Goddess.

"Okay, you gol'danged left-footed boobies, shut up and get in line! You *do* know what a *line* is don't 'cha? It's show time!" Pat hollered.

Pat's voice grated on Em's nerves like nails on a chalkboard.

Em inhaled, closed her eyes, and slowly counted to ten. When she opened her eyes, she found herself staring up at Nat Clark, a full time television script writer and part-time Kauai resident from L.A. Nat owned the refurbished plantation cottage on the beach next door to the Goddess. A tall hedge separated his property from their parking lot.

"You look like you need a break already," he said.

"I was thinking about hiding at your place," Em said. "It would serve you right if the camera crew followed me over."

Nat watched the commotion across the barroom where the Maidens were trying not to fidget while a cameraman balanced a huge handheld camera on his shoulder. He panned across them and then filmed the three-piece band on the stage.

"You realize I haven't had a minute of peace since this whole thing started." Em opened a new box of colorful cocktail umbrellas and set it on the bar near the garnishes. Ever since the pilot for a reality show based on the Goddess had aired, the lives of everyone connected with the place had been turned upside down. The show had aptly been named *Trouble in Paradise.*

"Back the dancers out of the way. I want a close up of the Tiki Tones."

The cameraman fought to be heard over Pat's hollering.

"She takes her job seriously," Nat said.

"She does," Em agreed. "With little success."

They watched Pat try to herd the Maidens away from the stage. Outfitted for a full dress rehearsal, all of the dancers were garbed in pink cellophane grass skirts tied over neon-yellow spandex cat suits—very large, very neon, cat suits.

Pat waved her arms. "Move back, ya'll. Let the cameraman in, would'ya? Back up, I say. Can't cha hear?"

The line of dancers fell apart as Pat urged them toward the center of the room. Dressed in the worn cowboy boots, white socks, cargo shorts, and baggy Aloha shirt over a bleach-stained, faded tank top, Pat's appearance was gender non-specific. Her close-cropped hair and lack of makeup made it impossible to tell if she was a woman or a young man.

Pat was the first to admit she "Didn't give a good gol'durned turd" about it.

"She was enlisted to save the Maidens from themselves, and despite the odds, she's bound and determined to succeed . . . whether they like it or not. Most of the time they don't," Em said.

Nat watched one of the heftier Maidens adjust her cleavage by yanking at the neckline of her top and heaving it up.

"I didn't know spandex had that much give," he said.

"You can see why I'm ready to get out of here."

"My door is always open," he told Em. "Make yourself at home anytime."

"I was serious when I said the crew would probably follow me over to your place. Every time I turn around there's a camera in my face."

"That bad?"

"Worse than bad. Yesterday the producer said he'd give me a co-producing credit if I kept Little Estelle from yelling 'Call me Cougar!' every fifteen minutes."

"Cougar? She's what? Ninety?" Nat laughed.

"Ninety-two. It's not funny. The woman is a sex maniac. Want some coffee?" She offered.

"I'd love some."

She filled a thick ceramic mug with a dark Kona brew that smelled like ambrosia. Em carefully slid the mug across the bar.

"Looks delicious," he said.

"Cream?" She thought Nat looked sort of delicious himself.

"I'll take it black. I need a good jolt."

Em glanced over at the stage where everything was at a standstill. The Maidens argued with each other in hushed tones while Pat shot them all stink-eye. Bandleader Danny Cook and the Tiki Tones were working out the chorus of a new Hawaiian song. Em didn't speak the language, but even to the untrained ear she guessed they were murdering the pronunciation.

She turned back to Nat. "Need a shot of something in your coffee? How about some Bailey's?"

"Nope." He took a sip. "This will do it." Nat glanced at his watch. "It's only nine thirty. They're filming early this morning."

"When *aren't* they filming? Such is life now, no thanks to you."

*Trouble in Paradise* had been Nat's idea. Who doesn't dream of an exotic escape from real life, and what better setting than the always unpredictable atmosphere of a tiki bar on the outskirts of nowhere? He had been certain, and it turned out he was right. A big cable channel had picked up the show. As Em re-arranged the lime wedges in the divided dish on the bar, she wished she could have talked him out of it before it was too late.

"I still haven't completely forgiven you for pitching the idea," she said.

"I thought you finally approved."

"Oh, big Hollywood writer, have you conveniently forgotten that I had reservations about this?" she shot back. "But once you told my uncle about it, Louie was so gung ho I couldn't stand in the way."

Nat set his mug down. "I'm sorry, Em. I really thought *Trouble in Paradise* would be great for the Goddess and the whole North Shore economy."

"Oh, there's no denying the show is helping everyone's business, especially ours," she admitted. "Ever since the pilot aired, tourists have been flooding in. The parking lot is always jammed. Of course, the neighbors absolutely hate all the traffic, and I can't blame them. Before we even open our lot is half full with the production crew's cars and their van. The Maidens are determined to be on every minute of air time, so they're always finding an excuse to practice or just hang around here. The overflow parking clogs the highway."

"It's hard to miss all the No Parking signs up and down the road."

"For all the good they do." Em shrugged. "They're painted on every-thing that doesn't move: surfboards, trash cans, light posts, derelict cars."

"I especially like the mannequin hanging from a noose in that old mango tree a few lots down," he said.

"The one dressed like a tourist holding a sign that says Park Here and Die?"

"Well, it's straightforward and to the point."

Em rested her chin on her fist. Before the pilot aired, the Goddess had been more than a setting for the latest hit reality show. It was not only a tourist destination, but a North Shore institution through good times and bad, a place so many in the community likened to a second home. The Goddess was their port in a storm.

"Some of the locals have shied away from all the action, but we're still making money hand over fist," she admitted. "The Maidens are all cashing in on the show's popularity, too. But that's created another problem."

"Celebrity gone to their heads?"

"You got it. They're so obsessed with checking the numbers of Likes they're getting on their Facebook pages that they've let their dancing slip."

"They didn't have very far to fall," he noted.

"We're talking about worse than ever. Those women spend more time preening in front of the camera or online promoting themselves than they do practicing. They've gotten so lax that Sophie refuses to help them anymore."

Sophie Chin, Em's young bartender and former hula dancer, had taken pity on the Maidens a few times when they were in a bind and asked her to choreograph for them, but that was before they'd been tainted by life in the spotlight.

"They're bickering all the time," Em said. "Worse than ever."

Nat studied the six older women of all shapes and sizes between the ages of sixty-two and seventy-two as they filed on stage. Little Estelle, or Cougar as she now insisted on being called, was the oldest of the group and confined to a Gadabout motorized scooter. For the moment, she was parked in the corner, snoozing away while her daughter Big Estelle, an Amazon in her seventies, joined the others on stage.

Not only were all the dancers outfitted in neon spandex and cellophane grass skirts, but their neck waddles were wreathed in flower *lei*, their heads crowned with huge sprays of flowers and ferns.

Nat took a sip of coffee. "If I didn't know better, I'd think a floral delivery truck had collided with a senior citizens' van in the middle of your bar."

"I miss the good old days," she sighed.

Five months ago, before their little corner of Kauai was illuminated by the reality show spotlight, this time of day she would have been out enjoying a morning swim and thinking about heading into the office to book catering gigs or to tackle the billing.

Now, instead of enjoying the sunny morning, warm water, and balmy trade wind breezes, she was longing for ways to escape the voyeuristic camera crew.

"What's your Uncle Louie up to this morning?" Nat asked.

"He and Marilyn are discussing the wedding plans, *again*, over breakfast on the *lanai* at the house. The producer gave up on any real action over there and brought the lead crew in to film rehearsals for tonight's show. I think there's another cameraman in the kitchen hassling Kimo about the set up for later today." She sighed again. "Last night he threatened to quit."

"Kimo or the cameraman?"

"Kimo."

"You're kidding? He's always so laid back. What happened?"

Their half-Hawaiian chef never got flustered, even when the place was "choke" with people and orders backed up.

Em said, "The kitchen is small enough as it is without a camera, boom, and assistant producer wedged in there."

"I really am sorry I got you into this," Nat said.

"You didn't even end up working on the show."

"I had no idea my agent would come up with another gig for me so fast after *CDP* was cancelled. I'd have been crazy to sign on for *Trouble in Paradise* over a big prime time network show."

Nat had been a head writer on *Crime Doesn't Pay* until the long-running show was cancelled. Now he was writing for another television who-done-it. No matter how bad things were at the Tiki Goddess, Em didn't begrudge him the chance to win another Emmy.

"I know," she admitted. "But I still wish you were here to inject some common sense into the hokey storyline ideas the producer keeps coming up with. It was a shock to find out there's nothing *real* about reality TV."

He finished the coffee and passed the mug back to her.

"More?" she asked.

"No, thanks. I'm good," he said.

"Do you like your new show?"

"Love it," he said. "It was that or writing for a new musical spin-off of *Glee*."

"Really? A *Glee* spin-off?"

"It's about a group of musical twenty-somethings who work at a theme park. Guess what they're calling it?"

"No idea."

"*Whee*."

"I can see how you'd prefer cops and murders." She dropped his cup in soapy water in the wash bin. "Thankfully, things have been really slow here. Other than Uncle Louie's wedding, the producer has had to come up with his own ideas for a storyline. Randy's always complaining that something exciting better happen soon."

Nat interrupted, "Randy Rich?"

"The head producer and director."

"I heard through the grapevine that he's a real wild card."

"You heard right. He came up with tonight's show idea. The Maidens are to compete in a hula-off dressed in all that spandex. They each get to do a solo, and members of the audience can give them the gong. The last one standing wins. It's going to be a train wreck."

"Not to mention dangerous. A couple of those women would kill to win," Nat said. "I can see what Randy's up to, though. Ratings will soar if the Maidens end up in a cat fight in cat suits."

"Ratings." Em scoffed. "You're just like the rest of them."

"The rest of who?"

"Hollywood types. *Industry* people. The oh-so-hip, so cool, so now."

"TV is my bread and butter, Em."

Em glanced out a side window. Kimo, their chef, was hurrying as fast as a heavyset short man with a well-nurtured party ball around his waistline could hustle across the lot. He jumped into his gecko-green pickup truck and pulled out of the lot.

"Kimo must really need something fast. When he preps for lunch he usually asks me to run errands for him," she said.

"How are Louie and Marilyn's wedding plans coming along?" he asked.

"Unfortunately, right on schedule," she said. "The only hitch so far is that she hasn't heard from her nephew Tom. He's flying in to give her away."

"The guy who was visiting a while back? He sounds like a nice guy."

Em nodded. "He was her sister's only child. Everyone in the family is gone but them. He's as protective of her as I am my uncle. He flew over to celebrate the engagement."

"So he's not against this marriage like you and everyone else around here?"

"Am I that transparent?"

"No, actually. You hide it pretty well. I just get the feeling you'd rather Louie not marry her."

"Everybody calls her the Black Widow behind her back. You know Louie is going to make husband number five? Kiki vehemently abhors her because Marilyn used to dance with the Maidens, but she quit. Kiki and the others doubt her motives for marrying Uncle Louie."

Kiki Godwin, leader of the Hula Maidens and wife of Kimo the chef, was as protective of Em's uncle as she was the bar, which she considered her turf.

"Maybe fifth time's the charm."

Em shrugged. "Marilyn likes being on camera 24/7. She kept plugging her event planning business during the tapings of *Trouble in Paradise,* and it worked. Lockhart's Luxury Events bookings are way up since the pilot aired."

"Just wait until the weekly episodes start."

"I can't imagine living with this for weeks on end. They shot two months of footage just to get enough material on film for a two hour pilot."

Nat shrugged. "Look at *Swamp People*. Who knew shooting alligators in the head over and over again would catch on? And what about *Honey Boo Boo*? If people get hooked on *Trouble in Paradise*, it could run for years."

Em groaned. "If this keeps up, I'll be hiring a 'gator hunter to 'choot' me in the head."

There was a blissful lull in the racket near the stage, but the silence was quickly filled by the sound of Sophie Chin's rust bucket Honda pulling into the lot. The ancient vehicle was held together with duct tape and Bondo, the air conditioner didn't work, and the whole thing rattled when it rolled. Sophie had named the car Shake and Bake and was always threatening to junk it and walk to work.

One of Kiki Godwin's many talents was car repair. She'd already replaced the carburetor and the timing belt before she declared Shake and Bake unworthy of any more spare parts.

Em glanced at her watch. If Kimo wasn't back in a few minutes, he'd be way behind on the lunch prep.

"How about we have dinner together soon?" Nat asked. "The least I can do is take you away from here for a few hours."

"The very least."

She'd gone out with Nat a couple of times. He was a genuinely nice guy, a great conversationalist, and easy on the eyes. As a writer he asked a lot of questions and had the ability to get her to open up more than she had with anyone else since she'd moved to Kauai.

With thick, wavy brown hair, square jaw and inquisitive blue eyes behind tortoiseshell glasses, Nat was undeniably attractive, but so far he hadn't ignited any real sparks. Then again, after her recent messy divorce, she wasn't anxious to get burned again.

Nat was waiting for an answer.

"I'd love to go out for dinner," she said. "As long as there's no camera crew."

"Positive."

"Great. How about Tuesday?"

A bloodcurdling scream stopped the uneven beat of the snare drum and instantly halted the Maidens' bickering. The silence was deafening.

Em and Nat ran into the kitchen and found Sophie standing over the body of Bobby Quinn, one of the two cameramen filming *Trouble in Paradise*.

The huge camera was on the floor beside Bobby, who was staring sightless at the ceiling. Blood oozed from beneath the knife in his chest, slowly forming a puddle.

Nat knelt down and touched the side of the man's neck, then gently closed the young man's eyes.

"He's dead." Nat looked up at Sophie.

"Oh my God!" Em turned to Sophie, too. "What happened?"

"Don't look at me." Sophie took a step back. She ran a hand through her spiked hair which was dyed black and tinted with neon-purple highlights. "I walked in and almost fell over him." Her dark almond-eyed gaze darted around the kitchen. "Where's Kimo?"

"Gone. I saw him." Em stopped abruptly and quickly lowered her voice. "I saw him run out and jump into his truck a few minutes ago."

"Uh, oh," Sophie said.

"You think *he* did this?" Nat asked.

"*Kimo?* No way," Em and Sophie both answered at once.

Pat Boggs appeared in the doorway, took one look at the body, and halted. Behind her, the Maidens, along with Randy Rich and his crew, were clamoring to get in. Kiki shouted Kimo's name over and over at the top of her lungs. Pat quickly assessed the situation, spun around, and blocked the doorway with outstretched arms.

"None of you suckers is getting by me, so just cool your jets. There ain't nothing in here you need to see *or* film."

"That's Kimo's special sashimi knife." Sophie pointed to the blade sticking out of the cameraman's chest. There were Japanese characters carved into the wooden handle. "The one *nobody* is allowed to touch."

"Kimo! Kimo, are you all right?" Kiki yelled over Pat's shoulder. Kiki and Kimo had been married for longer than anyone could recall.

"Let her in, Pat." Em knew Kiki would be frantic. Kiki on a tear was worse than letting her in.

Kiki came barreling in, a tempest in neon and shredded cellophane. She took one look at the dead man on the floor and shouted, "Where's Kimo?"

"He's not here." Em took her phone out of her shorts pocket and hit 911. The dispatcher came on immediately.

"There's been a murder," Em said. "This is Em Johnson. Yes, at the Tiki Goddess Bar in Haena. Yes. We're sure he's dead. A knife wound to the chest. Right. We're not going anywhere." She looked down. "And neither is he," she mumbled.

Bobby Quinn had only been a member of the crew for a couple of weeks. He seemed like a personable kid who was thrilled to be on assignment in Hawaii, but Em hadn't had much time to really talk to him.

The minute Em hung up Kiki said, "That looks like Kimo's sashimi knife."

"It is," Sophie confirmed.

"Nobody's supposed to touch it. *Ever*," Kiki said.

"Ever," Sophie nodded.

"Was anyone else here when you walked in?" Nat asked Sophie.

"No. There was no one in the parking lot. I didn't come directly into the kitchen, though. I walked in through Louie's office to ask Kimo if he needed help. I almost tripped and fell over"—she looked down at Bobby and shivered—"*him.*"

Louie's office door was still ajar. In a minute or two someone in the bar would remember they could get into the kitchen through the office.

Em gestured toward the office door. "Lock it," she said. "Quick."

Sophie closed the door and punched the lock on the handle.

Kiki clutched the sides of her cellophane skirt in her hands and pressed her fists against her temples. Pink cellophane appeared to be spraying out of her temples. Her eyes were bugging out.

"Kimo's been k-k-kidnapped," she stuttered. "Someone killed this guy and stole my Kimo."

"Who would want to kidnap Kimo?" Em wondered aloud. "Besides, I saw him drive away."

"They were probably hidden in his truck, on the floor or something. S-s-someone wants his recipes." Kiki was focused on a kidnapping. "They're all top secret."

Em averted her gaze from the body to watch Kiki with concern. The last time the woman had lost it, she started speaking gibberish.

"Have you got any Xanax in your purse, Kiki?"

Kiki shook her head. "No. But may-be-be some . . . vodka . . . woo-would . . . help."

"No vodka. Not yet." Em glanced down at Bobby Quinn. "Maybe we should cover him with a tablecloth," she suggested.

"Don't touch anything," Nat advised.

Em figured he knew best. He'd worked with forensics and police procedural experts for years on his last show.

Pandemonium had broken out in the bar. Randy Rich was at the door to the kitchen hollering around the stalwart Pat at the top of his lungs.

"Let me in there, or so help me I'll press charges! Your uncle signed a contract, Em. Nothing is off limits. You're violating the terms of the agreement. Let us through!"

"No one is goin' in until I get the gold-danged go-ahead." Pat clung to the door frame keeping Randy and crew at bay.

Em had never really appreciated Pat as much as now.

"Stand your ground," Em encouraged.

"You got it." Pat nodded without turning around.

Nat asked Em, "You agreed to let them film anything they wanted?"

"No, Uncle Louie did. He would let them film him cleaning lint out of his navel, which until a few minutes ago, was the most exciting thing going on around here."

"Wait until your detective hears *this* over the dispatch," Sophie whispered to Em.

Em pictured Roland Sharpe, a tall, dark, and hunky KPD detective, and groaned.

"He's not going to believe there's been another murder tied to the Goddess."

"Why not? There were five in the last year. This place is connected to more bodies than a morgue."

"Maybe we should have the place blessed," Sophie suggested.

"It's not the bar," Em reminded her. "Technically, only one body was ever found here, and it was dumped in our *luau* pit. It had nothing to do with us."

"What's going on out there?" Nat wondered. The barroom had gone deathly still.

Pat, still clinging to the door frame, called over her shoulder. "They're doing an end run around the outside of the building!"

Em was headed for the open back door but didn't make it before the *Trouble in Paradise* crew poured through with Joe Piscoli, the first cameraman, leading the way. Producer Randy Rich blustered in and tossed a clipboard at the young female assistant producer, Peggy Denton. Kiki was huddled in a corner, frantically tapping her cell phone.

The cameraman gasped when he saw the victim but quickly recovered enough to zoom in on his fallen comrade.

"Who screamed?" Randy Rich, shorter than the others, tried to see around Joe. "I think we caught it on the recording, but we may have to re-loop."

"Get a close up of all that blood oozing onto the floor." Peggy the PA leaned over Joe's shoulder.

"You people are sickos. I'll be behind the bar if you need me." Sophie nudged aside Pat who continued to hold the Maidens back, and slipped into the barroom.

"I heard you were an ass, Randy, but for the love of Pete, quit filming," Nat urged.

Somewhere in his mid-thirties, Randy Rich was producer, director, and the oldest member of the crew. He was short, already balding, and portly. "And who are you, exactly?"

Nat adjusted his tortoiseshell glasses. "Nat Clark. I live next door."

"Oh, yeah. I recognize the name. You write scripts for prime time, right? Well, this is real life, Clark," he told Nat. "Not the made-up crap you crank out for the networks."

Joe filmed their testy exchange while the young female PA looked like she was going to vomit.

Em felt sorry for her. Like Sophie, Peggy was in her early twenties, but in braids and a baseball cap, she didn't look a day over fifteen.

"Are you going to be sick?" Em asked her.

"Don't you dare!" Rich yelled. He nudged his cameraman. "Don't you dare puke until Joe can get a close up of it."

"What's going on in there?"

Em recognized her uncle Louie's voice outside the back door. The crew scooted around to film his uncensored reaction.

"Where's Em? Is she all right?" Usually laid back, Louie sounded almost frantic.

"I'm all right," Em assured him. "Don't come in."

Too late, seventy-year-old Louie Marshall had already reached the back steps. So had his fiancée, Marilyn Lockhart. She quickly scooted under the broad leaf of a banana plant near the building. The Black Widow was protecting her latest Botox and lip injections from the morning sun. The camera was rolling.

"I'm coming in," Louie said.

Em took a deep breath as he stepped over the threshold. "One of the cameramen is dead, Uncle Louie."

Louie Marshall stopped in his tracks and stared at the body. "Is that Bobby? He was only twenty-five. I told him he should quit smoking."

Em looked to Nat, silently pleading for help.

"Someone stabbed him, Louie," Nat said.

"To *death*?" Marilyn had also pushed her way in. She swallowed hard and covered her mouth with her hand.

"He's pretty dead," Nat nodded.

"Who did it?" Louie asked.

"No idea," Nat said.

"What about Kimo? Is he all right?" Louie's head was on a swivel. "Where is Kimo?"

"He's not here." Em had lowered her voice before she realized it didn't matter. The film crew was taping every word of their exchange. "Why don't you and Marilyn go back to the house, Uncle Louie?"

He ignored her.

Louie was growing frantic. "Whoever killed Bobby kidnapped Kimo!"

"Kimo drove away," Em said.

Kiki rejoined the fray. "Did you see for certain that Kimo was alone? I think Louie's right."

Louie drew himself up to his full six-three. With his deep tan, full head of snow-white hair, Hawaiian shirt, and white linen pants, he looked like an ambassador for the Hawaii Tourist Authority.

"Kimo is the best chef on Kauai," Louie said. "Since the pilot aired, people have been flocking in to taste his food. Everyone is raving about it."

"Exactly!" Kiki said.

Louie smoothed his hand over his white hair and turned to the camera, his expression somber. He pulled his cell phone out of the pocket of his baggy linen pants and held it up.

"I'll bet we'll get a ransom demand any minute now," he said.

Kiki turned to the camera. "If there's some kind of chef slave trade, they'll ask for millions. Or more."

"I'll pay it. I'll pay anything," Louie said.

Em rolled her eyes. Louie had a habit of spending money he didn't have.

"Maybe some egomaniacal billionaire will pay them a fortune and lock Kimo up in a mansion," Kiki said. "Force him to cook for them."

"Oh, the horror." Nat shook his head.

"He wasn't kidnapped, I tell you. I saw him leave in his truck a few minutes ago," Em said again. "Alone."

"That's odd." Marilyn licked her lips and made certain her best side was turned toward the camera. "He's supposed to be prepping for lunch."

The shrill whine of sirens sounded in the distance. Em glanced at her watch and tried to ignore the way Kiki was glaring at Marilyn.

"That was fast," Em said.

Within minutes, two KPD squad cars pulled into the lot with two officers in each. The production crew closed in on them until the senior officer told them to back off. Two uniformed policemen stepped into the kitchen. The younger one walked over to the body, knelt down, felt for the victim's pulse.

"Dead, all right." The officer stood up, then stepped to the back door. The Maidens had congregated outside in the parking lot and were clinging to each other, arms linked, faces shadowed with worry. Little Estelle was behind them driving in circles on the Gadabout.

"I'm going to walk all you folks back around to the main room. Nobody leaves the premises until an officer has interviewed you," the officer said.

Louie smiled up at the young man in his navy KPD uniform. He filled the kitchen doorway. "By now we know the drill, son."

Randy Rich gave him a keep-on-talking signal, and Louie went on without missing a beat.

"We're used to this sort of thing, you see. Last year our neighbor was killed." Louie made a hacking motion with his hand. "Took a machete chop to the head, and then his lifeless body was tossed into our *luau* pit. My niece was kidnapped by a psycho who killed Fernando, the famous pianist. He's the one who took over for Liberace in Las Vegas. We were catering

Fernando's party the night he was conked in the head with a rock." Louie executed an exaggerated conking move. "We catered his memorial. We have quite an extensive catering menu, from *pupus* to full-on four-course meals."

"Excuse me, Uncle Louie." Em cut him off.

Outside, two officers were closing off the parking lot with yellow crime scene tape. Cars were jamming the highway out front, so people were parking and walking up on foot. Between the Maidens making cell phone calls and the report going out on the police scanner, news was traveling on the coconut wireless as fast as Category 5 hurricane winds.

"Maybe you should stand on the front *lanai* and tell folks we're closed, Uncle Louie," Em suggested.

He blinked at her. "But . . . we *never* close."

"Believe me, nobody will want anything that comes out of the kitchen today." Em avoided looking at Bobby's bloody shirt front.

Louie stared into the camera again and smiled.

"No matter what happens here at the Tiki Goddess, we *always* serve drinks," he said. "Naturally, I'll start working on a commemorative cocktail to add to our already extensive tropical drink menu. But until it's been taste tested and approved by David Letterman, my expert taste-testing macaw, we'll be featuring our other beverage favorites. Two-for-one Mai Tais might be a good idea right now."

The youngest officer glanced at the camera and then pulled Louie aside.

"The less people we have in here the better, Uncle. Maybe talk about the drinks later, yeah?"

"But, if folks come by to see what's up, they need to know about the specials," Louie said.

"This isn't live, remember? We're taping," Randy Rich reminded him. "This stuff won't air for a couple months."

Marilyn stepped up and took Louie's arm. "Come on, sweetie. I'll go out to greet the crowds with you." She glanced over her shoulder at the camera crew. "My experience as owner of Lockhart's Luxury Events has taught me how to handle any last minute crisis, large or small."

Em pulled out her cell phone and turned her back on the camera crew. She punched in Kimo's number, but his voicemail picked up.

"Don't use your cell, Em," Louie advised. "We should keep all lines of communication open for the ransom call."

# 2

## Kiki Barely Hangs On

SWEATING WORSE than the day she'd gotten naked and wrapped herself in Saran Wrap to surprise Kimo at the front door, Kiki tugged at the plunging neckline of her spandex cat suit. She was dripping wet, fighting to maintain her sanity. Trapped in such close proximity to Marilyn Lockhart only added to her stress.

Looking far too smug and put together in a tropical silk ensemble, Marilyn paused on her way out the door and pointed at Kiki. "That's *her* husband's sashimi knife." She smiled up at young police office.

Silence thudded around the kitchen.

"Someone stole Kimo's kn-n-knife!" Kiki finally managed. "You don't think *he* did it, do you, Marilyn?" Kiki longed to close her hands around the woman's throat and squeeze.

Em stepped between them.

"I saw him get in his pickup and drive off a few minutes before Sophie walked in and found the body," Em said. "He was probably headed into Hanalei on an errand."

"Well, that's certainly odd for this time of day," Marilyn chirped.

"Shut up, Marilyn." Kiki opened and closed her fists. "Shut up now, or I swear . . ."

Glancing up at the boom mic suspended on a pole above her head, Kiki was suddenly aware of the camera again as Joe angled in on them. If she didn't get a grip on herself, someday in the very near future, the whole world would be watching her strangle the Black Widow.

Censoring herself had never been one of her many talents, but for Kimo's sake, Kiki clammed up and took a deep breath. She needed to get out of the spandex. She needed a four-olive vodka martini. It was only ten in the morning, but somehow her life had just careened off the rails.

"I've got to go," she decided. "Now."

"You can't," Louie reminded her. "The police have ordered everyone to stay put. They have to—"

"Interview us all. I know the drill. By now we all know it," Kiki said.

A small whimper escaped Marilyn. She batted her eyelashes at the camera. "I certainly hope this doesn't delay our wedding."

Kiki leaned in closer. "Working up some fake tears to go with those eyelashes, Marilyn? I can't imagine you letting a little thing like a murder stand in the way of your wedding. Besides, you're not holding the reception here anyway."

Kiki was still miffed that Louie had given into his fiancée and let her throw the wedding and reception at the St. Lexus, the ultra-swanky five star hotel in nearby Princeville, and not on the beach behind the Goddess.

Then again, the Goddess had been founded by Louie's late wife, Irene Kakaulanipuakaulani Hickam Marshall. As far as the locals were concerned, Louie getting married to a woman like Marilyn Lockhart in Irene's beloved establishment would have added insult to injury.

Kiki had suspected the Black Widow's motives ever since Marilyn started dating Louie. Kiki could never trust someone who could defect from the Hula Maidens in order to join a more highly regarded hula troupe.

Kiki turned to the officer. "I have to be the first one interviewed," she said. "I can't sit around. I have a million and one things to do."

*Like find Kimo and find him fast.* She was headed toward the door when a middle aged, heavy-set officer walked up to her. He was one of the musicians who jammed at the Wednesday afternoon ukulele sessions at the dump.

"You're married to Kimo Godwin, right?" the patrolman asked.

Kiki warned herself to stay calm. Last time she lost her cool in an emergency, she wound up speaking gibberish and nearly had a stroke. She opened her mouth, and nothing came out. She closed her eyes, took a deep breath, and tried again.

"Yes-s. I am . . . and I c-can assure you he didn't do this."

# 3

### Em's Private Detective Shows Up

By the time Em escaped into the shady interior of the bar, the sun was blazing down outside, and the air was thick with humidity. Kimo still hadn't returned. Looking worried and frazzled, her hair sticking out in all directions, Kiki had retreated to a table across the room. Nat was still outside with the officers.

Randy Rich and his PA were huddled at a table in the corner, frantically revamping their storyboards. One of the assistant directors was outside with Joe the cameraman taping individual interviews of the Maidens, calling the women out of the bar one by one. The uniformed officers had finally convinced Louie to shut down the Goddess.

Em hung the CLOSED sign out on the front *lanai*. She was turning away rental cars full of tourists, but they just kept coming. The highway was jam-packed.

The kitchen was just as crowded now that it was swarming with officers, a forensic specialist, and the coroner's crew. With the parking lot closed to all but official traffic, the highway in front of the Goddess was full. They may not have been able to get close, but everyone on the North Shore had to drive by and have a look anyway.

The Maidens were scattered around the bar in their dance costumes awaiting their turn for an interview with a police officer or in front of the camera. Some lounged with their feet up on the long banquette seats. Others were seated at tables. Danny and the Tiki Tones were still working out a new number. Pat Boggs was snoring with her head on a table by the front door.

Little Estelle Huntington had slept through the earlier commotion, but now she was wide awake. After parking her motorized Gadabout directly under a fan, she had propped her laptop on a tray attached to the front of the steering bar and was busy answering emails she received on various dating sites she had joined after the pilot aired.

Every few minutes the former Rockette would pump her fist over her head and yell, "Whoohoo! Another hit. Call me Cougar!"

"Disgusting," Sophie said as Em joined her behind the bar.

"The fact that she's getting online match ups? Or the way she growls after she yells 'cougar'?" Em asked.

"I've seen photos of some of her prospective dates," Sophie said.

"Bad?"

"Let's just say scary."

The Maidens waiting for turns to be interviewed were growing restless. Flora Carillo, on the light side of two hundred and fifty pounds, was a mountain encased in neon yellow. She had stripped off her cellophane grass skirt.

Since her sudden fame on cable TV, tourists were flocking into the trinket shop Flora had owned in Hanalei for years. She'd convinced Louie to go into producing a line of Tiki Goddess paraphernalia with her. The barware, cocktail napkins, coasters, and T-shirts were flying out the door faster than free bags of rice at the Walmart opening.

Big Estelle was one of the only Maidens who hadn't taken advantage of their sudden stardom. She spent all her time fending off her mother's online predators.

"We bettah get to leave soon. It's like a sauna in here." Flora fanned herself with a drink menu. "An' I gotta pick up an order of mugs at the post office."

Big Estelle turned to Flora. "Mugs?"

"Tiki Goddess mugs. I'm betting they sell better than the T-shirts and beer bottle openers." Flora called out to Em, "Is it okay if I use your Wifi? I wanna see how many new friends I got on Facebook today. Too bad I didn't take a picture of the dead guy to post."

"Can't anyone stop them?" Sophie arched her right brow. It was pierced with a row of silver rings. She turned away from the Maidens in disgust and filled a glass of ice water for herself.

"Overnight fame is ugly," Em whispered. "Dog ugly."

"Well, *there's* one thing that's not ugly." Sophie nodded toward the front door. "Your detective is here."

Sophie had started calling Roland Sharpe "Em's detective" the night they discovered their neighbor's body smoldering in the *luau* pit and the handsome *hapa* detective had showed up.

Em admired Roland as he crossed the room. If the heat bothered him, it didn't show. He was cool, somber, and all business as he slipped his sunglasses into his Aloha shirt pocket and pulled a small black notebook out of his back pocket. She watched him scan the room until his gaze stopped on her. *Spark time.*

Naturally a guy like Roland gave off sparks; he moonlighted as a fire knife dancer. Few men could compete with somebody who stripped down, oiled up, and twirled blazing knives.

He walked straight to the bar, nodded at Sophie, but never took his focus off of Em. She tried not to blush and give herself away.

"Really, Em? Again?" he asked.

"You think I like this?"

Suddenly Randy and the crew were headed toward them. The detective held up his hand like a traffic cop.

"Stop right there, and shut that thing off."

Randy kept coming. Joe kept filming.

Roland didn't take a step. Nor did he raise his voice. He didn't have to. His expression spoke volumes.

"Turn it off."

The camera light went off. No one moved.

Roland turned to Em. "Where's Kimo? Anyone seen or heard from him?"

"No. What have you heard?"

"Officer Shun briefed me. One victim. Stabbed to death. The weapon allegedly belonged to Kimo Godwin, and Kimo isn't around to explain."

Kiki was suddenly on her feet, pounding across the room.

"That doesn't mean anything, Roland," she said. "Someone obviously stole Kimo's knife."

"Not that obvious." The small black notebook Roland always carried was suddenly open, and he had a pen in hand. "Where did he go?"

"I have no idea." Kiki hiked her chin.

Roland turned to Em.

"Me, either," she shrugged.

"When did he leave?"

"No idea. We were almost on stage ready to rehearse for tonight's dance off," Kiki began.

"Dance off?" The pen in Roland's hand paused above the notebook.

"That was his idea." Kiki pointed at Randy Rich.

Roland glanced at the Maidens scattered around the room and shook his head at Randy. "A dance off? Between these ladies? You should be ashamed."

Roland turned to Em. "Did you see Kimo leave?"

Reluctantly, she nodded. "Yes."

"When?"

"Around nine thirty. I was at the bar setting up when I saw him walk across the side lot. He drove off in his truck."

"You're sure of the time?"

"I looked at my watch because he's usually busy prepping for the lunch crowd in the morning. I wondered where he was going."

"Thanks a lot, Em." Kiki glared.

"I figured he needed something from the store." Em shrugged.

"So is that usual?" Roland asked. "For him to take off while he's working?"

Kiki answered before Em. "If he ran out of something, of course. Why not?"

Roland waited for Em to respond. She wanted to help Kimo but pictured herself wired to a polygraph.

"Usually he just makes do. He's really creative." When she realized she might have incriminated Kimo, she added, "He's the nicest man alive, Roland. He didn't do this."

"Of course not," Kiki snapped. "Why would he?"

Em had nearly forgotten Sophie was there until the girl spoke up.

"For one thing, he hates the cameramen invading his space."

Kiki turned on Sophie. "Not enough to *kill* one, for heaven's sake!"

"Did Kimo have a beef with the guy?" Roland asked Randy Rich.

The producer shoved his thick glasses up the bridge of his nose.

"All the time. He didn't want us in the kitchen. Said it was too small for the crew. He couldn't work. Yesterday I told him we have the right to film, and if he locked us out he was violating the contract."

Em watched Roland make a note and wondered exactly what he was writing in his precise handwriting.

"So Kimo specifically had a beef with the cameramen?"

Joe Piscoli nodded. "Yeah, with both of us. He didn't exactly make it easy to film in the kitchen."

"What was the victim filming this morning?" Roland asked.

Joe shrugged. "All the action was in the bar. I have no idea what he was doing in there."

Randy Rich said, "I sent Bobby in to find out what the lunch special was going to be. It was taking a while, so I figured he'd gone to the john."

Kiki shook her head distractedly. "J-John who?"

"Not John. *The* john," Roland said. "The *lua*."

"Ah, *the* john," she nodded.

Em tried to come up with something to say in Kimo's defense when Kimo himself suddenly came strolling in carrying a box of mangoes. He was accompanied by a handsome young uniformed patrolman who was busy checking out Sophie. The word Shun was printed on his bronze nametag.

"What's going on?" Kimo asked Kiki. He gazed at the somber assembly. "How come we're closed?"

"Where have you been?" Kiki grabbed hold of his Tiki Goddess T-shirt sleeve. "Why didn't you answer your cell? I've been trying to call you."

"It's outta juice." He turned toward Roland. "What's up, bra?"

"Let's sit." Roland nodded toward an empty table in the corner near the front *lanai.* "I need to ask you a few questions."

"Sure." Kimo shrugged his beefy shoulders.

Kiki yelled, "No! Don't say anything. Not without a lawyer present."

Kimo's forehead creased with more rows of lines than a winter swell rolling over the ocean.

"What are you talking about?"

"Somebody killed the new cameraman," Kiki blurted. "Everybody thinks you did it."

"I don't," Em protested.

"Nobody does, Kiki," Sophie added.

Roland looked to Em for help.

"Come on, Kiki." She tried to pry the woman's fingers off Kimo's shirt. "Let Roland talk to Kimo alone."

Kimo started to hand the heavy box of mangoes over to Sophie. As she reached for the box, the young patrolman moved toward her.

"I'll take those," he offered.

Em couldn't help but notice the way the patrolman was smiling at Sophie.

"Thanks. You can set them on the bar," she told him.

As the young officer walked away, Sophie winked at Em and whispered, "Maybe I'll have my own policeman, just like you."

"I'm not leaving him alone," Kiki told Roland. "Surely you don't mind. I mean, we're all family, aren't we?"

Roland looked to Em. "You have somewhere we can all talk in private? How about Louie's office?"

"Sure." She led them into the office.

"Roland?" Kiki crossed her arms and tapped her foot.

"You can stay as long as you don't say a word. One word, and you're out," he told her.

Em started to leave, but Roland's expression all but shouted for her to stay and manage Kiki. Randy and the crew appeared on the threshold.

"Hold it right there. This is official police business." Roland closed the door in their faces. Em expected to hear sounds of protest, but none came.

"Anyone want to sit?" Roland waited. No one did. He turned to Kimo, ready to take notes.

"Tell me about your morning."

"All of it?"

"Right up until now."

Kimo rubbed his close-cropped dark hair. "I got up, came to work. Around eight this guy from some new vegetable supplier showed up. Gave me his card." Kimo pulled a creased business card out of his front pocket. "His name's on the back. You can keep it," Kimo said.

Roland glanced down at the card.

"How long was he here?"

"I don't know, a few minutes maybe. Brought in some samples, kale and Chinese parsley." Kimo shrugged. "I told him we like our current supplier just fine, but I promised to keep his card."

"What was he driving?"

"I dunno. I didn't see. Probably a van. They all drive vans."

"Did you see it in the lot?"

Kimo shook his head no. "Probably around the side of the building. Guys with big delivery trucks don't like to try to turn around or back out of the parking lot. The fish guy pulled in, and the vegetable guy left when I went out to pick up the fish order from the guy."

"You know him? The fish guy?"

"Who doesn't?" Kimo shrugged. "His company supplies all the restaurants on this side."

Roland asked for the fish distributor's driver's name and number and wrote them down.

"No one else went in and out of the kitchen this morning?"

"Just the veggie guy, the fish guy, and me. And the dead guy. But I guess technically, he didn't go out. He's still in there."

"Where was the cameraman when you went to get mangoes?"

"He was walking around the kitchen, trying to figure out where there was enough room for him and that humongous camera to fit."

"Alive and well."

"Definitely."

"I heard you had a beef with him."

Kimo shook his head. "I blew up at them all the other night. You saw how small the kitchen is. Can you imagine me trying to work, Em and Sophie running in and out, Kiki coming in for one thing and another . . ."

"Hey," Kiki said.

". . . and then there's the cameraman and that Peggy chick, and sometimes Randy wants to squeeze in too. Hell with it, I said. I'm under pressure now that we are so crowded. I don't do anything interesting enough to film. I told them so." He looked down at the floor for a second and then back at Roland. "I told them to stay out of my kitchen. Not in a nice way."

"Thanks, Kimo. That's all for now."

"For now?" Kiki had been about to burst. "What do you mean for now?"

"Come on." Em took Kiki's arm. "Let's go back out to the bar. Roland's got to help the officers interview everyone else too."

"Hey, Roland, I didn't do it," Kimo assured him. "And if I did. I sure as hell wouldn't have used my best sashimi knife."

THE REST OF the interviews were painfully slow. Em tried to keep the Maidens and Tiki Tones from revolting and charging out the door. Roland didn't want anyone inebriated before he and the other officers could interview them, so she served soft drinks and juices.

Kiki, cut off from her ten a.m. martini, was ready to blow and was fidgeting on a barstool, watching as Roland walked up to Kimo to say something she couldn't hear.

Kimo walked over to join her.

"What happened? What did he just say to you?" Kiki patted the carved tiki barstool next to hers. Kimo sat.

"He said don't leave the island."

"*What-t-t?*" Kiki's face flushed red as a rooster's comb. "What's that supposed to mean?"

Kimo shrugged. "Calm down. It'll be okay. Bobby was alive when I left. That's all I know."

"Don't worry, Kimo," Em said. "Everybody knows you're innocent."

"Don't *worry*? Somebody used my best knife to kill the guy," he said.

"We'll get you another one." Kiki patted the back of his meaty hand.

"You two might as well go home," Em said. "We're going to be closed until tomorrow. Maybe longer."

"You sure?" Kimo glanced toward the kitchen.

"Definitely," Em said.

"We never close." Kimo echoed Louie's earlier statement.

"We do today," Em said. "How about taking a few mangoes with you?"

Free mangoes. It was all the comfort she could offer.

"Naw." Kimo shook his head. "Not now."

"Let's go," Kiki urged. She glanced at her watch. "It's meatloaf Monday. We can have a nice lunch at C.J.'s. We'll leave your truck here, and I'll take my car up to Princeville."

"Meatloaf?" He shook his head. "I'm the number one suspect in a murder, and you want to go out for *meatloaf*? You go. I'm heading home."

# 4

## Strange Brew

Kimo and Kiki bickered over meatloaf as they walked out together. A few minutes later, Roland approached the bar and sat down in front of Em.

"If you'd like to come over to the house, I'll fix you lunch," she offered. "You can get away from this for a few minutes."

"Can't while the coroner's still here. I'm going to have a couple officers finish up the interviews. Basically none of the Maidens saw anything. They were all rehearsing in the bar together."

Em nodded. "Right."

"The rest of the crew was accounted for. Louie and Marilyn were together in the house."

"The only one in the kitchen was Kimo before he left."

Em toyed with a cardboard coaster with the Tiki Goddess logo on it.

"He didn't do it, Roland. I'll never believe it."

"He's the only one with even a hint of a motive. He had a beef with the guy, didn't want any cameramen in the kitchen with him. He took off somewhere right before or after the murder—within seconds either way. The victim was stabbed with Kimo's knife. We'll see what prints we can pick up."

"Of course Kimo's will be on it."

"Along with someone else's, if we get lucky."

"Hopefully."

"No one else was around. If someone on the crew had a problem with Bobby, no one is admitting it. Why would anyone want him dead?"

"He's new to the crew, hasn't been on island very long. Maybe someone followed him over from the mainland. Someone with a grudge," Em said.

Roland shook his head. "Doubtful that a hit man would try to kill him with all of you right here in the bar."

"There would be a lot more suspects, and the bar would be involved in more scandal."

"Anyone could have walked in on the murder."

"Thank heaven no one did. They could have been killed too." Em took a deep breath and let it go. "He seemed like a really upbeat guy. He didn't even mind that he couldn't stay with the rest of the crew."

"What do you mean?"

"The budget is tight, so they put him up at the Haena Beach Resort and not the St. Lexus in Princeville with the rest of them. He was so excited to work in Hawaii he didn't even care. I feel terrible for his family. We have to find whoever did this, Roland."

He stared at her for so long Em started to blush.

"*We?* I don't like the look on your face," he said. "It's making me nervous."

"What do you mean?"

"Do I need to remind you of the *pilikia* you and your friends get into whenever you start trying to help me do my job?"

"Last time you actually asked for my help," she said.

"And look how that turned out. I learned my lesson. Thanks for the offer, but no more, okay?"

"Hey, I . . . *we* were all instrumental in helping you solve a double homicide."

"Everyone on Kauai is still talking about the brawl between the Maidens and that Japanese hula *halau* at the competition. On stage."

"That wasn't my fault," she reminded him.

"Let's just say trouble follows you and the Maidens around like stink on . . ."

Before Roland could finish, Randy Rich joined them. He looked Roland over, then Em, and turned to Roland again.

"So, have you solved the case yet?" Randy asked.

"Working on it." Roland didn't smile.

"We'll need to notify Bobby's next of kin on the mainland. That's a call I don't want to make. Any information you can give me would help," the producer said.

Roland pulled a card out of his back pocket. "Here's the number his family should call to contact the coroner. It will be a while before we can release the body."

"Right." Randy paused, stared at the card. "If we're lucky, Bobby's camera was rolling. Maybe he caught the perp on film."

"Perp?" Roland stared back at Randy, who was nearly half as tall.

"Perpetrator. Where's the camera now?"

"Tagged as evidence."

"Did you play back the film?"

"Not yet." Roland glanced over at the patrolman leaning against the bar near where Sophie was working. The younger man, Shun, was sipping iced tea, but he had been listening to the exchange. Roland gave him a nod, and the man walked out.

"You want us to run it in the editing van? We can all go out and take a look and film your reaction as you watch it."

"Thanks, but we'll handle it."

"The film is the property of the production company. We expect its return no matter what's on it." Randy drew himself up, perhaps trying to appear taller. It didn't work.

"This case could take years to solve and then prosecute," Roland warned.

"At the very least we should have access to a copy. I'm going to call L.A. and get our lawyers on it ASAP."

Em was appalled. "You wouldn't actually air the murderer stabbing Bobby, would you?"

"Honey, you bet your bottom dollar. This is a reality show wet dream."

"Sicko." Disgusted, Em watched Randy walk away. "There has to be a way out of that contract."

Roland stared out the door at the traffic backed up on both sides of the highway. They watched Officer Shun walk back in, his expression grim as he tucked latex gloves into his pocket.

"What's up?" Roland asked.

"Nothing on the camera."

"Which means the victim hadn't filmed the killer."

# 5

## Shut Down But Not Out

For the first time since 1964, the Tiki Goddess was closed during business hours.

Even on holidays, Louie fed locals and tourists alike who had nowhere to go, including Thanksgiving and Christmas Eve. For St. Patrick's Day, Kimo cooked up a boiled corn beef and cabbage special. Patrons wore insane costumes at the Goddess Halloween Party, and photos from the event made the *Garden Island News*. They hadn't even closed when a body had been found smoldering in the *luau* pit a year ago.

But today, because of the murder in the kitchen, the local institution was forced to shut its doors. Roland told Louie the forensic crew couldn't have a crowd wandering around, so there was no option but to shut down.

Eventually the Maidens had all been interviewed. Nat went home, and Em gave up trying to convince Marilyn to go back to the beach house. As long as Louie lingered in the bar and the cameras were rolling, his fiancée wasn't leaving his side.

"What about all the lookie-loos?" Louie watched the parade of traffic outside. "They're parking half a mile away now and walking up the road. The least we could do is serve cold drinks when they get here."

"I asked Buzzy to plant himself on the *lanai* and explain what happened then turn them away."

Buzzy was a fixture at the Goddess. The aging hippie with only one name and long, gray hair lived up the road somewhere in the jungle. No one knew exactly where, but rumor had it he made his home in a tree house behind an old Hawaiian graveyard.

"You sure he won't mind?" Louie wasn't budging.

"I'll leave him with a six pack of Longboard in a cooler, and we can go back to the house."

Louie finally agreed. "Okay. Maybe giving him some responsibility will take his mind off his recent breakup. It's been hard on him."

"I think it was probably inevitable," Em said.

"Me, too. When he first told me he'd fallen in love with a dolphin, I thought it sounded kinda nuts."

"Uh huh." *What sane person wouldn't?*

"But eventually I started hoping it would work out for them. They probably never should have gotten engaged, though. He said she didn't understand him and was always nagging him to spend more time under-water. I guess after a while communicating telepathically didn't cut it."

"I can see where that would pose a problem."

*Only on Kauai would I be discussing someone's break up with a dolphin.*

She decided not to worry until this kind of conversation started to sound normal.

On the way back to the house, she and Louie passed the coroner's van parked behind the bar. The van doors were open. Inside was a gurney with an occupied body bag. Every KPD squad car on Kauai appeared to be parked in the lot.

"Well, an afternoon off will give me a head start on a commemorative cocktail," Louie said. His Booze Bible was filled with legendary tropical drink recipes inspired by major events in his life and at the Goddess.

Em scooted between two police cruisers and looked for Roland in the parking lot but didn't see him. They stepped off the gravel lot and onto the soft green grass that surrounded Louie's long, low beach house, a wooden structure that fronted the ocean.

"Don't you think it's kind of disrespectful to commemorate murder victims with cocktails? I mean, most people would find celebrating murder disturbing."

"These are chapters in the history of the Goddess, Em. Life is full of ups and downs, honey. We have to celebrate every minute before we drain our last tiki mug."

They reached the screened-in *lanai*. As Louie opened the door, his macaw, David Letterman, housed in a huge cage inside the main room, squawked, "Alooooooha! Suck 'em up!"

Em was about to follow her uncle inside when she spotted Nat Clark walking along the beach out front.

"I'll join you in a minute, Uncle Louie. Nat's headed this way." She walked the few yards to the sand and sat on a low slab of coral worn smooth over the eons.

"How are you doing?" Nat sat down beside her.

"Okay, all things considered. How long do you think it will be before the police clear out?" she asked.

"Most of the rest of the day, for sure," he said. "Where are Randy and his crew?"

"They packed up and headed to their hotel. "I think what happened finally hit them. They seemed pretty shaken up when they left, especially Joe."

"Is your uncle okay?"

"He's already thinking about creating a new cocktail to commemorate the murder. Marilyn is acting like it's the worst thing that could ever have happened to her. She's afraid they'll have to postpone the wedding."

"A lot of people might be delighted about that. You included."

She shrugged. "I gave up hoping Louie would come to his senses. The wedding is inevitable. Kiki hasn't been able to sabotage their plans, so I don't think even this catastrophe will put them off."

Em adjusted her sunglasses and gazed out over the green and turquoise waters of the Pacific. Cloud shadows floated across the surface and turned the water a deep dark blue.

"I'm going to grill some *ono* around four," Em said. "You're welcome to join us."

"Nothing I like better than fresh fish," Nat said. "But I think I'll pass."

"Coward."

"I figure there'll probably be some high drama going on with Marilyn around, and there's always the chance Randy and the crew will show up to film you all having dinner. So thanks, but count me out."

A nagging suspicion forced Em to speak up.

"You don't think Randy would have orchestrated this, do you? He's been coming up with some crazy concepts, hoping something spectacular will happen. He even suggested some of the locals stage a bar brawl, and when Louie put his foot down he mentioned bringing in some young, sexy hula dancers."

"Let me guess," Nat smiled.

"Kiki went crazy. That idea was nixed."

Nat frowned and stared out to sea. "Randy's a putz, but I can't believe he'd stoop to murder."

Em's cell phone went off playing "Crazy," the ringtone she'd assigned to Kiki.

"I should take this one," she told Nat. "Kiki might have some news."

"I'll go." He started to rise. She waved him back down.

"Hey, Kiki." Em barely got the words out before Kiki started shrieking. Em pulled the phone away from her ear. Even Nat heard her loud and clear.

"Kimo's been arrested!"

"But why?"

"He's the only suspect. His were the only prints on the knife. He was last one to see Bobby alive. They don't have any other suspects. He didn't do it, Em. He didn't do it!"

"Of course not." Em had to shout over her.

"We've got to *do* something. We've got to picket the police station. Hold a sit in. Make some Free Kimo signs. The Maidens need to start calling everyone they know and get them out to stage a protest. Would you please call Flora and tell her to start the phone chain? We'll need a fundraiser ASAP.

We'll have to sell *laulau*. Or how about a naked car wash?"

Kiki was always threatening a naked car wash. She had convinced the Maidens that people would pay them to keep their clothes on.

"I'm sure Kimo will be out on bail before the phone chain is done. How about you take a deep breath and try to calm down?" Em worried Kiki's brain would blow.

"That's easy for you to say. Don't tell me not to worry, Em. It's not *your* husband facing the electric chair."

An image of her ex, Phillip, strapped to an electric chair flashed through Em's mind. There had been many dark days during her divorce that she would have relished the idea.

"Tell her that Kimo's not going to get convicted," Nat said.

Em put her hand over the phone. "I can't tell her that. Who knows what might happen?"

"So far the police don't have any proof other than Kimo's fingerprints. Naturally they were on his knife."

Em could hear muffled yelling beneath her palm. She uncovered the phone.

"Kiki. Kiki, listen. Don't worry. Of course I'll call Flora and have her start the phone chain, okay? Just calm down. She'll let all the Maidens know what's happening. You call Flora in an hour or so and update her. If you need bail money, just let me know. Uncle Louie and I will stop by the bank and meet you in town."

Kiki's *mahalo* came out like a garbled sob, and the call abruptly ended.

"Naked car wash? Say it isn't so," Nat said.

"Only as a last resort."

# 6

## The Final Cut

It took hours before the police eventually cleared out of the parking lot, and the coroner's van was gone. Buzzy had passed out on the front *lanai* of the Goddess, but not before he grabbed the CLOSED sign and propped it on his chest. Anyone who ventured onto the *lanai* got the message.

As Em manned Louie's huge built-in barbecue on a covered pavilion in the yard beside the beach house, she reveled in the momentary calm. But she knew it was like standing in the eye of a hurricane. The calm would only last so long. She kept wishing there was a way out of the *Trouble In Paradise* contract, but despite the murder, Louie was still enthusiastic about the project. The Hula Maidens would no doubt continue to bask in the glow of their celebrity and newfound prosperity and want the show to go on.

Em knew she didn't stand a chance of fighting them all, let alone tackling the network lawyers.

She used long handled tongs to turn chicken thighs she'd marinated in teriyaki sauce and then shifted veggie kabobs to a cooler spot on the grill. Forbidden black rice was steaming in coconut milk in the rice cooker inside the house. A green salad was chilling in the fridge.

*"Yuck! Yuck! Patooie!"* When David Letterman let out the blood curdling squawk, Em nearly dropped her barbecue tongs.

"Uncle Louie?" She called over her shoulder. "What in the world did you give him?"

Letterman was temperamental at best, vicious at worst, but he loved nothing better than taste-testing Louie's beverage concoctions. If the damn parrot could predict the weather as well as he could judge the quality of a cocktail, they'd be rich.

Five minutes later, Louie appeared on the screened *lanai* with a cobalt tiki mug in hand. He opened the door and walked out to join her.

"Sorry about that," he said. "Dave still hates tomato juice based drinks. I thought I could sneak it by him, but he's not having it." Louie shrugged. "So I switched to orange juice. Want a taste?" He offered the mug for a sip.

"No thanks. I'll wait until Dave gives it his vote." She started to turn the chicken again. "Have you come up with a name?"

"How about Final Cut? Do you like it?"

She pictured Bobby with the sashimi knife sticking out of his chest. "Maybe too graphic."

"You know how Randy is always yelling 'Cut!'? That's what I meant. The Final Cut. The final take. It was Bobby's final cut."

"I know, but still."

"Have you heard from Kiki again? Any updates on Kimo?"

"Not yet, but I called Flora, and she's started the phone chain. The Maidens are on high alert."

It was the one thing Em admired most about the old gals; they were definitely one for all and all for one. If one of them needed help, they all showed up.

As if on cue, her phone beeped. When she saw it was a text from Kiki, she handed Louie the tongs and motioned at the kabobs. He automatically started shifting them around on the grill. Em read the text and then slid her phone back into her shorts' pocket.

"Kimo's out on two hundred dollars bail. That doesn't sound like much for a murder suspect."

Louie shrugged. "Everybody on the island knows Kimo. Besides, where would he go? They know he's innocent."

"Roland said he's still working on a couple of other leads. Let's hope he comes up with something sooner than later before Kiki snaps."

Em grabbed the platter on the barbecue shelf. Once the thighs and kabobs were arranged, she turned off the grill and headed for the house. Louie reached around and opened the screen door for her. As they passed Letterman's cage, she noticed David listing against the bars.

"You must be getting closer to the perfect mix," Em told Louie. "Dave's half gone."

Marilyn was on the sofa with her laptop on her knees. "My Facebook page is on fire since I posted the murder news," she said.

Em put the platter on the rattan table she'd set earlier and headed into the kitchen to take the black rice out of the cooker.

"What's wrong, sweetie?" Louie leaned over the back of the sofa to comfort Marilyn.

Em came around the corner of the open kitchen, set the rice pot on the table, and noticed the tears streaming down Marilyn's face, streaking her thick peach blush. Em glanced back at the platter of perfectly cooked chicken and kabobs, and her stomach growled. She sighed.

"I just got an email from my nephew, Tom. He can't come to the wedding after all." Marilyn's voice broke, and she buried her face in her palms.

Louie walked around the sofa and sat down beside her. He lifted the laptop off her knees and gently set it on the coffee table.

"Is he all right?" Louie awkwardly patted her shoulder.

Marilyn hiccupped and nodded yes. Em sat on a low footstool nearby.

"He . . . he's in India," Marilyn wailed.

"India?" Em said.

Marilyn nodded again. "He was going to give me away."

"I know. He seemed so excited when you asked him to."

Marilyn wasn't Em's favorite person in the world, but she sure hoped Tom Benton had a good excuse for breaking his aunt's heart. He'd visited twice since Marilyn and Louie had started dating, once shortly after they'd announced their engagement.

"He promised to be here," Marilyn sniffed.

"What happened?" Louie asked.

"He had to leave at the last minute. His company is outsourcing something." She leaned forward and opened her laptop and turned it toward Em. "See? Here's a photo of him in front of the Taj Mahal in Agra."

Em was more impressed with the Taj Mahal than Tom, a balding, non-descript forty-something-year-old. What brown hair he did have was already fading. As Marilyn dried her tears on the back of her hand, Em actually felt sorry for her, but dinner was hot and on the table.

"We should eat," Em said. "You should at least try."

Marilyn sniffed. "Something sure smells good."

"Em has dinner all ready. Sit with us, even if you don't feel like eating." Louie got up and extended a hand.

"I'll try for you, sweetie." Marilyn batted her matted lashes at him. As they walked toward the table hand in hand, she gave Louie a tremulous smile. "The show must go on, you know. I'll guess I'll just have to do this without my Tommy."

*Show?* Em frowned as she retrieved the chilled salad from the fridge.

Marilyn slipped into her place at the table. Louie stepped behind the mini tiki bar in the corner of the room, quickly mixed a cocktail and then opened a bottle of white wine. He poured a splash into the drink cup attached to Letterman's cage. Em took a seat across from Marilyn.

"Are you sure you're all right?" Em unfolded a napkin and spread it over her lap as Louie joined them.

"Things come up. Life gets in the way." Marilyn snuffled a bit and dabbed at the corners of her eyes with her napkin. "I understand. Everything will work out." She looked up at Louie. "Won't it, sweetie?"

Em started the rice around. "What would you think of asking Nat to stand in for Tom?" Em figured Marilyn would jump at the chance to have an Emmy award winning television writer give her away, and she was right.

"That's a good idea." Marilyn cut a miniscule piece of chicken and stared at it a moment. "The only other possibility is Orville Orion."

"Orville Orion?" Louie, about to shovel a fork full of rice into his mouth, paused. "Didn't you date Orion before me?"

"Why, yes." Marilyn batted her tear-spiked lashes again. She may have been frowning too, but a healthy injection of Botox made that impossible. "I guess I did."

"Who is Orville Orion?" Em put some salad on her plate and handed the bowl to Louie.

"He's a neighbor in Princeville," Marilyn said. "He's *chairman* of the homeowners' board." She made it sound as if the position was as important as Secretary of State.

*Let me guess*, Em thought.

"Wealthy?" Em picked up a veggie kabob and tried to sound mildly curious.

"Oh, very," Marilyn said.

"A widower?" Em looked down at her plate.

"Of course, he's not married. I don't go there." Marilyn finally popped the sliver of chicken into her mouth and smiled. "Actually, he'd be perfect for you."

"He's as old as I am." Louie looked appalled.

"That's not why I asked." Em quickly changed the subject. "I'm sure Nat would love to help out."

"Would you mind asking him for me, Em?" Marilyn was staring at her.

"Of course not. I'll talk to him first thing tomorrow," Em promised.

A feeble squawk followed by a distinct thud came from the refrigerator-sized birdcage in the corner near the bar. David Letterman had passed out and fallen off his perch.

Louie did a fist pump. "Looks like we finally have a winner!"

# 7

### Kiki Strikes a Bargain

Only the Maidens and the film crew were in the bar the next morning when Kiki arrived. Outfitted in a new *pareau*, a wrap-around sarong of vibrant red fabric splashed with yellow and purple orchids, she adjusted the massive *lei po'o* encircling her forehead as she walked into the bar.

Unable to sleep, she'd spent the night weaving the green and white Song of India leaves together with orchids into the intricate *lei*.

Puana Kimokani, a local *kahuna*-for-hire, showed up to bless the building as soon as the front door was unlocked. Everyone hoped the blessing would dispel any bad energy stirred up by the murder. He was still carrying a small calabash, wandering around mumbling chants and sprinkling water into the corners of the room.

Kiki headed for the table closest to the stage. Pat Boggs had taken off work for the morning and already had the other Maidens lined up at tables waiting for Kiki to begin the emergency session. She was relieved—if not completely worry free—this morning because Kimo was in the kitchen again puttering around.

He had called earlier to tell her that Em tried to send him home, but Louie stepped in and insisted he stay and cook despite what had happened. Uncle Louie was proud as punch that the Goddess was the *only* Kauai establishment that could boast that their chef was the island's number one murder suspect.

Randy Rich wasn't there, but he'd sent the van and a skeleton crew of two: Peggy and Joe the cameraman. Both were drowsing with their chins propped on their fists at a table near the bar.

Suzi Matamoto, Hula Maiden and one of Kauai's top realtors, was waving her hand around in the air. Kiki knew Suzi wouldn't put up with be ignored very long, so she quickly called the meeting to order.

Peggy and Joe snapped to life and sat up. Joe shouldered the camera, and they hustled closer.

"What is it, Suzi?" Kiki stifled a yawn.

"Why are we here? What's the big emergency? Kimo's in the kitchen.

All's right with the world." The diminutive realtor eyed her hula sisters and gave voice to what they all wondered. "Will there be a show tonight? Are we going to have to have that dance-off after all?"

Kiki glanced at Peggy, who signaled no by shaking her head and drawing her finger across her throat.

"The dance-off has been tabled for now," Kiki announced.

"Dance-off's been tabled," Pat Boggs boomed. She made a note on her clipboard.

"So what's up?" Flora wanted to know.

"I'd like to hold a fundraiser to help pay for Kimo's defense team, and we need to hold it ASAP. This weekend."

Pat hoisted the clipboard again and shouted, "Listen up, pee-pole! Fundraiser ASAP!"

"Pat!" Kiki turned to Pat, who was seated on her right. "Enough. Just take notes. Stop repeating what I say."

"Got it!" Pat hollered. "Just take notes!"

"Saturday is the Surf and Sun Swap Meet in Hanalei. Lots of folks turn up for that," Suzi Matamoto said. "We could hold a Keep Kimo Free parade up and down the sidewalk."

"Hanalei Town is only two blocks long," Trish Oakley, Maiden and professional photographer, reminded them. "How about a flash mob? Only we could do the hula instead of whatever you call the kind of dancing they do for those things."

"Beep bop?" Lillian Smith, a recent Iowa transplant and rhythmically challenged Maiden, pursed her lips.

The door to Louie's office suddenly flew open and banged against the wall.

Marilyn, red-faced and frantic, ran across the room yelling, "Absolutely not! Not on the day of my wedding!" She ran up to Kiki and started beating on the table in front of her. "You will *not* ruin *my* wedding! No, no, no way. There will be no parades and no mob flashing!"

Joe hustled across the room with Peggy behind him wrestling the long boom mic. For the moment, the sparring women were oblivious that they were being filmed. Kiki turned on Marilyn.

"Spying? You were in the office *spying* on us? Again? You tried to record and steal one of our dance numbers once, and you got caught. Have you learned nothing, Marilyn? And I think it's odd that you always refer to it as 'my' wedding, not 'our' wedding. This marriage was all your idea, Marilyn, not Louie's. Admit it. You've been leading him around by his weenie for two years, and you know it."

"His weenie?" Marilyn choked. "His *weenie*? You aren't fit to talk about that man's weenie."

"Zoom in." Peggy hovered. Joe zoomed.

Kiki wasn't about to back down. "I've known Louie Marshall for over forty years. If he wasn't under your evil spell, he'd *never* let you talk to me this way or pull these stunts."

"I know you hate me," Marilyn shouted back. "Ever since I left your stupid hula group, you've held a grudge. I know you'd like nothing better than to ruin my wedding, but I won't have it, do you hear me? You're not throwing a fundraiser that will draw the whole North Shore and steal *my* guests." Since most of her face was immobile, her lower lip quivered wildly. But there were no tears in her eyes.

Marilyn glared, but it didn't scare Kiki a bit.

"Don't you dare look at me like I'm insane," Marilyn shouted.

"Insane? You said it, not me." Kiki threw back her head and laughed so hard her head *lei* almost slipped off and fell on the floor. She made a one-handed grab and shoved it back into place.

"Want me to haul her outta here?" Sarge Pat puffed up at the ready, as official as a presidential bodyguard.

"I can handle this," Kiki assured her. She stared Marilyn down. "I'm not scared of her."

"What's going on? What's happening?" Em rushed in from the office. "I could hear you two yelling across the parking lot." She tried to step between the two women, but neither of them budged.

Kiki batted her long false lashes and sniffed. "I'm simply trying to organize a fundraiser for Kimo's defense, that's all."

"No naked car wash," Em said. "No matter what."

Marilyn grabbed Em's arm. "She's trying to sabotage my . . . *our* wedding."

"We were just discussing options for a fundraiser this weekend when she came flying out of the office all *pupule*. I thought she was going to kill me. Didn't you, ladies? Wasn't she acting all crazy?" Kiki gazed around the room at her hula sisters. The Maidens nodded in unison.

"You've been against me from the beginning. I *love* Louie," Marilyn protested. "How can I convince you of that?"

"What's love got to do with it?" Kiki shot back. "You're trying to steal the Goddess and turn it into an uppity upscale restaurant." When her head began to throb like it was about to explode, Kiki clenched her fists and took a step back.

Em was suddenly beside her, grabbing her arm, leading her toward the bar. "Kiki, you need to *calm down*."

Sophie was working behind the long *koa* wood bar. Em called, "Chablis, Soph. On ice. Quick."

Marilyn trailed them across the room. "Kiki knows a fundraiser on the day of the wedding would draw a crowd. She'll ask everyone on this side of the island to help her out, and they'll choose her stupid fundraiser over the wedding and reception."

Kiki glared over her shoulder.

"*Stupid* fundraiser? We're going to need the money to save Kimo. Can I help it if I've got more friends than she'll ever have? She doesn't even have a best friend. I heard she had to ask her hairdresser to be her maid of honor, for crap's sake."

Marilyn gasped. "I have time and money invested in this wedding. I've put down a huge deposit on the restaurant. We're having dinner for seventy-five." She ran a shaky hand over her brow and mumbled, "Steak and lobster at the St. Lexus. And my hairdresser *is* my best friend."

"Kiki, please." Em had a grip on her arm again. "Assure Marilyn you're *not* trying to sabotage the wedding. You can't hold the fundraiser on Saturday, but why not Sunday? That will give you one extra day to organize."

"What do I care what happens to her wedding?" Kiki reached for the glass of Chablis that Sophie had set on the bar. Her hand shook so hard the ice tinkled against the glass like a wind chime in a hurricane. "She thinks Kimo's guilty."

"Kiki, think about Uncle Louie for a minute. Please?"

Em obviously wasn't about to give up.

Kiki took a long, slow sip of wine. In a show of solidarity, the other Maidens had left their tables to gather around her.

Suzi Matamoto spoke up first. "Right, Kiki, think of Louie. He's let us perform here for years, long before anyone else wanted us to dance anywhere. We owe it to Louie not to ruin the wedding. If it wasn't for Louie and the Goddess, there would be no *Trouble in Paradise*, and we wouldn't be celebrities. Our businesses wouldn't all be booming, and we'd have no Facebook fans."

"Please." Lillian blinked back the tears magnified by her rhinestone-studded glasses. Sunlight streamed through the window behind her, backlighting her pink-tinted bouffant hairdo that was vintage sixties. Joe focused a tight camera shot on her.

Lillian's voice trembled. "Please, just don't argue anymore. Don't forget that *this* is the land of *aloha,* where we all love one another so much." She spread her plump arms wide, as if to encompass the whole island and enfold it with love.

Kiki was afraid Lil was about to burst into song and belt out something like the "Hallelujah Chorus." She started to tell Lillian to can the "Land of Aloha" speech when she caught a glimpse of the huge camera riding Joe's shoulder, remembered they were being filmed and was reminded of her twenty million viewers.

This whole affair, the murder, Kimo's arrest, the trial—if it came to that—would be televised. She not only had Kiki's Kreative Events, her own party planning business to run, but a growing fan base to think about. She couldn't let business suffer just because she had lost control and came off looking like a complete shrew.

Besides, no one knew how to wield power behind the scenes like she did. Staring at Marilyn's frantic, plastic-enhanced expression, Kiki knew she herself was holding all the cards.

So she pasted on a wide, fake smile and managed to appear remorseful at the same time. In a sugary sweet tone she said, "You're right, Lillian. This *is* the land of aloha. We won't hold a fundraiser on Saturday and chance ruining the day for you, Marilyn." She raised her chin a notch in defiance and toasted Marilyn with the nearly empty wineglass. "*If* you let us dance at the rehearsal dinner Friday night."

# 8

## Gimme a Head with Hair

Before Marilyn answered, she mugged for the camera, feigning an over exaggerated look of shock.

"You can't be serious. I won't allow it."

"You don't have a choice." Kiki flung her head back and wagged her finger in Marilyn's face to make sure Joe focused in on her and not Marilyn.

Suddenly, the assistant producer's cell went off.

"Freeze," Peggy directed. "Please don't say another thing. It's Randy."

The command caught Kiki with her mouth open. She snapped it shut and glowered at Marilyn while the young PA turned around and spoke to her boss in hushed tones. When Peggy finally snapped off the phone, her expression was grave.

"We've been ordered back to the hotel. We've got to pack and check out of the St. Lexus and be on the nine p.m. plane to L.A. Randy's going crazy. He said the network pulled the plug on the show. They're afraid we might all be in danger and want the whole crew out of here."

"Danger?" Kiki snorted. "What about us? We live here."

"You want reality?" Pat took a step toward Joe. "This is reality, buster, but I guess you panty wipes can't take it. Y'all Hollywood people are a bunch of wussies."

"You mean it's over? *Trouble in Paradise* is *pau*?" The color drained from Marilyn's already pale face, leaving behind two bright spots of blush high on her cheekbones.

The Maidens all held their collective breath.

Peggy cleared her throat. "I'm not in a position to comment right now."

Joe Piscoli lowered the camera. Right on cue, with a set of headphones still dangling around his neck, the technician from the production van parked outside ran into the bar.

"Did you hear?" he asked the others. "We're outta here. Pack up, and let's go."

"You shouldn't look so ecstatic," Kiki snapped at Em. "Not when we're all so bummed."

Em kept right on smiling as she turned to Sophie. "Run over and tell Uncle Louie what's up. I'll bartend if anyone wanders in."

Kiki motioned Pat closer.

"Announce that the meeting is adjourned and have the Maidens reconvene at my house in an hour. I'm holding a private rehearsal for Louie's rehearsal dinner show."

No way did she want Marilyn interfering or making any snide comments. Besides, with the television crew leaving, there was really no reason not to move the practice.

Pat tapped her pen against her clipboard.

"Y'all gotta get in your cars and go to Kiki's. No lollygagging."

"Kiki's house? We have to drive all the way out there? It's nearly at the end of the road," Lillian whined. "Why can't we practice here?"

"Because Kiki says we're practicing at her place." Pat eyeballed Lil. "What part of that don't you understand, Miss Lillian?"

Lillian sniffed and patted her pink bouffant. "Well, I suppose I could drive all the way out there. I'll have to call and tell MyBob I'm keeping the car a bit longer though. He was planning to go to the Albatross Protection Society meeting."

Big Estelle Huntington, the Cougar's daughter, said, "We'll be there, Kiki, as long as you assure Mother that your Wifi is working."

Little Estelle looked up from her Gadabout parked in the corner. "Gotta have Wifi. I've got a hot one on the hook," she called out. "He's a stripper from Des Moines. Don't wanna lose the connection."

"The Wifi was working just fine when I left this morning," Kiki assured them.

"I didn't know they had strippers in Des Moines, and I lived in Iowa all my life." Lillian's eyes were wide, her expression startled behind her black-rimmed glasses.

"I'll bet there's a lot you don't know, Miss Lillian." Pat winked at her, and Lil took a step back.

"Okay, ladies," Em said, "don't forget your purses and phones and notebooks on your way out."

"You going to pop a bottle of champagne when we're gone?" Kiki asked. "I'll bet you can't wait to celebrate the demise of the show."

"Not a bad idea. This day couldn't get any better."

"Yeah, but it could get worse." Kiki nodded toward the front door. "Here comes trouble."

Detective Roland Sharpe strode toward them, and Kiki couldn't help but notice the man never took his eyes off Em as he crossed the room. Kiki took a deep breath and reminded herself to stay calm. Roland rarely made house calls unless something was up. Surely he hadn't driven all the way out here unless it was to assure them Kimo was in the clear.

"So, Detective, are you here to tell us you finally found Bobby's murderer?" she asked.

He ignored her and greeted Em.

"Hi, Roland," Em returned.

Then he nodded to the Maidens and said, "Ladies."

Finally he turned to Kiki. "The murder happened yesterday, Kiki. We haven't finally solved it." Then he looked at the Maidens. "I'm glad you're all here. Among other things, synthetic wig fibers were found in the kitchen area and all around the bar." His gaze touched on each of them in turn. "Do any of you own a wig?"

Slowly, one by one, they all raised their hands. Roland rolled his eyes and leaned against the bar.

"Did you actually think this was going to be easy?" Em asked.

He shook his head. "There's always hope."

He turned back to Kiki. "So you all own wigs? Have you worn them here recently?"

"We wear them for certain dances, when we want to make a dramatic entrance and all have the same color and length of hair, just like the really well known dancers in the *halau* that compete at the Merry Monarch Festival. We wore them for a special number earlier in the week."

Roland's palm-sized notebook was in his hand, his pen poised above it. "So, are they black?"

"Yes. Long, black, waist-length fake hair."

"Do you own gray wigs?"

Little Estelle looked up from her laptop. "Gray wigs?" she shouted. "Who needs a gray wig? We have gray hair." She barked out a laugh and tooted the horn on her electric scooter. "All over."

"You're blushing, Roland," Kiki said.

"You really are," Em agreed.

"What about our silver wigs?" Suzi Matamoto asked. "The Cleopatra cut."

"I forgot about those." Kiki looked up at Roland. "You might mistake them for gray, but they're silver."

"You wear Cleopatra wigs for a hula?" Roland didn't hide his pain. "My Hawaiian grandmother is rolling over in her grave."

Kiki straightened her shoulders. "I choreographed a dance to 'Walk Like An Egyptian.' You have to think out of the box to have memorable performances. We actually performed it a week or so ago when Randy wanted to bring in some younger, sexier dancers. He thought it was great for the show."

"Kiki, you're so far out of the box no one could ever cram you back in." Marilyn sniffed.

"Marilyn, why don't you go back over to the house?" Em suggested. She lowered her voice. "Let things settle down in here."

Kiki turned her back on Marilyn. "Let's get back to our practice, ladies."

"Laaadeez! Off to Kiki's!" Pat yelled. "On the double."

# 9

Another Day Another Murder

Em waited until both Kiki and Marilyn had walked away before she turned to Roland. "What about the produce and fish delivery men? Anything turn up?"

"The fish delivery man's time is accounted for. He made all his stops that morning. I made calls to all of his customers, and I had a chance to talk to him personally. The produce man is a different story. I called Paradise Produce, and they said Keith Daws, the driver's name written on the card, left for Maui later that morning."

"So he couldn't have done it."

"He'd supposedly taken the whole day off. I got a hold of his flight number, and he could have had time to drive out here, kill the cameraman, then make it back to the airport and off the island," he said.

"So Kimo's in the clear. Are you going to arrest the guy?"

"For what? We've got no connection between him and Bobby Quinn and no evidence other than Kimo's word that he was here. I have the Maui police looking for him. He got off the plane and disappeared, because he didn't rent a car and he's not at a hotel. Probably because he's at a family reunion and staying with relatives. At least that's what his boss says. No one can remember the name of the folks having the reunion."

"If Daws did do it, what's to keep him from taking a flight from Maui to the mainland and slipping right through your fingers?"

"We have his name on a security watch list at the Maui airport. If he tries to fly anywhere but back to Kauai, he's out of luck. He's got a flight home on Tuesday."

"Can't you have the Maui police arrest him and bring him back over here now?"

"And ruin the family reunion? Listen, from everything I've found out about him, Keith Daws is a nice guy. Twenty-eight. Hard worker."

"So you're just going to wait until he moseys back to Kauai to question him?"

Roland shrugged. "Pretty much."

Just then the two-way radio clipped to Roland's belt squawked. He turned the volume down, but not before everyone in the bar heard the dispatcher on the other end.

"Ohmyword!" Lillian cried. "Not again."

"What did that just say?" Kiki wanted to know.

"Someone just found a body at the Haena Beach Resort." Em's hand went to her throat.

Haena Beach Resort was a small grouping of two-story condos on windswept Kepuhi Beach a couple of miles up the road from the Goddess. HBR, as the locals called it, had been built in the seventies and was a quiet, laid back resort with a pool and other modest amenities known for its off-the-beaten-path solitude and its stunning ocean front view of forever.

"Another murder?" Em spoke so softly Roland barely heard her over the chatter of the others. He scanned the anxious faces around the bar.

Pat Boggs cupped her hand around her mouth and yelled, "Laaaadeeez! Shut the bleep up. Let the man talk."

"I don't know any more than what you already heard," he told them and then headed for the door.

"Roland, wait." Em hurried to catch him.

He paused, and she reminded him, "Bobby Quinn was staying at HBR. The rest of the crew was up at Princeville at the St. Lexus. There wasn't enough in the budget for another high-end room, and Bobby was low man on the totem pole, so he had a condo out here."

Before the detective could say anything, Kiki called from across the room, "You can't pin this latest murder on Kimo, Roland. Before he came in to work, he had a six a.m. appointment at the spa for a pedicure. Having callouses filed off his feet is about the only thing that calms him down anymore."

# 10

## Louie's Big Event

Friday night, the night of the rehearsal dinner, Em was waiting for Louie in his office when someone knocked on the door. She smiled when she opened it and saw Roland.

"Hiding?" He stepped in. She shut the door, effectively cutting off the bedlam in the bar.

"I told Louie I wanted to walk into the party on his arm. He's going to join me as soon as he's ready. He's a little late because he and Buzzy carried Letterman over on his portable perch. My uncle thought it would be great to have folks meet the famous taste-testing parrot since there's a new write up about Dave on the drink menus. He was a real hit on the show pilot, but they had to take Letterman out of the bar because most of his dialogue had to be bleeped out. Besides, Louie was afraid Dave might really insult someone. My uncle is terrified of lawsuits."

"Does that thing bite?"

"Only if he doesn't like you, and there aren't many people he actually likes. Louie's also worried that David will make politically incorrect remarks to young women. He does that after he's had a couple of drinks."

Roland shook his head. "That's one for the books."

"If you pull out your little notebook and write that down, I'm going to have to ask you to leave." She was only half joking.

"Where is he now?"

"Louie or the parrot?"

"Your uncle."

"He ran back over to the house to change." She smiled up at him. "I'm glad you could make it, Roland."

He shrugged. "I'm here in an official capacity."

"Representing the mayor?"

"No, but I did see a couple of councilmen out there. Actually, I'm on duty. I thought someone should check out the crowd."

A chill ran down her spine. "You don't think the murderer would show up here tonight, do you?"

He shrugged. "I hope not."

"Still waiting for the vegetable delivery guy to come back from Maui?"

"He's supposed to be home on Tuesday. I talked to Kimo again and tried to get a description. He said he didn't really pay much attention. He was busy prepping and had his back to the guy most of the time, but he thought Keith Daws was wearing glasses, a baseball cap with the produce company's logo, some kind of uniform shirt. Said he had shaggy, black hair."

"What about the murder at Haena Beach Resort? There wasn't much in the paper."

"One of the maids, Esther Villaviejos, thirty-nine, was found dead in one of the condos. She was hit on the head with a blunt instrument we now believe to be a lamp. The receptionist said the guest who checked out of the room where the body was found had an ID from Indianapolis. His name was Dewey Smithson. The credit card matched up. She said he had washed out, stringy, long hair and wore it tied back in a ponytail. Looked like a nerd. He said he was a birdwatcher."

"So maybe the tourist did it and left the island."

"We checked the airline manifests, but there was no Smithson aboard any outbound flights. He could be out bird watching, maybe camping someplace. We have his name on a watch list. If he tries to leave the island, we'll bring him in for questioning."

"He could be anywhere."

"He's not our chief suspect." Roland looked over his shoulder then back at Em. "Ms. Villaviejos' co-workers said she's had a lot of beefs with her estranged husband and recently took out a restraining order. We hope to bring him in for questioning, but so far no one seems to know where the husband is."

Em pictured her own ex, Phillip. In their case, she'd most likely be the one doing the strangling.

"Maybe he's at a family reunion, too."

Roland ignored her comment.

"You think the maid's death was connected to Bobby's? He was staying out there."

He shrugged. "We tried connecting Mrs. Villaviejos to the cameraman. No one noticed anything going on. We tried connecting the husband, Victor Villaviejos, to the Goddess. One of the maid's friends said that when he and his wife were still getting along they sometimes stopped in here for a drink after he picked her up from work. We're trying to find out if maybe Victor was here the night before Bobby Quinn's murder. Maybe he and the cameraman had a run in."

"You think maybe this Victor Villaviejos came back and killed Bobby?"

"It's a long shot." Roland crossed his arms.

"What about the tourist? Smithson? I'd be surprised if someone staying that close to the Goddess didn't come in for a drink. Do you have a photo of him? Someone might remember seeing him."

"We're working on it."

"Do you think there's a serial murderer running around?"

"I hope not. I don't think the murders are connected."

Em tried to focus, but her gaze kept straying to the rock hard biceps beneath his Aloha shirt sleeves.

"Looks like having the TV crew pull out hasn't hurt business any," he said.

"You can't judge by tonight. Most of the people are here because of Louie and Marilyn's party. But you're right. Business is still great. But I don't miss the crew a bit. It's such a relief not to have that camera in my face," she said.

"I'm sure the Hula Maidens are despondent."

"Not so sad that they can't perform tonight. I've never seen Kiki so excited. She said she's got a big surprise number planned."

"Too bad I'm on duty and will be walking around with iced tea disguised as bourbon on the rocks. Her dance numbers would drive the Pope to drink."

"He probably does already. Please try not to look like a cop and scare off the customers."

"I am a cop."

She caught herself involuntarily taking a step toward him. Roland put his hand on the doorknob and smiled.

"Hold that thought," he said.

She blushed. "What thought?"

"My grandmother was psychic, remember?"

Or so he'd told her a few months back.

"What's that got to do with anything?" she asked.

"Even if I can't read your mind, the look in your eyes is gonna make me blush." He turned the knob and slipped out into the main room.

He'd inherited something special all right, but she doubted it was mindreading.

Em leaned against the desk, picked up a copy of a new sample menu, and fanned her heated face. Roland had barely closed the door to the main room when Louie walked in the back door.

"You look really nice, Uncle." Em tossed the paper on the desk and reached up to straighten the collar on one of his many vintage Aloha shirts. This one was silk from the forties and emblazoned with cocktail glasses of various shapes and sizes filled with colorful concoctions and garnishes.

"*Mahalo*, honey. Gotta be comfortable tonight. Marilyn talked me into wearing a monkey suit tomorrow."

"A tux?" Em eyeballed him. Tall, tan, and fit, her uncle's eyes were bright sky blue. He still had a full head of silver hair. "You're one of the most handsome grooms I've ever seen. In a tux you'll knock 'em dead. Marilyn is one lucky lady."

"She thought it would be great for the show. But I guess that's not to be now."

He looked so disappointed at the mention of the show, Em almost felt bad that the TV crew had pulled out.

"Have you heard anything from the production company?" she asked.

Louie nodded. "Randy called a little while ago. The show was definitely cancelled. The crew is flying back to L.A. tonight on the red eye. There's a chance that if they need to shoot any footage to wrap things up that they'll be back, but not until their safety can be assured."

"As Pat said, they're wussies."

"I'd rather not talk about it and spoil tonight. So, speaking of knockouts, you're looking pretty sexy yourself."

"Thanks." She'd pulled a dress out of her closet, a skinny little black cocktail dress she hadn't worn since she'd left the O.C. It fit even better than when she first bought it, which was a surprise since she'd definitely gained a few inches since she moved to the island of fat-filled pupu platters and high calorie cocktails. She had wound her hair up and anchored it to the top of her head with a black lacquered chopstick. A strand of white pearls and pearl earrings were added, and she was more dressed up than she'd been in forever.

Louie chucked her under her chin. "I sure wish you'd find Mr. Right. A great looking girl like you shouldn't be all alone. What about Nat? He seems interested. How was your dinner date with him the other night?"

She didn't dare tell him just how interested Nat was. After a delicious meal at Kauai Pasta and a nice bottle of wine, the writer had asked if she'd like to go home with him—and she could tell he wasn't just offering after-dinner coffee.

"I'm not looking for Mr. Right. I just got rid of Mr. Wrong not too long ago. Nat and I had a good time, but we're just friends." How could she explain there were no sparks? Where there were no sparks, no fire.

"What's wrong with the men on this island? I can't believe they haven't been lining up for you." Louie shook his head.

"Nothing wrong with them, Uncle." She couldn't help but think of one in particular. "I'm just picky."

There weren't many choices, and there was a disproportionate amount of surfers to choose from, not necessarily a bad thing, but on Kauai it was hard to tell the multi-millionaires from the bums. Then again, she'd been married to a wealthy white collar executive, a high-powered CPA in Newport Beach, but he was a player and far from a true gentleman. Phillip was a choice who looked great on paper, but that relationship had brought her nothing but heartache.

"Have you heard anything from Roland about the second murder? The one at HBR?"

She shook her head. "Only that someone hit one of the maids in the head and killed her. Her body was found in a guest's condo. The guy is a birdwatcher, which is all anyone remembers about him, except that that he also had long, stringy hair. No one has seen him since. Or she could have been killed by her estranged husband, who is also missing."

"I don't think the same person who killed Bobby killed that maid. It would be way too big of a coincidence."

"Neither does Roland. He's here checking out the crowd tonight."

"Does he think the murderer will show up here? Tonight? For gosh sake, don't tell Marilyn."

"It's a possibility. He's going to be on the lookout just in case. I hope things go smoothly. We don't need any more publicity—good or bad."

"Speaking of publicity, Marilyn is heartsick the TV crew couldn't stay until after the wedding tomorrow. I hope the festivities tonight will cheer her up."

"Speaking of Marilyn, we'd better go out and get seated. She's waiting for you," Em reminded him.

"She's already pissed off because our guests are here, but we're still open to the public tonight. She doesn't understand how I can continually have my 'life on display' as she puts it."

"That's odd. She certainly didn't shy away from the limelight during the filming."

"She doesn't realize playing host to the world isn't like having a real job to me. I enjoy meeting people and making them feel welcome and happy. As far as I'm concerned, there's nothing wrong with living life as one big party. It's too short for anything else."

Em paused before asking what so many others around the North Shore were thinking.

"Are you sure about this wedding, Uncle Louie?"

She thought she saw his smile dim just a notch, but if it had, he recovered in half a heartbeat.

"Sure, I'm sure. Despite what some folks think, Marilyn's a real fine woman. She makes me happy, and if this marriage will make her happy, I'm all for it."

"Great." Em felt less than great, but Louie was old enough to have his way. Kiki had convinced Em to move to Kauai by fabricating a story about Louie needing Em's help because he was losing his mental faculties, but Em had come to realize he was as sane as the rest of them.

"After you, Em." Louie opened the office door and stepped out into pandemonium in the main room.

# 11

Burnin' Ring O' Fire

The Tiki Tones were in the middle of one of their "tourist medleys" and were banging out "Little Grass Shack," "Goin' to a Hukilau" and "Pearly Shells." The tourists loved it and were singing along while the locals tried hard to look bored with the schmaltzy *hapa-haole* songs.

When Danny Cook saw Uncle Louie, he raised his hand, and the musicians beside him stopped playing to announce, "Ladies and gentlemen, *kane* and *wahine*, here he is, the groom, the Tiki Goddess's very own man of the hour, Louie Marshall!"

The crowd went wild. Tourists who had walked in for the first time tonight had no idea who Louie was or what was going on, but they were swept up by the enthusiastic crowd and were quickly cheering and hooting as loud as the locals.

Em followed Louie to the front table nearest the stage where Marilyn was waiting. Having agreed to give Marilyn away, Nat was there along with Buzzy, Louie's best man. Louie held out Em's chair for her. There was still one vacant place at the table beside Marilyn.

As soon as Em was seated, Marilyn leaned close and whispered, "So much for a classy, intimate dinner with the wedding party and a few out of town guests." Marilyn pursed her lips and stared down her nose.

"If you want classy, you're marrying the wrong guy. Besides, there aren't any out of town guests attending the wedding that I know of," Em reminded her. "Unless your nephew showed up at the last minute?" She looked around, expecting to spot the outsourcing Tom Benton. "If he's here, he should be seated with us."

"He's still in India. I got another email today wishing me the best. He attached a photo of himself riding on the back of an elephant." Marilyn's expression was sour. "Look around, Em. Even if he did show up, he couldn't get in the front door. This place was jammed at five o'clock. Once word got out about the celebration, all the locals who think they own this place started showing up."

Her sour attitude was lost on Louie. He was smiling and waving to

*51*

familiar faces in the crowd, and Em knew as soon as he finished dinner, he'd be on his feet circling the room with Letterman on his shoulder, meeting and greeting *kama'aina* and *malihini* alike. Old timers and newcomers were not only his bread and butter, he truly enjoyed people of every age and walk of life.

Em spotted what had to be a table full of Marilyn's neighbors from Princeville seated not far from the head table.

Marilyn leaned close to Em and said, "The tall distinguished-looking man you're staring at? That's Orville Orion. He's here with the homeowners' board. I invited them all."

"Where's your maid of honor?" Em noted the empty seat at their table.

Marilyn glanced around the room and then took a sip of champagne. "I don't know why she's not here already. I hope she's all right. Precious Cottrell is the most dependable person I know."

Em glanced over at the bar where Sophie was pouring drinks as fast as she could. She'd dyed the spiked tips of her hair gold for the occasion. Em had offered to hire a stand-in so she could have the night off to enjoy the party, but Soph said she'd rather work because she could still enjoy all the action from behind the bar and collect a mountain of tips by the end of the evening.

"Where is the great and magnificent Kiki and her collection of crazies?" Marilyn looked over her shoulder at the entrance to the bathroom the Maidens commandeered as a dressing room.

"She's got the Maidens corralled in the bathroom. They've worked up something really special for tonight."

Marilyn sniffed.

"I wish you two would bury the hatchet for Louie's sake," Em said. "Maybe even find it in your heart to compliment Kiki on the performance. If it wasn't for the Maidens, you'd only have the Tiki Tones for entertainment tonight."

Marilyn appeared to be ignoring her. She suddenly waved at someone near the door.

"There's Precious. She made it." Marilyn sounded relieved.

Precious Cottrell was exactly as Kiki had described her to Em earlier in the afternoon: a diminutive three-foot-six little person with auburn hair and a big smile.

The wedding party was served. Kimo's special panko and macadamia nut encrusted *ono* filets nestled atop mashed cinnamon sweet potatoes were not only delicious, but to Em's relief, the meal came off without a hitch. Marilyn was behaving as civilly as she could with Louie acting more concerned about David Letterman's behavior than the big event. Her uncle kept jumping up and down to make sure the parrot was content by pouring watered down cocktails into the cup attached to Dave's perch.

Em had to give Marilyn credit; it couldn't be easy sitting beside her fiancé beneath the life-sized portrait of Louie's late wife that was smiling down on them. Irene Kakaulanipuakaulani Hickam Marshall was a stunningly beautiful Hawaiian, if the portrait was an exact likeness. Irene had been Louie's one true love, the woman he called his tiki goddess. Together they established the bar and restaurant, and since Irene's passing, Louie had closed the show each and every evening by having the crowd join hands and sing the Tiki Goddess song he'd written in tribute to his wife.

Em wondered if he planned to skip the ritual closing tonight. And what about the future? She couldn't see how Marilyn would allow it.

More than once Em had gazed around and caught Roland watching her from across the room. She shrugged at him a couple of times as if to say, "Seen anything?"

He would only give the slightest shake of his head as if to say nothing.

Once the plates were cleared from the head table, Pat Boggs took the stage. Dressed like a man in black pants and a red and gold *kihei*, a square of fabric knotted at one shoulder and tied at an angle over a red long-sleeved shirt, she carried a gourd instrument called an *ipu*.

She stepped up to the microphone and waited for the crowd to settle down, obviously unaware that in a raucous bar, you could die trying to get everyone's attention. Two seconds later, Pat stuck her thumb and index finger in her mouth and gave an earsplitting whistle loud enough to send shock waves through Em's fillings. Some folks slapped their hands over their ears.

After the whistle died away, there wasn't a sound in the room.

"That's better." Pat rocked back on her heels. "You might wanna drink up," she began. "Y'all are about to see somethin' you won't believe."

She tucked the *ipu* under one arm and started in on a hypnotic rhythm, *dum dum thunk, dum dum thunk*. In a low, monotone pitch that reverberated in the mic, she began. "Tonight, in a tribute to Louie Marshall and his bride-to-be, Marilyn Lockhart, the Hula Maidens present for your pleasure an exotic, erotic hula they'll perform to the song 'Kalua.'"

*Dum dum thunk. Dum dum thunk.*

All eyes turned toward the bathroom door as Kiki stepped out and started slowly walking into the main barroom, moving in time to the beat of the *ipu*. Encased in a form fitting, off the shoulder gown of blood-red velvet, her real hair was hidden beneath a waist-length black wig studded with plastic hibiscus gilded with gold spray paint. Her expression was set in a zombie-like stare, her kohl-rimmed cat's eyes focused on the stage. Her arms were spread wide.

Balanced on each palm was a half coconut shell filled with flaming oil.

From each wick trailed a stream of black smoke that snaked toward the ceiling. If she was forty years younger, Kiki would have looked like she'd just stepped off the cover of Martin Denny's classic *Exotica* album.

*Dum dum thunk. Dum dum thunk.*

"Oh no," Em whispered.

"God help us." Louie's perpetual smile faded.

"I'm going to kill her." Marilyn started to stand.

Em grabbed her by the wrist and yanked her back down.

*Dum dum thunk. Dum dum thunk.*

Pat's drumbeat never faltered. Her monotone droned on.

"'Kalua' is a song from the film *Bird of Paradise*, which was about a *haole* guy who comes to the islands, falls in love, and goes native. He marries Kalua, an island beauty, which angers the volcano God who can only be appeased by a . . . *human sacrifice!*" Pat leaned close and yelled the last two words into the mic, which caused it to give off a high-pitched whine.

Em's fillings twanged again.

"Human *sacrifice?*" Marilyn pursed her lips. "I volunteer Kiki."

Pat glared down at her from the stage.

Slowly, one by one, the Hula Maidens filed out of the restroom like a procession of fallen vestal virgins. They were all dressed identically to Kiki, each in red velvet off the shoulder gowns, each wearing a long black wig and balancing flaming coconut shells on their open palms.

Six counts later, Suzi Matamoto, first in line behind Kiki, stepped out. Suzi had perfected her walk. Step, step, pause. Step, step, pause.

Next came photographer Trish Oakley, whose face was so flushed her freckles had disappeared. Flyaway strands of bright red hair peeked out from beneath the hairline of her wig. The Maidens were moving along, evenly spaced, until Flora Carillo stepped out. She gave the impression of a hobbled monk seal in her skintight crimson gown. Flora kept turning her head and smiling at the crowd and was soon out of step. The allotted space between her and Trish quickly dwindled to less than two feet.

Big Estelle appeared next, moving to the drum beat with head high and hands steady until Little Estelle laid on the Gadabout horn. When a tourist tried to shush her with a scowl, Little Estelle stuck out her tongue and gave him the raspberries. She kept on tooting the horn until Roland walked over, flashed a badge, and leaned down to whisper something in her ear.

Pat started her narrative again. "The island *kahuna* convinced the lovely Kalua to throw herself into the raging volcano to save the island from destruction . . ."

After Big Estelle walked on, all of the other dancers were in position in front of the stage, all but Lillian Smith, who finally appeared. Be-wigged like the rest of the Maidens, the skirt of her gown was so tight it bound her knees together, forcing her to take mincing steps across the room. Her hands were shaking so hard that hot oil threatened to slosh out of the flaming coconut shells.

*Dum dum thunk. Dum dum thunk.*

Em closed her eyes and tightened her death grip on Marilyn's wrist.

Unaware that Lillian was in distress, Pat droned on. "Now the world famous stars of TV and the Tiki Goddess stage, the Hula Maidens, will begin their dance, which they lovingly dedicate to Uncle Louie Marshall." She looked down at Louie and winked. "This one's for you, Uncle Louie."

The dedication made it more than obvious the Maidens could care less about Marilyn.

Danny and the Tiki Tones started playing, and Pat joined in singing along with them. "This is the night of love . . . this is the hour of . . . Ka . . . looooo . . . aaahhh."

The Maidens began to move, but there wasn't a soul in the room who would remotely call what they were doing dancing. Obviously all of the dancers were acutely aware of the flaming oil precariously sloshing in the half shells teetering on their palms. The women's movements were limited to swaying back and forth while they slowly raised and lowered their hands and arms. Their movements set off a tidal wave of sagging underarm undulations.

The usually riotous bar patrons watched in shock and awe the way spectators closely view a car chase or a forest fire, holding their breath and awaiting disaster, afraid to look and yet compelled to watch. No one in the audience moved; no one took a bite of food or sipped a drink as Pat continued to pound out the beat, the Tiki Tones played, and the Maidens jiggled and swayed.

Em was so nervous she kept forgetting to breathe. She noticed Lillian's glasses were fogging up. The woman's husband, MyBob, as Lillian always called him, had made his way to the front of the room and was videotaping the dance.

Em glanced up at her uncle. Louie was scanning the stage.

"There ought to be a bucket of water up there," he mumbled. "Just in case."

No sooner were the words out than Lillian let out a sharp cry that sounded like a yelp.

"Fire! Lil's hair is on fire!" MyBob yelled.

Sure enough, the right side of Lillian's long wig appeared to be melting as flames licked at it, slowly making their way toward her head. Lillian started screaming and tossed her coconuts in the air. They flew backward toward the band. Danny and the bass guitarist held their guitars over their heads for cover. The drummer vaulted off the stage.

"Water! Water!" MyBob was running in circles beside his wife, waving his hands in the air. "Her hair's on fire! *Her hair's on fire!*"

On the other side of Lil, Big Estelle stopped dancing and had the presence of mind to blow out her coconuts. Further down the line, the gravity of what was unfolding hadn't yet reached Flora, Trish, Suzi, or Kiki. They danced on in a hypnotic trance with smiles pasted on their faces and far off looks in their eyes as they continually raised and lowered their arms.

Everyone at the head table except Marilyn had jumped to their feet. Precious had scrambled to stand up on her chair and covered her mouth with both hands. Her eyes were about to bug out of her head. Nat instinctively grabbed a tall glass and was about to toss a drink at Lillian's head.

"Not alcohol! Don't throw any alcohol!" Louie threw himself in front of Nat's arm.

Nat was already in motion. Louie ended up with a sticky Mai Tai in his face and was blindly feeling around the table for a napkin. He grabbed the tablecloth instead and upended everyone else's drinks.

Pat Boggs was still on stage. She turned toward Lillian and yelled into the microphone, "Stop! Drop! Roll! Stop! Drop! Roll!"

"Her hair's on fire!" MyBob kept hollering. "My wife is on fire!" He tried fanning the flames with his hands.

"It's not *her* hair." Em tried yelling over the chaos, but no one heard her. "Pull off her wig! Pull off her wig!"

The coconuts Lillian had flung backward had ignited the carpet on the stage. Danny and the Tiki Tones were trying to stomp it out, melting the soles of their rubber flip flops.

Across the room, Sophie had climbed up on the bar and was wielding a fire extinguisher. She pulled the pin and aimed, but all that came out was a puff of white powder.

David Letterman, also behind the bar, was pacing back and forth on his perch screaming, *"Save me! Hunka Hunka Burnin' Love! Hunka Hunka Burnin' Love!"*

Buzzy leapt up from the table and headed for Dave's perch.

Lillian was screaming, "I'm melting! I melting!"

Precious let out a squeal and yelled at Marilyn. "I gotta get out of here before this turns into a flaming inferno! I'll be trampled if there's a stampede!"

She grabbed her purse, clambered down off her chair, and the last Em saw of Precious was her auburn head bobbing toward the front door as she skirted around and under tables.

Wanting to do something for Lillian, Em tried to push her way around

Louie and the others but was trapped on the wrong side of the table. By now tourists were headed for the door, colliding with locals pushing their way toward the front to get a better view of the commotion.

Just when Em was certain the Goddess was about to go up in flames and they should all head for the exits, she spotted Roland, towering head and shoulders over everyone in the room. He parted the crowd, striding through them like Moses wading through the Red Sea.

He reached Lillian before the flames neared her neck, yanked off her wig, and tossed it on the floor. After Roland ground it beneath his foot and moved on toward the stage, MyBob started jumping up and down on it.

Kiki and the others were still dancing. Big Estelle was paralyzed with terror. The fire on the stage was spreading.

Suddenly Kimo ran up to Roland and handed him the kitchen fire extinguisher. The detective pulled the pin, aimed, and thankfully this canister was full. White foam shot out, and Roland quickly coated everything, including Pat Boggs and the Tiki Tones. Then for good measure, he turned the spray on Kiki and the rest of the dancers.

Little Estelle pounded her Gadabout horn in a series of long-short-long SOS beeps. She kept it up until someone yelled, "I hear sirens. The fire truck is coming!"

Louie sank into an empty chair. The hem of the tablecloth was still pressed against his eyes.

"Damn it," he cursed. "My eyes are still stinging. What did I miss?"

"Sorry, Louie." Nat leaned over Louie and gave him a pat on the back. "I tossed a full Mai Tai at you. I wasn't even thinking. If you hadn't jumped in front of me, I would have blown that poor woman up."

"How is she?" Louie tried to open his eyes and then slammed them shut. "You think she'll sue?"

Marilyn, who'd buried her face in the crook of her arm, lifted her head and looked around. "Why would she? No one told her to play with fire. Those idiot women. Look at Kiki. She's covered in foam and still waving those damn coconuts around."

Em looked. Sure enough, Kiki, Suzi, Trish and Flora were still in line. Shock had finally registered on their foam-covered faces. They blinked and looked around as if awaking from a coma.

"What about Letterman?" Louie wiped his eyes with the corner of the tablecloth. Finally able to see, he looked around in a panic. "Where's my parrot? Someone stole my parrot."

"He's fine," Em assured him. "Buzzy tossed a bar towel over him, grabbed the perch- and carried him out."

"Thank heavens." Louie shook his head. "What if I'd have lost him?"

"Lost your *parrot?*" Marilyn screeched. "*Lost your parrot?* What about me? Those women could have burned the place down. Not that it would have been a great loss. This dump is a fire trap. It should have been condemned years ago. A termite roast, that's what it would have been. Snap, crackle, pop." She threw back her head and gave a maniacal laugh.

Louie rounded the table to sit beside her. When he tried to slip his arm around her shoulder, she shrugged him off.

"Oh, now sweetie, everything's all right. You know how much I care about you. Why, I'd never let anything happen to you. You're just a bit hysterical is all."

Marilyn sniffed and glowered at Kiki and the others. Covered in foam, they were carefully being led toward the bathroom by Kimo and MyBob.

"That woman should have never been allowed to perform tonight. She has it out for me. This is all her fault. She's ruined our rehearsal dinner. She's ruined everything!" Marilyn let out a heart-wrenching wail, folded toward the table, and buried her face in her arms again.

"Now that's not true, sweetie," Louie comforted between pats on the back. "The wedding is going to go off without a hitch. The reception will be beautiful. You know what they say, if you don't want problems with the show, then hope for a bad dress rehearsal."

Marilyn's head popped up. "Who? Who says that?"

Em realized her knees were knocking and plopped back down into her chair. She could have killed for a drink, but Louie had managed to dump every glass on the table. She watched as a squadron of handsome KFD firefighters made their way through the crowd toward the stage. Their captain conferred with Roland for a minute or two, and then the detective started toward her table.

He hunkered down beside her and rested his arm on the back of her chair.

"You okay?"

Em nodded. "I'm fine. Will the Maidens be all right? Is that stuff you sprayed on them toxic?"

"It's just $CO_2$."

"Thanks for saving Lillian. For saving all of them. And for saving the Goddess."

Even though Marilyn was right, that the place was a termite-infested dump, Em couldn't imagine what Uncle Louie, let alone the rest of them, would do without their beloved watering hole.

She was almost too upset to notice that Roland's hand had moved from the back of her chair to rest on her knee beneath the table. *Almost.*

"Are you going to be all right?" he asked.

She nodded, not quite able to form a complete sentence with heat radiating from beneath his hand from her knee up to her thigh. Even the sound of Marilyn moaning in the middle of her own little pity party wasn't enough to cool her off.

When Roland finally unfolded his six-three frame, Em was forced to crane her neck to look up at him. It was that or stare at the waistband of his pants and parts south.

"Everything's under control," he assured her. "But I'm going to stick around for a while, make sure everyone's okay. I'll check with you again before I head out."

Em finally found her tongue.

"*Mahalo* again, Roland. I can't thank you enough for being here and for the quick thinking."

"No worries."

As he walked away, Em looked at the wall behind the once smoldering stage. Smiling down on them all was the serene image of Irene Kakaulanipuakaulani Hickam Marshall. There was not a drop of fire extinguisher foam nor trace of smoke on Louie's late wife's portrait.

# 12

## And a Bottle of Rum

Em stared up at Irene's portrait for a moment or two until Louie asked, "Will you sit with Marilyn while I announce we'll be serving drinks on the house for an hour?"

"Drinks on the house? Are you sure?" Despite the fire, the place was still packed. Em was too shaken to tally up how much offering free drinks to smooth over this latest fiasco was going to cost them.

"A little rum will go a long way to help dull the memory of the trauma folks just witnessed. So will slices of that coconut sheet cake we've got in the kitchen. It's as big as a twin mattress."

Em doubted it. "You know, the drunker they get, the more they will embellish the story."

"Nothing wrong with a little free happy juice once in a while. We've got an overabundance of rum in the back. I'm going to have Buzzy help Sophie out at the bar." He reached over to squeeze Marilyn's hand. "Stay put, sweetie. I'll be right back."

Marilyn didn't look up.

Louie had no sooner made the big announcement that they'd be serving free Mai Tais for an hour than Kiki walked out of the bathroom carrying her red velvet gown over her arm. She was still wearing her wig, but a few of the gold plastic hibiscuses had fallen out. Her dark kohl mascara was so smeared she appeared to have two black eyes. Her jaw was set in a determined if not firm line.

She marched over to the table and stood there looking down at the top of Marilyn's head.

"Sorry, Em," Kiki said. "I really thought the fire element would add to the festivities and that Louie would be pleased. I have to admit the number didn't quite work out the way I planned, except I think the dancing was pretty good, don't you? I mean, we were all pretty much in step. I had my doubts about Lillian, though. She's not the pro the rest of them are. A little too soon for her to be using fire maybe."

Suddenly Marilyn was up, not just looking up, but on her feet, pushing out of her chair.

"You!" She pointed at Kiki. "You planned this entire disaster. You've been trying to break us up for two years now. You want me out of the picture so that you can keep this truly tacky tiki bar alive." Marilyn was so upset her jaw was quivering.

If it hadn't been for Louie's free round of drinks, there might have been an audience to witness the exchange, but folks were lined up three deep around the bar, some already clamoring for a refill.

Kiki planted her hands on her ample hips.

"Maybe so, Marilyn. You've got me there. I *have* wanted to get rid of you, but you can bet on your four late husbands' graves that I would never, ever burn down the Tiki Goddess to do it. A move like that would be more your style."

"You are not allowed at our wedding," Marilyn screamed.

"*As if.* As if I'd want to be there to see Louie Marshall brought so low."

"Drop dead, Kiki."

"No, you drop dead, Marilyn!"

Em shot to her feet and held out both hands. "That's enough. Kiki, if you're sure the Maidens are all right, it's time for you to go home."

"They're fine." Kiki avoided looking at Marilyn.

"What about Pat? She got a mouthful of $CO_2$."

"As if that could shut her up," Kiki rolled her eyes. "She's fine. She's back there telling the firemen how to do their jobs."

"Then you should leave. With Kimo, if he's still here," Em added.

"He's not finished cleaning up in the kitchen." Kiki looked over toward the bar. "Looks like Louie is still holding court. Please, tell him I apologize, but I really thought it would be great."

"I'll tell him," Em said.

"I mean it," Marilyn called out as Kiki walked away, "I don't want to see your face anywhere near the St. Lexus tomorrow. Just leave us in peace."

Kiki walked out without looking back.

Marilyn grabbed her sequin-encrusted evening bag. The poor little thing looked as out of place in the Goddess as a monkey in an igloo. She turned her gaze on Louie.

"Look at him," she sniffed. "He's actually enjoying this."

Louie did indeed appear to be the man of the hour, laughing and talking to the folks jammed around the bar, making sure everyone had plenty to drink and reminding them that the free rum would stop flowing after forty-five minutes. As if he sensed she was watching him, he turned and waved and gave Marilyn a big wink.

"You see?" she said.

"What I see is a man who is a genius when it comes to public relations. He's making sure no lasting harm was done and that none of these people will go home and file lawsuits claiming he put them in harm's way."

"What I see is a man who is ignoring me in my time of need."

"How about I walk you out to your car, Marilyn? Louie is going to be at this until closing time. Why don't you stay here tonight?"

She shook her head. "No. It's bad luck to spend the night together before the wedding. I just have to run over to the house and get my notebook and freshen up my make-up before I head home."

Em really couldn't afford to spend any more time smoothing Marilyn's ruffled feathers. From the sound of squawking coming from the direction of the beach house, they were going to have their hands full enough calming David Letterman.

She walked Marilyn out to the parking lot, and the woman headed toward the beach house. As she turned to go back to the bar to help clean up, she spotted Roland crossing the pavement headed her way. Em waited for him just beyond a puddle of light spilling out of Goddess window near the edge of the lot.

"You shouldn't be out here alone, Em."

"I just walked Marilyn out. She's inside getting her things together before she heads home to Princeville. Will you be here much longer?"

"I'm going to take off. I think it's too much to hope that Smithson or Villaviejos will show this late. I still like the husband for the maid's murder."

Even though it was a balmy night without the usual hint of a passing trade wind shower, a shiver went down Em's spine. She realized that sometime during the mayhem she's lost her chop stick, and her hair had tumbled down around her shoulders. She tucked a lock behind her ear.

"I like your hair down," he said. "Better than when it's all folded up."

She laughed. "Folded up."

"What's so funny?"

"I guess I do wear it folded up a lot. I just never thought of it that way."

An awkward silence fell, and though she knew she should get back inside, Em couldn't bring herself to walk away. Apparently Roland wasn't ready to go anywhere either.

"Is there anything I can do to help?" she finally managed.

"With the case? I had hoped you would swear off playing junior detective."

"This has hit close to home. If there is anything I can do to help clear Kimo's name, I will."

"Just keep Kiki from pulling any more stunts like tonight." He turned to look at the bar. "This place is not only a matchbox, but it was crowded. That could have been a real disaster. Thankfully no one was seriously hurt."

"Haven't you ever caught anything on fire during one of your fire knife performances?" He had to be one of the only cops in Polynesia who moonlighted by twirling and tossing burning knives strapped to long sticks into the air.

"Only my hair."

"You're kidding."

"I wish. But that was a long time ago."

He still made no move to leave, which was fine by her. Looking up into Roland's dark, exotic eyes, she recalled telling her uncle earlier that she was picky. Roland was employed, honorable, responsible, educated, well spoken, and to top it off, handsome. Not just good looking, but show stopping handsome.

The same could be said of Nat Clark, but even though Roland had never said or done anything to give her any indication that he was more than a little attracted, she was drawn to Roland in a way she wasn't to Nat.

She took a deep breath and quickly scanned the parking lot. There was no one else in sight. She took a step toward him, rested her hand on his forearm but couldn't think of a thing to say.

A second later when he kissed her, it didn't matter.

# 13

Bad News Comes in Threes

An hour after Louie stopped passing out drinks, they finally cleared the bar. It was close to one thirty a.m. The stench of melted, mildewed carpet lingered on the air. Em wished they could leave the windows open, but with all the liquor inside they battened down everything and headed home.

She was ready to collapse from exhaustion, but Louie was whistling like a man without a care in the world. Her uncle's effervescence and love of life was a rare gift. Em figured some of it was programed in her DNA, and she hoped it kicked in soon.

She bid him goodnight, changed into some knit shorts and a hot pink Goddess tank top and fell into a deep sleep only to be awakened by flashing blue and white lights spinning reflections around the walls of her bedroom.

Em sat up and shoved her hair back out of her eyes. She glanced at the old clock on the bedside table. It was a little after three in the morning. She accidentally kicked the table leg when she got out of bed and hopped a few steps to the window.

She tugged the bark cloth curtain aside and squinted into the pulsing lights atop an unmarked police cruiser. Just as she left her room, she heard a knock at the screen door.

Em unlocked the door into the house and then crossed the screened *lanai* to a second door. The beach house was oriented so that it faced the ocean with the Goddess parking lot behind it. The sound of the surf echoed in the stillness of the moonless night. She saw the dark shadow of a tall man silhouetted against the starry sky.

"Hello?"

"Em, it's me."

She recognized Roland's voice, quickly unlatched the door, and ushered him in.

"I take it since you brought a squad car with lights flashing this isn't a social call."

"I wish." He looked over her shoulder into the main part of the house.

She was about to ask who died when he said, "Is your uncle here?"

"He's asleep."

"I need to talk to him."

"What's going on?"

"I'll tell you together."

"But . . ."

"Please, get your uncle, Em."

She hurried through the house and tapped on Louie's door. When he didn't answer, she opened it. His snores filled the room.

"Uncle Louie," she called from the doorway.

The snoring abruptly turned to a sputter, and then he sat straight up in bed. "I'm awake."

"Roland's here to see you."

There was rustling in the darkness as he threw off the sheet.

"Roland? What the heck time is it? What's going on?"

"It's after three. I think it's urgent."

Louie moved toward her through the shadows, pulling on a *yukata*, a long, cotton Japanese robe with wide sleeves, over his floral print baggies.

"Must have found the murderer," he mumbled. "Did we say we wanted to know the minute the guy was caught? Couldn't this have waited until morning?"

Roland was waiting for them on the front *lanai*. As Louie poured himself a glass of water, Em ushered Roland into the open living/dining/kitchen area.

"Would you like something?" she asked. "I can make you some tea or coffee."

Roland shook his head. "Nothing."

"Have a seat." Em waved him toward the rattan sofa.

Roland remained standing in the middle of the room. Louie walked in with a tall glass of water.

"Did you get the guy?" He sat down on the sofa and ran his fingers through his thatch of white hair. "Kimo in the clear?"

Roland turned back to Em. "Have a seat," he said.

"You are scaring me," she said.

A carved wooden tiki had more facial expression than Roland in that moment. She tried to read behind his dark eyes and found herself automatically taking a seat beside her uncle on the sofa. Whatever Roland had come to say, it wasn't good.

"Is this about Kimo? Please don't tell me he murdered Bobby Quinn."

Roland sank into a rattan chair across the coffee table from where they were seated.

"This is one of the things I hate about my job," he said. "Every now and again I have to deliver bad news. I'm afraid I've got some for you tonight."

Em realized she was twisting a lock of hair around her finger and stopped.

Roland looked at them both in turn and then said, "Marilyn Lockhart has had an accident."

"No. Oh, no." Louie sat up and leaned forward. "Is she going to make it? Is she at Wilcox? How bad is it, Roland?"

Em tried to swallow around the lump in her throat. She didn't realize she knew Roland as well as she did until she was convinced by his expression that he was here with the worst kind of news. The kind of news no one ever wants to hear in light of day, let alone the middle of the night.

"Her car went off the road at the curve above Wainiha Bay and plunged into the ocean. She's dead."

Em knew the spot well. There was already one roadside memorial at the top of the hill for a local surfer who had tragically lost his life in the bay. Friends and family still studded the concrete guard rail with flowers in remembrance. Just past the guardrail there was a section where there was nothing to stop a careless driver from plunging over the side of the cliff.

Whenever Em drove around the curve, she found herself clutching the steering wheel and reminding herself not to look over the edge.

"Dead? Marilyn's *dead?*" Louie appeared to age before their eyes. His skin paled beneath his tan, leaving him a jaundiced yellow. He looked over at Em in confusion. "But the wedding is tomorrow."

She took both of his hands in hers. "I'm so sorry, Uncle Louie."

"So am I, sir," Roland said.

"I should have made her stay over."

Em said, "You had no way of knowing this would happen." She felt her uncle's hands begin to shake beneath hers.

"She's a great driver," Louie went on. "She was so proud of her new car." He shook his head. "Maybe she fell asleep at the wheel."

"Possibly," Roland said. "There will be autopsy, and the toxicology reports will tell us whether or not her blood alcohol level was over the limit."

"I know she wasn't drunk. Marilyn hardly ever has more than a glass or two of champagne."

"I'm going to get you a drink," Em told Louie. She got up and skirted the coffee table, heading for the tiki bar in the corner of the room. David Letterman's cage was covered with a sheet for the night, but she heard the big bird rustling around.

She grabbed a rocks glass, poured her uncle two fingers of gold rum, and carried it back across the room. Roland had his little black notebook in hand.

"Did Ms. Lockhart have any next of kin? Anyone we should notify?"

Louie nodded and took a long swallow of rum.

"She has a nephew, but he's in India on business," Em said.

"Do you know how to get a hold of him?"

"She gave me his number." Louie's expression was pained. "Said since we were all going to be family I should have it."

"Would you like me to call him?" Roland offered.

"It's probably better coming from us," Em said.

"I'm not sure where I put the number right now." Louie stared into the bottom of his glass as if the answer was hidden beneath the ice. "What if I can't find it?"

"If we recover Ms. Lockhart's phone, it may still work. He's probably one of her contacts."

"My cell phone went through an entire wash machine cycle once." Louie shook his head. "It still worked once it dried out."

"If we find her phone, we'll see if his number is on it. What's his name?"

"Tom Benton," Louie said. "How are we going to let everyone know the wedding's off?" he wondered aloud. He turned to Em, his expression one of complete loss.

"First thing in the morning I'll have the Hula Maidens start spreading the word, and then I'll alert the hotel. It won't be long before everyone knows."

Roland got up and slipped his notebook into his pocket. "I'm sorry I had to bring you such bad news."

Em stood to walk him to the door. Louie appeared to have sunken deeper into the sofa. He sat there in his *yukata* staring between his knees at the *lauhala* mat on the floor and didn't say another word to Roland.

"I'm sorry, Em," Roland said again.

"I can't believe Marilyn's gone." She rubbed her arms and shivered as the slightest breeze blew in off the water and gave her chicken skin. "Just like that. Here one minute, gone the next."

Roland crossed the *lanai* and was on the steps outside the front door before he turned to face her again. She saw him glance through the open windows into the living room and watch her uncle for a moment.

When he spoke again, his voice was so low she barely heard it.

"I'll call you tomorrow. Sooner if we find anything suspicious."

"I thought it was an accident," she said.

"More than likely it was. There was another vehicle traveling behind hers, but it was at the bottom of the hill as Ms. Lockhart reached the curve, so they only saw her tail lights. According to the witness, her brake lights went on, but she drove straight across the road without slowing down, and then the Mercedes launched into the air. They were at the top of the hill in seconds, but by the time they got there, her car was about twenty-five feet off shore and submerged upside down. There was no way they could climb down the cliff, so they called 911 and waited until the firemen and a fire boat got there."

"What about Marilyn?" Em didn't want to think about her still trapped in the car underwater.

"Divers retrieved the body. Soon as it's light, they'll out hoist the car, and we'll know more."

"Who would want to kill her?" The minute she'd voiced the thought she was sorry.

"Did she have any enemies?" he asked.

"But no one hated her enough to kill her," she said.

"I can think of one person who's had it out for her for a long time."

"Kiki," she whispered.

"Right. Kiki. She nearly burned the bar down just to get back at Marilyn."

"Kiki would never burn down the Goddess. Her main objection to the marriage was that she was convinced Marilyn only wanted to get her hands on the bar. Lillian accidently set her wig on fire, and that's what started the whole fiasco last night."

"That dance number was Kiki's idea. She's the one who put those coconuts in the hands of inexperienced dancers. She had to know better."

"There is no way Kiki would intentionally burn down the Goddess or harm anyone, especially one of the Maidens," she said.

"She's been under a lot of stress since Kimo's arrest. Maybe she snapped."

"I won't believe that she had anything to do with Marilyn's accident."

"I wasn't the only one in the place who heard her say she wanted to get rid of Marilyn. You were still at the table when they had their big argument tonight." He reached out and smoothed her hair back off her face. "Look, try to get some rest if you can. For now, don't worry about Kiki. We'll find out what happened sooner or later. For your sake and Kiki's, I hope you're right."

# 14

## A Sign From Beyond?

By the time Roland left, it was three thirty in the morning, and unfortunately, Em was wide awake. She Googled the time in India and found out it was six p.m. There was no sense in putting off the call to Tom Benton.

"Let's look for that phone number," she told Louie. He still hadn't budged from his spot on the sofa.

"I need another drink." He held up his glass.

*"A drink! Another drink!"* David Letterman squawked from beneath the sheet covering the cage.

"Enough for both of you," Em mumbled.

Louie remained uncooperative but gave her permission to look for Tom's number in his top dresser drawer where he kept "important" things. She found various receipts, faded, dog-eared photos, some coconut buttons off his Aloha shirts, shells he'd picked up off the beach. A rubber band held a stack of business cards, and one was Marilyn's. Tom Benton's address and cell number was written on the back.

Em carried the card back into the living room where her uncle was stretched out on the sofa sipping a rocks glass full of golden rum and staring mindlessly at the television screen. An infomercial with overly made up male and female announcers stood in front of a line of ovens filled with silently rotating chickens. The sound had been muted.

Em took a deep breath and dialed Tom's cell number.

"You've reached the voice mailbox of Tom Benton. I'm out of the country at the moment, but your call is still important to me. Leave me a message, and I'll return your call as soon as possible."

Em left her name and number, said she needed to talk to him urgently about his aunt, and asked him to call her as soon as possible. She set her cell phone on the counter that divided the kitchen and living room area. Worried about Louie, she stood at the foot of the sofa staring down at him. The couple on television was carving up one of the roasted chickens.

"Uncle Louie, maybe you should turn off the TV and try to get some sleep. There'll be a lot to do tomorrow."

His deep-set blue eyes were shadowed and forlorn. "Tomorrow was going to be my wedding day."

She sat down on the edge of the sofa beside him.

"Do you believe in fate, Em?" He watched the ice cubes float around in what was left of the rum.

She shrugged. Never in a million years would she have moved to Kauai to manage her uncle's bar if she hadn't found out about Phillip's cheating and divorced him. If she hadn't married Phillip in the first place, she would have never had to divorce him and would have never ended up on Kauai.

"Yeah, maybe some things are fated to be," she said. "Why?"

"Tonight, before the Maidens performed, I stared up at Irene's portrait and wondered what she thought about me marrying Marilyn. I asked her for a sign, something to let me know that it was all right. Then Lillian caught her wig on fire, and one thing led to another, and I figured since everything turned out all right and no one was hurt, well, that was the sign. No matter what, things would turn out all right. Now this. Marilyn is dead."

"You don't think . . ."

"What if Irene knows marrying Marilyn wasn't such a hot idea and decided to keep me from making a mistake?"

"Impossible. Besides, Uncle, from what you've told me of Irene, she wouldn't wish harm on anyone."

"You're right. I don't know what I was thinking."

He gave her hand an awkward pat. "I'm not sleepy, but maybe you should go to bed. Try to get some shut eye."

She thought it might be his way of asking to be alone, so she agreed to try. Picking up the cell phone on her way to her room, she realized just how hard Louie was taking the sudden death of his fiancée; he'd yet to talk about concocting a memorial cocktail in Marilyn's honor.

# 15

### Strength in Numbers

Though she hadn't thought it possible, Em dozed off and slept until her cell rang and woke her up at seven thirty.

"Hey, Em. It's Trish."

Em sat up and twisted her hair around her hand. Before she could say anything, Trish went on.

"Listen, I just got a call from the feature editor at the *Garden Island,* and she told me about Marilyn. I can't believe it. It's just awful." Trish did freelance photography for the newspaper and was well known for the feature article photos they often ran. "Have you contacted the Maidens yet?"

"I was waiting until eight," Em told her.

"I'll get the phone chain started," Trish volunteered.

"I'd really appreciate it. I'm hoping for a call from Marilyn's nephew."

She thanked Trish and once she hung up, Em grabbed a bath towel and headed through the house to the outdoor shower.

"You're up," Louie said. He was still on the sofa in his robe hitting the television remote, rotating through the channels.

"And you're still down."

"About as far as a man can get. Did you talk to Tom? I heard your cell ring."

"He hasn't returned my call yet. I'm not even sure he has cell service in India. That was Trish. She's going to call the Maidens. I'll get a hold of the hotel as soon as I've showered and let them know about the wedding."

"Mmm."

She knew Marilyn's death was a shock, but she hadn't expected Louie to completely fold up the way he had. It wasn't like him to just give up and do nothing. His eyes were bloodshot, his hair was sticking out all over his head, and he needed a shave.

"Would you like me to make coffee before I shower?" she offered.

"Nope. I'm good. Maybe when you get out. That's soon enough."

As she passed Letterman's cage and noticed it was still covered, she knew her uncle was far from "good." He and Dave were always up at the crack of dawn. She uncovered the parrot's cage. Sensing something was wrong, the macaw paced over to the edge of the perch, stuck one eye between the bars of the cage, and stared at Louie.

Em took a quick shower in the lava rock walled outdoor garden, slipped back into her shorts and a tank top, and wrapped the towel around her head. She stepped out of the private shower garden area and paused to stare out at the endless rolling waves.

"Aloha, Em. I just heard."

Em watched Sophie cross the yard toward her. She reached for Em and gave her a long hug and then air kisses beside each cheek, then she pulled back and studied Em's expression.

"You doing okay?"

"Sure," Em nodded. "I think I'm still in shock. You're here early."

"I came to see what I can do. I figured folks would be coming to pay condolences soon."

"Really? You think so soon?"

Sophie shrugged. "Somebody just died. That's what we do."

Em had no idea what Sophie meant until within the hour, the house was full of people and a mountain of casseroles. So many people showed up and trooped through that they ran Louie right off the sofa, forcing him to retreat into his room.

Once the Maidens had started to pass the word, the news spread on its own as fast as guava jelly on hot toast. Suzi, Trish, and the Estelles arrived. Since there was no wheelchair ramp into the beach house, Little Estelle volunteered to drive around the parking lot and direct traffic.

"Only if you wear your collapsible umbrella hat, Mother," Big Estelle told her. "That hot morning sun will fry your brains, and you're loony enough already."

There was much shouting exchanged, but eventually Big Estelle managed to get the umbrella hat strapped to her mother's head, and Little Estelle rolled away to the parking lot.

Flora arrived toting a forty cup coffeemaker and set it up in the kitchen. Suzi dug into her briefcase and pulled out masking tape and marking pens and made sure names were attached to every casserole dish that wasn't disposable. Trish shifted things around in the refrigerator and told Em that she hoped they had space over in the big double wide in the bar because they were already out of room.

Neighbors and Goddess patrons she knew and folks she'd never met continued to stream into the house. Em was in awe of how everyone started pitching in to help the minute they arrived.

"Em? 'Scuse me." A short, dark-haired Hawaiian lady spoke in such thick pidgin English that Em wasn't sure what she'd said, but it sound like, "Pickup truck wit da tables is here. Where you want 'em?"

"Tables?" Em had no idea what tables the woman was talking about.

Suzi suddenly joined Em in the living room. "Have the guys set them up under the awning, Duchess."

"What tables? What awning?" Em said.

"The wooden tables and benches for folks to sit on. The awnings are up already. Some of Kimo's buddies put them up half an hour ago."

Em hurried out to the front *lanai* with Suzi at her side. Sure enough, a huge awning covered a good portion of grassy lawn that bordered the sand. The table crew was already unloading long collapsible wooden tables and benches from the back of a pickup someone had driven onto the yard. Two men were scraping the barbecue, and a couple of younger guys were unloading a long white cooler the size of a tugboat.

"I don't get it," Em said. "It looks like we're having a *luau* out there."

"Everyone knows you need help feeding all these people," Suzi said.

"But I don't even know all these people. They haven't only brought food, they've lugged in everything but their kitchen sinks."

Flora was suddenly beside Em too. She threw an ample arm around Em's shoulders.

"Eh, Hawaiian style. You need help, we show up."

Show up they did, all morning long. More than once Em paused to wipe away tears witnessing such an outpouring of aloha.

Close to ten in the morning, Sophie found her. "It looks like you have plenty of help. I'll go over and get things set up at the bar. Kimo should be here soon."

"What if the place still stinks from the fire?"

"No worries," Soph said. "We'll get it cleaned up. I'll see if I can find Buzzy and have him bus tables. Don't you or Louie worry about the place today. We'll manage."

Suzi had her phone in hand. "I'll call Pat and have her bring over her cleaning crew. I use them for the rentals I manage."

Em didn't know how to thank them. She couldn't imagine there would be anyone but tourists in the bar today. The whole North Shore would end up in the yard soon.

In all the hubbub, Em had forgotten all about Kimo and Kiki until Sophie mentioned Kimo. So far she hadn't seen either of them. Surely they'd been notified about Marilyn's death. Everyone else on this side of the island apparently knew. It wasn't like Kiki not to be right in the middle of things, and Em wondered why she wasn't.

Sophie had no sooner walked out than the wedding coordinator from the hotel in Princeville finally called back. Em had left her a cryptic voicemail message trying to explain the situation.

"Did I hear right?" The young woman's French accent sounded decidedly thicker than the first time Em had spoken with her. "*Ze* wedding is *oof?*"

"*Oof?* Yes, I'm sorry, but the bride died, so the wedding is *oof*. I don't know what else to say."

"Miz Marilyn Lockhart signed a contract for *ze* expenses."

"Today definitely isn't the day for us to deal with that. I called to let you know that the wedding is cancelled."

Em stepped aside as an elderly little Japanese-American woman hustled through the door carrying a huge rice cooker. There had to be thirty pounds of cooked white rice in the kitchen already. Flora and Trish continued to hover at Em's elbow and direct the flow of aluminum pans.

Outside, the men were almost finished pounding the pile of tables and benches together. In a corner of the parking lot beyond the lawn, Little Estelle zoomed up to block a parking space and began to make threatening gestures until she succeeded in waving away a white van.

The Cougar remained at her post, guarding the space until Kimo pulled into the spot in his gecko-green pickup a minute later. He hopped out of the vehicle alone.

"I'm terribly sorry," the hotel wedding coordinator said, "but Miz Lockhart and Mr. Marshall will definitely lose *ze* deposit. Unfortunately, *ze* food has already been purchased, so you will be responsible for *zat* expense as well."

"Is it really too late to cancel the food? You surely haven't cooked the steaks and lobster yet?"

"I am afraid it's too late regardless."

Em was so flustered she said goodbye and hung up. Flora grabbed the cell from her, hit redial, and asked for the wedding coordinator.

"Eh," Flora said. "You the lady who just hung up? You know the woman who just talked to you about the cancelled wedding? She changed her mind. She wants all the steaks and lobsters she's payin' for. Cook 'um and bring 'um to the Tiki Goddess. Yeah. Today. *Wikiwiki.*" Flora hung up and handed Em her cell.

"What are we going to do with seventy-five steaks and lobsters?"

"You kidding me?" Flora waved toward the yard. "We got a lotta folks to feed. Everybody needs plenty food in a time of grief. What we don't eat, you sell over at the bar. You gotta pay for them anyway."

Em nodded. "You're right. Good thinking."

"For sure. I'm a darn good businesswoman." Flora walked over to the corner where she'd left her big woven plastic purse. "It's gotta be close to ten."

Em and Suzi watched her pull a Gatorade bottle full of green liquid out of her bag, open it, and take a swig. Flora smacked her lips and smiled.

Suzi and Em watched Flora head into the kitchen.

"You can bet that's not straight Gatorade," Em said.

"Will you be okay? I'm going to make sure the kid I put in charge of labeling the casseroles is not screwing up," Suzi said.

"I'm fine." Looking around, Em felt as if Marilyn had somehow managed to take over their lives from the great beyond. "I need to check on Uncle Louie."

Suzi left, and Em was about to go find Louie when she saw Nat headed for the house. He waved at a neighbor he recognized and then smiled her way when he saw her standing in the doorway.

"What's going on?" He looked around, bewildered. "Did you have to move the wedding? Are they getting married on the beach?"

The men standing near the barbecue overheard and fell silent. Em shook her head no and motioned him inside. She lowered her voice.

"Marilyn had an accident last night. She drove off the road just past Wainiha Bay and was killed."

His eyes widened behind his tortoiseshell glasses. "No way."

Em nodded. "It's true. She's gone. Uncle Louie is taking it pretty hard, as you might imagine, and now this place is as crowded as a mall on Black Friday."

# 16

## When the Going Gets Tough—Eat More

Before Em could tell Nat more, her cell phone rang, and she glanced at the caller ID.

"It's Randy Rich," she told him. "I'd better take this one."

The producer asked to speak to Louie. Hoping a conversation with Randy might get Louie moving again, Em excused herself and found Suzi in the kitchen with a couple of high school aged girls. The realtor was pointing at covered dishes.

"Put the side dishes over there." Suzi fanned her hand toward the far corner of the counter.

"We've got seven potato-macs," one of the girls said.

A mix of potato and macaroni salads was a staple at any gathering. Em had yet to get used to the combo, but everyone else managed to put away mounds of it.

"I've got to get this call to Uncle Louie," Em told Suzi. "You're in charge."

"Of course. I thought I was already," Suzi said.

Em knocked on Louie's bedroom door, and when he didn't answer, she poked her head in. The dark, floral-print curtains were drawn. The sun shone through, casting the room in green and yellow shadows.

"Uncle Louie?" she whispered.

"I'm awake," he said, sitting up. He still had on his robe and was in about the same shape as when she last saw him.

"I'm sorry to disturb you."

He shook his head. "Plenty of noise out there. I can't sleep anyway."

"I think the whole North Shore is here."

"Nice to know they care."

"Randy's on the phone." She held her cell out to him.

Louie waved it away. "I don't want to talk to him. You do it."

"Are you sure?"

"Positive. I'm not up to it."

She stepped out into the hall and heard Flora yell, "Who moved my Gatorade bottle?"

Em headed for her own room in the back corner of the house. She had her own private covered *lanai* that faced the ocean, so she stepped outside and sat in her favorite reading spot.

"Hi, Randy," she said. "Sorry about that. Uncle Louie's not up to a conversation right now. Can I help you?"

"Sounds like you're at the wedding. Wish we were there." He sounded disappointed.

"Actually, we're at the house. The wedding's off."

"I didn't think it would last. I hate that we didn't get the break up on film."

"It's a bit more complicated than a break up. Marilyn is dead."

"*What*? I can't believe it. What happened? She have a heart attack or something?"

"No, she had an accident. Her car went off the road on the curve near Wainiha Bay and went into the ocean last night. She didn't make it."

"*Damn*! We just missed it. *Damn*."

The unfeeling bastard was the last person Em wanted to deal with. "Listen, we're very busy here. I need to go."

"Hey, don't hang up. I just called to say that I'm sorry about what happened to the show, but the insurance company hit the roof when Bobby was murdered. We'll put as many episodes together as we can, right up until that last day of filming. In a perfect world, maybe we'll get the okay to come over and add a postscript before we're finally all done editing. If the show turns out to be a big hit, and once the murder is solved, we'll be back."

*I hope not*, Em thought. She was careful not to tell him about the death of the maid at Haena Bay Resort.

"Speaking of solving the murder, do you know if anyone on the mainland was out to get Bobby?" she asked.

"From everything we're hearing over here, he was an all-around great guy. It's a shame this had to happen to him."

"That's for sure."

"Listen," he said, "I'm sorry about Marilyn, but boy, what a twist. I sure wish we were there. What a great season finale . . ."

She hung up on him without a goodbye and watched a white cloud drift across the deep blue sky. At first she thought it looked like a billowy wiener dog. As the cloud moved slowly over the ocean, its shape shifted until it reminded her of a sashimi knife. Then it gradually morphed into a penis.

Em glanced at her watch. It wasn't even ten thirty in the morning, and she had already lost it. Par for the course around here. She thought about talking to Louie again. Maybe if she reminded him Marilyn deserved a memorial cocktail, he might snap out of it, but she decided to give him a little more time before she tried to get him out of his robe and his room.

"Kiki's here." Suzi found Em as soon as she walked back into the main room.

"Where is she?" Em straightened the hem of her tank top, wishing she had changed.

"Over there with the midget."

"Midget isn't the politically correct term."

"Okay, she's over there with the *Menehune*."

*Menehune* were the legendary little people of Kauai who inhabited the island before the Hawaiians arrived. Small in stature, they were capable of lifting heavy stones and magically completing rock walls when no one was looking, or so the legends claimed.

"She's not a *Menehune*," Em said. "Precious is a little person or LP."

"Whatever." Suzi pointed. "They're over there."

Em spotted them on the sofa. "Come with me," she told Suzi. "I need to make some decisions, and I need help."

Kiki jumped up when she saw Em, and by the time Em crossed the room, big alligator tears were streaming down Kiki's face. She grabbed Em and pulled her into a hug.

"I can't believe it. I just can't believe she's gone," Kiki wailed while rocking Em back and forth.

It had been a long night and even longer morning. Em wasn't about to respond to Kiki's dramatics and start trouble. She pulled out of Kiki's grasp. Precious had no such reservations.

"How about turning off the waterworks, Kiki? We all know there was no love lost between you and Marilyn," Precious said.

Kiki batted her eyes, forcing a few more tears to fall. In a high, thready voice she said, "Marilyn and I may have had our differences, but we were hula sisters once. That's a bond that's hard to break. Some of us have literally walked through fire together," she sniffed. She turned to Em. "Do you know what really happened? I heard she drove right off the curve at a hundred miles an hour."

"All I know is what Roland said. Her car flew off the road and ended upside down about twenty-five feet off shore. Divers pulled her out."

"It's a shame about her car. What happened to it?" Kiki reached into her bag, pulled out a tissue, and blotted the corner of her eye, taking care not to dislodge her false eyelash. "That Mercedes was only a few months old."

"They were going to hoist it out today."

"I passed a trailer truck in Kapa'a on my way out here," Precious said.

"It was hauling a black Mercedes. I wondered if it was hers."

Em knew the tears Precious tried to blink away were real.

"Who would want her dead?" Kiki said.

"Besides you?" Precious shrugged.

Kiki pointed a finger toward the ceiling. "I did not kill that woman."

"Did you want to talk about something, Em?" Suzi was watching the volunteers milling in the kitchen. "I really need to oversee all those casseroles."

"I hope there's enough food." Kiki watched two teenagers try to find room on the counter for another huge aluminum pan.

Em said, "I can't reach Marilyn's nephew, and I'm worried that crucial decisions will have to be made about . . . well, about what do with her until he gets here."

"They'll have to keep her on ice."

"Kiki!" Em almost told her to shut up for her own good.

"Well, what do *you* suggest?" Kiki was digging in her purse again. This time she pulled out a small mirror and inspected her lipstick.

"What about Louie? Shouldn't he be the one to decide?" Suzi's cell went off, but she ignored it.

"I can't get him to get up."

"That's no surprise at his age. Maybe he should try Viagra." Kiki snapped the mirror shut and dropped it into her purse.

"What are you *talking* about?" Precious was nearly engulfed in the deep rattan sofa cushions.

"Em just said Louie can't get it up."

"I said I couldn't get him to *get up out of bed.*"

"Oh."

"He's taking this really hard." Em wished she'd walked over to the Goddess to consult Sophie instead of this bunch.

"So what do you think?" she asked them. "We don't even know if Marilyn wanted to be buried on Kauai or not. I don't think we should hold a funeral or a memorial until we hear from her nephew."

"She adored Tom. He was the son she never had," Precious told them. "She even brought him into the shop to meet me last time he was on Kauai. He'll be heartbroken. I think you should wait until you talk to him."

Kiki zipped her purse closed. "Where did you say he is? Indonesia?"

"India. Outsourcing something. Do you know who he works for?" Em asked Precious.

"No, but he has a good job. Marilyn said he was recently promoted. Something about banking."

"How about cremation?" Suzi suggested. "That way the nephew can take her ashes back to the mainland if that's where she wanted to end up."

"Maybe she has a burial plot near one of her late husbands," Precious said.

"Maybe she's got 'em all lined up in a cemetery somewhere on the mainland. Black Widow Gardens." Kiki laughed but then quickly sobered. "Thank heaven Louie escaped."

Em wondered if she should tell Kiki that in the wee hours of the morning she had defended Kiki to Roland. For her own sake, she should stop making jokes about dearly departed Marilyn. Why risk more trouble? If Kiki thought she was under suspicion, and with Kimo out on bail, she could get hysterical. Hell had no fury that could match Kiki in hysterics.

Suzi interrupted Em's thoughts. "I've got to get back to the kitchen."

"Thanks for your input," Em said. "I'll think about what you said."

"I'll help." Precious climbed down off the sofa and followed Suzi. "What should I do?"

"Go out and tell the guys we're going to need more than one serving table for all this food."

"Got it. Do you know if anyone brought any bottled water? If not, I can run into Hanalei and get some," Precious offered.

"No need," Suzi said. "I saw a stack of Fiji water cases out there."

"Great. I'm dying of thirst."

Em held up her hand. "Please, don't use the word dying. I can't take any more."

"I'll head out and help set up the serving tables," Kiki said. "Least I can do."

"It's too bad Marilyn isn't here to see how much people really cared," Em noted.

A pained expression crossed Kiki's face. "Em, all these folks aren't here for Marilyn. They're here for Louie."

Em looked around and realized Kiki was probably right.

Kiki had no sooner left her side than Lillian walked into the house on MyBob's arm. The man Marilyn had pointed out as Orville Orion at last night's party was with them. He was definitely a tall, well-dressed senior of about Louie's vintage.

Lil, MyBob, and Orion paused on the threshold between the *lanai* and the living room until Em caught Lil's eye and waved them over. Lillian's upper left arm was bandaged to her shoulder.

"Oh, Lil, how are you?"

Lillian sniffed and glanced down at her wounded arm. "I'm fine, all things considered."

"She's lucky she didn't go up in flames. As it is, her arm is as cooked as *hulihuli* chicken." MyBob patted Lil on her good shoulder. "I'm just thankful I pulled her wig off before the fire reached her neck and face."

Em blinked. "Um, as I recall, Roland pulled her wig off."

"Whatever," MyBob said. "Thank goodness my little Lil survived. We're hoping she'll be able to dance without any residual trauma."

"Oh, I'm sure she'll be just as good as before," Em said. The way Lillian danced, Em figured she couldn't get any worse.

"I posted pictures and videos of Lillian dancing and the fire out on her Facebook fan page. You can't believe the response. A group from our hometown in Iowa is already planning a pilgrimage to Kauai."

"A pilgrimage?"

"They're coming all this way to cheer her in her time of need. Some of them have never been out of the state. I'll bet none of the other Maidens have gotten as many hits since last night."

"It would be interesting to find out." Lillian patted her pink bouffant. "Remind me to ask around."

Em could tell Orville Orion was hovering nearby, waiting for an introduction. He reminded her of her uncle in that he stood straight and tall for his years and appeared to be in great shape. Though he had less hair than Uncle Louie, he had enough for a comb over that was only borderline tacky. His green eyes were filled with sadness.

She smiled directly at him and held out her hand. "I'm Em Johnson. I don't believe we've met. Things were a bit hectic last night."

"I'm Orville Orion." He wrapped her hand in both of his. "Marilyn was my neighbor. She was a close friend."

Em recalled Marilyn mentioning his name the night she found out Tom was in India.

Her uncle had said the two once dated.

Orville let go of Em's hand and shook his head. In a voice so low Em barely heard him, he said, "I can't believe she's gone."

"It's terrible," she said.

He gazed around the room. "Is your uncle here? I'd like to extend my sympathies."

"He's . . . indisposed right now. You can imagine this was quite a shock."

"The night before the wedding. So sad."

"Has Uncle Louie started on a commemorative cocktail yet?" MyBob wanted to know.

"Not yet. That just shows you how far down he really is."

"I've got a great name for a cocktail in Lillian's honor. You know, it's not every day a hula dancer sets her hair on fire. That's something that needs commemorating if you ask me."

"I'm sure Louie will be interested in your idea. Some other day, though." Em noticed that across the room, Suzi had organized a conga line to help carry the casseroles outside.

"I'm thinking of coming up with the ingredients myself and naming it 'Light My Fire' after the song." MyBob laughed. "Then again, maybe you shouldn't tell him. I don't want him to steal my idea. Lillian's become such a celebrity, I should probably have the idea copyrighted."

# 17

## Roland Returns

By three in the afternoon everyone at Louie's house had already eaten at least twice, and a contented lethargy had set in big time. Folks were sitting around the tables beneath tents constructed out of aluminum posts and blue oil cloth tarps that protected them from the passing trade showers that misted the island and painted rainbows across the sky. No one was moving much at all.

Em listened to the lilting strains of slack-key guitar and ukulele music that lightened the mood. Her uncle had finally changed into board shorts and an Aloha shirt covered with illustrations of century-old maps of the Hawaiian Islands and joined the group. He was seated at a table with some of his cronies. None of them were saying much.

Kiki had stationed herself at the serving table where she could chat with one and all while alternately sipping white wine on ice and ladling out *lomilomi* salmon. Pan after pan of mac-potato salad, teriyaki chicken thighs, *kalua* pork, ribs, fish, rice, rice, and more rice covered every inch of three long tables. One lonely little bowl of mixed green salad had made an appearance in the sea of carbos.

Aware of Roland's arrival from the minute he walked across the yard, Em watched him stop to chat with everyone who hailed him. Like Louie, even though he was all business while on duty, he still had a smile ready for those who wanted to talk story.

After stopping for much *wala'au* along the way, he crossed the yard and spotted Em. When it was clear he was headed over to talk to her, she got up and met him halfway.

"Any news?"

"Yeah, but not the good kind. Walk with me."

Together they slowly strolled toward the Goddess parking lot where Em noticed Little Estelle parked in the shade of a mango tree. She was sound asleep, slumped over the handle bars of the Gadabout. Her umbrella hat covered her head and shoulders.

Roland stopped as soon as they were out of earshot of the gathering.

He was no longer smiling.

"It didn't take long for forensics to find out the brake line on Marilyn's car had been tampered with. I figure it probably happened right here in the parking lot. Someone punctured or cut through it just enough so that it eventually severed completely while she was on the road."

Em was stunned. It was one thing to speculate someone may have killed Marilyn, but it was another to find proof of foul play.

Island life was portrayed as being laid back and tranquil, but because of human nature, paradise was as hectic and dangerous as anywhere else in the world.

"Do you remember where she parked last night?"

She walked him a couple of yards down the lot and pointed. "Right about here, I think."

"Do you know whose van this is?"

"Big Estelle's. The lift on the back is for her mother's Gadabout. Do you want me to ask her to move it?"

"Not yet." He got down on one knee and studied the ground.

"See anything?" Em asked.

"Stains. Something dripped here, but not necessarily brake fluid. Could just be oil. Whatever it was has been driven through and tracked around, so it would be hard to prove anything."

"Sophie parks on this side of the lot all the time, and her car is always leaking something. If it wasn't for Kiki, that thing would have been hauled off to the county yard months ago."

He straightened, brushed his hands together. "Kiki?"

"She's repaired Sophie's Honda a couple of times. Put in some parts."

"Kiki repairs cars?"

Too late, Em realized what she'd just done.

"That doesn't mean she cut Marilyn's brake line."

"No, but it does mean she probably knows where to find it, what one looks like, and how to damage it."

"You don't even know if that's brake fluid under there," she said.

"I could call out a team to make sure, but there doesn't appear to be a substantial amount of anything left. Whatever they found would be corrupted."

"There has been a lot of traffic in and out of here all day long."

"You look exhausted, Em."

"Why, thank you." She reached up and tried to smooth her hair into place. "I was awake almost all night."

"Is Kiki here?"

"She was at the serving table when we left the yard." She didn't have to ask why he wanted to know.

"Is there anywhere I can talk to her alone?"

"The house is a zoo. How about Louie's office? Just pop into the bar and tell Sophie you'll be using it. I'll send Kiki over."

"By the way, we retrieved Marilyn's phone and her laptop. When the phone dries out, hopefully it'll work. Have you heard from her nephew yet?"

"Not yet. I found the number, and I'm going to leave him another message."

Em thought Kiki would take the news that he wanted to see her better from her than to have Roland walk up and take her away from the party.

"I'll go tell Kiki to meet you there," she said.

As Em walked back to the yard alone, she saw a child lying on her back just inside Nat's yard. Curious, she moved closer and discovered it wasn't a child, it was Precious. Stretched out in the full sun, the hairdresser was spread-eagled in the grass with her skirt hiked up her thighs. The exposed skin on her legs, arms, and face radiated with sunburn.

Em stood over her. Precious was so still that Em couldn't even tell if the woman was breathing.

"Precious?"

Nothing.

*Not another one. Not another murder.*

Em knelt down. "Precious!"

She shook Precious, who finally sputtered, started to sit up, and then flopped back onto the grass.

"Whazit? S'goin' on?" Precious's eyelids fluttered but didn't open.

"Are you all right? You're getting burned to a crisp."

Precious mumbled something Em couldn't understand and rolled onto her stomach, exposing a crushed Gatorade bottle beneath her. The cap was gone. Em reached for it and took a sniff of the contents. The smell of alcohol nearly knocked her out.

She knelt down beside Precious and rolled her onto her back again.

"Wake up." Em shook her shoulders hard.

"Wazzz?"

Em held the bottle close to Precious's nose. "Did you drink all of this?"

Precious's eyes opened for a nano-second. She took one look at the bottle and smiled.

"Found it on the laaammmai. Gatoade shur packsh a mean punsh."

Precious promptly passed out again, tongue out, head lolling to one side.

Em was just getting to her feet when Nat walked over. Together they stared down at Precious.

"What happened? Is she all right?" he asked.

"I hope so. Last time I saw her she was looking for bottled water. She found Flora's Gatorade instead."

"Uh-oh."

"You know about Flora's Gatorade?"

"This is Kauai. Everyone knows about everything."

"Rumors keep the island afloat," Em said.

Precious's skin was turning redder by the minute.

"You think she'll be all right?" Em made sure Kiki was still at the serving table across the yard.

"We should at least drag her into the shade," Nat suggested. "Grab her legs. I'll take her arms before she goes from medium to well done."

# 18

## Kiki Gets Grilled

Kiki filled her wine glass with ice and then reached beneath the serving table to grab a bottle of white wine out of the cooler she'd stashed there. She filled the glass, replaced the bottle, and when she looked across the yard she saw Em headed her way. Last time she saw Em, the young woman had been with Roland.

Em smiled at Kiki from across the serving table.

"Any news?" Kiki asked.

"Roland wants to talk to you." Em kept her voice low.

"Me? Now?" Kiki's pulse jumped. She took a sip of wine. "Something's up. I can tell by the look on your face. Is this about Kimo?"

"No."

"Surely Roland doesn't think Kimo had anything to do with Marilyn's accident."

"It's not that."

"Then what?"

Em looked around and whispered, "Someone cut the brake line on the Mercedes."

"What? Why would someone ruin such a great car?"

"Shh. Louie doesn't know yet. Besides, that's not the point. The point is that someone meant to harm Marilyn, and they succeeded."

"So why does Roland want to talk to me about it?" She waved her hand toward the crowd around them. "Out of all these people?"

"Please, Kiki. Go talk to him, and try not to bad mouth Marilyn."

Kiki grabbed both sides of her head. "He thinks I did it!"

Em shushed her again. "Calm down. He just wants to talk to you. I'm sure he'll be talking to a lot of people today."

"Like who?"

"Like me. He already talked to me."

"Ha. He always talks to you."

"I'll go with you if you want me to. Maybe that would be better. I can keep you from taking things from bad to worse."

"Aha! Things are already bad? Things are *bad* for me?" Kiki wondered what Em knew that she wasn't telling.

"That's not what I meant," Em said. "You were upset with Marilyn last night, and you two had it out right in front of everyone. Just talk to Roland, convince him you didn't do anything rash."

"Maybe I need our lawyer."

"Kiki, don't be ridiculous."

"That's not so ridiculous. Kimo's already been arrested. What if Roland hauls me out of here on suspicion of murder? Are you going to tell me I'm being ridiculous then?"

"I think you're making this bigger than it really is. You have nothing to hide, so go and talk to Roland. Get it over with."

Kiki polished off her wine.

"All right," she said.

"I'll walk you over to Louie's office."

"I've got my big girl panties on," Kiki said. "I can go by myself."


AS KIKI CROSSED the parking lot, everything seemed surreal. Hawaiian music floated on the air around her, light mist was falling, creating a rainbow that arched over the mountains in the distance. She took a deep breath and shook out the skirt of her *muumuu*. Kimo was in enough trouble. No need for her to fall apart or get defensive with Roland. She reminded herself to smile as she opened the back door into Louie's office.

"Hi, Roland."

He was sitting on the corner of Louie's desk, looking as delicious as a can of toasted macadamia nuts.

"Have a seat." He waved her toward a chair in front of the desk. She sat.

Too late she realized he was perched above her, looking down on her from a power position. Her stomach flipped, flopped, and then somewhat settled.

"So." She forced herself to smile. "What do you want to know?"

"What time did you leave here last night?"

She shrugged. "I don't know. Around midnight maybe?"

"Was Marilyn already gone?"

"No, her car was still in the lot."

"What time did you leave again?"

"Midnight. I think around then. I helped clean up for a while."

"Did you go right home?"

"Where else would I go that late? After the dance fiasco I called Lillian when I got home to make sure she was all right. Then I checked some emails and went to bed. Kimo was still here." She wished she hadn't said it, but it was true. She'd gone home first.

"He drove his truck to work yesterday like he always does, so we had two cars. He stayed late cleaning up the kitchen. Sophie and Em and probably Buzzy worked late too."

Roland nodded but didn't say anything. He walked over to the window overlooking the parking lot, Louie's crowded yard, and the ocean beyond. Then he turned around again.

"So, you repair cars along with your event planning and hula? You're one talented lady."

"Where did you hear that? About the car repairs?"

"Em said you've kept Sophie's junker running."

*Mahalo, Em, for that.*

Enough is enough, she decided. She raised her chin a notch.

"I've helped Sophie out, sure. My dad had an auto repair shop and taught me to do some basic stuff. So what?"

"Carburetors are basic?"

"Pretty much." She wasn't about to let Roland Sharpe railroad her into a murder charge.

"You fix any other stuff?"

"Besides cars? I fixed a toaster oven last week."

"I meant cars. Do you fix brakes?"

"I know a little about brakes, but my dad did those jobs himself. Liability and all that." She leaned forward. "Look, Roland, there was no love lost between Marilyn Lockhart and me, but I didn't hate her enough to kill her."

"You just hated her a little."

"I disliked her. I never trusted her. I know she was after the Goddess. She wanted it way more than she loved Louie, but I did not kill her." She stood up and looked him square in the eye. "If you're going to arrest me, then do it. If not, then I'll leave. I'm missing one hell of a party next door."

# 19

### The Shake Off

Two days later, and another week was already well underway. Em was still waiting to hear from Tom Benton when the coroner's office called that morning to tell them Marilyn's body was ready to be released. Em tried to rouse Uncle Louie from his permanent horizontal position on the sofa long enough to ask what he wanted to do.

"I can't stand the thought of leaving her in a mortuary until we hear from Tom," he said. "She told me once that she wanted to be cremated, so I guess there's no need to wait around. We can keep her ashes in a safe place until Tom arrives or he calls and can let us know what to do with them."

"True," Em said. With any luck at all, Tom would take over when he arrived on island. *If* he arrived on island.

While Louie stared at the ceiling, Em made the arrangements. When she was finished, she asked, "What about a paddle out?"

Along with traditional funerals and burials, many families opted for memorials at the beach. Armadas of outrigger canoes filled with paddlers, flowers, and friends ventured out onto the water to pour a loved one's ashes into the ocean.

"That's a definite no." Louie shook his head. "Marilyn never went to the beach, and she hated the ocean." He reached for the TV remote, turned on the television, and hit the mute button. On the screen, an anorexic blonde was doing some kind of dancer-cize.

"I'm worried about you, Uncle Louie. You need to get up and move around."

Em missed the old Louie. This spiritless man melting into the sofa was not her uncle. She hoped he didn't feel responsible for Marilyn's death.

"Not yet. It's only been three days."

"We need you at the Goddess. People come in expecting to meet you."

"You and Sophie can handle it for a while."

"We aren't you. You have more friends than you can count, and now you have so many fans since *Trouble in Paradise* aired. And what about Dave?" She glanced across the room to where the parrot was staring forlornly through the bars of his cage. "You haven't put his perch outside since the gathering on Saturday. He needs to get out in the fresh air, and so do you."

"Not today, Em."

"At least get up and get dressed. Let me wash that robe."

His cotton *yukata* was a crumpled mess.

"I'm fine."

"You haven't even mentioned making a commemorative cocktail in Marilyn's honor."

"You were right. It's macabre."

"I never said it was macabre."

He shrugged and stared at the ceiling again. "It seems like it now."

"But it's the way *you* honor someone. Celebrate life before we drain the last tiki mug or something, isn't that what you said? Marilyn would expect it, wouldn't she? She'd want you to come up with something classy and timeless that would be on the menu where everyone would read it."

Louie scratched his neck. "Do we have any more of that *haupia* pudding?"

The slick coconut pudding was an island favorite.

"We had about four trays of it, but they didn't last through the day on Saturday. We have about twenty-five pounds of potato-mac salad left, though."

"Okay, I'll have some of that."

Since he made no effort to get up and dish it up himself, Em fixed him a big bowl of potato-macaroni salad and opened a bottle of Pellegrino water. He turned off the television and sat up. Em handed him the bowl and set the water on the coffee table. His thick silver hair stuck out around his head in all directions. Em made an attempt to pat it down.

"You need a shampoo and shower." She stood over him while he ate a couple of bites of salad.

He finally looked up at her. "Did you tell me Precious drank a Gatorade bottle full of tequila? Or did I dream it?"

"She did. It was Flora's. It was a lot of tequila watered down with a little limeade. By the time Precious realized what was up, she'd already guzzled down most of it and passed out in Nat's yard."

"How is she? Do you know?"

"I called her earlier. She said she'd had a two day hangover and went through a bottle of aloe vera gel for her sunburn, but she's all right." Em didn't mention she feared the poor woman might have suffered brain damage. "She says she's thinking of joining the Maidens. She's always wanted to hula."

"Great!" He did a fist pump in the air.

Em smiled at the first sign of the old Louie.

"You think that's great? She was Marilyn's best friend, and she wants to join the Hula Maidens?"

"I think it's fabulous. Nobody else has a hula show with a dancing midget."

"Little person, Uncle Louie."

"Nobody else has a hula dancing little person either."


EM LEFT HIM shoveling down potato-mac salad and headed back over to the Goddess.

The place had been packed for lunch, but the weather was great, so most tourists were still at the beach soaking up sunshine. Kimo was in the kitchen prepping for the dinner crowd. If the trauma of the three murders had shaken the chef, he had never let it show. Em had only heard from Kiki once since half the island turned out for the sympathy gathering on Saturday. Roland hadn't called at all.

"Hi." Sophie was wiping off tabletops, moving around the room with the ease and energy of her youth. "Is Louie doing any better?"

"No, and I'm worried about him. He feels responsible for what happened and thinks he should have stopped Marilyn from going home so late. Not to mention calling down the wrath of his first wife, Irene, upon her."

"What?"

Em explained about his asking for a sign from the legendary Irene that night.

So far he hadn't looked at a newspaper, nor had word gotten to him, which was a miracle in itself, that Marilyn's car had been tampered with. Obviously it was the only news Kiki had ever kept to herself. If telling Louie about it would have helped, Em would have passed on what Roland said, but the way her uncle was feeling right now, she was afraid he'd somehow take responsibility for not protecting Marilyn.

The phone rang, and Em walked behind the bar to answer it, told the caller they no longer took reservations and that dinner seating was on a first come, first serve basis and then hung up.

"I've got to get Louie up and moving," she said. "He's not interested in anything but infomercials and staring at the ceiling. You have any idea how to get him out of his funk?"

"Actually, I do." Sophie walked back to the bar, tossed the dirty towel into a bin. She disappeared into the office and was back in no time with a newspaper article in her hand. She handed it to Em.

"I was going to give that to him once he was in a better mood, but maybe you should show it to him now."

"What is it?" Em unfolded the colorful clipping. There was a photo of a row of bright tropical cocktails lined up along a bar top. The banner headline read "National Cocktail Shake Off Coming to Honolulu."

"There's going to be a national cocktail contest with a Tropical Tiki Drink division. In six months, the winners from the western region will compete in the regional finals in Long Beach, California," Sophie said.

"California? Why not Hawaii?"

Sophie pursed her lips. "I guess there is a tiki resurgence in Southern California. Or so the article says. People are getting into tiki and the tiki lifestyle in a way that hasn't happened since the fifties. What I can tell from the photos in the article, the contest is run by a bunch of nerdy guys with goatees and retro midcentury clothes. But Uncle Louie is the real deal. He should enter."

Em scanned the article, folded it, and slid it into her back pocket. "Thanks, Sophie. Maybe it'll work. It's worth a try anyway."

Two couples walked in, paused just inside the door, and looked around. The wives were sporting fresh spray tans, plenty of gold jewelry, and new resort wear. Their white shorts were perfectly pressed—a dead giveaway they were tourists.

"Would you like a table?" Em grabbed four menus and walked over to greet them. "Or would you like to sit at the bar?"

One of the men looked at the others and asked in a deep southern accent, "Are you sure this is the place? It sure doesn't *look* like it could be the place."

The tall blonde beside him had been checking out the faded barstool covers before she turned her attention to Em.

"Is this the place on that *Trouble in Paradise* show?" Her accent was as thick as gumbo. Apparently they all hailed somewhere in the lower forty-eight.

"This is the place," Em said. "The world famous Tiki Goddess Bar."

"It sure looks better on television." This from a short, dark-haired woman who was a good fifty pounds overweight.

Em kept smiling. "That's the magic of film."

"Do you think we should eat here?" The first man was staring up at the dusty, antiquated *tapa* cloth that Louie had tacked to the ceiling sometime in the 1970's.

"Maybe just one drink." The short woman was no longer making eye contact at Em. "Just to say we've been here."

"We'll take a table," the blonde said. "By a window. Could you turn on the fans? It's stiflin' in here."

Em reinforced her smile and led them to the banquette near the window. Both women grabbed napkins from the basket in the center of the table and wiped off the vinyl chair seats before they sat down.

Em took their order and walked back to the bar.

"They want a round of Mai Tais. Make 'em double fisted. This bunch needs to loosen up."

"No worries." Sophie reached for the rum. "I'll make sure they walk out on their lips."

More people started rolling in, and it was a while before Em had a chance to fill a glass of ice water for herself. She stood beside the bar, looking around to see if anyone needed anything. Buzzy was at his usual table in the back corner engaged in his favorite sport of tourist watching. Since his break up with his fiancée, he'd taken up hunting for girls in resort wear again. He and the rest of the patrons in the place appeared content for the moment. The quartet from southern Missouri were no longer worried about a little grime. The women were shoving paper parasols from their drinks into their hair, and the men were arm wrestling.

"Better start watering down their Mai Tais." Em nodded toward the table of four.

"Good idea," Sophie told her. "Wanna bet they order dinner in a minute? They're not going anywhere."

"No doubt about it," Em agreed. "By the way, before this place gets slammed again, I wanted to tell you I have to go into town tomorrow morning. Hopefully it won't take long."

"No worries."

"Thanks. With Louie still out, you may be on your own for a while," Em said.

"If Buzzy comes in I'll have him help out. You running errands?"

"I may need to go in and pick up Marilyn."

# 20

### The Ride Along

Em was on her way out the door when Roland called and invited her to meet him for lunch at Mark's Place, a small take-out restaurant in a Lihu'e industrial complex. She ran back into the house, changed from a tank into a top with sleeves and a V neck and added a little eyeliner.

Traffic was the usual back up through Wailua, but it smoothed out after that. She made it to Mark's before Roland, parked and waited for him at one of the picnic tables out front. He pulled up to the curb in a white unmarked cruiser that wouldn't fool a four-year-old, rolled down the passenger side window, and called across the front seat, "I've got an appointment. Come with me."

She grabbed her purse, walked over to the curb, and slid into the car.

"You still owe me lunch," she said.

"For sure." He pulled away from the curb.

"Where are we going?"

"Talk to the Paradise Produce vegetable distributor. The rep is back from Maui."

"Do I have to wait in the car like a good girl?" Em batted her eyelashes and thought she saw a flicker of a smile.

"You can go in as long as you don't say one word."

"Really?" She was shocked.

Roland shrugged. "Let's just say I don't trust you to wait in the car. You'll find some excuse to follow me in. Besides, you know as much as we do right now."

"Have you found any connection between the murders?"

"Still fishing, but I have an interesting detail about Ms. Lockhart."

They pulled up in front of the warehouse, and she knew she'd have to wait to hear the interesting detail. The sign on the front of the building read Paradise Produce, and there was a painting of a bowl full of fruits and veggies.

"This is a new company that's been going after accounts."

"You think the rep was so gung ho he drove all the way out to the

Goddess to try to land some new business before he took off for Maui? Or maybe the trip to Maui was just a cover up?"

"I have no idea. Can you remember not to talk?"

Em mimed locking her lips and throwing away the key.

They walked across a parking lot full of trucks and vans painted green with the Paradise Produce logo. The huge warehouse was divided into cold storage rooms and crates of produce on the ground floor. A narrow wooden stairway led up to a loft.

A young female secretary seated at a desk at the top of the stairs waved them up.

"Are you Detective Sharpe?" she asked.

Roland nodded. "This is my assistant." He didn't give Em's name, but she nodded and tried to look official.

The young woman picked up the phone and pushed a button. "The detective is here," she said into the phone. When she hung up she smiled up at Roland again. "They'll be right up."

The loft was full of desks, some folding tables, and chairs. Em looked around while they waited, and within two minutes a local man in his fifties came up the stairs followed by a stocky, younger man in a uniform shirt that was green with the Paradise Produce logo on it. Neither smiled, but the older man was polite when he greeted Roland.

"I'm Edson Shihara, owner of Paradise Produce. This is Keith Daws, the driver you wanted to talk to."

"Thank you. Is there somewhere we can all sit?"

Shihara glanced at the secretary. She jumped to her feet and started pulling chairs away from the desks. After a second Keith helped. Once the chairs were arranged, the men and Em sat.

The secretary went back to her desk, but Em noticed she was doing more listening than actual work.

"How was your trip to Maui?" Roland asked Keith Daws.

"Great. My auntie came over from the mainland, so we had a big family reunion. Sixty people showed up."

"You lived on Kauai long?" Roland was jotting down notes. The way he danced around the real questions drove Em crazy, but she knew by now that's the way he worked. Slow and steady. Kauai style.

Keith shook his head no. "A couple years."

"You know why we're here," Roland said.

Keith swallowed. "Something about a murder at the Tiki Goddess."

"Right. It occurred the morning you left for Maui. Do you know a man named Bobby Quinn?"

"Never heard of him," Keith said. "I don't know what any of this has to do with me. I wasn't anywhere near the North Shore that morning."

"Were you with anyone? Somebody who can vouch for your whereabouts that morning before you left for Maui?"

He shook his head no. "I live by myself. I got up, watched some TV, took a shower, packed, and then went to catch my flight."

Roland pulled the Paradise Produce business card out of his pocket and held it up. "Supposedly you gave this to the chef at the Goddess that morning."

"Couldn't have been me." Keith shook his head.

"Your name is on the back," Roland told him. He handed Daws the card.

Daws turned it over. "That's my name, but it's not my handwriting."

His boss leaned forward to look at the card. Daws handed it to him. Edson turned it over, carefully studied the card front and back.

"We keep a box of these sitting right by the door downstairs for the drivers. Anyone could have come in and picked one up before one of us noticed."

"The chef said you gave him a free crate of kale and Chinese parsley. Said you were trying to get him to start an account."

"We don't give out free samples," Shihara said.

"Listen, all you have to do is show the guy my photo," Daws said. "I was never there that morning. If he says I was, then he's lying."

"Which is why I requested photos of all of your drivers when I called," Roland said.

"I have them right here." The secretary had stopped pretending not to be listening. She opened a desk drawer, pulled out a manila envelope and handed it to Roland. He handed it to Em without opening it.

Then he stood up and so did Em. Roland thanked Shihara and Daws for their co-operation. Before he started down the stairs Roland paused, his expression thoughtful. He was studying Daws.

"Do all your drivers wear those shirts?" Roland asked Shihara. Roland's notebook was out again, his pen poised above it.

"They do," Edson nodded. "All the shirts are green with the company logo on the back."


EM HELD HER silence as they crossed the parking lot to the car. She could tell Roland was lost in thought, no doubt going over the interview, putting the pieces together. Once they were in the car and she'd clicked her seat belt, she turned to him.

"I believe Daws," she said.

He turned the key in the ignition. "Why?"

"He just seemed really sincere." She shrugged. "I dunno why."

"I think so too. I don't think he was at the Goddess that morning."

"You don't think Kimo lied, do you?" There was no way she could be wrong about Kimo, but either he was lying or the veggie guy was. No one but Kimo had seen Daws there that day.

"No one saw any produce van that morning," Roland said. "We have no car description. It would sure help if there was one person who could back Kimo up."

"What now?"

"Now we eat."

In two minutes they were back at Mark's Place. Em's car was right where she left it in the parking lot. They went inside, waited in line. If they'd come in before the interview there wouldn't have been such a long wait, but Em decided it was worth it as she carried a plastic take-out box filled with a huge salad made with fresh greens out to the picnic tables in front. Roland swung his leg over the picnic bench and set down a *katzu* chicken plate lunch.

"I'm worried about Kimo," she said.

"Nothing to worry about. I'll show him the photo. I don't think he'll recognize Keith Daws."

"Which leaves us with a bigger problem. Who would impersonate the veggie man? And why?"

"Maybe someone else from Paradise Produce. Someone trying to frame Daws."

"Which is why you wanted photos of all the drivers."

"Exactly." He cut another bite of breaded fried chicken fillet, shoved it in his mouth, and chewed it up. "But Shihara already faxed me a schedule, and all of the other drivers and trucks were accounted for that morning. Supposedly none of them were on the North Shore until well after noon, and then it was just one truck and one driver."

They ate in silence for a few minutes before Em remembered.

"So what's the interesting detail about Marilyn?"

"We found her cell in the car and dried it out. She called someone named Orville Orion in the early morning hours just before she died. Does that seem odd? What's their connection?"

Em picked up a tomato wedge with her fingers, dipped it in the plastic dressing cup.

"He's a friend and a neighbor of hers. He was at the rehearsal party that night with a bunch of other Princevillians. He's the president of their homeowners' association." She popped the tomato into her mouth.

"He called her a couple of times but didn't leave messages. She called him back around 1:15 a.m."

Em paused with her plastic fork halfway to her mouth. She lowered the fork.

"She called him that late?"

"Wasn't that right before she left your place?"

She nodded. "She left the bar and went back to the house to get her iPad and . . ." Em suddenly paused.

"What?"

"It's probably nothing."

"But you're thinking it might be something."

"She said she was going back to the beach house to get her things and freshen up her makeup."

"So?"

"So who freshens up makeup at one a.m. when they're planning to go straight home?"

"So she could have been headed somewhere else."

"Orville Orion's place. Maybe she called to let him know she was on the way."

"The night before her wedding," he said.

"To my uncle."

Roland glanced at his watch and downed two scoops of fried rice in six bites. Em could tell he was anxious to take off. She closed the lid on her salad container.

"I'll take the rest home." She finished what was left of her soda.

Roland got to his feet, empty take-out box in hand. He picked up her soda cup to toss it in a bin along with his rubbish and waited at the edge of the parking lot near the trash can.

"Thanks for lunch," she said. "And for letting me sit in on the interview."

"Don't get any ideas about going into crime fighting on your own," he told her, finally smiling.

"Don't worry."

"Where are you headed?"

"I have to go by the mortuary and pick up Marilyn."

His eyebrows headed toward his hairline.

"She's been cremated."

"Ah."

"I'm still trying to connect with her nephew. He finally called me back, but I missed him. He left a voicemail. I called him back and asked him to call me tonight around six, that's around ten in the morning in India."

"Good luck. I'll probably see you soon. I'm going to head up to the Goddess with those photos of drivers and talk to Kimo again," he said.

"What if he IDs Keith Daws?"

"Then one of them is lying big time."

# 21

### Back to the Looney Bin

"Okay, so . . ." Em looked at the cardboard box she'd belted into the passenger seat. "Why did you call Orville Orion at one fifteen in the morning a few hours before you were going to marry Uncle Louie? Answer me that, Marilyn."

The box was silent.

"Freshen up your makeup? *Really?* Something's up, and we'll get to the bottom of it one way or another."

Em started humming the old Blondie tune "One Way Or Another." She was really into it the last quarter mile to the Goddess, tapping the steering wheel, singing at the top of her lungs, "I'm gonna get 'cha, get 'cha, get 'cha, get 'cha."

She turned into the parking lot and instantly recognized Big Estelle's van and the other Maidens' cars.

"Welcome back to the loony bin." She parked and unclicked the seat belt around the box. "Welcome home, Marilyn."

She waited until there was no one in the parking lot. Her flip flops slapped against the pavement as she hurried over to Louie's office door. Inside, she opened one of the old rusted lateral file drawers still full of years of receipts she hadn't gotten around to tossing or filing yet and tucked the box safely inside. Filing and organization were at the bottom of Louie's things to do list. Marilyn would be perfectly safe in the drawer until Em went over to the house.

Trying to enter the bar without being noticed, she opened the interior door wide enough to slip out and discovered there was no need to worry about being noticed yet. Kiki had all the dancers gathered around tables, and they were deep into conversation. Precious was seated beside Kiki in front of the group. The LP was jotting down notes on pink lined paper.

"Here's the name and phone number of our dressmaker." Kiki handed Precious a slip of paper and Precious copied the information as Kiki kept talking.

"You'll need to call her ASAP and tell her you're a new member. She'll make an appointment with you so that she can take your measurements and will keep them on file. You'll only need half the fabric we do, so there's probably enough left over yardage to make most of the costumes you'll need." Kiki turned to Suzi. "Do you have the list of dresses?"

Suzi nodded and turned on her iPad. "She'll need the white ruffled *muumuu*, the turquoise gown with the taro leaves, the group *pareau*, the off the shoulder blood-red dress we just used for Kalua."

"That's a lot of dresses." Precious stopped writing and looked at the women.

"Oh, there are even more. They aren't cheap, either," Flora assured her.

Em noticed Precious didn't respond to Flora and figured there was probably no love lost after the Gatorade incident.

"So they're expensive?" Kiki said. "So what? Cut some more hair. Raise your prices at the salon. We don't let just anyone become a Hula Maiden." Kiki lowered her voice. "Considering you were a good friend of Marilyn's . . ."

"You do want to be a Maiden, don't you?" Suzi paused with iPad in hand. "Because we can't go wasting fabric if you're going to up and quit right away. Have you thought about all the practicing you'll have to do? Especially before a big show. Can you take time off work?"

"I own my own salon. I set my own hours," Precious assured them.

"Just saying, it takes a *big* time commitment."

"Right. So is that it? That's all the dresses she'll need?" Kiki was digging in her bag.

Suzi nodded. "That's it for now. Do you think we'll ever do the Kalua fire dance again?"

There was a gasp from Lillian whose arm was still bandaged. "My dress is singed. I think it's ruined."

"Singed? It could have gone up in flames. Thank goodness it was treated with fire retardant," Big Estelle said. "Good thinking, Kiki."

Kiki shrugged. "Of course. I believe there's extra fabric."

"So?" Suzi was waiting. Precious looked terrified.

"Not everyone will have to do the fire dance from now on." Kiki bit her lip, thinking a minute. "Maybe just volunteers from the girls who've been dancing longest should handle flaming coconuts."

"I'm out," Lillian said.

"Me, too." Precious appeared relieved.

Em walked over to where Sophie was drawing beer for three big guys seated at the bar staring at a TV mounted in the corner. They were watching a surf contest, completely ignoring the Maiden meeting.

"Did you pick up the package?" Sophie asked her.

"I did. Mission accomplished. I had lunch with Roland."

Sophie paused to stare at her. "Really?"

"Nothing fancy. Take-out."

"Still."

"Yeah." Em tipped her head toward the ongoing meeting. "How long has this been going on?"

"An hour. Precious decided she wants to learn hula, and the Maidens talked it over, and she's going to join them. Kiki went over the history of the group . . ."

"Oh, no."

"Oh, yes. That took about forty minutes. About halfway through, Little Estelle threw the Gadabout into gear and roared out, sloshing her Blue Hawaii all over the floor. Said she was going to wait for Big Estelle on the beach."

"Have you seen Roland?"

Sophie said no. "Is he coming up here?"

"He needs to talk to Kimo again."

"Don't let Kiki know. She's worried."

"I can't say as I blame her."

"Has Roland got a lead?"

"All I can say is that he found out someone's lying big time," Em said.

Sophie glanced toward the kitchen door. "I hope it's not Kimo."

"You and me both."


EM WAS IN the office when Roland finally walked in. She'd just copied Orville Orion's name and phone number out of the phone book.

"I thought you'd get here long before me," she said.

"I thought so too, but they needed someone near Kalaheo, and the guys on patrol were stretched pretty thin. I answered the call."

"Not a murder, I hope."

"Nope. Seems like those are reserved for the North Shore."

"Not funny. Robbery?"

He shook his head no. "You know the place on the *makai* side of the road with the big Jesus Coming Soon sign on the roof?"

"Uncle Louie said it's been there since the seventies."

"At least. Some guy convinced himself Jesus really is coming soon. He took a beach chair and climbed up on the roof to wait. He wouldn't come down."

"What did you do?"

"The fire department was already there, but he wasn't budging. I climbed up and finally convinced him that if he didn't come down that we'd forcibly remove him, and if I threw him in jail he'd miss the second coming."

"So . . ."

"He climbed down."

"Don't you wish all your cases were that easy."

"For sure." He was carrying the envelope of photos. "Kimo here?"

"In the kitchen. Would you like me to have him come in?"

"Sure." He looked around at all the framed photos of Uncle Louie with famous dignitaries, movie stars, and royalty who had visited the Goddess at one time or another. "I'm starting to feel like this is my annex."

"Good thing there's never much actual work going on in here." She went to get Kimo and then went back into Louie's office with him. Roland didn't ask her to leave so she tried to disappear into the board and batten wall paneling.

Roland had the photos spread out over the desk. He greeted Kimo and then asked, "Recognize any of these guys?"

"None of 'em," Kimo said after taking his time to study each photo.

"None?"

"Not one."

Em was so relieved she wanted to hug him. She didn't make a peep.

"What's up?" Kimo asked Roland.

"These are all the Paradise Produce sales and delivery men."

Kimo shook his head. "The guy I met had on a brown shirt, like the UPS man."

"And that's who gave you the card."

"Right. And the kale and Chinese parsley."

Roland picked up a photo. "This is the real Keith Daws."

"That's not the one who was here."

"Then somebody is impersonating a Paradise Produce deliveryman," Roland said. "Somebody who doesn't even have the right color shirt."

"Why?" Kimo wondered aloud.

"To get into the kitchen?" The question popped out of Em without warning.

Kimo and Roland had obviously forgotten she was there.

"Just detecting. Sorry," she said.

"Go on," Roland said.

"Maybe whoever killed Bobby that morning came here looking for something else, and Bobby got in the way."

"Looking for what?" Roland started to pile up the photographs.

"My sashimi knife?" Kimo scratched his head.

"I have no idea," Em said. "It's just a thought." She was still so relieved that Kimo hadn't pointed out Keith Daws she had to really focus.

"So who killed Bobby Quinn and why?" Roland shoved the photos back into the envelope. "I'm starting to think that his murder must be connected to the murder of Esther Villaviejos."

"The maid at the resort," Kimo said.

Roland nodded. "Bobby was staying out there. Let's say he met Esther, and they had an affair. When Victor Villaviejos found out, he came here and killed Bobby. His wife suspected and confronted him, so then he killed her and got off the island."

"You said the maid was thirty-nine. Bobby was a good ten years younger, if not more."

"She was still good looking, a little frazzled though."

"She had a problematic husband. Anyone would look frazzled," Em said.

"How did Villaviejos get off the island?" Kimo asked.

"Boat?" Roland replied.

"You have a photo of him?" Kimo asked. "Maybe he posed as the deliveryman."

Roland used his cell phone to have Villaviejos' DMV photo emailed to him. When it came through he showed it to Kimo.

"He has dark hair like the guy I talked to, but that picture's not very clear," Kimo said. "I can't tell for sure."

Kimo went back to the kitchen. Em was alone again with Roland.

"What now?" she asked.

"I'm going to stop by Mr. Orion's on my way back to town."

"I'd love to be a fly on the wall for that." She didn't ask if she could ride along.

"I'd rather talk to him alone. He might not open up in front of you."

"Will you let me know what he says? I know you're not obligated. I promise I'd never do anything to jeopardize the case."

"I'll call you as soon as I get a chance."

# 22

## Frothy Fang

At six p.m. Em's phone rang right on time. She left the noisy bar and walked outside. The sun wouldn't set for another hour, but it was riding low in the sky as she headed out toward the sand. She didn't know she'd be so relieved when she heard Tom Benton's voice at last.

"Em? It's me. What's up? I couldn't get a hold of Aunt Marilyn. Is she all right?" Strains of East Indian music pounded in the background.

"I can hardly hear you. Are you in still in India?"

He laughed, and the music went down a few decibels. "Bollywood."

"Where's that?"

"Not where, that's a kind of music. From Indian musicals."

"Oh, right." *Bollywood.* Megawatt smiles, vibrant rainbow colors, lots of jumping around.

"I'm back in California. Just got in. How was the wedding? Where's my aunt? Are she and Louie on a honeymoon?"

Em took a deep breath and decided not to beat around the banana tree.

"I'm sorry, Tom, but Marilyn was in a terrible wreck. She died Saturday night."

"What? When did you say? She died? Saturday? The night before the wedding?" He made a choking sound. "Is Louie all right?"

"Louie is fine. He wasn't with her. It was the night of the rehearsal dinner. She was driving home to Princeville alone after a rehearsal dinner party, and her car went off the road."

He mumbled a curse and then she heard him say, "No."

"There's more."

"That's not enough?"

"It wasn't an accident, Tom. The police discovered that someone tampered with the brakes on her car."

By now Tom Benton was cursing a blue streak. "I told her not to move to f-ing Kauai. I *told* her she'd be over there all alone."

"She wasn't exactly alone, and what does that have to do with anything?"

"She didn't have family there. No one to watch over her. I'm her only family now that my mom is gone. Now someone has *killed* my Aunt Marilyn? Why?"

"They don't know yet."

"I'll hire a private investigator if I have to. I'll get to the truth. One way or another I'll get to the bottom of this."

"Listen, Tom, the KPD is working the case. I know the lead detective personally."

"Right. Don't forget you're on an island, Em. In the middle of nowhere. It's practically a third world country. The police are probably a bunch of hicks at best. Good old boys. My aunt was an old, rich *haloe* lady. They're not going to prosecute one of their own to avenge her death. Mark my words." His anger pulsed across the air waves.

"Listen, Tom, I know you're upset . . . ."

"What do they know so far? Or is anyone saying?"

"They did an autopsy. Her blood alcohol was in legal limits. She went into the ocean and died on impact. The brake line was cut."

Suddenly he made a choking sound, and his anger dissolved into despair. "She was so happy. She said she'd found someone who could make her so happy. Of course, she always said that before one of her marriages. I can't believe she's gone."

"My uncle is broken-hearted. I've never seen him so down."

"Where . . . where is she now?"

"In the office. Locked in a file drawer."

"What?"

"We couldn't get a hold of you, and a decision had to be made. We had her cremated. I have the ashes here. We were waiting for you to decide on the style of memorial you think would be fitting. Do you know what she wanted?"

"I can't think at all right now. I really can't think about *that* right now. We'll talk about it when I get there. I'll be on the first flight that I can get."

"You're welcome to stay with us," she offered.

"'I have a key to my aunt's house. I'll stay there."

"Call as soon as you're settled."

"Don't worry, I will. Rest assured I'm not going to let anyone get away with murder."


EM WORKED alongside Sophie until closing that night. When Sophie asked how Louie had responded to the article about the cocktail shake off, Em admitted that with everything else that was going on, she'd forgotten to show it to him.

Exhausted, she went back to the house wanting nothing more than to take a quick shower and drop into bed, but a few yards from the back door, the sound of Arthur Lyman singing "Puka Shells" accompanied by the sound of vibraphone music came floating toward her in the dark.

Apparently Louie was still up and hopefully making some progress toward recovery. She called out hello as she walked inside, but he didn't answer. The TV was still on, but the sound was muted. There was a vinyl LP record playing on an old turntable in a teak cabinet. Louie refused to get rid of the stereo system because he owned a huge collection of vintage Hawaiian and exotica albums that were not available in CD or MP3 formats and probably never would be.

*"Oo ,oo, oo. Ah, ah, ah."*

Arthur Lyman was making howler monkey sounds on the recording. Not for the first time, Em was glad the popularity of the exotica music genre had been confined to a limited audience.

Louie came walking out of the back of the house in an Aloha shirt in a traditional tapa cloth pattern of brown and black. He also had on long, purple flannel pajama pants.

"I brought you some garlic shrimp and mashed sweet potatoes." She held out the take-out box for him. "I figured you hadn't eaten."

"Tonight's special? Yum." He took the box and shuffled over to the kitchen, slid open the drawer, and pulled out a fork. He walked back to the bar and set down the box.

"How was your day?" he asked.

"Long." She realized she hadn't even come over after she returned home from town earlier. "I'm so sorry I didn't come over when I got back, but we were slammed. I was hung up waiting tables and helping out all night."

"I saw all the cars in the lot."

"Kimo did a great job on the shrimp. It's excellent. Try it." She'd given up trying to force feed him. "You look like you're losing weight."

"Did you . . . you know?"

"I picked up the box at the mortuary. It's locked in the file cabinet." Thinking of Marilyn reminded her of Tom Benton. "Tom called," she said.

"How did he take it?" Louie stared down at the recycled paper take-out box but didn't open it.

"He was upset, of course. He'll be on the first flight he can get."

"From India?"

"From California."

"That's good. Marilyn would be happy to know he'll be here to take care of things. She would have wanted that."

Em didn't want to bring him down any lower by telling him about

Marilyn's middle of the night phone call to Orville Orion and was wondering what she could possibly say to cheer him. Then she remembered the article.

"Pour me a drink," she told him. "I'll be right back."

"What would you like?" He sounded listless and less than enthused, but he was headed for the tiki bar.

"Surprise me."

She went into her room, dug through her dirty clothes basket, and found the shorts she had worn when Sophie gave her the article. Luckily she was behind on the laundry. She pulled it out, shoved it into her back pocket, and returned to the living room.

Her uncle was putting the lid on a cocktail shaker when she walked back over to the bar and sat down on one of the swivel stools. As Louie shook the shaker and the ice rattled against chrome, David Letterman started running back and forth on his perch bobbing his head.

*"Shake. Shake. Shake."* The parrot was so excited that Louie was back in action, he was screaming at the top of his lungs. *"Shake your boobie. Shake your boobie."*

"I thought it was 'shake your bootie,'" Em said.

Louie shrugged. "He's getting hard of hearing."

He poured the contents of the shaker into a low glass and handed it to her. She took a sip, closed her eyes, and said, "Ahhh."

"Like it? It's an old favorite, a Frothy Fang." He held up his left hand and showed her the missing digit on his little finger. "Commemorates the time I was bit by a loose pit bull. It attacked me when I was out hiking up the *Okolehau* Trail behind Hanalei."

"I thought you told me you lost the tip of your finger snorkeling."

He shrugged. "Did I?" He stared at his left hand. "Hmm. Maybe it *was* the time I stuck my hand between two rocks, and an eel bit it off."

Em took another sip, savoring the refreshing mint flavor. She pulled the article out of her back pocket. She smoothed it out and turned it around so that Louie could read it.

"What's this?" He barely glanced at the page.

"An article Soph tore out of the *Hawaiian Airlines* magazine. There's going to be a national contest for the best tropical drink cocktail in the country. The first state round will be held in Honolulu, then the winner will go on to Long Beach for the western regionals." She pointed at the text. Louie was staring at the photo.

"You'll win the state round hands down," she added.

"That looks like my 'Blood on the Beach.'" He pointed to a photo of a drink that resembled his version of a Bloody Mary. Louie leaned closer and read the caption aloud.

"The 'Tropic of Tomato' is a heady blend of vodka, tomato puree, and rosemary oil with the slightest essence of lime. What?" He scanned the page and frowned. "What the heck's that supposed to mean? It sounds more like soup or spaghetti sauce than a drink."

"It means you can win this thing. I read the whole article. Some of these guys couldn't tell a classic tropical cocktail from a can of gasoline."

He stared at the page, scratched his head, and then looked at Dave. "What do you think, buddy? Do we have it in us?"

Afraid to get prematurely excited over his reaction, Em said, "You should seriously think about it. You could enter one of your old favorites off the menu or come up with something new."

He reached beneath the bar and pulled out a thick, tattered binder labeled Uncle Louie's Booze Bible. He tapped the cover.

"You realize this is worth a small fortune?"

She nodded. No doubt it was to someone. The binder contained every tropical drink her uncle had ever come up with, each accompanied by its own outrageous legend that told the origin for his inspiration.

"If I croak before I find a publisher, it's yours. You have my permission to publish it posthumorously."

"You mean posthumously."

"Right. After I'm gone."

She watched him stroke the cover of the binder and thought about the day she'd arrived on Kauai. Her shattering divorce had left her not only broken but broke. When a letter from Kiki had arrived, she'd used the one way ticket the Maidens pitched in to buy and mailed to her. They had begged her to answer their emergency plea. With nothing to lose, she headed for Kauai under the impression her uncle was feeble-minded.

What she discovered was that the bar accounts were in the red because Louie was running the Goddess into the ground by loaning money to the locals and offering too many "on the house" rounds. What Kiki had really feared was that Louie would fall so far into debt that he would lose the Goddess before he lost his mind.

Most of the time Louie Marshall was as sane as the rest of them.

"You're not going anywhere, Uncle Louie," Em said.

"That's what Marilyn thought on her way home Saturday." He shook his head. "You never know, Em. You just never know."

# 23

### Roland Calls with the 411

"ARE YOU BUSY?"

Em smiled when she heard Roland's voice on the Goddess line.

"Busy? I'm always busy. Why?"

"I'm right up the road. I hoped you could meet me for a few minutes," he said.

She covered the receiver, stuck her head out of the office, and waved at Sophie. "Can you spare me for a while?"

Sophie glanced at the clock behind the bar.

"Sure. Long as you're back by eleven when that tour van gets here."

Em ducked back into the office again. "Where are you? I can leave for about an hour and a half." She'd forgotten a tour company had called to arrange a special group lunch.

"I'm at the kayak rental stand."

"The one by the river or the one on the highway?"

"Neither. The one by the surfboard rental stand."

"The one in the park or the one on the beach?"

"Park."

"I'll be there in twenty minutes." She started to hang up and then said, "Is this an emergency?"

"No. I just wanted to tell you what Orion had to say and thought you might want a slice of pie to help you swallow it."

"That bad?"

"We'll talk when you get here."

Twenty minutes later she spotted Roland on the beach where the Hanalei River emptied into the ocean and watched him cross the sand that had been beaten down as hard as pavement by all the cars and pickups that vied for parking space on the beach between the pier and the river.

"What happened?"

"A couple from Montana has either stolen a kayak, or they're lost somewhere on the ocean. Honeymooners. Rented a double kayak yesterday afternoon, said they'd only be gone for an hour. They aren't back yet."

Em studied the endless horizon. Near the shore the water was as placid as a lake, but outside the bay, the swells were deep and relentless, a challenge to anyone unfamiliar with the ocean.

"Isn't this a job for the Coast Guard? Or the lifeguards?"

"The manager of the kayak rentals called and reported a theft, not a missing persons report. It got turned over to me."

"So you have to detect what happened."

"Until we find an empty kayak somewhere, I do. I doubt they know a thing about the ocean."

"I can't believe all you need is a driver's license and a credit card and away you go."

"No qualifications needed to launch into some of the most dangerous water in the world."

"Kind of like getting married or having kids," she said.

"Kinda."

"You mentioned pie," she reminded him.

"Come with me."

They walked over to his car. He opened the door and took out a brown paper bag, then closed the door and headed for a green picnic table under the shade of an ironwood pine tree in Black Pot Park.

She looked around. Thinking he might not want to be the subject of more gossip than necessary, she sat across the table instead of next to him.

Roland methodically opened the bag, took out two individual mini fruit pies, two bottled waters and two forks then smoothed out the bag. He tore it down two seams and handed her a section to use as a placemat.

"Wow. From the Pie Lady?" Em's mouth watered.

He nodded. "Mango blueberry."

She was chewing a forkful before he'd taken his first bite.

"So, you like pie, I take it?" He was actually smiling.

"Luff it," she mumbled around another bite. Em swallowed, opened her water, and took a sip. "So what did Orville have to say?"

"You realize this is confidential."

"Of course. I still haven't told Louie about Marilyn's one a.m. call. So what did he have to say?"

"He says all he wanted was to wish her luck."

"At one a.m.?"

"That's all he'd say. I questioned him for quite a while. His story never changed."

"Did he seem nervous?"

"Not really. He was cool, calm, and collected. From the looks of his house and his car, the guy doesn't need to worry about money."

"Maybe he was jealous." She stared at the pie for a minute. "Maybe he was so jealous he decided if he couldn't have her then neither could my uncle."

"He's seventy-four, Em."

"So? Do you think jealously is reserved only for the young?"

He shrugged.

"Maybe I should talk to him," she said.

"Because you could get the truth out of him?"

"Maybe I can appeal to his emotions. Tell him how broken up Louie is."

"If he was responsible, he'll trip up and we'll get him, but we have to have all our ducks in a row. Don't go treading in shark infested water, Em."

She didn't promise anything. She finished her pie.

"Did you ever hear from the nephew?"

"Last night. He's flying in as soon as he can and will call me when he gets here. He's going to stay at Marilyn's."

"Did you tell him everything yet?"

"I told him about the brake line being cut. Not about the other murders or the ever growing list of suspects or Orville's phone calls." She didn't dare tell Roland that Tom Benton had very little faith in the KPD. "He's furious as you can well imagine. He's even threatening to hire a private detective."

"If he hires someone on Kauai, he'll get a retired cop. He brings someone in from the mainland, and no one's going to talk to the guy."


AFTER THEY finished their pie, Roland left. Em checked her watch. Since she was already in Hanalei, she had time to run up to Princeville and pick up some flowers for Tom Benton before she had to get back to the Goddess.

Considering herself lucky, she only had to circle the Foodland parking lot twice before one of the miniscule parking slots opened up, and she slid her uncle's old pickup between two red Mustang rental convertibles. She grabbed a bouquet of tall tropical stalks of red ginger, heliconia, and ti on her way into the store, hurried back to the fruit department and chose some papayas, and then got in the ten-items-or-less line.

Counting herself lucky not to have run into anyone in the store or parking lot, which would mean another ten minutes would have been spent on talking story, she jumped back into the truck and threaded her way back through the parking lot. She turned left and passed the library and Princeville community center. Before she turned left again and started to weave her way into the bowels of the planned development, she pulled the slip of paper with Orion's address out of her purse, determined to drive by and check out his house.

It didn't matter how many times she'd driven around Princeville, there were so many Loops and Drives with similar Hawaiian names that she always got turned around and had no idea where she was. Laid out around three nine hole golf courses, the resort community was lovely if you enjoyed a pristine environment. Nearly every home had a view of the lush green mountains, and some looked out over the ocean and had incredible sunset views.

Somehow she turned onto Orion's street, one of the Loops, and slowed as she drove past his house. The garage door was down so there was no telling if he was home or not. The landscaping was well-trimmed and tasteful, professionally laid out. His home appeared to be in pristine condition. It was painted a light sea foam green that stood out amid an ocean of beige on beige homes.

At the corner she was deciding whether to turn left or right when she noticed the low lava rock wall street marker with a Princeville logo that bore the name of Marilyn's street. It was on the left, so Em turned onto it and started winding around. Eventually, she came to Marilyn's home.

Both garage doors were down, and there was no sign of a rental car out front. She pulled into the driveway, grabbed the fruit and flowers, and headed for the front door.

The door was painted with red enamel. Em recalled Marilyn had chosen it because according to Feng Shui, "good chi" supposedly flowed in through a red door. In an additional touch of drama, one foot high brass initials, MML, for Marilyn Marlene Lockhart, were attached to the center of the door.

Em rang the bell and looked in the long beveled windows in the sidelights beside the front door. There was no sign of anyone inside.

"Tom?" Em knocked on the door and called his name again.

She tried the knob, but the door was locked. Louie and his friends in Haena were still in the habit of leaving their doors unlocked. When taking something over to a neighbor, no one thought anything of walking in and leaving it in the house. Now and again whenever a rash of burglaries broke out, depending on who was in or out of jail that week, folks tried to be more vigilant about locking up. If they could find their house keys.

She decided to take the welcome gifts around back and leave them on the covered *lanai* rather than out on the sunny front steps. She headed around the side of the house, using the stone path that ran along the evenly trimmed mock orange hedge. When she reached the shaded concrete *lanai*, she put the flowers and fruit on an outdoor dining table. Then she walked up to one of two sets of wide glass pocket doors that, when pushed open, completely disappeared from view. She cupped her hand above her forehead and looked into the living room.

As anyone who knew Marilyn would suspect, the inside of the house was perfect. There wasn't so much as a throw pillow out of place. Em had only been inside once when Marilyn had invited her to dinner after the engagement was official. The house was filled with Marilyn's art collection, colorful glass vases, and oil paintings done by artists from all over the islands.

Em felt a twinge of sadness seeing the place exactly the way Marilyn had left it, knowing that Marilyn would not be coming back and how much all the things inside meant to her. She walked over to the next set of long, wide glass doors that opened into Marilyn's room.

Again, everything was just as she left it. An ivory silk dress on a padded clothes hanger, her wedding gown, was draped over a wing chair. A pair of shoes in the same ivory color were side by side on the plush carpet beneath the chair as if waiting for Marilyn to step into them.

Em sighed and turned around to face the yard. Like the inside of the house, it was perfectly manicured. There was not an overgrown shrub or a dead leaf to mar the perfection. The house and garden were perfect if you liked living in gated, planned communities.

Princeville reminded Em too much of the community and house she left behind in California, a place where she thought she had everything she ever wanted until she found out everything she believed about her life with Phillip had been a lie.

She thought of all the friends who'd felt comfortable enough to show up and take over Louie's beach house to mourn with him on Saturday morning. She pictured the cozy old place full of gently worn and lived in furniture that represented a lifetime of living. Going out and purchasing "Designer Package A" wasn't his style. She looked around and realized it wasn't hers anymore either.

She checked the flowers again to make sure they were right where Tom would see them when he opened the *lanai* doors. When she turned around and faced the hedge directly across from the *lanai*, the color sea foam green caught her eye, and she realized she was looking at the back of Orville Orion's house.

Not only did he live directly behind Marilyn, but looking closer, Em noticed there was an opening in the hedge between the two houses. It wasn't anything well defined, not a real gateway with a path lined with stepping stones, but it was wide enough to be obvious as an opening that connected the two yards.

Did Orville and Marilyn use it to go back and forth? Or was Orville some kind of peeping pervert who got his kicks out of sneaking through and staring into Marilyn's bedroom?

Before she knew she'd taken a step, Em was already across Marilyn's yard. She stopped at the hole in the hedge, leaned through to better see the back of Orville Orion's house.

"Em? Is that you?"

# 24

### Bad Cop

It was too late to duck back behind the hedge. Orville Orion was standing not four feet from the opening, staring at her.

"Oh. Hi, Orville."

Em forced a smile and acted as if she popped through his hedge every day. He looked as shocked to see her as she was him. Dressed in a white golf shirt, black Bermuda shorts, and leather flip flops, he held a tumbler full of amber liquid and ice.

Unless he'd just become a Hula Maiden, it was a little early for a cocktail.

Behind him, a crew of at least three men were on ladders, unlatching window screens, spraying water on the glass, and wiping them down.

"I didn't know this was your place." Em casually strolled through the hedge. The yard was immaculate, what there was of it. A large pool with a smaller, heated spa at one end took up most of the space. Smooth jazz music floated outside from the windows that were open to the *lanai*.

"I had no idea you lived so close to Marilyn," she said.

Seeing him looking so very together in his pristine environment, knowing now that he and Marilyn were much closer than either of them had let on, made Em want to shake the truth out of him. She decided to ignore Roland's warning.

"This is pretty convenient." She nodded at the hole in the hedge.

"Marilyn was more than welcome to use the spa. After she would put on a big event, she'd sometimes like to come over and soak. Since I have so many social commitments, I'm not here a lot. I'm head of the homeowners association, you know."

"So I heard."

"She wasn't one to sunbathe though. She liked to use the spa in private."

*Of course not*, Em thought. Marilyn was afraid her face would melt in the sun.

"Do you have any plans for the memorial?" He winced on the word memorial as if it truly pained him.

"Not yet. Her nephew Tom is due to arrive as soon as he can get a flight out of California. I stopped by to leave him some flowers."

"I'm sure poor Tom is really torn up about this. He was like a son to her."

Even though Marilyn had been engaged to Louie, Orville acted as if Em wouldn't have known about Tom.

Orville glanced at the window washers on the other side of the pool.

"I'm glad Tom's coming soon. Did you tell him everything?"

Em barely knew the man, but she thought Orville seemed nervous.

"What do you mean by everything?"

"I heard a rumor that her car was tampered with."

"Really?" *Had he heard or had he done the tampering?* she wondered. "Where did you hear that?"

He shrugged. "Everyone's talking about it."

"Yes, I told Tom," she said. "He was furious."

"Rightly so."

"So furious in fact, that he said he's going to hire a private detective to get to the truth."

Orville paused with his drink halfway to his lips. "A private detective?"

"He wants to find out who murdered her as much as we do. Tom promised to leave no stone unturned to find Marilyn's killer." Em watched him closely as she said, "I still can't believe someone would actually kill Marilyn."

Orville took a drink. "Someone would have to be crazy to have done it, but we all know who's crazy enough, don't we?"

Aware of the window crew, Em lowered her voice. "What are you saying?"

"Kiki Godwin. Marilyn always said the woman had it out for her, and she was right. The poor thing had no idea how far Kiki would go, though. I can't believe they haven't arrested her already. And that husband of hers. He killed that young cameraman, and he's out on bail that wouldn't even buy a dinner around here. Justice is a travesty on this island. I was just taking a break from writing a letter to the editor of the *Garden Island*. It's like the wild, wild west around here."

"You think Kiki did it?"

"Everyone thinks Kiki did it. I'm *sure* she did it," he said.

*Oh sure*, Em thought. Save yourself and throw Kiki under the bus.

Roland told her not to tell anyone about Marilyn's last phone call, and she'd fully intended not to blab to anyone, but now here was Orville Orion trying to pin the murder on Kiki and take the heat off himself.

"*Everyone* doesn't know the whole story," she shot back.

"What *whole* story?"

On Nat's old show, *CDP*, the first cop to question a suspect always played the good cop. Roland had already questioned Orville about Marilyn's one a.m. phone call and had gotten nowhere.

*Time for the bad cop to step in.*

Em took a deep breath. *Here goes nothing.*

She looked toward the house, paused long enough for Orville to follow her gaze, silently reminding him they were not alone. She felt safe enough with the window washers a few yards away.

Em lowered her voice. "What everyone doesn't know is that in the early morning hours before her wedding, you and Marilyn were exchanging phone calls. The last person she spoke to before she died was *you*."

The color drained from his face faster than Flora could suck a Gatorade bottle dry.

"How do you . . . ?"

"How do I know? She was my uncle's fiancée. The police recovered her phone and found her calls to and from you in the middle of the night."

The ice in his glass started to tinkle. She noticed his hand was shaking.

"You called her first," Em pushed. "So whatever you wanted must have been very important for her to call you back after one in the morning. Why is that, Mr. Orion? What did you want that couldn't wait?"

He took a step back. "I've already answered that this morning when I spoke to the detective."

"Then you don't mind telling me what it was all about." She hoped to catch him in a lie.

"I wanted to wish her luck, that's all."

She laughed. "Did he believe you? If he did, maybe you should have tried to sell him the Hanalei Bridge while you were at it."

"It's the truth." He took another step back, watching her as if she was crazier than Kiki.

With all of the window washers there, no way would he dare touch her, so Em pressed him again. She planted her hands on her hips.

"Come on, Mr. Orion. Do I look that stupid? You're not dealing with some nice-guy Kauai detective here. I'm a woman. I know all about crimes of passion. My uncle is suffering over this, and I'm not going to let it go."

He tossed the drink in a nearby planter. "I did not kill Marilyn."

"I think you did. I think you wanted her all to yourself, and that's why you tampered with her brakes. If you couldn't have her, then you didn't want anyone to have her, especially my uncle."

His suave demeanor vanished. His face was mottled red and he was sweating.

"That's not true. I would never kill Marilyn. I loved her. I wanted one more chance to talk her out of going through with the wedding. We were going to be togeth . . ." He stopped in midsentence, his eyes wide and startled.

"*Together?*" Em finished for him. "You were going to be together? How is that possible? She was planning to marry my uncle that very morning. Her dress is still laid out and ready for the wedding. She ordered seventy-five steaks and lobsters for the reception. That doesn't sound like she wanted to back out and be with you, Mr. Orion."

Suddenly he was backing away.

"I didn't mean it that way. We *were* going to be together, before she met Louie."

"That's a lie. You might as well tell me the truth. Or would you rather I tell Tom what you just admitted? He's determined to get to the bottom of this. I'd love to speed things up."

Orion ran a hand over his hair and glanced at his house.

One of the men on the roof near a second floor window was watching them and called out, "You okay, Mr. O?"

"I'm fine." His answer sounded lackluster. He turned back to Em.

"Okay. Okay." He took a deep breath. "If I tell you what the call was all about, will that satisfy you?"

What if he admitted to murder? What then? Once she was out of sight of the crew, she'd be in danger until she could get back around Marilyn's house, into her car, and on her way home.

He ran a hand over his sweaty forehead. "I did call Marilyn that night after the rehearsal dinner, which was a fiasco, by the way."

"Unforgettable."

"She didn't call me back until a few minutes after one. We planned to rendezvous one more time after the rehearsal dinner. In my heart I hoped I could talk her out of going through with the wedding. I kept calling to see if she still planned to come over."

Em thought she heard wrong. "She was going to be with you after the rehearsal dinner?"

He nodded yes. "She loved me, not Louie Marshall. But she was obsessed with getting her hands on the Tiki Goddess. She wanted to own that place more than anything, and it cost her her life."

"*What?*" If what he was saying was true, Kiki had been right all along. "She was willing to marry my uncle just to get her hands on the Goddess?"

"It's the only restaurant on that end of the island, *and* it has a liquor license. It's close enough to the water that with a second story addition it would have a quite a view. She knew Louie would never renovate the place because it's so sacred to him. She said it was filled with forty years of memories, dust, and termites. The only way she would ever see her plans finalized was to marry Louie."

"But my uncle would never hand it over to her." The truth was hard to swallow. Marilyn had been marrying Louie under false pretenses.

"Marilyn can be very persuasive," Orion said. "She told me she had ways of making him sign the place over to her. Ways that always worked before. She was quite a savvy business woman. You know she was worth a fortune."

"Of course she was," Em said. "Louie was going to be her fifth husband." Em paused. "I have a feeling there was not going to be much persuading going on," she said.

"What do you mean?"

"I think she was going to marry my uncle, pretend to be the adoring wife while you waited patiently in the wings, and then once she had the deed to the Goddess, she would get rid of Uncle Louie. Just as she no doubt got rid of her first four husbands."

Orion blinked. "She'd never do something like that." He didn't sound all that certain.

"No?" Em held up her hand and started counting off on her fingers. "She planned to cheat on her fiancé the night before her wedding. She's been married four times. Not two or three but four, and probably inherited a fortune from each husband. You've practically admitted you were part of her scheme."

His reaction to the accusation was so immediate that Em's gut told her he wasn't lying.

"I was *not* part of her scheme. I was just waiting in the wings, hoping she wasn't playing me for a fool. When I begged her not to go through with it, she gave me her word she'd only stay married to Louie until she was in control of the Goddess, then she'd divorce him, and we could be together. That's why she wasn't selling her house."

"She told Louie she was holding on to her house so she could run her business out of it," Em said.

"We were still going to meet here whenever she came up to work."

"Convenient," Em said.

"Adultery is one thing, but I would never, ever, condone murder." He took a deep breath, let it go, and then squared his shoulders, visibly pulling himself together. "After all, I *am* the president of the homeowner's board."

# 25

### The Lillians Arrive

As Em turned into the Goddess parking lot headed for her private parking place behind the beach house, she saw Lillian walking up the steps to the Goddess *lanai*. Lillian minus her bandages.

She waved, but Lillian didn't wave back, which Em thought odd until she saw not one but three more Lillians seated at tables on the *lanai*. They all had the same pink hair, curled into perms and backcombed into cotton candy bouffant dos, frilly white blouses, and hot pink pedal pushers.

When Em spotted a *Holoholo Holiday* tour van parked in the lot she remembered that Lillian's fan club had rushed in from Iowa to help cheer their idol. If she'd seen a bus load of clones of women impersonating *her*, she would have run screaming into the hills.

She parked and ran back to the bar, which was full of even more Lillians. They were seated at tables around the room, some with husbands or traveling companions. All of them had the same hairdo and black rhinestone-encrusted frames on their retro glasses. Buzzy was busy delivering prefix hamburger and fries lunches to a table for six. Trish and Suzi were hurrying out of the kitchen carrying orders.

Sophie shot her a where-have-you-been look as Em hurried to help. She grabbed an apron from a hook near the kitchen door and tied it on.

"Sorry I'm late," she told Sophie. "I forgot about the Lillians."

"Me too. That sure took a while. Hope it was fun." Sophie didn't look pissed, just swamped and more than a little curious.

"I met up with Roland. Then I went to Foodland and ran an errand."

"Playing *with* the detective, not detecting, right?"

Em wasn't about to admit she had been doing just that by trying to get the truth out of Orville Orion, so she changed the subject.

"What's this?" Em picked up a tray Sophie had filled with pink cocktails.

"Something I made up for the occasion. They're called Pink Lillies. Pink lemonade and lime flavored Caribbean Rum."

"Pink Lillies. Cute," Em said.

"I asked Louie to come up with something, but he said he was too busy."

"Busy watching infomercials, I'm afraid. Good thing the Maidens are here."

"They are going to back Lillian up while she does a couple of dances for her fans. For The Official Lillian Smith Fan Club, that is. As opposed to the unofficial one, I guess." Sophie shrugged.

"Where is the real Lillian?" Em didn't have time to study each and every Lillian in the room. Seeing them all together was like double vision magnified. It was making her lightheaded.

"She's in the restroom getting ready to go on as the featured dancer."

"That's big of Kiki. Is Lil's arm all right?"

"Miraculous healing. Her bandage came off just in time for her to appear before her adoring fans."

Kimo started hammering on the ship's bell he kept in the kitchen. Em ran in and came back out with three more hamburger specials. She set them down and then asked the table of Lils and their mates if they needed anything else.

One of the Lillians lifted off the top bun, stared at the hamburger, then poked it with a fork.

"That's not fish, is it?" She wrinkled her nose.

"No. It's a hamburger."

"They tried to give us fish at the hotel last night. I hate fish. There's fish all over the place."

"We're surrounded by water," Em said.

"Fish, fish, fish," another Lillian agreed. "I only like fish sticks."

"There is no actual fish shaped like a popsicle." Em never, ever considered fish sticks fish.

"We're from Iowa. We don't like fish." The first Lillian's husband wrinkled his nose.

"Too far from the ocean." The second Lillian nodded.

"Catfish." The first Lillian said, "I kind of like catfish."

Em was on her way back across the room when she noticed Big Estelle hovering by the bathroom door.

"Where's Little Estelle?" Em asked her. "I don't see her anywhere."

"She stayed home. The perfect match she met on the dating site hadn't shown up yet. She's really bummed. She wasn't in the mood to come along. I usually don't leave her home alone. Not after what happened last time."

"Last time?"

"She put on her bathrobe and flashed the gardener from her upstairs window."

"I can see why you wouldn't want her home alone."

"No kidding. The guy quit. Naturally the word got out. I can't find a gardener to save my life. Oh, Kiki said to tell you we're ready," Big Estelle remembered. "Since we're dancing to the boom box we need someone to MC and then push the start button. Louie still won't come out of the house."

"What are you dancing?"

"Just two numbers. *Keep Your Eyes on The Hands* first, then we're teaching the Lillians *Going to a Hukilau*. Trish and Suzi are going to waitress."

"You got it," Em said. Then Kimo started ringing the bell like crazy. "Give me two minutes." She ran after three more orders. Once they were delivered, Em stepped up to the mic and tapped it.

"Testing." She turned up the mic. Kiki popped out of the restroom, waved at Em, and cued up the boom box. Then she gave Em the high sign and scurried out of sight.

"Welcome to the Tiki Goddess." Em decided to keep it short but sweet. "You all know the Hula Maidens from the reality show *Trouble in Paradise*, and now you'll see them in action." Em nodded at Kiki.

Kiki whispered back, "Tell them it's me, Flora, and Big Estelle, and we're spotlighting Lillian. When we get on stage, push the start button."

As the women filed on stage, Em leaned toward the mic again.

"Maidens Flora and Big Estelle, along with their leader, Kiki, will be dancing behind your favorite Hula Maiden, Iowa's own Lillian Smith!"

Lillian stepped out of the bathroom into the bar, and the room went wild. All the Lillians started screaming and jumped to their feet. The husbands who had been brave enough to come along rolled their eyes at each other.

When Lillian walked onto the stage and stood front and center with the other dancers behind her, a hush fell over the room. The Lillians from Iowa had come three thousand miles to witness what they'd only seen on TV. Their hometown idol was about to perform.

Em pushed the start button, and the boom box blared, "Whenever you're watching the hula girls dance . . ."

Having done her part, Em walked back to the bar.

Sophie said, "I can't watch."

Em couldn't look away. The three back-up Maidens went right. Lil went left. There was a definite rhythm running through the melody. Lillian was oblivious to it.

But the crowd went crazy. Not once did the real Lillian do anything resembling the performance going on behind her. Kiki, Flora, and Big Estelle kept right on smiling and dancing until the song ended.

The faux Lillians remained on their feet, screaming the entire time.

When it was over, tears of joy streamed down the real Lillian's face.

Kiki turned off the boom box and took the mic.

When the crowd heard that they too were now going to learn a hula, their enthusiasm knew no bounds. Even the women who hated fishing didn't seem to mind that they were learning a song about fishing the old Hawaiian way. They joined in, swaying to and fro while they mimed tossing out fish nets and pulling them in.

If any of them noticed their idol was completely hula-challenged, they didn't let on.

Em was weaving her way through the crowded room to clear tables when she recognized Tom Benton. He was standing in the open doorway, surveying the room.

She waved, and he threaded his way through and took the only empty seat at the end of the bar. Em walked over and gave him a hug.

"Oh, Tom, I'm so sorry." She had to shout to be heard over the ruckus.

He frowned and shook his head. "It's your loss too, Em. I'll go over and pay my respects to Louie, but I wanted to talk to you first."

"Did you just get here?"

"I haven't even been to Marilyn's yet."

"Would you like lunch?"

He shook his head no. "I'd love a beer though."

Em drew him a draft beer. There was no sense in trying to carry on a meaningful conversation yet, but Lillian's clones were slowly calming down. As the frenzy subsided, they dropped into their chairs. Their tour leader, a woman far younger than the real Lillian but proudly sporting a poufy pink wig, blew a whistle to get their attention.

The room fell almost silent. The tour leader proceeded to read off the rest of the day's activities. Much to everyone's joy and amazement, the *real* Lillian had agreed to accompany them as they toured the North Shore. Afterward they would return to their hotel for a cocktail party and a "We Love Lillian" banquet.

"So finish up!" the tour leader shouted. "We Lillians have to get moving."

Em let Tom wind down with his beer and started clearing tables. The Lillians were up and out of the bar in ten minutes. She left Suzi and Trish and Sophie finishing up and joined Tom at the bar again.

"Want another?" she asked him.

"Why not?"

Em filled another glass and handed it to him then went back to clearing the tables.

When she joined him again he was staring into his second empty beer glass.

"I still can't believe it," he said.

"I know. This has really shaken up my uncle. I'm worried about him."

"I'm sure he wants Marilyn's murderer found as much as I do. But don't you worry." He looked around the room, and his gaze stopped on the stage where Kiki was still dancing a solo to the boom box music even though no one was paying attention. "I'll get to the bottom of this one way or another. I'll bring in experts the likes of which this island has never seen."

Em studied him for a moment. He was truly hurting, and his hurt had turned into anger.

"Let me give you a little tip, Tom."

"Sure."

"You might want to ease into this. If you start pissing off the wrong people with a kick-butt-take-no-prisoners mainland attitude, you're not going to get anywhere. Neither will your experts. I hate to see you waste your time and money when the local police can handle it."

She watched the muscle in his jaw twitch.

"Point taken," he said. "But Aunt Marilyn was the only family I had. I want her killer brought to justice."

She could sympathize. Louie was all the family she had since the divorce.

"Is this place always this crowded?" He watched a carload of tourists walk in as the last straggling Lillians walked out.

"Since the *Trouble in Paradise* pilot aired, we've been slammed."

"For such a tired dump this place is quite the little moneymaker."

Em bristled and tried to excuse his rude remark, which only proved he and Marilyn shared DNA.

"I sat next to a really chatty old guy from Kauai on the flight from Honolulu," he said.

"Everyone likes to *wala'au*. Especially the *kupuna*."

He stared at her. "I have no idea what you just said."

"Everyone likes to talk story. Especially the old folks."

"Yeah, well, he valla-howed all right."

She didn't try to correct him.

"I said I was coming over because my aunt had been killed in a car crash, and he'd heard all about the recent murders and said they were big news over here. He went on to tell me some really disturbing things."

"There was a murder, yes but . . ."

"*Murders*, Em. Not murder. Not just Aunt Marilyn. When I called, you failed to mention there had been *two other* recent murders here."

"Technically, only one of them was connected to the Goddess. A maid was killed out at Haena Beach Resort the same week, but the police haven't actually found anything to tie it to Marilyn's or Bobby the cameraman's murders."

He looked pained. "Would you like to explain?"

Every stool at the bar was full. She lowered her voice. "One of the cameramen working on the show was stabbed in our kitchen a few days before your aunt died. So far there's only been one arrest, our chef Kimo Godwin, but he's innocent. He was released on bail."

"Out on bail? He's still a suspect?"

"But he has no real motive. Oh, we all knew the cameramen were both driving him crazy but certainly not enough to kill one of them."

"The old man on the plane heard there was some kind of a cat fight in here the night my aunt died. Said Aunt Marilyn was terrified of some crazy woman."

The power and swiftness of the coconut wireless never ceased to amaze Em.

"There was an argument, but I saw your aunt afterward, and she certainly wasn't terrified. She and Kiki argued all the time."

"Kiki? Kiki Godwin?"

Sorry she'd mentioned Kiki's name, Em could only nod.

"I had a feeling it was *that* crazy woman. Aunt Marilyn was always complaining about her. If her husband is a suspected killer, what makes you think this Kiki is so innocent? They may have been in it together."

"That's ridiculous."

"Do the police have a better theory?"

She'd promised Roland she wouldn't tell anyone about the phone calls between Marilyn and Orville Orion. After talking to Orion earlier, she was convinced he hadn't killed her, still, dropping Orion's name might take the heat off of Kiki for a while.

But Em couldn't do it.

"I can't say," she said.

Tom was staring at the stage. "That's her, isn't it? That's Kiki Godwin."

"Yes, but . . ."

Suddenly he was on his feet, advancing on the stage.

"Tom, wait." Em went after him. He didn't turn around.

The song on the boom box ended, and the only sounds in the room were the laughter and conversation of patrons. Flora and Big Estelle walked out of the restroom. They'd taken off their *muumuus* and stuffed them into the big straw bags they now carried. They joined Kiki just as Tom reached them.

"Tom." Em kept her voice low. "Please."

Kiki was still in her white *muumuu* covered in huge red hibiscus flowers. She noticed Tom, and her smile lit up.

"A-loha. I'm Kiki. Can I help you?"

Kiki always turned on the charm when she was pitching a prospective Kiki's Kreative Events client.

"Only if you confess to murder," Tom shot back.

Kiki's smiled dissolved.

"What?" She turned to Em.

"Kiki, this is Tom Benton, Marilyn's nephew."

"If you think you're going to get away with murder, Ms. Godwin, think again," he said.

Giving new meaning to someone tossing her weight around, Flora stepped up to Tom and got right in his face.

"Hey, *haole* boy. Who you think you are, being all rude like that?"

He shrugged her off. "Don't *haole* boy me. You will all know I mean business soon enough." He ignored everyone else and focused on Kiki. "I know you had it out for my aunt. She used to tell me all about you, and how you hated her for leaving your little dance troupe of misfits. She knew you were trying to talk Louie out of marrying her."

"Mmfuupp." Kiki tried to speak. Her mouth was open, her eyes bugging out of her head.

Em tried to grab Tom's shoulder. "Tom, please don't. She could have a stroke. When she gets really upset, she loses the ability to talk."

He shook her off.

"She doesn't have to talk to me. All she has to do is listen. Here's what I think." He stepped closer and pointed at Kiki. "I think that cameraman was killed as part of a scheme to throw the police off your trail before you killed my aunt. You and your husband were in on this together. She was getting too close to the one thing you love most in the world. This place. So you plotted to kill Aunt Marilyn on the night before her wedding. First your husband killed the cameraman, and then one or both of you caused Aunt Marilyn's wreck. Now the police are running around in circles, just the way you planned."

"Want me to call 911, Em?" Behind the bar, Sophie had the phone in her hand.

Kimo walked out of the kitchen wielding a meat cleaver.

"Step away from my wife," he said.

A tourist at a table near the stage hoisted his drink and said, "This is great, isn't it, hon? I wonder when this episode will air?"

"This is no show," Flora told them. "This is the real thing. For sure."

Tom noticed the cleaver and stepped away from Kiki.

"Take it back," Kimo said. "Take it all back."

Tom may have backed up, but he didn't back down.

"I'm not taking anything back because it's the truth. The world will know it too, just as soon as the private detective gets here."

He turned around, and without a word to anyone, not even Em, he stalked out of the bar.

People seated at nearby tables burst into applause.

# 26

### Kiki's Big Plan

Kiki's legs were shaking so violently Kimo handed the meat cleaver to Big Estelle. He grabbed Kiki by the arm and led her away from the applauding crowd and into Louie's office. Em, Flora, and Big Estelle followed close behind, and once they were all inside, Kimo closed the door.

She opened her mouth to voice her outrage. "Muffluffer."

Kimo led her over to Louie's office chair behind the desk and helped her sit.

"Close your eyes. Remember what the doctor said after the last time this happened. Close your eyes and take long, deep breaths," he said.

"In and out." Flora started taking long deep breaths. Inhaling and exhaling through her teeth. She sounded like a runaway steam engine.

"In and out." Big Estelle copied her.

"Whuhuh lamuuph cuz?" Unable to get her lips to work right, Kiki had meant to say, "Where are we, a Lamaze class?"

"Close your eyes and sit back." Em patted her shoulder. "Please, Kiki."

The door opened, and Sophie, bless her, entered carrying a chilled martini glass full of vodka. There were four olives skewered to a plastic sword in it.

"Here you go, Kiki."

Kiki held out her hand for the drink, but she was shaking so hard Sophie set it on the desk in front of her.

"When you're ready." Sophie went back to work.

"You want the drink?" Kimo was leaning over her.

Kiki bobbed her head up and down.

"Then sit back and close your eyes," he ordered.

She leaned back and closed her eyes.

"And don't worry," Em added.

*Don't worry!* All she could do was worry. Kiki's thoughts were tumbling over one another faster than water in a waterfall during a rain storm. She snapped her eyes open and glared at Em.

"Okay, so worry. Just don't try to talk yet," Em advised.

They hovered over her until she'd stopped quaking like a volcano about to blow. She opened her eyes and pointed to the martini.

Flora handed it to her. Kiki barely sloshed any vodka as she raised it to her lips.

Calmer now, she said, "Mudluker."

"Kiki. I mean it. Don't try to talk." Kimo wiped his brow with his T-shirt sleeve. For his sake and his alone, Kiki shut up and downed half the martini.

She took deep breaths. Closed and opened her eyes a few times. She caught Kimo staring at the cleaver on the desk.

"Orders are backing up," he said.

"This is an emergency," Em told him. "Don't worry about it."

Kiki pointed toward the kitchen and nodded.

"Will you be all right?" He didn't look like he would leave her.

Kiki nodded and held up the martini. *No worries*, she wanted to say. *I'm feeling better.*

All she could do was nod and smile.

Em sat on the corner of the desk. Flora went out to get their straw bags, and when she came back she had drinks for both herself and Big Estelle.

Sophie brought in a second martini, and once half of that was gone, Kiki was ready to try again.

"I will . . . mot be . . . shang-roaded."

"You mean shanghaied?" Big Estelle said.

"Or railroaded?" Flora laughed.

"Either one," Kiki assured them. "I'm not going down for a brime I didn't commit. Crime," she amended.

"No one thinks you will," Em said.

"He does. That nephew does. I'm not going to jail. Not on his life. Private dick or no private dick."

"What?" Em was staring at her.

"It's from the old movies," Big Estelle told her. "They called detectives private dicks."

Em looked puzzled. "Why?"

Big Estelle shrugged. "I don't know. I'll ask my mother."

"Hey! I'm in rubble. Trouble." Kiki took a deep breath. "I won't sit here and do nothing and end up in prison for life in Arizona or some other godforsaken place."

"Good lawyers are *waiwai*." Flora pulled a lime wedge out of her drink and started chomping on it, rind and all.

"Not to mention expensive."

Flora swallowed. "That's what I said."

"Are you going to be all right, Kiki?" Em stood up.

"Of course. I'm all right. I'm sure Sophie and the others need you. Get back out there and make money." Kiki faked a huge smile. She reached up and made certain the flowers anchored on her head were still in place.

"You're sure?"

"Really."

"Tom Benton is just in shock, and he's angry," Em said. "He'll calm down. There's no way anyone can prove you did this, even some imported detective."

Kiki wished she could be as certain.

"I think one of the girls should drive you home," Em suggested. "How about you, Big Estelle?"

"I'd be happy to, of course."

"Nonsense," Kiki told them. "You have to get home and make sure Little Estelle isn't up to any of her tricks. Flora, you have to get back to your store. Make sure those Tiki Goddess items are still moving."

"No worry there," Flora told them. "People are hoarding T-shirts and mugs since the murders. The Lillian Fan Club is stopping by in a couple hours though. I should be there when they make a run on the store."

"You go right along," Kiki said. "I'm feeling much better."

The world always looked better after a couple of good stiff martinis.

"You all go on."

Flora and Big Estelle picked up their bags and headed out into the bar. Kiki stopped Em and asked her to tell Kimo she needed to talk to him for a minute.

She sat alone in Louie's office, tempted to kick back and put her feet up on the desk for a while and stare at all the photos of Louie with politicians and celebrities. The shot of Louie and Irene with Elvis on the set of *Blue Hawaii* was one of her favorites.

As much as she hated to admit it, she wasn't a bit sad about Marilyn's death. The Goddess and Louie would be better off without her.

Kimo stepped into the office wearing his stained apron and carrying a wire whisk. With the tour van there along with the usual lunch crowd, he'd had one heck of a morning in the kitchen.

"What's up? Feeling better?" he asked.

"Of course. I don't want you to get upset, but I need to tell you something."

His face creased with worry lines. "What?"

"I don't know of any other way to save ourselves. We have to get out of here."

"What have you done, Kiki?"

She gasped. "Nothing! I haven't done anything, but we have to run,

Kimo. We need to hide out for as long as it takes. We have to hide like Ko'olau the Leper and his wife, Pi'ilani."

"Don't be crazy."

"I'm not crazy. I'm thinking clearly for the first time in a couple of days. That nephew of Marilyn's is as evil as she was. He's going to try and pin her murder on me and the cameraman's murder on you."

"He'll never prove it."

"I'm not going down for a crime I didn't commit, and neither are you. I have a plan."

"What kind of plan?"

"We have to get off the island."

"I can't leave. I'm out on bail. How far would I get?" He shrugged. "They'll have my name at the airport. If I did manage to get off Kauai it would only make things worse. I'm not going anywhere."

"Boat. We could take a boat."

"I'm not running, Kiki."

Kiki started to gnaw on her lower lip. "You really won't even consider it?"

"Count me out." He pointed the wire whisk at her. "You are not going anywhere either. Go home and take a nap. Things will look better after you get some rest."

One of the hardest things she ever did was smile back and agree.


KIKI TOLD everyone at the Goddess goodbye and assured them the full effects of the martinis were nearly gone. Sophie made her drink a glass of water and gave her a handful of olives tucked in a napkin, and she was on her way.

Once she was home, she pulled into one of the parking spaces beneath the house. Because it was located in a tsunami area, the single structure was a good twenty feet off the ground, floating above vast open space below. Adding an elevator had been Kimo's idea, and now she didn't know what they would have ever done without it. She couldn't imagine schlepping groceries, not to mention all of their hula adornments and costumes, up and down the long flight of stairs to the living quarters.

Once inside, Kiki headed straight for her bedroom. She opened the closet and dug around on the floor for a nylon backpack she hadn't used in years. It was small and lightweight and would hold a few essentials but little else. She carried it into the master suite bathroom and tossed in some nighttime wrinkle remover, a tube of eyelash glue, toothbrush and toothpaste, and a big bottle of Tums. Then she hurried into her craft room and grabbed a package of raffia off the table. She opened a drawer and stared at a pair of scissors and some short-handled pruning shears and tossed them in thinking, *you just never know.*

After rolling up two batik *pareaus*, wide colorful lengths of fabric she used as sarongs, she shoved them into the pack, pulled a sweatshirt and a pair of yoga pants out of a drawer, and put those in too.

*Almost done.*

Writing a note to Kimo was the hardest part. She didn't want him following her, nor did she want him to panic. She stared at a blank page of lined paper for a couple of minutes. She picked up a pen and started tapping her front teeth with it. It took her a while to compose, but once she was finished she was satisfied.

She purposely left her cell phone charger on the kitchen table near the note where he'd see it. If she didn't answer the phone he'd think she forgot the charger and wouldn't panic. She opened the freezer and took out a zip lock that was marked prime rib. There was a block the size of a thin brick of cash inside wrapped in foil. Kiki tucked it in her backpack and picked up her car keys and purse. On the way out of the kitchen, she opened the liquor cabinet in the dining room and grabbed a half gallon of vodka and a jar of olives.

Less than twenty minutes after she got home, Kiki was on her way.

# 27

## Uncle Stirs Again

Em didn't get a chance to run over to the house until seven that evening when she took Louie a plate of barbecue ribs, garlic mashed potatoes, and steamed string beans tossed with mac nuts. She was pleased and surprised to find him up, dressed, and behind the tiki bar making notes in his three ring binder, the Booze Bible.

"Hi." She held up the plate wrapped in foil. "Brought you tonight's special with extra barbecue sauce and some croutons for Dave."

"*Yo, ho, ho!*" Letterman squawked.

"*Mahalo.*" Louie reached for the plate.

Em pulled a little paper sack with croutons out of her apron pocket and tossed a couple into Dave's food dish before the parrot could dart over and take off one of her fingers.

"I'm starving," Louie said.

*Another sign of recovery.* She was relieved to hear it.

"Let me get you some silverware." She headed for the kitchen while Louie pulled out a chair at the dining table and sat down.

"Tom Benton stopped by earlier today." Louie carefully opened the foil.

"I wish I'd had time to walk over with him." Hopefully he hadn't been rude to Louie after his confrontation with Kiki. "How was he?"

"He's furious, you know. He's convinced Kiki tampered with Marilyn's brake line."

"He really upset Kiki earlier. I thought she was going to croak."

"Is she all right?"

Em nodded. "Hopefully. It took a couple of martinis to calm her down. She left for home hours ago." She handed Louie a fork and knife. He dug into the mashed potatoes.

"I tried to tell him Kiki did no such thing," Louie said between bites. "I couldn't convince him otherwise. He had a couple of valid points though."

"Such as? Surely he didn't convince you that Kiki's capable of murder."

Louie tore a rib off the half rack. "Who else had motive?"

She debated telling him anything about Orion, but the truth would come out sooner than later.

"Actually, Roland found something a little suspicious."

"What?" He stopped eating.

"There were a couple of one a.m. phone calls on Marilyn's cell right before she died. Calls from Orville Orion."

"Orion? No kidding?"

She could see the wheels turning in his mind as Louie stared back at her. Then he merely shrugged and chewed the meat off a rib.

"So," he said.

"Aren't you even curious about what Marilyn and Orion had to discuss at one a.m.?"

"They were friends. I wouldn't worry about it. Will it clear Kiki?"

"I don't know."

"Those calls were probably about nothing that matters."

The truth would no doubt hurt her uncle. She didn't want Roland to know she'd confronted Orion either, so she gave up and shook her head.

"No, I guess not."

He picked up another rib.

"Do you have plans to use your truck tomorrow morning?" she asked.

"No. Go ahead if you need it."

"Nat has to go back to L.A. for a writers meeting. I volunteered to drive him into the airport. His flight leaves at nine, so I'll be heading in early."

"No problem."

"Would you like to ride along? We could go out to breakfast afterward."

"No, thanks. Some other time." Louie made short work of the meal. After he took the plate to the kitchen sink and rinsed it off he headed back to the tiki bar.

"Dave and I have been working really hard on a couple of new drinks," he said.

"I thought you both had a sparkle in your eyes."

Letterman was in his cage munching on a crouton.

"I played catch up first, finally got around to putting the finishing touches on the Final Cut in honor of Bobby Quinn. Then I refined Marilyn's favorite, the Fizzy Lady, with champagne and *liliko'i* syrup. Now I've cleared the decks to work on a drink for the state competition in Honolulu."

"That's great news. Are you ready to share the details yet?" He sometimes kept the details between himself and Dave until a drink was perfected.

"I'll tell you the name, if you'll promise to keep it under wraps."

"Shoot."

"Flaming Inferno."

She smiled. "I like it. Inspired by the Kalua dance number, of course."

"Oh, yeah."

"Can't wait to hear more." She glanced at the clock on the stove. "I'd better get back."

"How are things going over there?"

It was the first time he'd even asked about business since Marilyn's death, another sign that he was coming out of his depression.

"We had three van loads of Lillian's fans from Iowa in for lunch. Thankfully things settled down after that. In fact, we're a bit slow. Kiki and the Maidens didn't come in to perform tonight since they were here to entertain the tour group. Trish and Suzi waited tables at lunch."

"Kiki didn't even come back tonight to dance solo?"

"She was really upset."

"She must have been. I've never known her not to show up."

"Tom really got to her. I hope he calms down. He's going to step on a lot of toes and never get to the truth."

"He even seemed pissed that I wasn't doing more to find Marilyn's killer." Louie walked across the room to the small bar and picked up his reading glasses. "I told him that's what Roland and the KPD are for."

"Good thinking."

"Besides, if someone around here is nuts enough to cut a brake line, not to mention stab someone with a sashimi knife, I don't want to be out looking for him. Or her. Or whoever." He tipped his head and peered at her over his glasses. "I don't want *you* out looking for them either, young lady."

Em nodded. "Got it."

She was almost at the front door to the *lanai* when she thought of something he'd said earlier. She paused and turned back.

"Uncle Louie? About that drink for the contest."

"Flaming Inferno?"

"Promise me you won't blow yourself, the house, or Dave to smithereens."

# 28

## Em Confesses

The next morning it was pouring rain, the sky full of gray clouds hanging so low they looked close enough to touch. Em was up early, dressed and ready to drive Nat into Lihue to the airport. She called and told him to stay put and that she'd drive the truck across the lot and pick him up so that he didn't get soaked.

He was waiting on his *lanai*, ran out, and tossed his leather backpack in the back seat of the truck cab. Then he took off his glasses and was wiping the lenses dry as Em started to pull out on to the highway.

"Click it or ticket," she reminded him.

He fastened his seat belt. "Are you sure I'm not taking you away from your duties?"

"We open late on Sunday," she reminded him. "I re-stocked the bar last night before I left. It's nice to get out of the hood once in a while." Without traffic it was an hour drive to the airport, and the long stretches with fantastic views helped Em clear her mind.

"Hope you don't mind riding in this thing." Her uncle's truck was old but he loved it.

"Not at all. For once I might look like I belong here."

"I thought you could do most of your work over here, even take meetings."

"Usually," he said. "But this is a biggie with the producers and network. I have to be there."

"Will you be gone long?"

He had another home in the L.A. area as well as an apartment in Honolulu. Sometimes Nat was away for weeks at a time.

"I never know," he shrugged. "Boy, the rain is really coming down."

"We needed it. I just feel sorry for the tourists who came to get tan."

They went around a curve, and a flagman at the side of the road beneath a huge day-glow orange umbrella slowed them to a standstill. Up the line of cars ahead of them, they could see a bulldozer moving rocks off the highway.

"Must have been a rock slide," Em said.

Nat nodded and then said, "I was thinking about using the murder in the restaurant kitchen as a storyline, but there's no ending yet."

"It's still a mystery, for sure." She filled him in on what Roland knew and then said, "I keep thinking about who and why someone might impersonate a produce deliveryman."

"Maybe it was a robbery gone bad. The guy shows up intent on a robbery, he discovers the place full of crazy hula dancers and a film crew. Maybe Bobby confronted him, and the killer stabbed him."

"But who didn't know filming was going on? There was a tech van outside. All the Maidens' cars were there, too," she said.

"If it wasn't a bungled robbery, why would someone kill Bobby?"

They both sat in silence, thinking and watching rain pour down the windshield.

The bulldozer finally pulled to the side of the road, and the flagman waved them on. Rainwater was running down the mountain side in small streams, taking the iron rich, red Kauai dirt with it. Em held her breath, hoping they made it before more rocks decided to slide.

"Maybe the guy was there to kill someone else. Like Kimo," she said.

"Then why didn't he? Maybe he posed as a deliveryman to have access to the kitchen without looking out of place."

"But something like that is easy enough to check out here. It's not like the mainland where there's a delivery van with a driver in some kind of uniform on every corner." Nat thought a while longer. "Why kill Kimo? He's not the obvious choice, you know."

"Then who?"

"Marilyn. Maybe someone wanted her dead all along and finally succeeded."

"So whoever killed Bobby might have been there to kill Marilyn instead? That certainly leaves Kiki out of it," she said.

"Unless Kimo killed Bobby and Marilyn. Or, as Tom contends, the Godwins were in it together."

She stared at the road stretching out ahead of them. The rain had let up as soon as they left the North Shore behind, but thick smoke-gray clouds were still blanketing the island.

"I just can't and won't believe it."

"I can't either, but right now there are no other suspects."

They chatted all the way to town. Nat suggested Em hire another waitress or two since the Goddess was obviously out of the red.

"That's an idea," she said, "but good, dependable help is hard to find. Bottom line is that the Goddess is a family owned and operated business. I'm just thankful Sophie fit in so easily. Not everyone could put up with the craziness around there. Still, finding good part-time help might be worth a try."

It was no longer raining when they reached the airport. She turned onto Ahukini Road and entered the roundabout.

"I'm on Hawaiian," Nat said. "Stopping in Honolulu first."

She pulled up to the curb in front of the security check in. He reached into the back seat for his backpack. There was an awkward moment as Nat paused with his carry on backpack in his lap.

"Thanks for driving me in." He leaned closer. "See you soon, I hope."

"Bye," she whispered.

When he leaned close enough to kiss her, it seemed natural to let him. He kissed her on the lips, not her cheek.

"Bye, Em."

Nat stepped out and waved as she pulled away from the curb. Em waved back, remembering to smile. Deciding to head over to Costco to pick up a package of microfiber cleaning rags, she turned left out of the airport onto Kapule Highway. As she drove past police headquarters, she couldn't help but think of Roland.

She reached the corner of Kapule Highway and Rice Street, made another left, and a few yards down the road heard the short *whoop whoop* of a police siren. She glanced at her speedometer. Well within the speed limit. Em glanced in the rearview mirror and saw a white unmarked car with a rotating light on the dashboard behind her.

*Roland.*

How long had he been following her?

She pulled over, cheeks were on fire as she glanced in her rearview mirror and watched him get out of the car and walk up to the truck. She lowered the window and blessed the rush of cool air on her face.

"Sorry, officer." She looked up at him when he stopped outside her door. "I don't think I was speeding."

"That's what they all say." He leaned his forearm on the window. His face was inches away from hers. "Where's the fire?"

"That's what you all say." *Is it a guilty shame to be so happy to see him?*

"How about breakfast? Have you eaten?" he asked.

"Don't you want to see my driver's license and registration?"

"Maybe later. Right now I'm hungry."

She couldn't think of a reason in the world to say no.

"I'd love breakfast. Where?"

"Follow me." He walked back to the cruiser, and she followed him on down the hill toward Nawiliwili. When they reached the Harbor Mall shopping center, he turned into the parking lot. She pulled in beside him.

"The Feral Pig all right?" He held the truck door open for her.

"Great. I hear it's good."

She grabbed her purse, and together they walked across the lot and into The Feral Pig, on the ground floor of the two-story mini mall of shops and restaurants. Em hoped that passengers from the various cruise ships berthed in the harbor up the road were able to see more of the majesty of Kauai than just this one stop.

The attractive young waitress acting as hostess knew Roland, and they were seated right away. While Em perused the menu, she felt his gaze on her. She made a choice, closed the menu and looked up at him.

"I just dropped Nat off at the airport."

"I know."

She blushed and wished she had more control. "How long were you following me?"

"Long enough." He dropped his gaze to her lips.

Em had the urge to slide out of the chair and run out the door. Thankfully the waitress appeared and claimed their attention.

"Ready to order?" she asked them.

Em ordered the banana bread French toast and scrambled eggs.

"I'll have the kalua pork breakfast burrito." Roland closed his menu.

The waitress nearly fell all over him while thanking him for his order.

"Nat said something interesting." Em fiddled with her napkin.

"It was a long drive. I hope so."

"He wondered if Bobby's killer might have been there to kill someone else."

"Go on."

"Maybe he came that morning hoping to kill Marilyn. When he didn't get the chance, he cut her brake line later."

"So why was he posing as a produce deliveryman?"

"Maybe he was casing the place," she said.

"It's a possibility," he said. "Maybe he wanted to kill Marilyn at the Goddess so the blame would fall on someone close to her. The murder could be pinned on your uncle, or Kiki, since everyone knew about their animosity toward each other."

"So, you've already thought this scenario through. The murderer might have been there to get Marilyn and ended up killing Bobby."

"That's why I have a badge. They pay me to figure this stuff out."

"So you really don't think Kiki killed Marilyn."

"I'm not entirely convinced. I know she didn't kill Bobby. She was in the bar when he was murdered, but that doesn't let Kimo off the hook."

"He didn't do it."

"So what happened to set the murderer off? Why kill Bobby Quinn? Other than Kimo, no one else had motive."

"That we know of."

Their breakfasts arrived. Em dove into her banana bread French toast. "This is really good. Like eating cake."

He was staring at her and hadn't even picked up his fork yet.

"What?" She stopped eating.

"So you and the neighbor. Is this a thing?"

"A thing?"

"Are you two in a relationship?"

*So he did see the kiss.* "No, Detective Sharpe. I am not in a relationship. Nat and I are friends."

"You kiss all of your friends goodbye like that?"

"We've dated a couple of times. That's all. Not that I owe you any explanation."

Roland was still staring.

"Your burrito will get cold."

He ignored his plate.

"I'm not sleeping with him, if that's what you're asking."

"I wasn't asking, but thanks for the information." He dug into the *ono* looking burrito.

"You're quite a detective. Don't you always manage to get to the truth?"

"Eventually. I take my time, but I'm worth the wait."

Em focused on her scrambled eggs so he wouldn't catch her smiling.

"We've got new information on the murdered maid. Her husband is back on Kauai. Victor Villaviejos has been questioned and released," he said.

"Why am I not surprised?"

"He couldn't have killed his wife. He'd been fishing off of Kona since the morning of her death. He wasn't on island when she died. He flew out early that morning."

"But, I thought you checked the plane manifests, and he wasn't on any flights out. How did he get to the Big Island?"

"He used his cousin's ticket and driver's license to get on the flight."

"Isn't that against the law?"

"Definitely there are security issues, but that's up to DHS to follow up on. The cousin had paid for the fishing trip and couldn't go, so he gave Victor the non-transferable ticket. They look like brothers more than cousins. So much so that Victor was able to use the cousin's ID to get through security."

"Because the name on the ID has to match the name on the ticket," she said.

"Right. When Victor's wife was murdered, and we were questioning his friends and family as to his whereabouts, the cousin was too scared to come forward."

"With good reason. So Victor is off the hook," she said.

"He didn't find out about his wife's death until the fishing boat got back to Kona. He's pretty broken up about it. He came right into headquarters with his cousin and explained. He was trying to work things out with his wife, just like her friends at the resort said. So now we're back to square one on that one."

"Unless you can tie Bobby's murderer to Esther Villaviejos."

"When we found those phone calls from Orion to Marilyn, I thought we had something. Still might have," he said. "I'm going to show up at his place again, see if I can press him."

Em swallowed the last of her coffee and stared down into her empty mug.

"What?" he asked.

"What?"

"I can tell there's something you're not telling me. Say it, Em."

"You are psychic."

He shrugged. "Your expressions always give you away."

"Remember when you told me to leave the detecting up to you?"

"I have a feeling I'm not going to want to hear this."

"I ran into Orville Orion."

"Accidentally, of course."

"I was dropping some flowers at Marilyn's for her nephew, Tom, and discovered their backyards were connected by an opening in the hedge."

"Discovered?"

"I went around back to leave the flowers in the shade on the *lanai*. It was all perfectly innocent on my part."

"I'm sure it started that way."

"When I saw the opening in the hedge I realized Marilyn and Orion were closer than any of us suspected. I was checking it out when I ran into Orion on the other side. So I started pressing him about that phone call in the wee morning hours, and he admitted that Marilyn was marrying my uncle just to get her hands on the Goddess."

Roland's plate was empty. He sat back, set his napkin on the table. "How did you get him to admit it?"

She had to clear her throat and tried to gauge just how upset Roland was going to be. *Maybe not so much now that he was full of food.*

"I told him that he was still a suspect as far as you were concerned. That's not too far off the mark, is it? He got all panicked and told me that there was no way he killed Marilyn because he loved her. He believed she loved him even though she was going to marry my uncle, and he was trying to talk her out of going through with it."

"And you believed him."

"You should have seen his face. He was telling the truth, Roland. I know he was. I was so upset I still haven't told Uncle Louie what Orion said. I did tell Louie about the phone calls they exchanged that morning, but I said that Orion was just calling to wish Marilyn luck. I didn't want to break my uncle's heart."

"I wish you'd have left Orion to us. We have no idea what's really going on. Things could have gone really bad, Em. Have you forgotten that not too long ago you were kidnapped, ended up in the trunk of a car, and dumped in the jungle?"

"How could I? But I wasn't worried. There was a window washing crew at Orion's. They were only a few yards away. He was a wreck anyway. I'm glad I confronted him. But now I don't think he killed Marilyn."

"So we're back to Kiki. Only she had motive."

"But she didn't do it. So, who did?"

He leaned across the table and lowered his voice. "That's for me to find out, not you. Don't be fooled by all the palm trees and rainbows outside, Em. There's a killer or killers out there, and I don't want you putting yourself in danger again."

# 29

Where's Kiki?

The next day Em set her alarm early enough to get in a walk on the beach before she had to go to the bar. The weather was still drizzling rain, but it was light enough to ignore. She was in the outdoor shower when Louie called over the rock wall.

"Some of the Maidens are milling around in the parking lot."

It was too early for Sophie or Kimo to be in yet. Too early to have the Maidens show up, but as Em rinsed shampoo out of her hair she called back, "I'll get the key and go over as soon as I get dressed. Can you go out and tell them I'll be there?"

Em heard indistinct grumbling and took it as a yes. Within fifteen minutes she'd thrown on a pair of capris and a top, grabbed the key, and was headed out to the lot. Suzi hurried over to her while Flora and Trish waited out of the drizzle beneath the overhang by the back door.

"We're having an emergency meeting," Suzi said. "Hope you don't mind."

"Not at all." Em opened the back door into Louie's office and Suzi, Trish, and Flora filed through into the bar.

Em walked through the room to unlock the front door. "Where's everyone else?"

"On the way, I hope," Suzi said. "Lillian's the only one who can't come. She's still touring with the official Lillian Fan Club."

"Where's Kiki?"

Suzi shrugged. "That's why I called the meeting. She's missing."

Trish stopped in the act of pulling out a chair at one of the larger tables. "What do you mean missing? If she's missing, then we should call the police."

Suzi waved toward the chair. "Sit down, Trish."

Trish sat. So did Flora.

"No calling the police," Suzi said. She looked at each in turn. In a whisper she said, "She's on the run."

"Why?"

The only thing that would send Kiki running was if she had heard Roland intended to arrest her. Em figured he would have told her about it yesterday at breakfast, unless some startling new evidence had been uncovered overnight.

"She's afraid of Tom Benton's detective," Suzi said. "Tom's out for revenge, and Kiki's sure he's going to frame her."

"Is he even on island yet?" Trish asked Em.

"The detective? I don't know."

Pat Boggs came stomping into the bar, her cowboy boots hammering against the wooden floor. She was carrying Precious under one arm like a sack of potatoes. She set Precious down on her feet before she noticed everyone was staring.

"What?" Pat held out her arms and shrugged. "She walks too slow. Thought I'd help her make up some time."

Precious tugged on the hem of her blouse and patted her hair into place.

"What's up?" Pat asked. "What's the big emergency? It better be good. I've got dirty condos waiting to be cleaned. Work is stackin' up out there." Pat pulled out a chair for Precious and one for herself. Precious climbed up and set her purse on the table. Pat sat down.

"Kimo called and told me that Kiki has been gone for two days, and he's worried." Suzi had taken over as their leader and remained standing at the head of the table.

"He's just getting around to telling someone now? Suspicious!" Flora shouted.

"No, Kiki left him a note so he wasn't worried at first, but he hasn't heard from her yet. He said she always checks in with him at the end of the day. Her cell isn't picking up, but he wasn't too worried, because she left the charger on the kitchen table. He brought me the note she left him." She pulled it out of her purse, unfolded it, and began to read.

*Kimo honey,*

*I've driven to Wailua to teach Meno'ok Lodfort from the senior center to make that special chicken* hekka *we all made and served at the last Annual Hanalei Slug Festival. She's cooking challenged so I may have to spend a couple of days with her, but that's probably for the best. You told me to calm down so this will be a good way not to think about you-know-what. I have my cell phone with me. Don't worry. I'll be back as soon as I can.*

*Aloha, Kiki xoxoxo*

Suzi didn't have to wait long for a reaction.

"Who the heck is this Meno'ok Lodfort she went to help?" Flora wanted to know. "I don't know anybody by that name."

"You might not know everybody Kiki knows," Pat said.

Suzi nodded. "We do."

Pat wasn't convinced. "If she bothered to leave a note then she's probably right where she said she would be. If ya'll got me over here for nothing, I'm gonna be madder than a wet sittin' hen."

Flora leaned over and whispered to Trish, "What does that mean?"

"I have no idea," the photographer shrugged.

Precious didn't look any happier than Pat. "I ran out of the salon and left a woman sitting with dye on her hair."

"Uh, oh," Flora said. Then she burped.

"I told my receptionist to finish up. Hopefully she's not going to fry the woman's scalp."

"Then why are you here?" Pat asked her.

"I was afraid if I missed this, you would all think I wasn't committed to being a Hula Maiden."

Suzi stared at the note in her hands. "I think Kiki is trying to throw us off her trail. I don't remember ever making chicken *hekka* for the Slug Festival." She looked at the women gathered around the table. "Do you?"

They all shook their heads no.

"Who was she going to see?" Pat wanted to know.

"Meno'ok Lodfort."

"What the heck kind of a name is that?" Pat scratched her head. "Sounds like it's one of those Eye-ran-yuns."

Trish stared at Pat. "One of those *what?*"

"You know, somebody from Eye-ran."

Trish sighed.

"Maybe that's code for something. Give me that thang." Pat held out her hand. Suzi slapped the note in it. Pat pulled a pen out of her shirt pocket, grabbed a handful of napkins out of the basket in the center of the table, and started writing.

"Where could she be?" Trish frowned. "She has to be somewhere on the island."

"Unless she flew away." Flora was clutching a Gatorade bottle.

Em said, "She'd never leave Kauai with Kimo out on bail. He wouldn't be able to follow her."

The sound of a motor revving drew their attention to the front door. Little Estelle rolled in followed by Big Estelle. Trailing behind them was a huge blond Viking with curly hair, ice blue eyes, and muscles bulging out of bigger muscles. He was oiled to a high shine, and his miniscule red shorts and tight white T-shirt left nothing to the imagination.

Little Estelle idled near the table and snapped her fingers. The giant moved one of the chairs away so she could park beside Precious. Big Estelle sat as far away from her mother as possible without staying out on the *lanai*. The giant folded his arms and stood behind Little Estelle.

Everyone else exchanged questioning looks. Little Estelle barked out a laugh. "This is Lars, everyone. He's my soul mate. We found each other on *iLoveCougars.com*. He's eye candy, and he's mine. So you can look, but you can't touch." She reached over and squeezed Lars' butt cheek. He leaned down and patted her on the head.

"Eye candy?" Trish whispered to Em. "Is that anything like an Eye-raniun?"

"I heard that, missy." Pat didn't look up from where she was hunched over open paper napkins that took up most of the table top in front of her.

"Lars is from Norway. He doesn't speak English," Little Estelle said. "You can say anything you want in front of him." She gazed around the table at the assembly. "Any of you have any questions for me? Wondering what sex is like between a Cougar and a thirty-year-old?"

"Mother!" Big Estelle yelled.

Pat finally looked up. "This meeting's not about you, Little Estelle, though I'll have to admit I got a lotta questions. This is about Kiki. She's gone missing. At least we think she's gone missing."

"She'll be back," Little Estelle assured them. "That woman can't stay away from here."

"She will if she's afraid."

Little Estelle sniffed. "She's not afraid of anything."

Em glanced out the window and saw Kimo's truck drive past.

"Kimo just drove in," she said. No one was paying attention.

Suzi was saying, "Kiki's convinced she's going to be arrested for Marilyn's murder. The Black Widow's nephew hired a private detective to find her killer."

"A private dick?" Little Estelle smiled up at Lars.

Pat's arm shot up. "Stop it, y'all! This is no joke. Kiki is *missing*."

"Kiki ran off, she's not missing," Flora said.

Just then Kimo walked in. He said, "Either way, she's out there somewhere all by herself. She hates to be alone. She needs people. She needs her friends."

"She needs an audience," Little Estelle said.

"I've got it!" Pat jumped to her feet and waved the napkin around. "It *is* code."

Her chair clattered backward. Kimo righted it. He looked at the napkin in Pat's hand.

"What kind of code? What are you talking about?"

Pat tapped the center of the paper napkin so hard she poked her finger through it. "If you unscramble the letters of Meno'ok Lodfort, they spell Don't Look For Me! *Don't look for me*, get it? Kiki is warning us not to look for her."

Kimo sank into a chair at the table behind them. "I should never have fallen for that note. She tried to get me to run off with her, but I refused. She was talking crazy after Tom Benton came in the bar. Said we should head off into the jungle like Ko'olau the leper and his wife Pi'ilani."

"Like *who*?" Em worried she'd stumbled into the middle of an old *Twilight Zone* episode. Either that, or she was having a nightmare. Any minute now she'd wake up, and it would be time to start the day with a walk on the beach.

"Ko'olau the leper," Flora said.

"More code?" Pat reached for more napkins.

Suzi said to Flora, "Let me explain." She turned to Pat. "Ko'olau the leper and his wife Pi'ilani ran from the Hawaiian government back when they exiled people with Hanson's Disease to the island of Moloka'i. The couple hid in Kalalau Valley, and when the law came to get them, Ko'olau shot and killed the sheriff. Ko'olau eventually died hiding somewhere up in one of the valleys."

Flora shook her head. "If Kiki's up in Kalalau, we can't follow her. We'd never make it."

"Do you think she took a gun?" Little Estelle wondered.

"No kidding," Pat said. "Even if we could get a boat to drop us off, I hear that trail is steep, eleven miles long and less than three feet wide in some spots."

"No toilets," Em said.

"No bars," Flora added.

"No hula," Little Estelle said.

Suzi nodded. "Good points. So Kiki's probably not there. My guess is that she's somewhere comfortable. I just hope she's safe and not the murderer's latest victim."

"Me too." Kimo looked defeated until he finally noticed Lars, who was still standing behind Little Estelle's Gadabout. "Who the heck is this?"

Little Estelle pinched Lars' butt again, winked at Kimo, and said, "Call me Cougar!"

# 30

### Hiding Out in Style

The rain hadn't let up for three days in the Kokee forest area of Kauai. Thirty-six hundred feet above sea level, the air was thinner, the pine trees thicker, and the temperatures cooler. As Kiki sat under a shelter in the park area, fashioning a rain poncho out of an extra large, black plastic trash bag, she found herself wishing she'd packed flannel pajamas.

After she wrote her note to Kimo, she'd left the North Shore and headed for the west side of the island. Stopping in Waimea, she ran into Ishihara Market, bought a Styrofoam cooler, and stocked up on deli items and plenty of sushi rolls before she drove up the winding mountain road into Kokee.

She ditched her car on an unpaved road, having driven on gravel as far as she could make it before she turned onto a spur road open to hunters. She left the car and the bulk of her supplies and hiked out. The cold and rain forced her to return to the car to sleep in it her first night on the mountain.

The second morning, she made a pack of essentials. It wasn't all that exciting to have to use nature as a toilet, but she hadn't earned every Girl Scout camping badge way back when for nothing.

"Kiki Godwin, you are a high achiever," she told herself as she slipped the trash bag over her head. "You play to win and don't ever forget it."

None of the contestants on *Survivor* had anything on her. So what if she was sixty-seven? She could have beaten them all and walked off with a million dollars every season. No way was she going to get railroaded on some trumped up murder charge. No way O.J.

She left the shelter in *Kanaloahuluhulu* Meadow where the Hula Maidens performed at the annual Queen Emma Festival every fall and slowly trudged up the road toward Camp Sloggett. Eventually she turned off the road in search of a deserted cabin where she could spend the night. Most of the privately owned or leased cabins were only used on weekends when locals could escape their everyday lives.

Her feet and knees were killing her from too much hula, but what's a girl to do? She kept plowing along uphill, stopping now and again when she got winded. Finally she glimpsed a rusting tin roof through the trees and headed up a small driveway that wound its way through the bush. The cabin wasn't visible from the road, and the driveway was overgrown with weeds, so she doubted anyone had used it in a while.

As she suspected, the cabin was uninhabited. Once she was inside, the place appeared not to have been used for some time. There was an old sofa that didn't look like it housed many rats. She picked up a piece of wood on the hearth and beat it on the sofa cushions, and thankfully nothing ran out. Even the rats had deserted the place. She dumped her pack on a rickety table and then sat down and stared at the empty fireplace. No way could she build a fire and chance the smoke being seen.

She had what she needed in her pack to build a mean martini. She pulled out the martini glass she'd wrapped in her pareau, the bottle of vodka, and a sushi roll.

When the cocktail was ready, Kiki raised her glass.

"Here's to someone getting arrested soon so I can go home."

# 31

## True Confessions

The Hula Maiden's "Kiki's Missing Emergency Meeting" had gone on way longer than it should have.

As soon as Sophie arrived, she started prepping the tables, refilling ketchup and soy sauce bottles, and setting up the room for the lunch crowd. Kimo, with worry lines marring his usually jovial expression, left the Maidens to their own devices and was soon in the kitchen working on the special of the day, grilled *mahi mahi* sandwiches with fries on the side.

At ten o'clock Em started serving the Maidens drinks. By eleven thirty she was ready to pull the plug and free up the tables for folks coming in for lunch. She was behind the bar when she looked up and spotted Tom Benton in the doorway. None of the Maidens had seen him yet. She tried to signal Suzi to stop talking, but the realtor was in high gear and focused on the women staring up at her.

"So, should we hold a fundraiser ASAP?" Suzi asked. "If so, we need a theme."

"Free Kiki!" Flora hoisted her plastic bottled beverage.

"She'd not in jail yet," Trish reminded her.

"Find Kiki!" Big Estelle called out. "Or Where in the World is Kiki? That might be better."

"She doesn't want to be found, remember?" Pat said.

"Maybe a fundraiser is a bad idea," Suzi decided.

Tom walked straight across the room toward Em.

"What are they talking about?" He stopped at the bar. "Find Kiki? Where's Kiki? What's going on?"

Em finished wiping down the bar and then tossed the towel.

"Em?"

"Kiki left a note for Kimo. She took off, and no one has seen her since."

Tom Benton focused on what Em said for a second, then his eyes widened, and he smiled.

"So, she's on the run. I knew it! I knew that woman was guilty."

Little Estelle was the one closest to the bar and had overheard. She put the Gadabout in gear. Followed by Lars, she rolled over to where Tom was standing.

"Who are you exactly?" Little Estelle blinked behind her wire-framed glasses and stared up at him.

"I'm Tom Benton. Who are you?"

"Call me Cougar. Are you the guy with the private dick?"

"Not if the right woman comes along," he said.

Little Estelle pursed her lips in disgust. "Not *that* one. Are you the guy with the private detective?"

"That's me. Marilyn Lockhart's nephew."

All the Maidens were silently staring at him now. He turned and slowly eyed them one at a time.

"So, Kiki Godwin is on the run." He had the nerve to look smug about it.

"She's not on the run." Suzi grabbed the note from Pat Boggs and read it aloud. "See, she said she'd be back when she finished. She's on an errand of mercy."

Tom sneered then said, "Call it whatever you want. You all know and *I* know that Kiki has disappeared because she is guilty of murdering my aunt. This sudden disappearance of hers might be all the proof I need."

Little Estelle revved her motor and threatened to run over his toes. Lars flexed and unflexed his collection of well-oiled muscles.

"You'll never find any proof that Kiki killed your aunt." Suzi folded the note and tucked it beneath the neckline of her blouse and then shoved it in her bra as if that might keep it from being used as discovery in a murder investigation.

"Nobody really liked Marilyn," Flora said. "Not on this island. It coulda been any one of us killed her. Maybe *I* did it."

"No way you did it, Flora." Trish was on her feet. "Maybe it was me. Maybe I killed her."

"Think I'da let ya'll have all the fun?" Pat Boggs slapped her hands on the table top, turned, and took a step in Tom's direction. "If they did it, I did it."

"I helped 'em!" Little Estelle said. "Had Lars hold the wire cutters and hack the brake line. My daughter was in on it too." She pointed to Big Estelle.

"Mother! This isn't funny." Big Estelle covered her face.

"I didn't do it!" Precious was waving her arms over her head. "I was going to be her maid of honor. We were friends."

"You were the *only* friend she had," Suzi clarified.

"Okay, okay, that's it." Em held up both hands. "Enough of the crazy talk. Either ask for menus and be prepared to order lunch, or pick up your things and go so we can accommodate the lunch crowd. I can't have you all taking up any more free space here today."

A family of tourists in the doorway had witnessed the spontaneous burst of murder confessions. They were about to turn and walk out when Sophie grabbed some menus, turned on her charm, and talked them into taking a table on the *lanai*.

Tom promised the Maidens he was going to have Kiki's head on a platter if it was the last thing he did and stormed out. The women spent ten more minutes arguing about what they should do to help Kiki, then collected their purses and belongings and filed out of the bar.

Em worked without a break until around two thirty when she headed over to the beach house to check on Uncle Louie and take him a sandwich. When she reached the front steps she heard voices over the sound of the surf and found her uncle in conversation with Orville Orion.

Her stomach did a back flip. *What now?*

"Hi, Mr. Orion. Uncle Louie." Uneasy, she glanced over at her uncle and then back to Orion. "Is everything all right?"

"I was just leaving," Orville Orion said with a hang dog expression on his face.

"*Mahalo* for coming by," Louie told him.

"It's the least I could do under the circumstances. No hard feelings then?"

"I'll get over it." Louie turned to gaze out at the ocean for a moment before Orion offered his hand. Louie shook it, then Orion walked out. Em closed the screen door and handed her uncle the to-go box.

"Thanks." His shoulders slumped as he turned around and led the way into the main room.

"Hard feelings?" Em knew what her uncle was about to say and wished she didn't.

"He came clean about his 'friendship' with Marilyn. Said he tried to talk her out of marrying me, but she was determined to go through with it. Apparently she led him to believe she didn't really love me as much as she wanted the Goddess."

"Oh."

"You're not surprised." He was watching her so closely she could have squirmed.

"Well, actually no. I'm not surprised."

"He told me that he confessed everything to you already. If you knew about Orville and Marilyn, why didn't you tell me? I felt like a fool when he broke it to me just now."

"I'm sorry I didn't tell you the minute I found out." Seeing his expression, she was truly sorry. Avoiding the truth had hurt him more than the truth itself.

"Why didn't you, Em? Why weren't you honest with me?"

"I didn't want you hurt any more than you already were by Marilyn's death. I didn't see what difference it would make now that she's gone."

He set the Styrofoam box on the kitchen counter and ignored it.

"So you were just going to let me be happy living a lie."

"You didn't know it was a lie."

"I trust you above all people to be honest with me, Em. You're all I've got."

"I'm so sorry, Uncle."

"If you'd found out right before the wedding, would you have stopped me, or would you have let me make a fool of myself?"

She didn't even pause to consider. "Of course I would have stopped you if I found out before the wedding, but I *didn't* know. I had no way of knowing. I wasn't thrilled that you were going to marry Marilyn, but I trusted that things would work out. I continually hoped Kiki's suspicions were just that. You were so in love, I wanted you to be happy."

"Kiki was right all along. Marilyn only wanted the Goddess. I'll have to tell Kiki I'm sorry I doubted her."

"She's missing."

"Missing? *Kiki?*"

"She's not actually missing, but no one knows where she is. That's what the Maidens' meeting was about this morning. They're convinced she's hiding out in the jungle somewhere like some legendary Hawaiian outlaw leper. If I know Kiki, more than likely she's checked into a hotel in Po'ipu under an alias."

"What's she hiding from?"

"Tom Benton's private detective."

"Is anyone going to look for her?" He studied the take-out box, reached for it, and opened the lid.

"Not yet. She's not around because she doesn't want to be found. Kimo would sure like to hear from her though. He's really worried."

"Kiki always lands on her feet," he reminded her.

"How's the Flaming Inferno coming?"

"So far I'm still figuring out the lighting process. Dave throws a fit when I light the shots on fire. I've got the contest application ready to go out with tomorrow's mail." He opened the silverware drawer and took out a fork.

"That's great," Em smiled, relieved that he'd forgiven her and that his appetite hadn't diminished again.

"Is the guy on island yet? Tom's detective?"

"It could be a woman detective, you know."

"Right." Louie picked up the *mahi mahi* sandwich, took a bite, and swallowed. "Wonder what people call a woman detective? Certainly not a private dick."

AFTER THEY closed for the night, Em poured Sophie a glass of wine, and they finally got off their feet.

"We need to hire a waitress," Em told her. "That way Louie can cut back, and you and I can take a day off once in a while. Since the murder you've been working way too hard."

"I sure don't mind the extra money," Sophie said.

"I can't risk you burning out. I don't know what we did without you as it is." Em had taken a chance on the young woman with no references who had been living in her car, and it turned out to be one of the best decisions she'd ever made.

"*Mahalo* for that."

"Maybe we should put the word out. I'll download a work application form."

"Before you do that, let me make a call. I know someone who might be interested."

"Not Buzzy."

"Heck no. Not Buzzy. It's Tiko."

Tiko Scott, the owner of Tiko's Tastee Tropicals, lived in Wailua Homesteads and owned a line of fruit smoothie powders. Louie had approved carrying a few of Tiko's specialties on the drink menu as non-alcoholic beverage choices, and the smoothies had quickly become a staple.

"I hope she's not giving up on her smoothie business." Em took a sip of wine.

"Not the dream. But the reality is she can't make enough just working festivals. Her dream is to own a shop in town, but with a big blended juice corporation in the shopping center, it's just too hard to compete. She's not looking for more than a few days a week. She might even consider filling in at the last minute whenever things come up. Like a murder or two." Sophie winced. "Sorry. Not funny."

"But pretty close to the truth, unfortunately. There's always some kind of emergency around here lately." Em finished her wine, more than ready to call it quits for the day. "I'll give Tiko a call in the morning," she said.

"I hope it works out for all of us." Sophie picked up their empty wine glasses and headed over to the bar.

When Em's cell rang, she wondered who could be calling at one in the morning. She glanced at the caller ID, thinking it might be Kiki with one of her hysterical phone calls, but it was Roland.

"Hi." She realized she was smiling and glanced over at the bar. Sophie had caught her expression and mouthed, "Roland?"

Em nodded.

"I didn't wake you, did I?" he said. "I thought you were probably closing up."

"Just finished."

"We've had calls from a couple of Kokee cabin owners near the Camp Sloggett Road. They've found obvious signs that someone has broken in and used their homes. Nothing has been stolen, but they can tell someone has been there. Someone who keeps leaving neat little piles of olive pits on coffee tables."

"Kiki," Em said.

"That's what I was thinking. Her car was found deserted on a hunting trail. The forest service had to tow it. Do you have any idea what's going on?"

"Me?"

"That's what I figured. What's up?"

*No way out*, Em thought.

"She's afraid Tom Benton's hired detective is going to frame her for murdering Marilyn, so she's on the run like the legendary leper."

"She's not doing a very good job of hiding."

"I guess not."

"Is there any way you can contact her?" He sounded tired.

"She left a note written in code. It said not to look for her."

"You deciphering codes now?"

"Not me. One of the Maidens. It makes sense, sort of."

"Only if that bunch has gotten to you, Em."

"Don't worry about me. Do you think Kiki's all right?"

"Personally, I think she's crazy, but I hope she's not putting herself in danger. It's easy to get turned around on those trails. I can't believe I'm asking, but do you think you can find her and bring her home before someone presses charges, and we have to arrest her for breaking and entering?"

"I can try. How long before you have to do something?"

"I can't stall long."

"I'll leave in the morning."

He thanked her and said goodnight. Em hung up and turned to Sophie.

"Can you call Tiko for me first thing in the morning? Ask if she can come in tomorrow? We've got another emergency on our hands."

"Emergency? Is Kiki all right?"

"As far as we know, but she's broken into some cabins in Kokee and is leaving a trail of olive pits. I have to go find her before the owners want her arrested."

"Are you going by yourself?"

Em stared at Sophie in disbelief. "I hope you aren't suggesting I ask the Maidens to help."

"At least call Suzi. You shouldn't be running around up there alone."

# 32

## Hunting Kiki in Kokee

Em felt Suzi was probably the most level-headed of the Maidens, so she called the realtor as early as she dared the next morning, told her about Roland's call, and asked if she would meet her at the Princeville Library. The plan was for the two of them to carpool to Kokee.

After digging out some old hiking boots, long cargo pants, and a flannel shirt to wear over a tank top, Em was ready. She cranked up Louie's truck and took off. When she pulled into the lot at the library and realized what was going on, it was too late to turn back.

Suzi's new Prius was parked beside Big Estelle's handicap-equipped van. Big Estelle was waiting in the parking lot beside Suzi and Trish. Little Estelle was in the van watching from the back window. She waved when she saw Em, and then the panel door slid open and Lars climbed out dressed from head to toe in camouflage pants, shirt, jacket, and a hat with ear flaps.

Too late. They'd all seen her. When Em parked and got out of her car, they all ran over. She gave Suzi what she hoped was the look of death.

"Sorry," Suzi shrugged. "One for all, and all for one."

"We have it all figured out. Suzi and I will ride with you, Em," Trish said. "Big Estelle will bring Lars and her mom, and they'll pick up Precious in Kapa'a. She's going to wait for us on the side of the road."

"Flora can't go," Suzi added. "An order of plush parrots came in for her store yesterday. You should see them. They're little stuffed David Lettermans, and when you push the button in the tummy they actually spit and squawk, '*Yuck, yuck, patooie!*'"

"Just like David does when he hates a new drink," Trish said. "Each one comes with its own little plastic shot glass."

"They're so cute. Flora wants to get them unpacked and on display right away."

Thank God for small favors, Em thought. Better than having Flora and her Gatorade bottle lost on a hunting trail.

"Ve go?" Covered in camo, Lars was sweating buckets.

"Why don't you take off the hat?" Em asked him.

He smiled and nodded. His English was obviously limited. She pointed to her head. "Too hot?"

"Ya!" He smiled and nodded some more. "Hot."

"He won't take it off. Mother told him he had to wear it. It's part of the outfit," Big Estelle said.

They all piled into their vehicles. Sure enough, when they reached Kapa'a they saw Precious standing on the highway in front of the ABC liquor store. Big Estelle pulled over, and Em pulled in behind her. Precious walked up to the van, the door slid open, and Lars jumped out. He scooped up Precious and lifted her inside. The door slid shut, and they were off.

The caravan made three more stops before they even reached Waimea town where Big Estelle pulled over again and pointed at the Shrimp Station, a brightly painted square building with a take-out window.

"What now?" They'd left Princeville at eight in the morning, but Em was beginning to wonder if they'd make it to Kokee before sunset.

"I think they want to stop for shrimp tacos."

"Shrimp tacos? Good grief. We had to stop for malasadas at the stand at Kmart, then for *liliko'i* chiffon pie in Hanapepe not fifteen minutes ago. Now they want shrimp tacos?"

"I could eat one myself," Trish said. "Besides, it's more like twenty minutes now. When was the last time you had sautéed, beer battered, coconut flaked grilled shrimp in a tortilla?"

"How are you going to make it up on the mountain without buying food every half hour?" Em said. "I was planning on roughing it with bottled water and granola bars."

"That's because you still think like a *haole*. We could always have lunch at the Kokee Museum restaurant when we get to the park."

"I was kidding," Em said. "You all need to realize this is an emergency. If we don't find Kiki, the police are going to be called in and nothing good will happen if they have to spend time tracking her down."

"Sheesh, Em. Don't be so uptight. We'll find her," Suzi said.

"We can't find her if everyone is too full to walk."

Big Estelle refused to go on until they all piled out and had shrimp tacos. Em hated to admit she was glad they did. In Waimea they took Route 55, Waimea Canyon Road, then drove up a steep grade with a stunning view of the ocean and the island of Ni'ihau in the distance. The foliage began to thicken, and soon they were driving through the forest of *koa* wood and pine trees. On the right side of the road, the land abruptly dropped off toward the floor of the Waimea Valley over three thousand feet below.

The highway twisted up the side of the canyon through the forest, the air grew cooler, and the vegetation thickened. Em kept her eyes on the road until Big Estelle pulled over without warning in a turn-out, and Em whizzed by. There was no one behind them, so she backed up and parked behind the van. Lars, in all his camouflage glory, was on the side of the road puking his guts up.

Big Estelle rolled down her window, stuck her head out, and yelled, "Car sick!"

Trish stuck the huge telephoto lens of her camera out the window. She took aim at Lars and then photographed the stunning view of the canyon.

Somehow, they made it to the meadow at Kokee. Em pulled into the parking lot, hoping no one would seriously want to eat at the lodge restaurant.

"So what's the plan?" Suzi waited to ask Em until everyone but Little Estelle had gathered in the parking lot next to Louie's truck.

"Does anyone know where the Camp Sloggett road is?" Em asked.

All but Lars pointed toward the road going up the hill across from the Kokee Lodge.

"We should drive in as far as we can," Big Estelle suggested.

Em stared at the steep road. "How far is that?"

"Pretty darn far as I recall. I used to have a map in the van, but I couldn't find it. Maybe we can buy one in the museum."

"I've got GPS," Suzi said. "We should have driven the Prius."

"Does it work up here?" Em's cell had been out of range since early on. Trish said that was because they were near the military's Makaha Ridge Tracking Station, which was connected to the Pacific Missile Range Facility.

"Better known as Star Wars," Suzi added. "My GPS still works up here though."

"But this old truck has four wheel drive," Em reminded them.

They started up the dirt road to Camp Sloggett and turned into the driveways of each cabin nestled in the forest along the way. Some driveways were overgrown, so it meant getting out on foot and prowling around empty cabins looking for signs of Kiki, knocking on doors, and calling out, "Hoo-ee!"

The others waited in their van as Em, Suzi, and Trish went to the doors of occupied cabins. They realized they were on Kiki's trail when they ran into some owners who had called to report a break in. None of them had actually seen anyone fitting Kiki's description.

"We found a pile of olive pits, though," one woman said. "They were stacked like a little pyramid. Why would someone leave evidence behind like that? You'd almost think she wanted to be found."

"Maybe," Em said, "she wanted to leave us a sign that she'd been here, that she was all right."

"She's not thinking clearly right now," Suzi said.

"Medication," Trish quickly added. "She . . . she's off her meds and a bit disoriented. It's not her fault. Kind of sad actually. I sure hope you can forgive her."

The cabin owner's expression saddened. "Oh, that's too bad."

"That's why we're searching for her. We hope you understand she needs help and that you won't call the police again."

"Not at all," the woman said. "No harm done. I hope you find her, poor thing."

As they walked back down the driveway, Em whispered, "Medication?"

"It's all I could think of," Trish said.

"Sounds good to me. It'll buy her some time," Suzi decided. "But Kiki will be furious if she ever finds out."

"She's not here," Suzi told Big Estelle and the others when they reached the van. "But she has been."

"You don't think she'd be at Camp Sloggett, do you?" Big Estelle leaned out of the driver's side window.

"It's not really her style," Trish said.

"Maybe it's worth a look after coming all this way," Em said.

They loaded up and drove up to the sign at the entrance to Camp Sloggett and turned down the long drive. The *Holoholo Holiday* tour van was parked in the open meadow near a long bunk house. Em saw a flash of hot pink in one of the windows.

"Oh, no," Suzi said.

"The Lillians," Trish said.

"Let's hope Kiki found them or they found her." Her marriage might have ended on a sour note, but Em was ever hopeful things would work out for the best.

As the Maidens approached the bunk house, a few of the Lillians filed out, all wearing matching hot pink sweat suits.

The real Lillian separated herself from the group. She was all smiles.

"What a nice surprise!" She welcomed them with open arms. "I'm so glad that you're all here. The Lillians have been talking about you all since the show at the Goddess."

More Lillians poured out of a building that turned out to be where the dining hall and central kitchen was located. Soon Em and the others were surrounded by visitors from Iowa.

Big Estelle opened the van and lowered the lift where Little Estelle was seated on the Gadabout. She appeared like a Cougar goddess, descending with arms spread wide. Sometime between the Kokee Lodge and now, she'd donned a camouflage cat suit.

Standing behind her like a personal Adonis, Lars flexed, though his camo gear hid most of his muscles.

Em took Suzi and Trish aside.

The Lillians burst into applause. Little Estelle preened.

The real Lillian was in tears, as usual. "I can't tell you how much it means to me that you drove all the way up here. You simply must stay for our pot luck dinner!"

"Have you got enough?" With Lars occupied, Precious had to climb out of the van on her own. "We're kind of last minute."

The Lillians all started laughing. "We have so much food we couldn't close the refrigerator doors."

Em pulled Suzi and Trish aside. "We're burning daylight here."

"Too bad we're going to have to burst Lillian's bubble and tell them why we're really here." Trish glanced over her shoulder at the cloud of women in pink.

"I'll try to make it gentle," Em said. She clapped her hands, trying to get their attention.

"Ladies . . ." When no one stopped talking, Em found herself wishing Pat Boggs was there.

"Lillians!" Em yelled. "Listen up."

One by one they finally settled down.

Em said, "Not only are we here to see you all, but we are on a mission. We're trying to find Kiki. She is up here in Kokee somewhere, and it's imperative that we find her."

"Kiki?" The real Lillian wiped her eyes. "Why, she spent the night with us last night."

"Really?" Em looked around. "Is she still here?"

"No, she had to go. Said she had to keep moving."

"Did she tell you why?" Suzi asked.

"She said there was a bounty on her head. She was never going to let them bring her in."

"A bounty on her head?" Precious laughed.

"The legend grows," Trish said.

"You have no idea where she went?" Em had hoped this was going to be easier.

Lillian said, "No, she left just after dawn. We gave her a little water, some food, enough for a day or two if she's careful. She didn't want it to weigh her down. And we gave her a bottle of vodka. We brought plenty of booze with us, of course."

"Great," Em mumbled. "Now what?"

Trish suggested, "Let's leave Big Estelle and her bunch here to party, and the three of us can take the truck up the road. Tell them we're going where we need four wheel drive."

"Good idea. Besides, from the looks of the road past this point I don't think that's a lie," Suzi said.

Em explained the plan to the others, and then she and Trish and Suzi drove as far up the road as they thought Kiki could walk in a few hours, which wasn't far. They'd driven about twenty minutes when they passed two large pickup trucks full of empty cages.

"Uh, oh." Suzi said.

"What?" Em stared at the trucks. "What in the heck belongs in those?"

"Hunting dogs," Trish said. "The hunters let them out to track down wild boar."

"Pig hunters," Suzi said.

Just then two hunters came out of the woods carrying rifles. Leather sheaths with long knives hung from their belts. One of them came to talk to Em when she waved them over.

Em stared at the huge man standing next to the door of her truck. "Have you seen a woman up here? She's in her sixties."

"Why you wanna know?"

"We're her friends. She's in trouble, and we came to help her." Trish, riding in the small back seat of the truck cab, leaned over the window ledge.

The other hunter joined the first. "You talkin' about Auntie Kiki?"

"You know her?" Suzi sounded amazed.

"Sure. Saw her a couple days ago. Told her she should be wearing day-glow orange. We'd hate to shoot her accidently."

"Orange isn't really one of Kiki's colors," Trish said.

"You haven't seen her today, have you?" Em hated to go back down the mountain and tell Roland that she hadn't found Kiki. She had no idea it would be this difficult to find a sixty-seven-year-old woman who was on foot. Nor had she realized how immense the forest was. Kiki could be anywhere.

"Thank you," Em told the men. "If you see Kiki again, will you please tell her that her friends are looking for her and she needs to go home?"

They nodded, but Em wasn't sure Kiki would get the message. She headed back down the road, stopped by a couple more cabins before they returned to Camp Sloggett in defeat.

"Please stay for dinner," Lillian begged. "We're eating early."

"I'd like to head back down the mountain before dark," Em told her. "But I guess we can stay."

There was a pay phone in the communal dining hall. Em wondered if it was the last pay phone in existence. She picked up the receiver, and there was a dial tone so she dropped in some coins and dialed Roland. Across the room, the Lillians were dragging pot luck pans out of the kitchen and lining them up on long folding tables. The *Holoholo Holidays* van driver sat outside at a picnic table smoking cigarettes and watched the crazy *haoles* run around inside the hall.

Big Estelle was in a corner with Suzi and Trish deciding which songs they would perform for the Lillians. Big Estelle always carried a box of hula CDs and a small boom box in the van. Her mother had parked the Gadabout at the front of the dining hall near the buffet table. She and Lars were signing autographs in between making goo-goo eyes at each other.

Em had to look away.

"We haven't found her yet," Em told Roland when he answered.

"It's getting late. Do you think you will?"

"I hope so. We just spoke to some hunters who had seen Kiki. Lillian is up here, and we ran into her. In fact, there are thirty Lillians here at Camp Sloggett on a *holoholo*."

"Lillian is the one with pink hair who caught herself on fire? Isn't one enough?"

"Not since the "Trouble in Paradise" pilot premiered. Her fan club flew in from her hometown in Iowa after the big burn incident. They've morphed into clones of Lillian."

She thought about Kiki's dilemma again. "Listen, Roland, can you give Kiki more time? We spoke to some cabin owners, and it turns out they aren't very upset. We explained that she was a bit disoriented."

"A bit disoriented? If only. One of the owners did call in after talking to you and said she's not going to press charges. I can't guarantee the rest of the homeowners will feel that way, especially if Kiki keeps it up."

"It's going to be dark soon." Em looked out the window. There was a mist rolling in, covering the deep green shades of the forest in milk white. She didn't relish driving down miles of winding road in the dark if the fog thickened.

"Get out of there as soon as you can," he said. "No one's pressing charges right now. It's my guess the cabin owners up there will talk to one another. They'll all realize their mystery house crasher is a 'disoriented' senior, and with any luck they'll try to help by bringing her in."

Em tried to imagine Kiki going for that. Not to mention how she'd react to someone calling her a disoriented senior.

She told him goodbye and hung up. By now the Lillians were seated at long folding tables. Their plates were heaped with piles of pot luck dishes, most of them various forms of pasta smothered in red tomato-based sauces and oozing thick layers of cheese.

Big Estelle, the real Lillian, Trish, and Suzi were lined up and already dancing hula at the open end of the hall. Precious took her first official job for the group seriously and was standing beside the boom box with her finger poised above the stop button.

Em wasn't hungry. She'd eaten more that morning that she had in days, but she did have to use the *lua*, so she headed out toward the bunk house across the meadow. On her way back out of the bunk house, she had just stepped off the porch headed for the dining hall when she heard a low hissing sound.

*Rattlesnake.* She froze and heard it again, closer this time.

"Psst. Psst. Em!"

*There are no snakes in Hawaii*, she remembered. *There are no talking snakes anywhere except in the Bible.*

Em looked around but didn't see anything. Worst case scenario was that the Maidens had finally succeeded in driving her crazy.

A hushed voice said, "Over here. Behind you."

Em looked over her shoulder and studied some low bushes at the edge of the forest. She glanced toward the communal building where the Lillians were cheering, and then she began to walk backwards until she could slip behind the bunk house. Once the building blocked her from view, she turned and sprinted across the grass to the bushes. Ducking behind a shrub she tried to locate Kiki.

"Where are you?" she whispered back though there was no one close enough to hear.

"I'm on your three o'clock!"

Em turned that direction and headed deeper into the trees and bushes. She picked her way along until she thought she spotted Kiki crouched behind a tree trunk. Kiki waved and stood up, then walked gingerly toward Em.

Em hugged her. "We've been so worried about you. We've been looking all over."

"I left a note. Didn't anyone figure it out?"

"Pat did."

"I said don't look for me. So, why are you looking?" Kiki sounded miffed.

"Roland wanted me to take you back home before a cabin owner presses charges."

"For what?"

"Breaking and entering, for one thing."

"Breaking and entering! All I did was use the *lua*, sleep on the sofas, and have a martini or two. Most of those people didn't even lock the doors. What do they expect?"

"You were uninvited, Kiki."

"They would seriously press charges against me?"

Em shrugged. "Hopefully not now. We told them you were off your meds."

"What meds? Now I'm not just a murder suspect on the run, I'm a *crazed* fugitive?

"We had to think fast."

Kiki smiled, looking almost pleased. "Who is we? Are all the girls searching for me?"

"Most of the Maidens. Little Estelle and Lars, too."

"Who the heck is Lars?"

"Her soul mate. They met on the *iLoveCougars.com.*"

"Stop." Kiki held up her hand. "Don't tell me."

Em figured if they all had to suffer, so should Kiki.

"Lars is twenty-three if he's a day, and he's straight out of some Viking DNA gene pool." Em wanted to get going, so she motioned toward the camp hall. "You've got to come home with us, Kiki. Please. You're just making your situation worse."

"No. I can't. Not while there's a chance I'll end up in prison. Please don't make me. I'm fine up here. Just give it a few more days."

"But Roland said . . ."

"Roland. So that's why you're here. Did he send you?"

"Yes. He wanted me to bring you back before any of the cabin owners got mad enough to press charges. You should be happy he called me first. Do the smart thing, Kiki. Come down off this mountain."

# 33

### Hiding in Plain Sight

Exhausted, Kiki leaned against the tree trunk. She was cold and tired, and her feet and legs ached from three days of hiking around on uneven ground.

The mist was lifting, but it would be back, passing like ghosts through the trees. She heard the shrill frenetic barking of a pack of hunting dogs hot on the trail of a kill in the distance. Em's eyes widened at the sound, and then the younger woman gazed longingly toward the camp dining hall.

"There's only one way I'll go back," Kiki told her.

"How?"

"I need everyone to think I'm still up here. Everyone. Including the Maidens. If one of them knows, the whole island will know I'm home. You, I can trust."

"How do you suggest we pull that off?"

Kiki had the feeling Em was such a do-goody-goody that she'd probably never agree to anything the least bit sneaky.

"Does your uncle have a tarp in the truck?"

Em frowned a minute. "I think there's one folded up in the back of the cab. He uses it to keep things dry in the truck bed if it starts raining."

"The Lillians were having dinner." Kiki glanced at the building. "Are they almost done?"

"Not yet. The Maidens are dancing."

"Even better. Go back and get them to teach the Lillians another hula. A group lesson. That'll keep them all occupied. It's almost dusk now. When the light fades, I'll sneak over to your truck, wrap up in the tarp, and hide in the truck bed."

"In plain sight."

"If you wait until dark to leave, no one will notice me. I'll just be a lump. A shadow."

"A big lump. I wanted to drive down the mountain while it was still light."

"Don't be such a chicken, Em. You can make it. I'll ride covered up in the truck bed, and when we get back to the Goddess I'll slip into   Kimo's

*167*

truck and hide there. You can tell him what's up, and I'll ride home with him when he's done for the night. As far as everyone else is concerned, I'm still up here hiding out."

"I won't lie to Roland."

"Not telling isn't exactly lying."

"He's going to ask if I found you. I'll have to tell him."

"All right. You can tell Roland, but nobody else. Tell him that until he has a reason to arrest me, then he needs to leave me alone. I don't want Tom Benton to know I'm back."

"What if you bounce out of the truck bed? The road out of here has more holes in it than Swiss cheese."

"Let me worry about that. Will you do it?"

Em stared out into the thickening gloom.

"This is against my better judgment, but okay, I will."

# 34

## Keeping Kiki Undercover

Jumpy as a frog in a frying pan, Em went back to the dining hall where the Maidens were tuned up and dancing their toes off. Instead of insisting they pack up and take off, she let them cavort, even suggesting they teach the Lillians another easy hula.

Em watched twilight deepen to darkness in the meadow.

If anyone noticed she'd given up leaving before dark, no one reminded her. Lars disappeared and came back with dried twigs and fallen branches and piled them into the fire pit under a pavilion in the meadow.

"Come on, everybody!" Little Estelle rolled the Gadabout out of the dining room and down the ramp outside. "Lars is about to light the campfire."

"Time for s'mores!" The real Lillian waved a huge bag of marshmallows in the air.

Em prayed Kiki was wrapped up in the truck as the women all poured outside. She stopped Trish and Suzi on their way out.

"I'm heading back to Haena," she told them. "If you want to ride back with Big Estelle, that's all right with me."

"I've got a photo shoot in the morning," Trish said. "I'll go with you."

"Me, too," said Suzi. "I've got some property to show. Besides, I heard Big Estelle say the rest of them were thinking of spending the night. There are plenty of empty bunks."

The Lillians and the others were seated on log benches around the fire pit roasting marshmallows and singing "Ninety-nine Bottles of Beer on the Wall." Em, Trish, and Suzi said their goodbyes, and Em made sure she was the first to get to the pickup.

Sure enough, there was a mound beneath the tarp in the back. The truck was in a shadowy spot far enough from the fire that neither Trish nor Suzi noticed. As they climbed in and Em honked and waved goodbye to the others, a low cloud drifted into the meadow, shrouding them in mist.

Em gripped the wheel as they left the grassy meadow behind and hit the dirt road. She leaned toward the windshield, straining to see. Visibility was down to three feet beyond the glow of the headlamps when she hit a pothole. If they hadn't had their seat belts on, she and the other two would have hit their heads on the top of the cab.

There was an audible thud behind them.

"What was that?" Trish craned her neck to look out the small window behind her.

"What?" Em pictured Kiki lying on the road behind them. "Probably hit a rock."

She fought to stay on the smoothest sections of the road, but it was nearly impossible. Kiki would be a mass of bruises, if she made it back.

The left rear tire sank into another pothole and there was another thud from the truck bed. This time it was even louder.

"There is goes again," Trish said.

"I heard it this time," Suzi added. "Did you just hear a whimper?"

Em turned on the radio, but there was only static. She pushed the CD button, and the music from one of Uncle Louie's exotica collection CDs filled the cab. The classic 50's music was filled with the sounds of a vibraphone, monkey calls, bird screeches, and what sounded like a woman in pain howling, "*Ooo-ooo. Wa-ooo-ooo.*"

They hit a bump. A screech followed.

"Amazing. That sounded really lifelike. They did a great job of re-mastering those old records." Trish said.

Em saw a pothole looming and hit the brake. Kiki rolled and thudded against the back of the truck bed. Em mentally cursed Tom Benton. Poor Kiki wouldn't be in this situation if he hadn't threatened her and sent her on the run with his quest to avenge Marilyn's death.

Suzi bounced along with a grip on the door handle. "Wow. I hope your uncle's truck is going to be all right. Sounds like you might have a broken axle."

"I'm sure it's all right." Em wasn't sure about anything, but at least she could tell by the thuds and the yelps that Kiki was still in the truck bed.

Fifteen minutes seemed like forever, but they finally reached the paved road and started down the hill. They passed Kokee Lodge which was dark for the night, driving through a misty cloud that refused to lift. Em's grip never loosened on the wheel as they snaked their way back down the mountain.

At one point the fog was so thick Em nearly pulled over to wait it out.

"Suzi, hang your head out of the window and tell me if I start to get too close to the edge of the road. I can't see a thing," Em said.

"Good thing the canyon is on the other side of the truck going down-hill." Trish was clutching her camera in her lap. "If we go over the edge, it's a long way down."

Em didn't loosen her grip until they were safely back at sea level in Waimea and she had started the long haul around the island to the North Shore. Despite the monkey calls and odd whining siren sounds coming out of the CD player, Trish and Suzi soon fell sound asleep.

As Em drove along she thought about the life she'd left behind in Orange County where trendy shops and restaurants lined the streets. Fantastic food could be had for a tenth of what it cost on Kauai. Upscale shopping centers and boutiques were the norm. Luxury cars filled every garage in her Newport Beach neighborhood. But she had quickly discovered after the divorce that her husband had gotten custody of their friends. As time passed and she no longer heard from any of them, Em realized it wasn't such a great loss.

It was impossible to imagine any one of her old friends getting involved in smuggling a middle-aged murder suspect around in the back of a pickup, chatting up pig hunters, or going on covert assignments to help a fire dancing detective.

Em relaxed and found herself smiling and humming to the strains of her uncle's eclectic midcentury cocktail party tunes. The miles whizzed by, and she made it back to the North Shore in record time. Avoiding the lights in the Princeville library parking lot, she let Suzi and Trish out and pulled away before they spotted the lump that was Kiki in the back.

She drove down the road, crossed the single lane Hanalei Bridge, and continued on around the coast line to Haena. There were very few cars in the Goddess parking lot, so she drove on through and pulled into the beach house driveway, which was not well lit.

Climbing down out of the pickup, Em made certain no one was around before she reached out and shook the lump. There was no response.

"Kiki? We're here."

Kiki groaned.

"Are you all right?"

"Help me." Kiki sounded so weak Em could barely hear her.

Em looked to see if Uncle Louie might be standing near one of the windows in the back of the beach house, but it was all clear. She uncovered Kiki and found her curled into a fetal position around her backpack.

"I can't feel my legs," Kiki croaked. "I'll never dance again. I'm dying."

"Try to uncurl them very slowly," Em encouraged. She rubbed Kiki's lower legs and then gripped her arm and tried to help her sit up.

"I feel like I've been bouncing around in an aluminum blender. I'm going to be black and blue all over."

After much moaning and groaning on Kiki's part and much shushing on Em's, Kiki was finally able to sit up. Once more, Em found herself mentally cursing Tom Benton.

Five minutes passed before Kiki could crawl out of the truck bed, butt first. Em had to hold on to Kiki to keep her upright. She took a few wobbly steps and then with Em's help, she hobbled over to Kimo's truck.

Once Kiki was tucked inside, slouched over out of sight, Em headed back to the house. She paused outside, pulled her cell out of her pocket, and punched in Roland's number. When his voicemail picked up she left a brief message.

"I'm back from Kokee and all is well. Call me when you can." She shoved her phone back into her pocket and went into the house.

Uncle Louie was sound asleep on the sofa. On the muted television, an actor in a white lab coat was busy rubbing a miraculous wrinkle remover on a model without a line on her face.

Across the room, David Letterman lay passed out on the bottom of his cage. Empty shot glasses were lined up on the tiki bar surrounded by sticky spillage and what appeared to be a quarter-sized burn mark on the bar top.

Em wiped excess alcohol off the bar and carried the shot glasses into the kitchen thinking, all in all, it had been a pretty darned good day. Kiki had been found, talked out of hiding, brought down the mountain and safely hidden in Kimo's truck. Uncle Louie's depression was lifting; apparently the Flaming Inferno had been perfected. The recipe had definitely passed the David Letterman test.

She covered the bird cage, turned off the television and lamp, and left Uncle Louie snoring on the sofa. Heading back to the bar to help Sophie close up and warn Kimo that Kiki was back and hiding in his truck, Em started humming, "Just Another Day in Paradise."

# 35

### Pleading Kiki's Case

When Em still hadn't heard from Roland by nine the next morning, she figured he had worked late at a *luau* gig. She didn't look forward to trying to convince him to let people believe Kiki was still in hiding. At least Em could report that the cabin break-ins were over.

The more Em thought about Tom Benton and how he'd zeroed in on Kiki, the more she thought that she should personally ask him to back off. Not that she would have much influence on him, but maybe it would be worth a try.

She was at the Goddess that morning waiting for Kimo to wrap up a couple of orders of wontons she'd called in from the house. She didn't dare tell him they were for Tom. While Em was looking over some receipts in the cash register drawer, Tiko Scott walked in.

Like Em, Tiko was in her early thirties, but with coffee-colored skin. She was petite and very thin with long black hair that hung past her waist and was as dark as her ebony eyes.

"I can't thank you enough for hiring me part time," she told Em.

"I'm just happy you were available and hope you can add as many hours as you can spare."

"This will give me a chance to see firsthand how my smoothies are received in a real restaurant. Maybe it'll help me come up with other ideas."

Kimo walked out with a foil covered take-out container of pork wonton that smelled great.

"Here you go, Em."

Em's mouth watered. "Perfect. *Mahalo.*" She gave him a meaningful look. "Is everything all right at home?"

"Good as it can be," he said. "Thanks."

"I hope somebody finds Kiki soon," Sophie said.

Em was embarrassed and wished she could tell Sophie the truth, but she had given Kiki her word.

"I've got to deliver these." Em held up the wontons. "I should be right back."

"I didn't know you delivered take-out," Tiko said.

"We don't." Sophie seemed to be waiting for Em to explain.

"I'll be back ASAP." Em hurried out the door before she had to tell Sophie what was up.

The morning was postcard perfect, and the sky appeared to have been hand-tinted a bright blue. White clouds scudded by on the trade winds. Em turned left into the entrance of Princeville where all was perfectly quiet. The emerald golf course was rimmed with generously sized houses. The yards were pristine, the hedges all trimmed to homeowner regulation height and not an inch higher or lower. It was the stuff of travel brochures.

Pausing to let a pair of golf carts cross the road, Em thought, *Cue the golfers.*

She wound around the various loops and drives and circles and somehow found Marilyn's former home. She wondered if and when Tom planned to sell it. There was no sign of a car in the driveway, but that didn't mean he wasn't there. She parked and walked up the stone path through an entry garden of various lush tropical flowers with red and yellow blooms.

Calling his name, she knocked and peered through the beveled glass sidelights that bordered the front door. She didn't see him inside, so she knocked louder and called his name again. When he still didn't appear, she decided to leave him a note with the wontons. She tried the knob and found the door unlocked.

She stepped inside and left the door open as she moved deeper into the interior, calling Tom's name as she went, thinking perhaps he was out on the back *lanai*.

Though it was customary to go into friends' homes to drop things off, Em still wasn't comfortable with wandering through someone's house if they weren't there. It was especially creepy to be walking around inside without Marilyn there.

On her way into the kitchen, she noticed an open laptop where Tom must have been working before he left. Beside it lay an uneven pile of what appeared to be pages of credit ratings on the glass dining table. Along with the credit rating pages there was a scattered pile of at least ten credit cards: Visas, MasterCards, American Express.

Curiosity got the better of her, and Em veered close to the table on her way into the kitchen. Expecting to see Tom's name on the cards, when she saw they belonged to others, she looked closer.

The name imprinted on one of the cards was Dewey Smithson. The minute she saw it the name rang a bell, and she remembered that Smithson was the tourist who had occupied the room where Esther Villaviejos' body had been found.

What was the birdwatcher's credit card doing there?

Em glanced over her shoulder, but there was still no sign of Tom anywhere. She picked up the card. As far as she knew, no one had seen Smithson since he checked out of the Haena Beach Resort. She set down the wonton box but then had to make a grab for it as it almost fell off the table.

She came to the conclusion that Tom's private detective had arrived on island and they had made more headway locating Smithson than the KPD. But how did they get the man's credit card? And why?

She fanned out the cards on the table with one hand. There were a good ten cards there, all with different names imprinted on them. Smithson's was only one of many.

Unless Dewey Smithson's accounts were part of a random credit check that Tom was working on for his company, then something was up.

A chill ran down Em's spine. She heard Roland's voice in her head as clear as a bell.

*"Don't be stupid, Em."*

She quickly pulled her cell phone out of her shorts pocket, left the credit cards fanned out and took a photo of them, then a photo of the credit rating slips and one of the computer screen, which she realized showed lists of Social Security numbers.

She was about to take one more shot of the cards when she heard men's voices coming from the direction of the backyard.

"Thanks for inviting me, Tom, but I'm not sure I can make it tonight." It was Orville Orion.

"I know it's last minute. I'm just having a few of the neighbors over. No need to let me know. You're welcome to stop by if you can."

Em quickly gathered the cards back into a stack, grabbed the wonton box, ran through the living room, and closed the front door behind her without a sound. She paused on the front steps to look up and down the street. Thankfully there wasn't a soul in sight. Not even a gardener. She heard Tom's footsteps inside now.

*"Don't be stupid."*

Em whipped around, faced the front door again, knocked, and called out Tom's name.

"Tom? It's Em Johnson."

There was a moment of hesitation before he answered.

"Just a minute, Em." Then she heard him moving around inside and saw through the sidelight that he was straightening his things on the dining table. He touched the laptop keyboard before he headed toward the front door.

When it opened, he ran his hand through his hair and smiled.

"Hi, Em. I hope you haven't been waiting long. I was out back talking to Orville."

"No, not at all." She handed him the carton of wontons. "I thought you might like these."

"Why, thanks." He seemed taken aback by the gesture. "Come on in."

He led her through the house to the kitchen. As they passed the dining table, she noticed the papers that had been all over the table must have disappeared into a manila folder that was there. The screen saver displayed a photo of the Taj Mahal.

Em started to smile, but then her heart almost stopped when she glanced down at the carpet and realized that when she'd juggled the take-out box, a wonton had slipped out. It was lying on the floor beneath the table. If Tom saw it, he'd surely wonder how it got there.

"You should probably put those in the refrigerator," she suggested. "If you're not going to have some right away."

*Keep walking. Please, keep walking into the kitchen.*

"Nice surprise." Focused on the wonton container, his back was to her as he headed into the kitchen.

Em did a quick squat and grab and then straightened and fell into step behind him.

She opened her palm. "This one slipped out. Sorry." She looked around for a trash can.

"Over there." Tom nodded toward a long thin cabinet that slid out to reveal a trash can.

She tossed the wonton and brushed her hands together.

"How's your uncle?" he asked.

"Doing all right. Thanks for asking."

Tom put the take-out box in the refrigerator. When he turned and smiled at her, Em hoped she'd recovered her composure. Her heart was beating faster than a Tahitian drummer on Red Bull.

"I'm really sorry about the way I acted at the bar the other day. It's just so frustrating to think that there's a killer on the loose. If it is Kiki Godwin, then she needs to be brought to justice. That's all I was saying. Is she still missing?"

"No one has seen her." Pretty much the truth. "Actually, Kiki is the reason I came by to see you." She saw his expression tighten and quickly added, "She's almost seventy, Tom. Your groundless accusations are taking a physical toll on her."

"They aren't groundless, and there is no age limit on killers," he said.

"The police questioned her and found no reason to hold her." Em couldn't stop thinking about the credit card on the dining table with Dewey Smithson's name on it.

The only thing she really knew about Tom Benton was that he was successfully employed at some kind of credit agency.

He certainly looked harmless enough.

"How was India?" she asked.

"What?" Confused by her abrupt change of subject, he blinked a couple of times. "India. Oh, it was great. The Taj is incredible."

"So I hear."

Was he watching her too closely? Her imagination was running wild, her gut screaming at her to get out.

*"Don't be stupid."*

"Has your private detective arrived on Kauai?" She leaned against the butcher block island in the center of the kitchen hoping she looked nonchalant.

"I'd rather not say."

Her mind careened down a wave of possibilities after that comment. Did he have someone out trying to solve the murders, or merely to frame Kiki?

Tom's glance strayed to the dining table, giving him away before he focused on her again. He shrugged. "You can understand my reticence to say anything, given your friendship with Kiki."

He was staring at her as if trying to figure out why the line of questioning.

"I understand where you're coming from, Em." Suddenly, his tone softened. "It's because of your friendship with Kiki and her husband that your perspective on this is so clouded. From everything my aunt told me about their rivalry, I think there's a very real chance the woman is guilty. Don't let your emotions get in the way of the truth."

Em forced a smile and pushed away from the kitchen island. This was not an argument she was going to win.

"You're right. I should be more open-minded, but so should you."

Tom suddenly paused in the opening between the kitchen and dining room, effectively blocking her way to the front door.

Em pulled her phone out of her pocket and glanced at it. "Look at the time. I told everyone at the Goddess that I'd be right back."

Tom smiled, as cordial as could be and stepped aside. "I'll walk you out."

Em told herself she was going nuts. Tom was no threat. Roland was right. Maybe spending so much time around the Hula Maidens was making her as crazy as they were. He reached around her to open the front door, and Em stepped outside. Tom followed, and together they paused on the top step. The soothing sound of the water feature by the door did its job, and Em felt her pulse rate slow.

"Thanks for hearing me out," she said.

"No problem. Thanks for the wontons."


ONCE SHE WAS in the car, Em couldn't get away fast enough. Tom was still on the front step, so she waved as she pulled out of the driveway and onto the street. She drove back down the hill from Princeville, crossed the Hanalei River Bridge, and when she reached the parking area in front of the Dolphin restaurant, she pulled over.

She tried to call Roland, but her call went straight to voicemail, so she sent him a text and emailed the photos, then she got back on the road and headed north.

When Em walked into the Goddess, Sophie took one look at her and said, "What's wrong?"

Em reached up and smoothed down her hair. Was the fact that Tom rattled her really so apparent?

She walked over to the bar and lowered her voice. "I can't say yet."

"Okay." Sophie watched her closely, and then she looked at the front door. "Should I be worried? Is anyone else dead? Is trouble about to walk in?"

"Not yet. Not that I know of anyway."

Em's cell went off. She mouthed the word "Roland" to Sophie, then she headed into Louie's office and closed the door.

"Where did you get those photos you emailed me?" he asked.

"I took them a few minutes ago at Marilyn Lockhart's house." She explained what she'd been doing there, how she'd found Kiki and talked her down off the mountain, and how Kiki was hiding at home.

"But please don't tell anyone Kiki's back, Roland. No one needs to know yet. The cabin owners have nothing to complain about now. Kiki doesn't want anyone to know she's around yet, especially Tom Benton's detective."

"So what were you doing at Marilyn's, taking photos of Smithson's credit card? Where did it come from?"

"I went to ask Tom to consider backing off Kiki. He wasn't there, but the door was open so I went inside."

"And?"

"There was stuff all over the dining room table. Credit card statements and credit cards and a laptop. At first I didn't think anything about it because the company Tom works for deals with credit ratings or something like that. But then when I saw Dewey Smithson's name on one of the cards, bells went off. I remembered that was the name of the missing birdwatcher at HBR. Maybe Tom found him, or his detective found him. Tom won't tell me if the detective is on island or not. All they had to do was ask at the resort about the room where the maid was killed to find out who'd been there. But I thought you'd like to see what he has."

"Dewey Smithson. Probably too much of a coincidence that Benton was just checking his credit for work. That's quite a stretch."

"I think so too. Tom had a Social Security site online. That's on one of the photos I sent you. I was in the middle of taking them when I heard him coming in from the backyard. So I ran back out the front door and knocked again as if I'd just arrived."

"You got away with snooping inside and went back in?"

"I hate to admit it, but I actually heard your voice in my head telling me not to be stupid."

"But you didn't listen, as usual."

"I went there to try to talk Tom into backing off Kiki. She really can't take much more of this. He's putting an old woman through hell for no reason."

"Did you stop to wonder why?"

"Because Marilyn poisoned him against Kiki."

"Maybe. Or maybe he's trying to shift the blame."

"Shift it to who?"

"Not *to* someone. Away from someone. What if Benton and Smithson are one and the same?" Roland asked.

Em sat down hard. She stared at the desktop, fiddled with a pen. "Are you serious?"

"I have to keep all possibilities open."

"But Tom wasn't even on island when the maid was murdered. And why would he do it?"

"Those are details I have to look into."

"What do we do now?"

"*We* don't do anything. Promise me that you won't do anything."

"Will you call me as soon as you know something?"

"I will but only if you promise."

She hesitated a second too long. "Okay."

"I wish you sounded like you meant it. I'm not kidding, Em. Stand down." He fell silent and after a pause added, "For me?"

*"For me?"* Em closed her eyes. Was she really at the point where he could talk her into doing just about anything for him?

"Okay, I promise."

# 36

## Sophie's Suggestion

After balancing the cash drawer, Sophie packed up the money and headed into Louie's office. She hadn't had a chance to talk to Em alone all day. She found her behind the desk, but Em was on her feet, bending over what appeared to be rows of sheets of papers all neatly laid out. There were some notes on some pages, lists on others. A couple of them only contained a name.

Em looked up. "Do you need me?"

Sophie shook her head no. "All closed up nice and tight."

Sophie indicated the cash box and set it on the corner of Louie's old file cabinet.

Em nodded absently. "Thanks. I'll take it to the house when I go over."

"It was manageable out there tonight, eh? Word is out that the *Trouble in Paradise* crew is pretty much gone for good. People aren't as willing to come out on a rainy night if they're not going to be on camera. Still, we had a good night. Lots of locals are coming back."

"That's good." Em had crossed her arms and was looking down at the desk.

"Tiko's a quick learner and a natural with people. I think she's really going to work out."

"She's used to handling the pressure of serving long lines at her smoothie booth at festivals," Em said.

"But do you think she can handle working with Buzzy?" Sophie noticed *that* got Em's attention. "He's been trailing after Tiko with goo-goo eyes for two days."

"So he's completely over dolphin fever?"

"I overheard him ask Tiko if she'd like to go snorkeling with him sometime," Sophie said.

"I hope he won't take her out to snorkel Makua. That's where his ex-fiancée lives."

"Maybe we should give Tiko a word of warning," Em said. "I know I'd hate to have a jealous dolphin come after me."

"I heard Tiko tell him that she's really busy with two jobs right now. She left it open though."

They laughed and then Sophie said, "What's up with all this?"

She stepped around to Em's side of the desk, took a closer look at the papers. "Uh, oh."

From this angle she could see the pages were organized into a huge moveable chart. There was nothing new in Em making lists. Before the reality show aired, when business was shaky, Em started making lists of goals and objectives for the bar. When the lists were done, she'd hold a meeting with Louie and Sophie.

Sophie didn't like what she was looking at right now. These were no ordinary lists.

Em was one of the few people Sophie truly cared about in her life, and as she scanned the carefully made notes and sheets that contained but a name or two, Sophie's protective instincts kicked in.

She had virtually raised herself on the streets of Honolulu. Troubles between her and her bad seed former boyfriend were how she'd ended up moving from Oahu to Kauai. She was a girl-on-the-run without references or any experience she could name when she asked for a job, yet Em had been willing to take a chance and hired her.

Since that day, Sophie knew she would walk through hot coals for Em, but she hoped it never came to that.

In her mid-thirties, Em was older than Sophie by ten years, but from things Em had told her, the recent divorce was the only terrible thing that had ever happened to her. Though her husband had played her for a fool, Em still tended to see the world through rose colored glasses.

"What's up with all these?" Sophie indicated the pages with a wave of her hand. "It looks like information about the murders."

"I was just messing around." Em stood beside her and stared down at the desk.

"You aren't one to waste time messing around. I saw the look on your face when you came in earlier today. Is this about Kiki? Is there some proof against her now? Is that really why she ran?"

The indecision on Em's face was easy to read.

"Em, you can trust me," Sophie said.

"I know. It's just that Roland asked me to keep some of this confidential. He's working on a lot of threads, trying to *wili* them together."

"Did he ask for your help?" Sophie asked.

They had started out on rocky ground, but Sophie was finally on better footing where Roland was concerned. He'd been suspicious of her once because of her past history on Oahu, but they had come to a truce because of Em. She was sure Roland wouldn't put Em in danger, but that didn't mean Em might not wander into it on her own.

"Not really." Em chewed her lip for a second. "But I stumbled onto something odd this morning." She pointed to some grainy print outs of credit cards spread out on a table. "I saw these credit cards when I stopped by Marilyn's place to talk to Tom Benton this morning."

Sophie leaned closer. "Credit cards. Other people's?"

Em shrugged. "Looks like it. Tom works for some kind of credit rating company or something like that, so at first glance it didn't seem suspicious."

"But . . ."

"One of the suspects, or at the very least a possible witness in the murder of the HBR maid, is a birdwatcher named Dewey Smithson." Em leaned down and pointed to a photo. "That card has his name on it."

"Yikes."

"Yeah. Yikes. No one has seen the man since the day of the murder when he checked out of HBR."

"So what is Benton doing with the guy's credit card?" Sophie wondered.

"At first I thought maybe Tom's private detective had found Smithson."

"But how would they get his credit card?"

"Good point. And shouldn't they tell the police they found Smithson? The KPD has been looking for him." Em paused, then looked up at Sophie. "I've been thinking, what if there is no Smithson?"

"What do you mean?"

"Roland thinks maybe Smithson and Tom Benton could be one and the same," Em said.

"But let's say Benton was posing as some guy named Smithson. Why? And why would Marilyn's nephew kill a maid?"

Em shook her head. "He couldn't have. He was in India until a few days ago," Em reminded her.

"For sure?"

"He emailed Marilyn a photo of himself at the Taj Mahal right before the wedding."

"Give me ten minutes on a computer with Photoshop, and I'll email you a photo of me at the Taj Mahal." Sophie ran her fingers through her spiked hair.

"You mean he faked it?"

"I mean he could have. Do you have a photo of him? Does Louie?"

"I don't know. I don't think so. Why?"

"Someone could take it out to HBR and ask around, see if anyone on the staff recognizes him."

"They'll recognize him if he's already been out there asking questions and trying to find Marilyn's killer."

"He wants to pin this on Kiki, so maybe he's not even looking."

"Maybe," Em said, "he only wants to pin this on Kiki . . ."

"To take the heat off of himself."

A chill went down Sophie's spine. She pictured Tom Benton yelling at Kiki in the bar the other day. He'd reminded her of a temperamental dough boy.

She and Em jumped when Kimo knocked on the doorframe.

"I'm all done," he said. "Ready to go."

Sophie noticed Em was staring at Kimo with a deer-in-the-headlights expression.

"Thanks," Em finally managed. "See you in the morning."

Kimo ducked out. They waited until they heard the back door in the kitchen close.

"I forgot he was still here," Em said.

"Me, too." Sophie glanced toward the window as Kimo drove by. "Do you think he heard us?"

"I don't know. Right now it's all just speculation stemming from what I found when I walked into Marilyn's house looking for Tom. I'm not sure that would hold up in court." Em started stacking up all the pages she'd laid out, carefully keeping them in order. "Right now, I'm not really sure of anything."

# 37

## Kimo Reports

Clouds that hung halfway down the mountain in the distance beyond Kiki's bedroom window spread a soft misty drizzle of rain. Drops dripped slowly off the eaves of the house, hitting wide banana leaves. Each and every plunk was like a steady stream of Chinese water torture.

It was a little after dawn. Still in bed, Kiki groaned and pulled the covers over her head. Hiding out at home had been next to impossible because it was boring as hell. The only thing that had kept her from bolting so far was that emails and inquiries were pouring into Kiki's Kreative Events. Now that Marilyn Lockhart was out of the picture, Kiki had an exclusive hold on the North Shore, at least until some other upstart tried to move in on her territory.

Just last night someone had emailed about booking a wedding on the *Jurassic Park* helicopter landing pad at the bottom of a waterfall. The bride and groom wanted to wear Indiana Jones costumes complete with whips and pith helmets and, if possible, they wanted a sound system blaring the trumpeting sound of a T-Rex along with the movie soundtrack.

It would be a pricy event that included their wish list as well as booking the Movie Tours vans for the guests and a helicopter to fly the wedding couple to the landing pad.

The challenge should have perked her up, but it only depressed her more. She wasn't as good at making deals on the phone as she was in person, and she needed to go to the helicopter tour office to finalize the details.

She was trying to think up a disguise she could wear if she snuck out when she heard the bedroom door open.

"Time to wake up, Kiki. Have I got a treat for you," Kimo said.

Kiki groaned. "I'm not in the mood."

"Not in the mood for macadamia nut waffles with sliced bananas and papaya and coconut syrup?"

"I'm too depressed to eat." Her stomach growled in protest.

"Come on. You need something in your stomach. When was the last time you ate?"

"I had a stuffed baked potato last night. I think it was last night." She rolled over and pulled the bed sheet down so she could peek over the edge. "That smells good."

"Sit up. It is good."

Kiki squirmed her way up the bed and leaned against the headboard. Kimo was holding a bed tray with a plateful of waffles, a small crystal vase with an anthurium and a sprig of fern, and hot coffee and a glass of champagne.

"Well," she shrugged, patting her lap, "maybe I'll have a little."

Kimo carefully situated the tray across her and stepped back. Kiki dug into the waffles and closed her eyes.

"Perfect. *Mahalo*, honey."

He didn't walk out as she expected.

"What?" Kiki took another bite.

"Last night I overheard something that might be important."

"Like what?" She plucked up a banana slice with her fingers and popped it in her mouth.

"Em and Sophie were talking in Louie's office. I didn't catch all of what they were saying, but they were talking about Tom Benton."

Kiki felt her arteries clench. "Please, I'm eating."

"I think it was something you should know."

"So talk." She put down her fork and picked up her coffee.

"The gist of it was about Tom posing as someone else. They were trying to figure out when exactly he arrived on Kauai. Sophie said it would be easy to fake photos of himself in India and email them to Marilyn."

"If he wasn't in India, where was he?"

Kimo shrugged. "Sounded like they are thinking he might have been here."

"Then why wasn't he at the wedding?"

"Good question. And why would he pretend to be somewhere else?" He was waiting for her to say something.

"Okay, I give. Why would he?"

"I heard Em say she thinks he's trying to take the heat off of himself by pinning Marilyn's murder on you."

"Em said that?" She quickly shoveled down more food and pointed at her purse on a chair across the room, snapped her fingers when he didn't move and pointed at it again.

Kimo retrieved her purse. He handed it over, and Kiki started digging for her cell phone.

"You'd better head into work," she told him. "We don't want anything to look suspicious. Do *not* tell Em that you told me what you heard."

"What are you going to do?"

"I'm getting out of this house, and I'm getting to the bottom of this once and for all. I'm not taking the fall for this guy. Not by a long shot. Now go."

He went. She tossed her purse aside and dialed Suzi, but the realtor's voicemail came on, so she dialed Trish.

"Trish? It's Kiki," she said when Trish picked up.

"Kiki! Are you still up in Kokee?"

"No. I'm home. Long story, but right now I need your help. I need you to round up as many of the girls as you can. We're going on a covert mission."

"Today?"

"As soon as we can gather."

"The weather's pretty junk."

"Trish, it's life and death. Forget the weather."

"Okay, then. You want me to round up the Maidens. Got it."

"Do you have paper and a pencil? They'll need to dress appropriately."

"Uh, oh. Hang on." Kiki heard Trish rustling around and then she was back. "Go ahead. I'm ready."

Kiki thought for a minute. "We're going on a stakeout at Princeville. The good news is the weather's junk, as you said, so there won't be a whole lot of golfers out today. Not many tourists anyway. Have the girls gear up in green. That way they'll help blend into the landscape. Do we have any green costumes so we can all dress the same?"

"You want them to do a stakeout in green *muumuus*?"

"We don't have green *muumuus*." Kiki snapped her fingers. "Ah! We do have those green harem pants we performed in at the Lion's Club Arabian Nights Dinner Dance a couple of years ago."

"Green harem pants. Got it," Trish said.

"Green on top. Hoodies if they have them."

"Kind of warm for hoodies today."

"No hoodies then." Kiki couldn't bear hearing them all whine about how hot and sweaty they were. "So let's go with ferns pinned on their heads."

"Got it. We all have to dress alike because why?"

"If anyone asks what we're doing prowling around up there, we can say we're on the way to a performance."

"What will we really be doing?"

"You're all on a need to know basis. Right now all you need to know is that we're rendezvousing at the Sunrise Loop Rec Room parking lot at Princeville in two hours. Make sure Big Estelle comes, no excuses. We need her van. Tell Pat to drop whatever she's doing." Kiki lifted the bed tray off of her lap and set it on the floor.

"Got it. Big Estelle with the van. Pat must be there. Everyone meet in two hours at the Sunrise Loop Rec Room parking lot in Princeville. Anything else?"

"Bring your camera," Kiki said.

"I never leave home without it."

# 38

Rendezvous Point: Sunrise Loop Rec Room Parking Lot 0:900

Kiki thought she'd be the first one there, but when she arrived at the parking lot, Big Estelle's van was already parked at the end of the lot behind a tall shrub that almost hid it from the golf course view. The minute Kiki pulled in and parked, the van door slid open, and Big Estelle waved Kiki inside.

"You look great." Kiki climbed in carrying a huge black duffle bag and settled into the shotgun seat.

As per Kiki's request, Big Estelle was outfitted in wide-legged, lime green harem pants gathered at the ankles. She had on a forest green blouse and had already pinned fern fronds all over her head.

Lars, outfitted in his green camo gear was crammed into the very back of the van with Little Estelle, also decked out in camo. She was seated on her Gadabout.

"Let us out," Little Estelle hollered. "It's gettin' hot back here."

"Hang on, Mother," Big Estelle shouted. "Prepare to launch."

Big Estelle hit the control button behind the wheel, and the lift on the back of the van slowly lowered Lars, Little Estelle, and her Gadabout to the pavement. Kiki rolled down her window and cautioned, "Keep the noise down. We're undercover."

"What should we do?" Little Estelle revved her engine.

"Reconnoiter. Cruise the perimeter of the parking lot. Let us know if you see anything suspicious." When Little Estelle headed for the far corner of the lot, Kiki rolled up her window.

"Are you expecting trouble? What kind of suspicious things are you looking for?" Big Estelle wanted to know.

"I just wanted to keep your mother out of trouble."

"That's impossible."

"So is Lars going to be here forever?" Kiki watched the long-legged Norwegian lope along behind the Gadabout. "Is he for real?"

Big Estelle shrugged. "Right now he's doting on my mother. She's happy, and he seems perfectly harmless."

"What about the future?"

"What future? Mother's ninety-two. The most he can get out of her is a green card."

Just then Trish and Suzi pulled up in Suzi's car. Kiki waved them over, and they hopped into the back of the van. Before Kiki could answer any of their questions, Pat and Flora arrived. Once they were all crammed into the van, Kiki unzipped the duffle, revealing three, two-way radios. Kimo had bought them a couple of years ago for hunting trips, and she was sure he would have happily loaned them to her had she asked, but she hadn't.

She handed one to Pat.

"This is your radio, Pat. You'll remain here in the van. From here on out we'll call this Command and Control Central, or CCC. I'll have another radio, and I'm giving one to Big Estelle." She handed one to the woman behind the wheel of the van.

"Pat and Flora, you two will remain in the van. Little Estelle and Lars will continue to watch the parking lot and discourage parking. Big Estelle, you'll walk two blocks over with Trish, Suzi, and me, but then we'll separate, and you'll remain on the corner. Find the biggest tree or shrub you can and hide behind it. Trish, Suzi, and I will continue on to our destination."

Pat was fiddling with the two-way. The others nodded in understanding.

"Where is Lillian?" Kiki looked out the van window.

Trish raised her hand. "The Lillians are still touring. Today they're taking the inner tube adventure down the irrigation ditch, and real Lillian is going with them."

Kiki glanced up at the sky. "In that case I hope it doesn't rain any harder. They could get decapitated in the tunnels if the water rises too fast."

Suzi rolled her eyes. "Can you imagine all those pink heads bobbing downstream?"

"What about Precious?" It irked Kiki to no end that all of the Maidens hadn't showed.

"I called her," Trish said. "She's sorry, but she had customers booked for the whole day. She really wanted to be here."

"People who have real jobs just irk me to death," Kiki grumbled.

Lars was tapping on the van door. Big Estelle opened it. "What?"

Little Estelle called up to them. "We checked the lot. Everything's a-okay. Now what?"

Kiki leaned out. "Cordon off the perimeter." She pointed at Lars and yelled, "No cars in! No cars!"

"Ya! No cars. Goot," he yelled back and clicked his boot heels together.

Big Estelle closed the door.

"So we're good to go," Kiki said.

Pat clicked on the two-way and said, "Roger. Copy that."

Suzi raised her hand.

"What?" Kiki was fumbling with the two-way, trying to clip it to the waistband of her harem pants.

"After we leave Big Estelle in a bush on a corner two blocks from here, what will we actually be doing?" Suzi asked.

"Here's what's up," Kiki said. "Long story short, Marilyn's disgusting nephew Tom is trying to frame me. Someone who shall remain nameless thinks he's been lying from the get go about when he arrived on island and probably about a lot more. We need to find proof we can take to Roland and the KPD to prove that he's up to something. We have to find out why he's so anxious to have me take the fall for Marilyn's murder. We three are heading over to his house to see if he's there, and if he's not, we're going in and we'll have a look around."

"Why am I *not* liking the sound of this?" Trish mumbled.

"So what do *we* do?" Pat wanted to know.

"Trish and Suzi and I will go around the block by cutting across the golf course to Marilyn's house where Tom is staying. Big Estelle will stand watch at the end of his street and radio to let us know if she sees anyone approaching his house."

"I just stand there?" Big Estelle wasn't happy.

"Watching the street," Kiki said.

"In the rain?"

"I'd do it for you." Kiki gave her a hard-eyed squint.

"Okay, but I'm taking a plastic trash sack to sit on and one to wear."

Kiki sighed and then continued. "If the coast is clear, we'll enter the house and look for evidence. Trish will take photos."

"Enter the house? Breaking and entering?" Trish was shaking her head no.

"This," Kiki said, straightening her spine, "is a matter of life and death."

"I don't know about this," Suzi said.

"What if he's home?" Trish asked.

"We wait until he leaves," Kiki said.

Suzi wasn't convinced. "What if we get in, and he comes right back?"

"Then you'll say you assumed he would be selling the place, and you already have some prospective buyers. You will say you are there to see if the house is in condition to show."

"I could lose my real estate license."

"And if we don't do something, I could spend the rest of my life directing hula shows in prison," Kiki shot back.

Trish shifted her camera strap. "What are we looking for exactly?"

Kiki shrugged. "Anything suspicious. We'll know it when we see it." She turned to Pat and Flora. "If any busybodies or Princeville security come nosing around and wants to know what we're doing in the neighborhood, tell them we're gathering *kukui* nut leaves for head *lei*. Point out that we are in costume because we're on the way to Happy Days Long Term Care Center to entertain." She had but one more instruction. She looked around the van at each of them in turn. "No matter who you talk to, no matter what comes up, *tell no one* about this. Ever."

"Tell no one. Got it!" Pat saluted and then reached into a battered briefcase at her feet. She pulled out a large map of Princeville and spread it open on the back of the center passenger seat. Then she clicked on the two-way.

"Command and Control Center is good to go."

# 39

## Identity Thief

Em was in the office that morning finding it hard to concentrate with Roland Sharpe's presence filling the room. He stood there in a white T-shirt and a bright red *lava lava* wrapped around his hips. His skin glistened.

*Nothing like the scent of a well-oiled fire dancing detective in the morning.*

"You haven't been home all night, I take it?" She was curious as to why he was still in his *luau* costume but wasn't sure she actually wanted to hear the answer.

"This is the new standard issue uniform for the KPD," he said.

"Lucky for Kauai, then. I hope all the other guys wear it as well as you do."

"You like this look? A man in a skirt?"

"You bet. There's something oddly sexy about it. Like a man parading around in a bath towel." She tried to focus but couldn't stop smiling. "If you'd like to use our shower and change, go right ahead. There are fresh towels in a basket near the entry."

"Thanks, but I'm headed home. Maybe some other time when you can join me."

If she thought he was going to fess up to where he was last night, she was wrong.

"You left a message, said it was important, and you needed to talk to me right away," he reminded her.

Em watched Roland cross the room, his coffee-brown skin highlighted by the stark white of his T-shirt.

She cleared her throat. "What?"

"You wanted to talk to me."

"Right. Last night Sophie and I were talking about Tom Benton, and I told her about the things I saw on his dining table. We were trying to figure out what they might mean. She thinks he could have been lying about being in India."

"That's a very accurate assumption. I checked the airline manifests, and he wasn't aboard any planes to Kauai on the day he supposedly flew in. Nor any time before that that I can find."

"What do you mean? He has to be. How did he get here?"

"Not by cruise ship, either."

"Why would he take a cruise ship? He was in a hurry to get here after Marilyn died."

"Something else turned up. Dewey Smithson has supposedly been on island for nearly a month according to flight manifests. We've been looking for him all over the island, as you know. But when I called his bank to check on that credit card number on the card in the photo, it turns out Smithson is still in Indiana. He's never been to Hawaii in his life."

"Are you sure it's the same Smithson? Dewey Smithson?"

"Yep." He perched on the edge of the desk, and his *lava lava* gapped open just enough to tempt her to glimpse a peek of the tattoo on his thigh. "Turns out he's not a birdwatcher. His identity was stolen a little over a month ago. He's been working on clearing things up ever since, but it's been slow going. Whoever did it is an expert. His Social Security and every other important number the poor guy had is now compromised."

Em had her movable chart laid out again. Roland glanced down at the pages.

"What's all this?"

"Names of the murder victims, possible suspects and motives, and any other clues I could come up with yesterday."

He frowned as he studied the pages on the desk but didn't say anything.

"I saw Nat working on one of his show plots once, and he had made up a moveable chart just like this one." She picked up the page with Kiki's name on it and moved it to the bottom of the suspect list across from the Motive column. "I thought it might help us see something we're missing. Something that will clear Kiki. I'm pretty convinced Tom Benton is in this much deeper than we know."

"This isn't a TV show, Em."

"I know," she nodded. "Do you think Tom has been posing as Dewey Smithson? That he's an identity thief?"

"If he is, then Benton was on island before Bobby's death, and before the maid's. Both of them were connected to HBR, and whoever posed as Smithson was staying there."

"Why would Tom kill Bobby? Why kill Esther Villaviejos?"

"Why hide his own identity?" Roland asked.

"Maybe it's just a coincidence that Tom has Smithson's credit card. Maybe he's working on Smithson's identity theft case."

"But then if he's innocent, why didn't Tom fly here under his own name? If he wasn't already here posing as Smithson, how did he get on island? On the other hand, what if he checked into HBR pretending to *be*

Smithson? If he did, that would put him on Kauai *before* his aunt's wedding, yet he told her he couldn't attend because he was supposedly in India. Again, why? He had to be up to something."

She told him about Sophie's photoshopped email photo theory.

"We still have Marilyn's notebook. I'll have our tech guys go over her emails from Benton. They'll know if the photos are fake."

"So we're back to why he hid the fact he was on island from Marilyn."

Em picked up the photo of the credit cards on Tom's dining table. "Maybe he was into identity theft big time. Maybe he came over here to hide out."

"That's possible," Roland said. "But he's not hiding now."

"No."

"You're overlooking something, Em."

She scanned the chart. "What? What am I missing?"

"Tom was here on the night of Marilyn's murder."

"Do you think he could have killed her? He loved her."

Roland shrugged. "Supposedly he loved her. Why else was he hiding from her? He is the executor of her estate and her only heir."

"So he had motive."

"Big time."

Em stared at Roland for a second. "Okay, so maybe Tom killed Marilyn, but what about the other two murders?"

"The only connection between them is Haena Beach Resort. Other than that, I have no idea why he would kill the cameraman or the maid. We may still be dealing with two murderers." He stood up. "Three is a long shot."

"What now?" Em stretched her neck, rolled her head.

"Those photos you sent yesterday were a big help, Em. You did good. Now it's time to step out of the way."

"And let the big boys handle it, you mean?"

"Right."

"Are you going to pick up Tom for questioning?"

"Yes. I want to find out if he came to Kauai posing as Smithson and why he has Smithson's credit card. I doubt he'll admit anything. We'll need to search his aunt's house, legally, for evidence, which involves a search warrant. We need to stick to the letter of the law so he can't slip off the hook." He locked gazes with her to get his point across then added, "I'm not going to do anything else today until I'm out of this skirt and I have a warrant in my hand."

# 40

## Deep Undercover

Kiki led Big Estelle, Trish, and Suzi along the perimeter of the Woods course, past golf course homes with wide *lanais* open to the view. Kiki gave the women the universal sign for *shh!* as they crept past an elderly couple having breakfast at a table under an awning.

The woman peered over the edge of her morning newspaper. Kiki froze and motioned for the others to duck behind some Song of India plants.

"I thought I saw some belly dancers running across the course," the woman said.

"What?" the man mumbled.

"Belly dancers on the course," the wife yelled.

"Most belly aches run their course," he said.

Kiki waited until the wife went back to reading. She signaled for the women to run, and off they ran. When they reached the corner of Marilyn's street, she waved Big Estelle over to the nearest yard, but Big Estelle hesitated.

"I don't want to do this by myself. Can't Suzi stay with me? Trish can go with you and take photos," she said.

Kiki shook her head. "I may need them both. Suzi is small enough to lift through a window, and Trish is my photographer. Hide behind that big schefflera over there." Kiki pointed to a nearby overgrown bush that was a good eight feet high and four feet wide.

"Are you sure nobody can see me? I feel stupid squatting back here." She carefully picked her way through wet leaves until she was behind the bush. Trish was watching the house behind them. There didn't appear to be anyone there.

"Most of these places are empty," Suzi said. "The snowbirds have flown the coop this time of year."

Big Estelle bent down to place a plastic trash liner on the ground. She fussed with it, trying to get it perfectly flattened on the leaves.

"Hurry up," Kiki prodded. "We don't have all day."

She was headed toward the street but froze when Big Estelle let out a bloodcurdling scream and grabbed her right foot. Hopping on her left leg, the woman kept screaming at the top of her lungs.

"What! What's going on?" Suzi ran away from Big Estelle as fast as she could.

"What happened? What's wrong?" Trish tried to help Big Estelle balance on one foot.

"Centipede!" Big Estelle's eyes bugged out. She clutched her throat and staggered back. "A centipede bit my foot! Help me! Help me! I'm gonna die!"

Kiki ran back to the bush and slapped Big Estelle so hard she was shocked into silence.

"What did you do that for?" Trish asked.

"Shut up! This is a covert mission. You're attracting attention," Kiki whispered.

Big Estelle was staring at her foot.

"It's already swelling," Suzi said.

"Wow. You can see the fang marks," Trish pointed the camera at Big Estelle's foot and took a photo.

"Not fangs," Suzi said. "Pinchers."

"Where is it?" Big Estelle hopped out of the debris around the bottom of the schefflera. "Is it on my cuff?" She shook out the blousy harem pant leg, kicked her foot around and screamed at the pain.

"Ow! Ow, ow, ow. It hurts like hell."

"I think we're supposed to pee on it," Suzi said.

"That's for a jellyfish sting," Trish said. "Or maybe that's the remedy for stepping on sea urchin spines."

Kiki was fed up with all of them. She stepped off the curb and looked up and down the street. Luckily there was no sign of Tom or anyone else, but time was wasting.

"I can't stand on my foot," Big Estelle was crying now, big tears rolling down her flat cheeks. "Really. It burns something fierce. I need to go to the hospital. The venom is pulsing through my veins. I can feel it. I'm going numb all over."

"You," Kiki said, "are hysterical. What you are going to do is go sit on that *lanai* behind us. There is no one home, so sit there and watch the street."

Big Estelle leaned over Kiki. They didn't call her Big Estelle for nothing.

"I am not. I am going to hobble back to the van and put my foot up. We have a first aid kit. At the very least I need first aid. You are on your own, Kiki Godwin. I've done enough this morning."

"You can't just walk away."

"No, but I can hop. Just watch me." Big Estelle took a step in the direction of the golf course but buckled as soon as she put weight on her injured foot. She moaned. She grabbed her head. "I can't even hop! I can't get back on my own."

"I'll go with you," Suzi volunteered. She slipped under Big Estelle's arm and turned to Kiki. "She can't walk."

"I see that." Kiki looked at the diminutive Asian nearly hidden beneath Big Estelle's frame. "If she topples over, she'll kill you."

"I'll go with them." Trish stepped up beside Big Estelle. "One for all, and all for one."

"What about *me*?" Kiki said. "What about the photos? I need to find some proof that Tom Benton is guilty of *something,* and I need photos of the proof."

"I'm dying here!" Big Estelle hollered. "Look at my foot."

There was no denying it had swollen to twice its size already.

"This sneaking into Marilyn's is a really bad idea," Suzi said. "Maybe this is a sign we should call it off."

"I'm going in with or without any of you," Kiki said.

Big Estelle clicked on her two-way.

"Emergency!" she yelled into the device. "Centipede attack. Pick me up on the corner of Emmalani Drive and Victoria Loop."

Kiki grabbed the two-way. "Abort! Abort! Stay in position. Stay in position. Over."

Pat's voice crackled over the speaker. "Roger that. We stay."

"How am I going to get back to the van?" Big Estelle sobbed. "How?"

"Take Trish and Suzi and go back the way we came across the golf course. It's the shortest route to Sunrise Loop. I don't need your help. I'm going in alone."

The three of them were staring at her as if she had lost her mind. She was pretty sure she was on the verge.

"Promise you won't do anything foolish, Kiki." Trish looked so torn that Kiki thought the photographer might change her mind and stay with her. Instead, Trish handed over her camera. "Be careful with this. It's my bread and butter."

"I will. Promise." Kiki turned the camera over and over in her hands. "How do you work it?"

"It's set to automatic. Just point and shoot." She touched the button on top.

Then Trish wrapped her arm around Big Estelle's waist, and the three women turned to leave. Before they could even get started, a golf cart bearing the Princeville Security shield turned the corner and rolled over to where they were standing at the curb. The local security guard hung out at the Goddess. He recognized them, waved, and pulled over.

"Hey, Kiki. Whazup? You folks shooting a segment?"

Kiki took a deep breath and forced a smile.

"Hi, Binky. No, we're just looking for some *kukui* nut leaves. Adornments. You know. Dancing at the Day Care center today."

"Plenty *kukui* trees on the golf course. Go back a few yards." He looked at Big Estelle. "You okay?"

"Centipede bite," Kiki said. "But she's fine."

"I am not," Big Estelle sniffed.

"Yikes. Bettah get that taken care of."

Big Estelle looked at Kiki. "I'm trying."

"Nice pants," the guard said. Before he put the cart in gear and headed back toward the course, he winked. "Good luck with the belly dance."

# 41

### Kiki Goes In Alone

"You can do this." Kiki realized she was mumbling to herself and swatted a mosquito away from her face as she knelt in the topical grotto near Marilyn's front door.

Two houses down, a yappy dog kept up a constant bark that started when she had walked by its house. The mutt hadn't let up yet. She was debating whether or not to call off the mission when a jogger came thudding down the middle of the street. Once he was well out of sight, the dog stopped barking, and Kiki breathed a sigh of relief.

She admired the water feature splashing merrily away near Marilyn's front door. It was a nice touch. Real classy. When she got home she was going to mention to Kimo that she wanted a fountain too. And maybe even some big shiny brass initials, K&KG.

She waited five more minutes, and there was still no sign of life in the house so she hit the transmit button on the two way, held it close to her mouth, and whispered into it.

"CCC, this is Kiki one. Kiki one here. I'm going in. Do not call me. Repeat. Do not call me until I call you. Copy?"

Pat's voice crackled over the line. "Copy that. No calls until you call us."

Kiki made sure Trish's camera was secure on the strap hanging around her neck. She crept along the narrow sidewalk between Marilyn's house and the one to the north of it, peering into windows as she passed. The place looked as cool and put together as Marilyn herself. The décor was slick and perfect. There wasn't a knick-knack or a keepsake that identified the owner. Every accessory matched the beige color scheme.

Kiki scanned the backyard before she went around the corner of the house. There was no sign of anyone there, no one seated at the table on the *lanai*. A six foot hedge surrounded the yard. There was an opening cut through to the house behind Marilyn's. Kiki couldn't see anything but a pool beyond the space in the hedge.

The slider was locked. At first she was bummed. It wouldn't be easy going back around to the side of the house and loosening a screen so that she could climb inside. If she'd have made Suzi stay, she could have hoisted her up, but too late for regrets now. She was willing to do what she had to.

Before she gave up and went to the side of the house, she lifted the welcome mat beneath the slider and sure enough, there was a spare key. She opened the door, stepped inside the kitchen and replaced the key before she closed the glass door and flipped the lock on the handle.

More than likely Tom would enter through the garage door at the side of the house, and she'd hear him coming in. Plenty of time to bolt out the front or the back.

She kept one hand on Trish's camera. The kitchen counters were clear. She opened the freezer, the perfect hiding place for cash, but there was only an icemaker full of ice. The bottom of the huge refrigerator was bare except for an open box of baking soda and the light bulb.

She wandered around in the living/dining room. There was no sign anyone had been there recently, and she found herself hoping that she wasn't too late. Maybe Tom had already left for the mainland. She hated to think he was going to get away.

There was nothing of interest in the master bedroom except Marilyn's wedding dress, which was carefully draped over a chair. She crept down the hall to the guest room and pulled up short when she saw a navy blue duffle bag open on the queen bed.

She was reaching for the bag when she heard what sounded like a cough down the hall and froze. Her heart started racing, her face flushed with heat.

*Keep it together, Kiki.*

She held her breath and waited. The only sounds she heard were birds singing in the garden and the far away hum of a weed blower. Kiki stepped up to the bed and fingered the zipper on the duffle, opening it wide enough to look inside.

"Bingo," she whispered. She wasn't quite sure what she was actually looking at, but taken as a whole, it was a lot of very weird stuff. Too weird to be normal. She started pulling things out as fast as she could

There was a long, gray, fake ponytail attached to a ball cap, a nondescript brown uniform shirt without any logos on it, the kind she'd seen on sale at the Humane Society Thrift Shop. She pulled out a Birds of Hawaii book with photos and descriptions of island birds. There were bits of paper in it, so she shook the book. Receipts sifted out and fell on the bed—credit card receipts with the name Dewey Smithson on them from the Haena Beach Resort.

She reached in and fished around and came up with a stack of credit cards held together with a rubber band. None of them had been issued to

Tom Benton. A roll of masking tape was there along with some heavier items in the bottom of the bag that clinked together. She felt around and came up with wire cutters and an ice pick.

"Gotcha, sucker."

Kiki laid them on the bed beside all the other items, found the button Trish had shown her, and quickly snapped off some photos. If only she was better with tech stuff she could use a phone camera and email the photos directly to Roland at the KPD.

She stuffed everything back into the bag and was headed out of the room when she heard a toilet flush down the hall. She had to hurry if she wanted to escape through the front door. She tiptoed down the hall, and the closer she got to the bathroom, the more certain she was that someone was inside. He had flushed the toilet, and that someone was headed for the door.

Kiki opened the louvered door directly across from the bathroom door only to discover it was a hall closet stuffed with cardboard file boxes that were labeled and contained various party and event supplies. She threw herself against the boxes and tugged the door closed. Sharp cardboard corners were piercing her ribs as she smashed herself up against the boxes.

The bathroom door opened. She could see out through the louvers. Tom Benton was directly across from her, so close she could hear him breathing.

He stood there for so long she thought he must have known she was there, but then he turned and headed down the hall toward the guest room.

*No*, she thought. *No, no, no.*

She cracked the door open and peered through a slit. When he disappeared into the guest room, she opened the closet door and slipped out. The carpet muffled her steps as she hurried back down the hall toward the living/dining room. Hopefully she could get out of the house before he came looking for her. At the very least, she needed to find a bigger closet to hide in.

She had almost made it through the dining room when she heard a click, and then Tom said, "Going somewhere, Kiki?"

She slowly turned, saw the gun in his hand, and raised her hands.

"Home?" she shrugged.

"I could shoot you right now and get away with it. You've broken in, obviously with the intent to harm me."

"I used a key. You're the one with a gun. I'm only armed with a camera." She lifted it to show him.

"You entered without permission. The way I'll tell it, you were here to harm me, steal from me, or both."

"Steal what? Your stack of stolen credit cards? Or the ice pick you used on Marilyn's brake line? Or your phony disguises? How very convenient of you to keep all the evidence in one place."

"You must be hallucinating."

"Your bag of tricks."

"No such bag exists."

"I saw it." She didn't have to tell him she had photographed it. He glanced down at the camera around her neck, and she could tell he knew.

"I was just about to get rid of that whole duffle bag. Now I'll have to find a way to get rid of two old bags at the same time."

She thought about making a run for it, but turtles ran faster than she did.

"They're on to you, you know. It's just a matter of time," she said.

"On to *me*? The poor bereaved nephew?"

"Em knows all about your credit card racket. By now she's told her detective boyfriend. You might as well turn yourself in. You'll never get off the island."

"Tom Benton might not, but I have plenty of other identities. With my dear departed aunt's money I can go anywhere in the world from here. I'll be in Honolulu in a few hours and then who knows? The world is my oyster." He closed the distance between them. "Too bad you had to do this to yourself, Kiki. I was all set to go, and they'd eventually have cleared you. Now I'll have to add you to my growing list of People Who Got In My Way, like that cameraman who opened the pantry at the Goddess and found me hiding there. I had to stab him to keep him quiet."

"What were you doing in the pantry?" She was shocked to realize Kimo might have been Tom's first victim.

"I went disguised as a produce deliveryman to check the place out, see if there was anywhere convenient to kill Aunt Marilyn. I had ducked back in the kitchen just as the cameraman was walking in. So I hid, thinking he'd leave, but he found me. Kind of hard to explain to anyone what I was doing in there in a black wig holding a sashimi knife."

"You are disgusting."

He shrugged. "I'm a victim of circumstance, just like the maid at the Haena Beach Resort. She thought the room was vacant, walked in, and caught me coming out of the bathroom without my Dewey Smithson birdwatcher disguise. She couldn't have been more apologetic."

"You killed her anyway."

He smiled. "Hit her in the head with a lamp. Had to. Didn't want her to identify me later. Didn't want anyone to know I was in Haena, not India where I was supposed to be."

"You're a cool customer, killing three innocent people." Fighting to stay cool and calm herself, Kiki took a small step backward.

"Hey, I didn't want to kill two of them. I had to. Now I'll have to deal with you, a busybody, hula-wanna-be who can't keep her nose out of where it belongs."

*Busybody?* She could live with that. *Hula-wanna-be?* That set her teeth on edge.

"How *dare* you?" She forgot herself and got in his face. "I didn't come up here alone," she said.

"Right. I'm not falling for that." He shoved the gun in her gut. "Hands up."

When Kiki raised her hands, he noticed the two-way radio hanging from her waistband and jerked it off.

"What's this?"

"I told you. I'm not alone. Hula Maidens are hidden all over your neighborhood."

For a split second she thought he was going to hit her. Instead, he marched her back to the bedroom.

"Sit," he commanded.

Kiki sat on the end of the bed while Benton paced back and forth thinking.

Suddenly he stopped, then reached down and yanked the camera strap from around her neck.

"Please, be careful with that. I borrowed it."

With one hand holding his gun, he awkwardly fiddled with a couple of buttons on Trish's camera then waited a second or two.

"There. No more photos on the card." He tossed the camera in the duffle. Then he picked up the two-way.

"Here's what we are going to do. You're going to get rid of your little friends. All of them. Say whatever you have to. Just get them to go home without you."

"What should I say?"

"That this was a stupid idea and you called a cab. I don't care. Just get them out of here. Fast."

"Or?"

"Or you'll make the People Who Got in My Way list right here, right now."

Kiki swallowed and stared at the gun in his hand.

"It would be a shame to mess up all this beige," she said.

"Ready?" he asked.

She shook her head no. "Give me another minute."

She closed her eyes and thought about what to say. Then she looked up at him and nodded.

"Okay. Push the button."

The radio crackled. Kiki leaned forward.

"CCC, this is Kiki. All clear here. Go ahead and take off. Do you copy?"

There was another crackle and then Pat yelled, "Copy that. What about you?"

"Get Big Estelle to the doctor. I'll call Kimo and meet you all at the Goddess later. Don't forget *pele h'me*. Copy."

"*Pele h'me?*"

"Right. The new song."

"Got it. See you later. Roger that."

Tom pushed the off button.

"*Pele h'me?*"

"A new dance. They're supposed to learn the words. I wanted them to play the CD on the way back to Haena. I've been nagging them about that."

"Nice touch. You're a better actress than you are a dancer."

Tempted to lunge at him and bite him in his puffy stomach, she looked away.

"Whatever."

# 42

## Pele H'me

At nine thirty that morning, Em and Sophie were setting up when Louie walked into the bar sipping a tall Blood on the Beach.

"Hey, Uncle," Em said. "Good morning." When she'd left earlier, he was still in bed.

"Wow. It's great to see you here, Louie." Sophie walked around the bar to give him a hug.

"Thought it was about time I got my head out of the sand and walked over to see what kind of damage you girls have done in my absence." He pretended to be studying the room. "Everything looks okay though."

"Everything is almost back to normal. Kimo's in the kitchen prepping for the calamari lunch special," Em said. "The drizzle is letting up, and it looks like the sun is going to shine later. Should be good snorkeling weather. There will be a lot of traffic up to Tunnels."

Louie stirred his drink with the tall celery stick garnish, took a swig, and smacked his lips.

Em heard the sound of a car pulling into the lot and looked out the front window.

"Family in a Jeep," she said.

"I'll go out and tell them we're not open yet," Louie volunteered. He headed for the door with a bounce in his step.

"He looks good." Sophie watched Louie cross the bar.

"I think he's snapping out of it. That contest article you found really helped. He's getting psyched to fly to Honolulu for the competition."

"You think he'll win?"

"He thinks so. I think he just might pull it off. He's even considering taking Letterman with him. That parrot is getting more fan mail than anyone else."

"I can't imagine loading that bird on a plane."

Em shrugged. "I'm sure Louie will think it through. He'd be heartsick if anything happened to Dave."

A couple with two tweens had climbed out of the Jeep and were chatting with Louie on the *lanai*. He had greeted them with a welcoming "Aloooha!" and told them that the restaurant would be open for lunch at eleven.

"The staff will be happy to sign autographs then," Louie said.

The kids were staring up at him in awe. The father asked directions to the nearest safe snorkeling beach.

By the time Louie finished regaling them with the story of his run in with a shark which was the inspiration for his version of a Bloody Mary, which he called Blood on the Beach, they decided maybe they would forgo snorkeling for a hike.

When Louie walked back into the bar, Em met him near a corner table.

"Have a seat for a minute," she said.

"Uh, oh. What's up?"

She sat. He pulled out a chair and joined her.

"I talked to Roland early this morning. He's going to question Tom Benton today." She lowered her voice. "There's some doubt about when he actually arrived on island."

"What do you mean?" Louie said. "He got here as soon as he came back from India."

"He may never have been in India," Em said.

She quickly explained a little about the things she'd seen at Marilyn's and Sophie's theory that he could have used Photoshop on the email photos. She said they weren't sure if Tom was on island the night of Marilyn's murder or not.

"Are you sure?" Louie's forehead wrinkled. "Marilyn loved him so much. I can't believe he's guilty of her murder."

"Hopefully Roland will get to the bottom of this quickly."

He finished his drink and set the glass down.

"I don't like you playing detective, Em. I don't know what I'd do if something happened to you. "

"Roland's already had this talk with me, Uncle Louie. I'm not going to do anything dangerous."

Just then Little Estelle roared in on the Gadabout followed by Lars. They were both in camouflage regalia. Big Estelle came limping in wearing wide-legged green chiffon pants cuffed at the ankles, a camo tank top, and a huge bandage around one foot.

They waved to Em, Louie, and Sophie and then chose a table near the front door. Louie left to go back into his office, and Em walked over to greet them.

"Good morning, Ladies. Lars," Em said. "Are you holding a practice this morning?"

She couldn't believe they would dare to hold a practice without Kiki in charge. The Estelles exchanged quick glances.

"Not really," Little Estelle said.

"Maybe," Big Estelle said.

Lars said, "Ya."

Big Estelle was fiddling with a two-way radio. Em asked her if it was a new toy, and she said no, but didn't explain.

"Where is the rest of the gang?" Em thought they were acting odd, but no more than usual.

"Busy."

"What happened to your foot?"

"Centipede bite." Big Estelle scrunched up her face.

"Ouch," Em said.

"Would you like some coffee?" Em asked. They all nodded.

Once she was behind the bar again, Em said to Sophie, "Something's definitely not right."

Sophie glanced at the three Maidens at the table. "What's new?"

"They haven't said a word about Kiki. Do you think she told them she's back?"

"Who knows?" Sophie shrugged. "We need more coffee." She held up the nearly empty pot. "This one is just dregs. I'll go get some."

"That's all right. I'll go." Em went into the kitchen for the refill pot. Kimo was chopping a pile of kale. "Did Kiki tell the Maidens that she's back?"

He glanced at her over his shoulder then went back to chopping.

"I don't know. Why?"

"Big Estelle, the Cougar, and her boyfriend are in the bar. They're acting strange."

"Strange? How can you tell?"

"Big Estelle is sitting there on stun, maybe from a centipede bite. She brought in a two-way radio. None of them have asked if I know where Kiki is."

"Uh, oh." He grabbed a towel and wiped his hands. Em picked up the refill pot and followed him.

Kimo walked up to Big Estelle's table and looked at the two-way. "Is that one of mine?"

Big Estelle swallowed. "Yup."

"I hate to ask. Where are the other two?"

"Huh?"

"The other two radios. Where are they?"

"Pat has one," she said.

"And . . ."

Little Estelle drove over to join them. "Don't tell them anything else."

"Don't tell me what?" Kimo focused on Big Estelle.

"You took an oath. A Hula Maiden oath," Little Estelle reminded her daughter.

"Ya," Lars smiled and nodded.

"Do you know what's going on?" Em asked Lars. "If you do, spill it. You're not a Hula Maiden."

"Ya." Lars smiled and nodded again. "Goot."

"I guess I can tell, since it might be a matter of life and death," Big Estelle said. "Kiki has the other one."

Em took a look at Kimo, and the worry on his face said it all.

"Where is Kiki?" Em was afraid to hear.

"I can't say," Big Estelle said.

"So you all know she's not up in Kokee anymore," Em said.

"Right." Suddenly Little Estelle looked up at Kimo. "Aren't you supposed to be picking her up?"

"What are you talking about?"

"She said she would call you to pick her up."

Kimo planted his hands on his hips. "Where is she?"

"Tell him," Little Estelle said.

"Everything?" Big Estelle looked befuddled.

Em was ready to scream. "Start at the beginning."

Big Estelle set the two-way down and folded her hands. "Trish called us a little after eight and told me to bring Mother and Lars and the van and meet her in Princeville for a covert mission."

"We were to rendezvous at the Sunrise Loop Recreation room," she continued. "Wearing our harem pants and green tops so we'd blend into the golf course. In case anyone asked, we were to say we were on our way to perform at the Happy Days Long Term Care Center."

"Maybe," Em said, though she was afraid to hear, "you should get to the plot. What were you all doing running around the golf course?"

"Not me. I wasn't on the golf course. Lars and I were guarding the van and the cars in the parking lot," Little Estelle said.

Big Estelle was sweating. She patted her upper lip with a cocktail napkin. "We were going undercover, to break into Marilyn's house and get evidence that would clear Kiki. She said Marilyn's nephew, Tom, is the guilty one, not her."

"What evidence?" Em had no idea how Kiki could have learned what she'd just discovered yesterday, not until Kimo turned to her.

"I overheard you and Sophie talking in the office last night. About Tom changing identities, and how he might have been on island when he was supposed to be in India. Kiki was in such a funk this morning that I thought she should know you were getting closer to clearing her name. I had no idea she'd come up with another of her harebrained schemes."

"Giving her that information was like handing a toddler a nuclear bomb detonator to chew on." Em shook her head.

"Suzi and Trish were supposed to go inside Marilyn's house with her," Big Estelle said. "I was going to be the lookout on the corner. Except for Kiki, we all thought it was a bad idea. Then I stepped into a pile of leaves, and a centipede bit me. I couldn't walk, so Trish and Suzi helped me back to the van."

"Where Pat was running the Command and Control Center," Little Estelle added.

"So you left Kiki on her own? Was she going in alone?"

"She didn't mind. She got in and then radioed and said that she was fine and that we should all meet up here. She decided to have Kimo pick her up."

"She never called me," he said.

"She said something that didn't make sense." A tear rolled down Big Estelle's cheek. "I hope she wasn't having one of her spells."

"What did she say?" Em asked.

"Not to forget the new song, *Pele H'me*."

"We couldn't figure out what she was saying. But then as Pat was getting out of the van, she yelled, 'Holy hot gecko poop! It's code!'"

When Big Estelle shouted, imitating Pat Boggs, Kimo grabbed his heart.

"What? What's happening?" he cried.

"It was code," Little Estelle said. "Kiki gave us a message in code again."

"Ya," Lars nodded.

"Pat started writing down letters and crossing them off over and over again and finally figured it out. *Pele H'me* is code for Help Me."

"She's in trouble." Em's stomach sank.

"Where is Marilyn's house?" Kimo stripped off his apron.

"Don't go running up there," Em advised. "I'll call Roland."

"Po-lice!" Lars shouted. "Ya. Goot."

"Okay, okay." Em pulled her cell out of her pocket and hit Roland's number.

"I'm not going to sit around here and wait for the police," Kimo said. "Tell me where the house is."

# 43

### Maidens To The Rescue

Kiki tried to stay positive and convince herself she would be all right, but there was a wild look in Tom Benton's eyes that was more than a little scary as he reached into the duffle and pulled out the masking tape.

"Put your hands behind your back and don't try anything."

As soon as she put her hands behind her, he grabbed her wrists and held tight. She felt him winding the tape around her wrists.

"Masking tape? Really?" she scoffed.

"It'll hold long enough. I don't plan on keeping you around." He finished winding the tape and then used some to seal her lips closed. When he turned away to toss the tape back into the bag she tried to open her mouth.

"Mphff." She tried to kick him.

"Don't push me. I've already murdered three people, Kiki. What's one more?"

He zipped up the duffle, picked up the gun again, and suddenly someone was knocking on the sliding glass door to the *lanai* off the kitchen.

The knocking didn't last long. They heard the door slide open. A man's voice called out, "Tom? Are you still here?"

Benton's expression was one of fury but not panic. He grabbed Kiki by the elbow and forced her to her feet.

"Damn this open house aloha crap. Doesn't anyone respect a closed door around here?" He continued to mumble to himself as he shoved Kiki toward the closet then tossed in the duffle bag. He pushed her inside and forced her down.

"Just a minute, Orville. I'll be right there."

Without the use of her hands for balance, she toppled over with an "*Oof!*"

It was impossible for her to struggle to her feet in the confined space. Lying on her side, she had a view of the windows above the carved headboard behind the bed. Her eyes widened in shock, and she blinked to make sure she wasn't hallucinating. Quickly recovering, she hoped Tom hadn't seen her reaction to what she'd just seen outside the window. She peeked up again.

Sure enough, there was Pat Boggs' face in the lower corner of the window. Pat had to be standing on a tree branch. The leaves around her were shaking.

Tom was too intent on scanning the room for anything he might have overlooked to notice Pat. Kiki nodded her head frantically, hoping Pat would realize Kiki knew she was there. Pat raised her hand and made thumbs up.

"Tom? If this is an inconvenient time, I can come back," Orville called from the kitchen.

"Coming!" Tom closed the closet door on Kiki.

She listened to his footsteps as he hurried down the hall. She stayed perfectly still, her shoulders resting on the lumpy duffle. She couldn't hear what Tom and Orion were talking about and wondered if Orville was in danger.

Two seconds later she heard a distinct thud against the side of the house beneath the window where she'd seen Pat. She hoped it wasn't loud enough for Tom to have heard. She fought with the tape around her wrists and tried rubbing her cheek against the duffle to loosen the tape across her mouth. Nothing worked.

Scrabbling sounds came from beyond the closet, and then suddenly the door swung open and Trish and Pat were standing there.

"Let's help her up," Trish whispered.

They reached for Kiki. Grunting and groaning, they finally got her on her feet. Behind them, Suzi tiptoed to the door that led out to the hallway and slowly closed it and pulled a chair in front of it. It wouldn't hold Tom back for long, but at least it was something.

"Mpff!" Kiki fought the tape.

"Hold still," Pat whispered. When she yanked off the tape, Kiki swallowed a yelp.

"We have to get out of here," Kiki whispered. "He has a gun."

Pat pulled out a pocket knife and began to saw at the tape around Kiki's wrists. Suzi pointed to the window they'd come through. Trish had already climbed back up on the polished surface of the dresser beneath it. She waved Kiki forward then held up her hand for Kiki to stop.

"Where's my camera?" Trish whispered.

"Grab that duffle," Kiki told Pat. "It's full of evidence. Your camera is in there too."

Pat picked it up as Trish disappeared out the window. Kiki climbed up on the dresser and looked outside. It was a good six feet to the ground, but she didn't have time to debate. She stuck her leg out the window, straddled the sill, then pulled her other leg out and half-jumped, half-rolled out. Thankfully, she hit the ground on her feet.

Suzi came next, then Pat tossed out the duffle, and Kiki grabbed it. Trish had already started around toward the front of the house. Suzi motioned for Kiki to go. As soon as Kiki saw Pat stick her leg out of the window, she took off after them.

As they crept down the side of the house toward the street, Kiki tried not to bump the duffle against the wood siding. When they reached the edge of the property, they stopped and silently high fived each other and then hid behind the hedge on the neighbors' side.

"Who has a cell phone?" Kiki said.

"We left everything in Pat's car," Trish said.

Pat headed for the SUV parked sideways across Tom's driveway.

"Stop." Kiki grabbed the back of Pat's green tank top. "If you leave it there, he can't get a car out of the garage. He's making plans to escape."

"Leave my car?" Pat stared at the burgundy rust bucket.

"He's got a gun," Trish reminded them. "We need to call the police right away."

"Fine, so let's cut across the golf course," Kiki suggested. "It's the fastest way to the main road and the security kiosk."

They argued for a minute over who was better fit to carry the duffle, but Kiki wasn't letting go. Pat led them down a narrow space between the hedge and Tom's house. On the street behind Tom's, the lot next to Orville Orion's home was still vacant. The wide green yard opened onto the golf course. They ran along the edge of the course like rats running around the edges of a room. Suzi soon darted into the lead, running as fast as her short legs could carry her. Trish was next. Weighed down by the duffle bag, Kiki was panting, bringing up the rear. Pat ran back, grabbed the bag, and this time Kiki didn't argue.

She was about to take off again when a golf ball landed two feet ahead of her, hitting the ground right between her and Pat.

She looked around and spotted a knot of golfers teeing off.

"Hey!" Kiki hollered and shook her fist. "Somebody could get killed out here!"

"Kiki, shut up and come on," Pat yelled back.

Kiki hiked up her harem pants and started running again. They hadn't gone ten yards when a golf cart suddenly turned off the cart path speeding toward them. The driver was honking and waving, and as he drew close, Kiki recognized the Princeville Security shield.

She waved back. When he roared up beside them, she leaned against the cart and fought for a breath.

"Binky, you're a godsend. Call the police."

"Why?"

"Because there's a murderer living in Marilyn Lockhart's house. He's planning an escape. The KPD needs to be alerted. He's got to be arrested before he can leave the island."

Binky smoothed his hand over his hair, smiled, and looked all around.

"We're on camera right? You're filming?"

"What are you *talking* about?" She grabbed her head. "Filming?"

"That *Trouble in Paradise* show. We're on it right now, aren't we? Where are the cameras hidden?" He scanned the tree line.

"Binky, so help me, you need to help us."

"Actually, I'm out here to pick you all up and take you to the manager's office. We've had more than eight complaints called in in the last ten minutes."

"What?"

"We had three calls about you trespassing in yards. One of you broke off a plumeria limb in another yard, and golfers are calling to report a bunch of crazy women in baggy pants running around loose on the course." He looked at them. "That would be you. Have you ladies been drinking?"

"Not yet," Kiki said, "but I could sure use a martini."

"We aren't the guilty ones here," Trish told him.

Pat held up the duffle. "We have evidence in here that's going to solve a murder."

"Three murders," Kiki added. "So call the police."

"I can handle this," Binky hiked up his pants. He pointed to the shield on his sleeve. "In case you haven't noticed, *I'm* the police up here."

"You are a security guard," Suzi reminded him.

"And you ladies are trespassing on private property."

Trish was staring in the direction they'd come from. "Oh, no, I think I just saw him over there." She pointed at some bushes.

"Who?" Binky turned around.

"The murderer, that's who. Tom Benton."

Trish was digging in the duffle for her camera. She squealed and jerked her hand out of the bag.

"There's something furry in there."

"Wigs," Kiki said. "Two wigs."

Trish tried again, pulled out her camera, and hung it around her neck. A gunshot popped behind them.

Binky turned toward the bushes. "Wow. That really sounds lifelike."

"That's because it is!" Kiki dove to the ground. Trish and Suzi joined her. Pat flew past Binky, grabbed him on the way down and shouted, "Heads down! That toad sucker is really startin' to piss me off!"

# 44

Kimo to the Rescue

Em called Roland and was forced to leave a message on his voicemail. Kimo asked her not to call 911 until they found out what kind of situation Kiki was embroiled in. Em insisted Kimo take her with him as he headed for Princeville.

"What if she's in danger?" She had asked him the same thing three times already. They'd just crossed the Hanalei Bridge.

"We'll know soon enough. Kiki's got more lives than a cat."

"I hope so." Em stared out the window. The sky was clearing toward the south where their weather came from. As soon as they entered Princeville, Em gave Kimo directions to Marilyn's house. When they arrived they noticed the garage door was up. There was a car inside, and parked crossways on the driveway was Pat Bogg's SUV.

Kimo pulled into the driveway behind Pat's car then grabbed the machete he kept in the side pocket of the driver's seat door and jumped out. He headed up the walk to the front door before Em could stop him.

Before she could talk herself out of it, she jumped out of the pickup and ran after him with her cell phone in hand. Beside the front door, Marilyn's water feature merrily bubbled on.

Kimo knocked twice, raised his machete, and opened the door.

"Now I know how you and Kiki have stayed together for so long," she mumbled. "You're both crazy."

The house felt as empty as a tomb. There wasn't a thing out of place in the main rooms.

"Kiki!" Kimo hollered as he headed down the long hallway to the bedrooms. Em stayed on his heels. "Kiki, where are you?"

He went through a doorway at the end of the hall and stepped into a bedroom. Unlike the rest of the rooms, things were scattered all over inside this one. A chair was on the floor near the door, the closet door was wide open and items that had been on the dresser—a clock, an empty vase, and a small, framed watercolor of a hibiscus bloom—were on the floor nearby. The window above the dresser was open, the screen was off, and the curtain was hanging half in and half outside.

"Looks like someone went out this way." Kimo stared up at the window.

"More than just one someone, judging by the scratches on top of the dresser and the marks on the wall." Em knew the place had to have been pristine before the escape. "At least Kiki isn't alone."

"Pat's car is still here," Kimo said. "So they have to be on foot."

"Surely they've gotten some help by now. Hopefully they've called the police."

Suddenly they heard a distinct pop in the distance.

"That's a gunshot." Kimo spun around and headed back down the hall.

"Sounds like it was close by."

He jumped into the truck, and as Em closed her door, he was already backing out onto the street.

Em hit 911 and talked to the police dispatcher as Kimo raced down the street.

"Gunshots have been fired near the Princeville Golf Course," Em said. "Send someone now."

"Can you stay on the line, ma'am? Where is your location?"

She tried to explain, but they were moving so fast she wasn't really sure. She gave them Marilyn's street name but then added, "The shot came from the golf course near that address. You need to send someone over here right away."

Kimo headed for the end of the cul-de-sac and drove over the curb, barely missed a For Sale sign staked on an empty lot and cut across the golf course. He turned onto the cart path.

When he rounded a curve, they were facing three carts full of golfers coming at him from the other direction. The golfers whistled and waved for him to move over, but he didn't budge. The cart drivers had to swerve off the path to miss him, and then they went bumping along on the grass.

Em kept her eyes peeled on the edge of the golf course that bordered huge two-story homes.

"There!" Kimo yelled. "I see a security cart. It's pulled over." He pointed to a spot up ahead of them. "No, there it goes. Security is headed for the club house."

"Look," Em pointed. "Right there near where the cart was parked. Is that them?"

One minute ago the Princeville security golf cart had been there, but then it raced away. Three familiar figures were getting to their feet. The fern fronds bobbing around their heads and their wide-legged pants gave them away.

"It's Kiki and the others. I don't know who the fifth one is."

Kimo strained forward, clutching the wheel. He squinted.

"That's Binky. He works security up here."

They hit a speed bump on the cart path so hard that Em flew up off the seat, and her head rammed into the roof of the cab.

"Yikes, slow down, Kimo."

They reached Kiki and the others, and he not only slowed down, he pulled off the path and headed for Kiki, who was running toward him waving her arms. Her hair had come unpinned and was standing out around her head like a wild nimbus.

Kiki ran up to Kimo's pickup. She pointed at the cart in the distance.

"Tom's getting away! Don't let him. Go after him!"

Kimo paused long enough to let Em climb out, and then he turned back toward the cart path and took off again, bouncing down the narrow road like crazy. Em heard a siren in the distance and thanked God for small favors. Finally, the police were on the way.

Kiki, Trish, Pat, and Suzi crowded around her. A security guard lingered a few feet away carefully studying the shrubbery along the edge of the course. He kept sticking out his chest and pulling in his stomach. Em wasn't certain, but he sure looked like he was posing.

"Are you all right?" Em hugged each of the Maidens in turn.

"We're fine," Kiki said. "No thanks to Binky."

"What's he doing?" Em whispered. "Is he all right?"

"We can't convince him this is all too real. He thinks we're shooting *Trouble in Paradise* and that the cameras are hidden just off the course."

"Binky's in for a shock when he finds out Tom fired a real shot into the air. Binky isn't allowed to carry any bullets." Suzi suddenly sat down on a lumpy black duffle near her feet. "Whew, I get dizzy just thinking about it."

"Binky said they won't issue him real bullets," Trish said. "Now I know why."

"Look! Here come the cops." Kiki pointed toward the main road through the resort that ran parallel to the golf course. Two police cruisers were flying along between speed humps with their sirens on and lights flashing. Kimo laid on the horn in his truck as he followed Tom across the course, quickly closing the distance between them.

Em and the others watched the chase and saw Tom careen off the path, make a wrong turn, and then his cart flew off the edge of a sand trap, was airborne for a second before it dropped, and came to a dead stop. He jumped out of the cart and carefully kept the sand trap between himself and Kimo's truck as he headed for the clubhouse a few feet away.

"Oh, no," Em said. "Looks like he's going to make it."

Tom reached the Makai golf club and disappeared from view. The two cruisers pulled onto the drive to the clubhouse and turned in.

"I wish we were over there," Kiki said.

"It's not that far, let's walk."

"It'd be faster if I ran back and got my car," Pat said. "I think I can cut right through a couple yards back there and end up at Marilyn's." She pointed in that direction.

"No trespassing," Binky said. "No cutting through yards."

Pat marched over to him until they were standing toe to toe.

"Oh yeah? Oh *yeah*?" She leaned even closer and whispered, "If you let me go, folks will sure be talking about this episode when it airs. Who knows? You might even get your own fan club."

Binky hiked up his pants.

"All right, go ahead."

Pat started to walk away.

He called after her, waved, and smiled toward the nearest shrubbery. "I'll let you go this time, but make sure it doesn't happen again."

Trish rolled her eyes. Kiki shook her head.

Pat had no sooner disappeared between two bushes than Suzi said, "Here comes Big Estelle."

Sure enough, the white van had turned off the main road and was headed toward the nearest golf cart path. Within a minute Big Estelle pulled up next to them. The side door slid open.

"Don't get out," Kiki called up to them. "Take us to the Makai golf club." She yanked the duffle out from under Suzi, who toppled onto the grass. Kiki tossed the bag into the van and climbed in after it. Trish, Suzi, and Em followed her. Em climbed up into the shotgun seat, and Lars slammed the door shut.

"What's in there?" Em pointed to the duffle.

"Everything Roland will need to convict Tom Benton. Wait until you hear the whole story," Kiki said.

They crowded into the van with the others. Little Estelle was in the back, strapped onto the Gadabout. Lars was in the backseat.

"How did you find us?" Trish asked Big Estelle.

"There aren't a lot of golfers out here in gauze harem pants." Big Estelle carefully negotiated the big van along the cart path. "What happened?"

Em looked forward to hearing too. Trish quickly filled them in.

"Pat figured out the code and that Kiki needed help. We went back and watched the house, and when we heard Tom's voice, Pat climbed a tree outside one of the bedrooms and peeked in. Then we heard someone call out to Tom from the kitchen and next thing you know, Tom tossed Kiki in the closet. Can you imagine somebody tossing Kiki in a closet? So we hustled around to a lower window and climbed in and rescued her."

"And ran like hell," Suzi said.

"Great idea blocking him in with Pat's car," Em said.

"That was my idea." Kiki looked exhausted, but she was beaming.

"Hand me my bag, Lars, baby," Little Estelle yelled from the back.

"Ya, Cougar." He reached over Trish and picked up a canvas purse and handed it back to Little Estelle. She dug around in it for a second and then held up a silver flask and waved it around.

"You girls could probably use a little toot right about now, so here you go."

They arrived at the Makai golf club before the flask had made it around to everyone.

"We can't get any closer," Big Estelle said. "The police have blocked off both ends of the street with squad cars already."

Em declined the flask when it reached her and looked out the window. Sure enough, the two squad cars had split up and were at each end of the road just beyond the golf starter's shack.

"Can we get out?" Suzi was on her knees on the seat trying to see what was going on.

"Why not?" Kiki motioned for Lars to open the door. As soon as it opened, she jumped out. Everyone in back followed. Big Estelle tipped the flask up and took a long swig.

"There's a little left," she told Em. "Want it?"

"No, thanks. I think I'll try to keep my wits about me. They're in short supply around here obviously."

"I'll take it!" Little Estelle shouted. "Lower the lift and let me out."

Big Estelle started to push the button to lower the Gadabout to the pavement.

"Do you think that's a good idea?" Em asked. "Things could get dicey out there. We might have to take cover."

Big Estelle turned to Em. "*You* tell her she can't get out."

"Point taken." Em saw Roland come driving up behind them. He was talking on his radio.

"Go find out what's happening," Kiki urged.

"I don't want to get in the way," Em said.

After what happened this morning she wasn't looking forward to seeing him. It was inadvertently her fault Kiki found out about their suspicions about Tom. As she watched two more squad cars pull up, followed by a fire truck and an EMT vehicle, she was fairly sure Roland would no doubt blame her for this whole fiasco.

Kiki was watching her and must have sensed her hesitation.

"Don't worry, Em. He won't be pissed long. We flushed out a

murderer for him," Kiki reminded her. "He should be grateful."

Somehow Em didn't think so.

Before she had to make a decision, Suzi said, "Looks like he's coming over here."

Sure enough, Roland was driving again, headed across the road. He parked near the van and got out.

"I'm going to have to ask you all to move back." His cool gaze touched each of them in turn.

Em noticed she got no more, no less attention than any of the others.

Kiki stepped to the front of the group. With a huge smile, she handed Roland the duffle.

"There you go, Roland. All the evidence you'll need to convict Tom Benton."

His only comment was a shake of his head.

"No need to thank me." Kiki's smile dimmed but didn't fade.

"I should have known when I heard the call that shots had been fired at Princeville you women were somehow involved."

"All we did was flush Benton out," Kiki said. "My reputation, not to mention my freedom, was on the line. Turns out he was about to leave the island under an alias."

"Then no doubt we'd have found out that he was guilty of his aunt's murder with or without this bag."

"He confessed to me that he also killed Bobby Quinn and the maid at Haena Bay Resort," Kiki said. "The disguises he wore while he was hiding out here, while he was supposedly in India, are in the bag along with a pile of credit cards that were not issued to him. Again, no need to thank me."

"Don't worry. We've now got a stand-off and a hostage situation on our hands," Roland said.

Em's heart sank.

"What hostages?" Suzi wanted to know.

"Two of the golf starters and a woman who works in the concession stand are trapped inside with him."

"I hear the chili dogs are great," Little Estelle said.

"Ya." Lars nodded. "Goot."

"If you're not leaving, which is what I'd advise you to do, then you'll all have to move back beyond that speed hump behind you. Move your vehicle, too. We're going to put up barricades back there." He pointed to a spot a good distance away. "We need to keep this area clear for more emergency vehicles."

Just then a male voice issued from a bullhorn near the clubhouse.

"Tom Benton. We advise you to let your hostages go and give yourself up."

Everyone held their breath. Even the breeze seemed to stop blowing. There was no response. Without another word to any of them, Roland shouldered the strap on the duffle and turned to walk away.

"Roland, wait," Em said softly.

He paused and waited for her. They walked away alone, stopping far enough away that they could speak without the Maidens hearing.

"I didn't know what they were up to, or I'd have tried to stop them," she said.

He looked back at the gaggle of women and Lars and didn't bother to hide his frustration.

Em went on. "Kimo overheard Sophie and me talking last night. He told Kiki our suspicions about Tom hiding the fact he was on island before the wedding."

"As usual, Kiki decided to take things into her own hands, and the rest followed," he said.

"She says the proof of his guilt is in that bag."

"The proof of his guilt is that he's armed and holed up in the clubhouse. I'm sure he didn't just hand it over to her, Em."

"She took off with it after he locked her in a closet and her friends broke her out."

"So she just went calling, asking for evidence?"

"Well, maybe she broke in, but you can't blame her for trying to clear her name."

"We'll worry about it later. Right now, if you can't convince them to leave, at least get them to move back and stay out of the way." He walked away, headed for the growing ring of police cruisers outside the clubhouse. Uniformed officers were crouched behind the cars parked nearest the low building. The captain in charge kept issuing demands that Benton give up and come out or at least release his hostages.

Em turned around and went to join the Maidens. Big Estelle had already moved the van to a position behind the speed hump. Traffic entering the road behind them had been halted. People were pulling over, leaving their cars and walking up the road. The parking lot near the main entrance had been blocked off to everyone except police, fire, and ambulance personnel.

A herd of golf carts were slowly gathering off to one side of the road near Big Estelle's van. Kimo's truck was there too. As more and more foursomes finished their golf rounds, they drove up, expecting to turn their carts in.

Despite the seriousness of the situation, there was a hint of excitement in the air fueled by adrenaline and curiosity.

It wasn't long before the beverage cart came putting up, and the attendant was soon selling beer out of a cooler strapped on the back. Big

Estelle opened the van doors and had taken out a couple of folding spectator chairs that she always carried and set them up on the road just behind the quickly erected KPD barricade.

Em had almost returned to the van when a resident from one of the houses fronting the golf course came running out. She was dressed in a flowing green and orange caftan and matching orange flip flops with green bows on the toes. When she raised her hand to shield her eyes from the sun, the row of gold bangle bracelets on her arm clinked together.

"Do you know what's happening?" she asked Em. Before Em could say anything, she went on. "My neighbor called and said it's a terrorist attack. An Arabian terror cell is trying to take over all of Princeville. Should I start packing?"

"It's not a terrorist attack," Em said.

"Someone saw a bunch of women wearing those puffy belly dancer pants running across the golf course. She said they looked really strange. Foreign even."

At least the really strange part was right.

"All I can say is there's a man in the clubhouse with a gun. He's got the starters and one of the concession ladies in there with him."

"Well, that's good," the woman said.

"Good?" Em wondered what exactly was good about it.

"At least it's just some crazy person and not a bunch of terrorists. That could really drive down the value of our home." Her gaze strayed to the gaggle of golfers swilling beer near the golf carts. "Oh, there's my husband. Freddy! Freddy!" She started waving and hurried away.

When Em reached the van she realized the Maidens were settling in for the long haul.

Pat had retrieved her SUV and was back. Suzi was on her cell phone but for once wasn't working real estate.

"Right," Suzi said. "We'd like four large combo pizzas, a case of Diet Pepsi, six bottles of Cabot Pinot Grigio. Yes. We have valid IDs. Oh, you'll find us. Just take the back entrance to Princeville, Hanalei River Road, the one that goes by the police station. Right. We're closest to the police barricade in the white van."

"Food?" Em said when Suzi hung up.

"We're hungry," Trish said. "We've been at this since early this morning, and it's already one thirty. Tiki Man Pizza said they'd deliver for twenty bucks."

Suzi tapped out some figures on her phone calculator then announced, "I'll be collecting twenty-two fifty from each of you," she said.

"Twenty-two fifty?" Big Estelle's brows shot up.

"That includes tax, tip, and delivery."

"Okay, I guess," Big Estelle shrugged.

"You're not going to pass up pizza," Suzi said.

By now the back road into the resort was backed up past the golf course, lined with cars parked in front of the newer luxury town homes behind security gates. Looky-loos were walking in on foot. Em realized there was no getting out unless she left on foot. From the sound of the bullhorn blaring near the KPD mobile command center that had just arrived, Tom Benton wasn't budging.

Em called Sophie on her cell and told her what was happening.

"I have no idea when I'll be back," Em said. "Kimo was part of the chase, and he's being questioned by the police. When they're done with him, hopefully he'll go back to work and won't want to hang around here like the rest of the world. Did you have to turn away a lot of lunch business?"

"Not too much," Sophie said. "We made do. Buzzy fried up a bunch of burgers. Louie waited tables and charmed almost everyone into staying even though we only had one choice."

"Unless I walk down the road and get a ride out of Princeville, I'll be here for a while."

"I can have Buzzy come pick you up. Things will slow down after lunch."

Em turned her back to the van and lowered her voice. "I'm kind of afraid to leave the Maidens. Someone has to be the voice of reason. Roland's pretty upset."

"Seriously? He's really pissed at you?"

"He hasn't said much, but I can tell he's not happy with me. I'll call and let you know if I need a ride back. Just make sure to tell Uncle Louie I'm all right."

# 45

## Hangin' at the Standoff

Seven hours later, beneath a sliver of a moon and a starry sky, the standoff was still underway. The scene on the Princeville golf course surrounding the clubhouse had become a carnival. Em suspected everyone was secretly waiting to see if there would be a shootout and if so, they weren't about to miss it.

Porta Pottys provided by Princeville Corporation had been set up in a neat row along the far end of the parking lot near the main road. Earlier in the afternoon a group of hippies had arrived and spread blankets under the trees. Now they were dancing beneath the stars, long hair flowing, dreadlocks bouncing as they swayed to lilting flute music and the jingling beat of tambourines.

Golf carts that couldn't be returned to the starter shack had been carefully parked in neat rows and then abandoned. Before the sun set, Princeville residents walked out of their homes with beach chairs, cocktails, and pupus and set up an impromptu party on the green.

The Mayor of Kilauea, the nearest town just down the road, commandeered a huge portable grill, hustled for donations from local stores, and called in Lion's Club volunteers to barbecue hamburgers and hot dogs to sell for a fundraiser. He had borrowed the police bullhorn to announce that they had nearly sold out of food.

Sometime that afternoon Precious and Flora had arrived and joined the other Maidens. Binky had driven them in on the security cart. He still wasn't convinced they weren't secretly filming an episode of *Trouble in Paradise*.

Em hadn't talked to Roland again though every forty-five minutes or so an officer would come by and inform the crowd what was going on. So far none of their efforts to extract Tom Benton from the clubhouse had worked. He'd demanded a helicopter and safe passage, but he intended to take the chili dog cook with him.

Little Estelle and Lars kept disappearing into the shrubbery. They'd just returned with smiles on their faces. Flora was lying on her back, a shadowy ruffled mound in a *muumuu*, with Precious beside her. Precious was pointing out the Big Dipper and the North Star until she abruptly stopped talking. She stacked her hands beneath her head and continued to stare at the night sky.

"Are you all right?" Em asked her.

"I'm just thinking of ways to get Tom Benton out of the clubhouse," she said. "We need to do something."

"Oh, I think we've done enough," Em said.

"I agree." Roland's voice came out of the dark. The Maidens gathered around when they heard him.

"Is Benton going to give up?" Big Estelle wanted to know. "I need a shower."

"Not any time soon, I'm afraid," Roland said. "We're worried that he had nothing to lose and would shoot a hostage if we didn't meet his demands, then he let one of the starters go because the guy is on medication."

"That's a good sign, isn't it?" Em wanted to cling to any positive shred of hope even though she was convinced the spark between her and Roland had been all but extinguished.

Precious edged closer to Roland and tugged on the hem of his Aloha shirt. He looked down at her and gave a nod of acknowledgement. "Marilyn Lockhart's maid of honor," he said.

"Precious Cottrell. I'm a new Maiden." She sounded so proud, as if joining the group was her life's greatest accomplishment to date.

"Can I help you?" He crossed his arms.

"I've been thinking about how to get Benton out of there. Have you thought of smoking him out with tear gas?"

"We're afraid for the hostages."

"They're probably pretty afraid for themselves by now," Big Estelle said. "This is taking forever. It's ridiculous."

"He should have taken me hostage," Little Estelle said. "I'd have devised an escape plan by now. He'd be toast." She turned to Lars. "Right, babe?"

"Ya, Cougar. Das goot."

"What about sleep deprivation?" Precious wasn't willing to give up now that she had Roland's attention. "It's used to break enemy combatants."

Roland surveyed the circus on the course around them. "If this goes on much longer, we're all going to be suffering sleep deprivation."

"She might be onto something." Kiki stepped up from the shadows. "Flood the place with blinding light to keep him awake. I saw that on a spy series. When he starts to nod off, you blast the place with heavy metal. It'll drive him insane."

"Not to mention all the neighbors," Em added.

"What's worse than heavy metal?" Big Estelle asked.

"Your singing." Little Estelle laughed.

"Hey!" Kiki snapped her fingers. "Now you're talking." In her excitement she'd grabbed Roland's arm. He gave her a frosty look, and she immediately let go, but her enthusiasm wasn't dimmed.

"Our singing is just terrible. All we need are a few more of those bull horns. Let us drive him out."

"We could dance, too," Suzi said. "Just for fun."

"Better to put the energy into singing," Kiki said. "If we try to sing and dance, we'll get winded."

"How bad is your singing?" Precious wanted to know.

"Like a bunch of feral cats screaming in a bag." Little Estelle shook her head. "Horrible."

"That pretty much sums it up," Em agreed.

"Could we keep it up long enough to drive someone crazy, though?" Suzi wondered.

Kiki laughed. "You actually think it would take that long? We don't know any heavy metal, but we could sing some of our hula songs, and if he doesn't come out we can try some campfire tunes like 'Ninety-nine Bottles of Beer on the Wall.'"

Roland turned to Em. "Tell me they're not serious."

"Their singing is pretty horrible. It makes their dancing look like they're ready to be pros on *Dancing with the Stars*. What have you got to lose?"

"I seriously want you to think about seeking professional help. You're getting as nutty as they are."

She couldn't help but smile. "Nothing else has worked. Do you want to end up giving Benton a helicopter ride out of here? How's that going to reflect on the KPD?"

"Of course we're not doing that."

She figured whatever they had going between them was long gone. She had nothing to lose, so she asked, "Got any better ideas?"

He studied the crowd and then all the cars lining both sides of every road.

"I'd be happy if they just cleared the crowd on the golf course." He shrugged. "Crazier things have been suggested today, believe me."

"Are you really thinking of letting them try it?" Em couldn't believe it.

"Is it a go?" Kiki wanted to know. "If so, we need to open that last bottle of wine *wikiwiki*."

Roland nodded. "Okay, go ahead and get tuned up, ladies. I'll go run it by the captain and see how many bull horns we have."

# 46

## Employing Torture Tactics

For the first time since Tom Benton tossed her in his closet that morning, Kiki felt back in control. Though the KPD had taken Roland's suggestion and agreed to let them try their caterwauling, she didn't actually hold much hope for success. But at the very least, the effort might make up for her having ignited this whole powder keg.

"Okay, girls, it's show time." She instructed Pat to line the Maidens up near Big Estelle's van. From there they would march down the road to the KPD mobile command and control van.

"We started this thing," Kiki said. "With any luck we can end it. I'm counting on you ladies to sing loud and stay off-key. Got it?"

"Loud and off-key, laaadeez!" Pat shouted in case any of them missed the directive.

"Right." Precious was all smiles.

"Ya. Goot." Lars had donned night vision goggles.

"We don't sing in any known key anyway," Trish said.

Kiki turned to Little Estelle. The Gadabout was charged up and ready to go. "Can Lars carry a tune?"

"Not even in a bucket."

"Great," Kiki nodded.

"He doesn't know what we're saying, let alone the words to any of our songs," Big Estelle said.

"Exactly," Little Estelle said. "And I mean to keep it that way."

"No matter," Kiki decided. "Let him sing in Norwegian or Finnish or whatever language he speaks. Let him sing a whole other tune, in fact. That'll just add to the confusion. Get him to sing loud."

"Can you sing, Em?" Kiki noticed Em standing off to the side of the group looking worried.

"Kind of," Em said.

"Then you can't join us. I don't want anyone who is *remotely* on key near those bullhorns."

"How long do you think they'll let us go on?" Suzi was looking at the time on her cell phone. "I really need to get back to work tomorrow. I've got houses to show and escrows to close."

"Depends on how well this works," Kiki told them. "All we can do is our worst."

They marched down the hill with Little Estelle leading the way on her scooter. The spectators scattered all around the course noticed that something was finally happening. Observers swarmed to the side of the road to watch.

When they reached the KPD mobile command and control van, Roland walked over to Kiki with one of the uniformed officers. He introduced them and said he'd already explained what the women were going to do and why.

"Hope it works, Auntie," the captain told Kiki. "Some fun today, eh? But it's time to end this thing. We're all ready to go home." He waved two younger officers forward. Between them they had rounded up five bullhorns which they passed out to the Maidens.

Kiki and the others pressed the buttons and familiarized themselves with the horns, then she decided they should get as close to the clubhouse as possible while staying out of range of Benton's handgun.

"What are we going to sing first?" Trish wanted to know.

"Let's start with all the old *hapa-haole* songs like 'Tiny Bubbles' and 'Little Grass Shack' and 'We're Going to a Hukilau.'"

"How about 'Sweet Leilani'?" Flora had huffed up the road with her Gatorade bottle in hand, bringing up the rear. "I hate that one."

Kiki picked up her bullhorn and held it out so that two of the others could sing into it with her. Down the line they all shared the other four horns. She raised her right hand, mouthed the words "Tiny Bubbles," and then motioned for them to start singing.

Amplified, their collective sound was worse than she'd ever imagined. The looky-loos on the golf course pulled back. Even the hippies held their hands to their ears.

The Maidens sang all the *hapa-haole* songs Kiki had mentioned and then some, so they launched into "She'll Be Comin' Around the Mountain" and then "Kumbaya." By now they were all leaning against police cruisers. Singing at the top of one's lungs after a tense day was not for the weak of heart.

Finally Kiki decided they were about done in. Halfway through their fifth song, a uniformed officer had passed out bottled water. She took another swig now, cleared her throat, and noticed she was getting hoarse.

"Time for the last resort. Let's go with 'Ninety-nine Bottles of Beer on the Wall.'" She lifted the bullhorn to her lips for what she hoped was the last time.

They'd just hit seventy-three bottles when the side door of the clubhouse slammed open. The police raised their weapons. The Maidens ducked behind the cruisers. There were no gunshots, just the cries of the chili dog vendor as she came tearing out into the night.

"Don't shoot! It's me!" the woman hollered. "Don't shoot." She ran toward the police cars. When she was out of Benton's range, an officer in riot gear ran out to grab her and pull her to safety.

"What's happening? What's going on?" Kiki yelled to the closest cop. He held up his hands and shrugged. Then Kiki heard the woman's voice again.

"Tell them to keep singing," the concessionaire waved. She called out to the Maidens, "Don't stop, Aunties. It's driving him crazy. He's in the corner with his gun in his lap, staring at it and sobbing. He was fine until you started singing 'Kumbaya,' then he slid down the wall and cracked up. I finally took a chance and slipped out of the main room and ran out the side door. He didn't try to stop me."

Someone in the crowd yelled out asking about the other hostage.

The woman called out, "He's hiding in back of the big walk-in refrigerator. Not inside it, behind it. The guy with the gun never even knew he had three hostages in there. He thought he only had two, me and the guy he let go."

"Sing!" The police captain signaled Kiki. "Sing, Aunties."

They picked up where they left off and sang as loud as they could. By the time they got to sixty-eight bottles of beer, a black chopper appeared over the clubhouse, and an officer swinging on a rope was lowered to the roof while the SWAT team, in full regalia, ran out in a line and hugged the sides of the building.

The last thing Kiki wanted was for Tom Benton to put a bullet in his head, no matter what he'd done. She wanted justice. She wanted him to stand trial for three murders and spend the rest of his life in prison with a big, burly cell mate with bad breath and no teeth.

"Fifty-four bottles of beer on the wall, fifty-four bottles if beeeeeeer," the Maidens howled.

The crowd had moved up as far as they could behind the maidens, and some of the folks started howling along with them. Kiki noticed Em standing not far away. She wished Kimo was here to see this, but by now he was busy with the last few dinner orders at the Goddess.

"Take one down and pass it aroooooound . . ."

There was a loud pop near the clubhouse, and then smoke suddenly billowed out of the windows. Three of the members of the SWAT team climbed through a window. Two ran in the door the chili dog lady had left standing open.

The Maidens' singing gradually faded away. Em moved closer to Kiki. "Do you think it worked?" Em whispered. "If it did, it's a miracle."

"If it worked, we're going to be even more famous than we are now. Randy Rich is going to eat his heart out over this one. He couldn't have scripted this scene in a million and one years."

"Think of all the dance gigs we're going to get now." Flora was so hoarse she could barely talk, but her croak sounded ecstatic.

"Hey, is that photographer here from the *Garden Island*?" Precious's head was on a swivel.

"I haven't seen him, but I'm here," Trish said. "I've been taking photos all day. I got some of you all lined up singing a few minutes ago. No worries. I took enough for a whole spread in the paper. I'll email you copies for your websites."

"Could life get any better?" Kiki lowered the bullhorn and sighed with relief.

"Have you all forgotten why we're here? Tom Benton was a cold-blooded murderer." Em was staring at the tear gas rolling out of the smoking clubhouse.

The rest of them immediately sobered.

"Way to bring down a party," Kiki nudged her with her elbow.

"This is no party, Kiki. Just pray the SWAT team makes it out all right."

"Look!" Little Estelle started tooting her horn. "Here they come! They've got Tom Benton with them."

Sure enough, Tom Benton's arms were draped over the shoulders of two SWAT team members. He was hanging between them, head down, and they appeared to be supporting him. His toes dragged on the ground.

When the police officers visibly relaxed and started slapping one another on the back, a cheer went up from the assembled crowd. The hippies started playing their flutes and frolicking in the grass again.

Kiki felt Em stiffen beside her, looked up, and saw Roland walking toward them. He wasn't smiling, but he appeared to have thawed a bit. Kiki wanted like hell to say she'd told him so, but she held her tongue.

Roland looked like he was about to swallow glass.

"I never thought I'd hear myself say this, but thank you, ladies."

Kiki was glad he thanked them, no matter how sparingly.

"No problem, Roland. If you ever find yourself in another standoff situation, you've got our numbers."

# 47

### All *Pau* for Now

After a day's respite, Pat called the Goddess at Kiki's request and asked Em to please reserve them a table for lunch. She said they were officially coming in to celebrate their success as the KPD's secret weapon deployed at what was quickly becoming the legendary Princeville Makai Clubhouse standoff.

"What time will they be here?" Sophie was busy wiping off chair seats and pulling tables together.

"Eleven." Em glanced at the clock behind the bar. They had ten minutes before the Maidens descended and they would open for lunch.

Louie came breezing in, his thick white hair still wet from the shower and slicked back. He walked over to Em. "I got your phone message. What do you need?"

"The Maidens are coming in for lunch to celebrate. I thought you might like to whip up a commemorative cocktail for the occasion."

"Great idea. I saw the article in the *Garden Island* this morning. Front page story and two pages of photos, most of them by our Trish. Super coverage."

"Wasn't it? The standoff ended too late for the story to run yesterday, but the paper wrote them up big time today," Em said.

"Probably not a good thing." Sophie had finished setting up the tables and headed over to the bar. "The reality show fame was bad enough. There will be no living with the old girls now that the whole island has read about them."

"I particularly liked the quotes included from all the bystanders," Em said. "Especially the one hippie guy who said the police should sponsor starlight concerts on the golf course once a month."

Louie got busy behind the bar. Kimo told Sophie to push the *mahi mahi* sandwiches. A carload of tourists walked in for lunch, and Em took their orders.

"Excuse me," one of the women asked. "What time do they turn on the waterfalls?"

Used to folks asking every kind of question under the sun including where they could see the Hawaiians who lived in grass huts, Em didn't even blink. She looked at her watch.

"They should have the waterfalls running in a couple hours. Now, how about a Mai Tai to go with that *mahi* sandwich?"

By eleven sharp all the Maidens had shown up and were poring over their copies of the newspaper while sipping hurricane glasses full of Louie's hastily concocted new drink, the Sour Note.

"Listen to this," Suzi read. "Police won't say what Kiki Godwin, local party planner and hula enthusiast, did to help, just that she was instrumental in bringing Tom Benton, alleged murderer of three people on the North Shore, to justice."

"Hula enthusiast?" Kiki sniffed. "That makes it sound like I'm just a fan of hula, not a professional dancer."

"Here's to Kiki!" Flora raised her glass. They were all toasting their leader, and not for the first time, when Lillian Smith breezed in followed by MyBob. She waved her copy of the *Garden Island* in the air.

"You're all so famous," she cooed. "I'm so proud of my hula sisters I could just burst." She pulled out the last empty chair at the table and sat with the girls. MyBob was forced to wander over and grab a stool at the bar.

"Where are the other Lillians?" Trish asked.

"Gone home, thank heavens." Lillian patted her pink bouffant. "What an exhausting group. We were playing the radio in the *Holoholo* van yesterday and heard about the standoff on KONG radio. It took forever to get everyone collected after tubing down the irrigation ditch, and then half of them wanted to drive all the way over to Hanapepe to walk across the swinging bridge, so off we went. Then a couple of tourists told one of them about the monk seals beached at the park at Po'ipu, so off we went again. By that time it was sunset happy hour at the Sheraton, and you know how that goes. I was soooo sad to miss the standoff and the singing. I was in the choir in Iowa. I could have really helped out."

Little Estelle piped up, "You wouldn't have been allowed to sing."

Lillian started to tear up. "Why not?"

"Only off-key singers allowed," Pat said.

Too late. Lillian was already crying.

"I could have tried to sing off key," she wailed.

"Here you go, dumpling." MyBob walked over and handed her a Sour Note. "That'll make you feel better."

She sniffed and wiped her nose with a napkin and then looked at the others' plates. "So would a *mahi* sandwich and fries."

"I'll give Sophie your order, honey." He walked back to the bar.

"Already got it," Sophie told MyBob before she turned to Em. "This is better than TV."

"Don't even think it." Em kept her voice low. "I'm afraid Randy Rich will call any minute to tell us the network saw the news and wants us back. Kiki said he's probably eating his heart out right about now."

Louie walked over to the Maiden's table.

"Congratulations, ladies. How do you like the Sour Notes?"

They raised their glasses high.

"Love, 'em," Kiki said. "I can't wait to read the legend you'll write for the menu."

Em joined her uncle and stood next to him at the head of the Maidens' table.

"I've got an announcement to make," she said. "Uncle Louie is heading to Honolulu in the morning to compete at the state level of the National Cocktail Shake Off. If he wins the state, he'll go on to represent Hawaii in Long Beach, California, at the Western Regionals."

The Maidens started whooping and slapping the table.

"Here's to Louie." Kiki raised her glass. "Bring home the trophy! Better yet, if you make it to the regionals, we'll all go with you."

Louie waited until the cheering subsided. "*Mahalo* for your support and confidence. In celebration, you can all have another round of Sour Notes, this time on the house."

"Das goot!" Already bleary-eyed, Lars raised his glass.

Once the fresh round had been served, Kiki got to her feet and asked for everyone's attention. Kiki's speeches were known to be unending. Em sighed and headed back to the bar. Louie mumbled something about needing to do something at the house and walked away.

With all the drama of a soap opera star, Kiki slowly let her gaze touch each and every one of the Maidens and then took a deep breath.

"If there's one thing I can count on in life, it's my hula sisters. From the first sign of trouble when Kimo became a murder suspect, and then the Defector was murdered and suddenly I was a suspect, you were there for us. Two mornings ago, I called for your help, and you showed up to help me clear my name. Pat, Trish, and Suzi risked their own lives to save me from a terrible, terrible end, I'm sure. And then, last night, we stood shoulder to shoulder to help the KPD bring in the real murderer, Tom Benton. You were there through it all."

She paused and blinked her false eyelashes. "Well, *almost* all of you were there. You, Lillian, were too busy with your fan club, but that's okay. I understand. Really. That's ok-ay." She raised her glass. "So here's to all of you. Here's to us!"

"Ya!" Lars shouted. "Us goot!"

Behind the bar Em told Sophie, "I called Tiko and asked her to come in tomorrow morning while I take Louie in to the airport."

"Did he decide to take Letterman to Honolulu?" Sophie was topping off Sour Notes with lime wedges and cherries on plastic swords.

"No, I get the wonderful privilege of bird sitting." Em reached for more hurricane glasses and had her back to the room. "With any luck I'll keep all my fingers."

"Well, look who just walked in," Sophie said. "Maybe he'll offer to light your fire while Louie's off island."

Em turned around in time to see Roland head directly for the Maidens' table. The women started toasting him, and Kiki announced she had a wedding reception gig for him if he wanted to book it. It was impossible for Em not to notice he hadn't even looked her way.

"Talk to me about that later," he told Kiki. "I've got a little something to say to all of you."

"Uh, oh." Sophie set down the tray she was about to carry over to the table.

Roland towered over the seated women, who were all staring up at him in awe.

"Ladies, on behalf of the Kauai Police Department, I'd like to officially say *mahalo* for your part in ending the Princeville clubhouse standoff. We appreciate what each of you did to help, and there will be a more formal presentation in the near future."

There were more cheers and more toasting. Flora's glass was empty, and she was looking toward the bar with anticipation.

Roland raised his hand, and they all quieted down again.

"On a personal note," he looked at each of them in turn. "I'd like to say that even though there is no doubt that your efforts helped us end the standoff and hostage situation and bring in a dangerous criminal, under no circumstances," he glanced over at Em and then away, "under no circumstances do I condone any of you interfering in KPD investigations in the future, whether the events are connected to you directly or indirectly. To make myself perfectly clear, no more amateur detecting. No more. You are all *pau* with that. Got it?"

One by one they all slowly nodded. All but one.

"Kiki?" Roland stared at her until she met his eyes.

Kiki actually looked a bit sheepish, but Em guessed it was simply a well-practiced expression.

"Oh, okay, Roland. I've got it. All *pau*."

Satisfied, he nodded, then turned and headed for the bar, leaving them to polish off their drinks in silence. He surprised Em by sitting on a barstool directly in front of her. Feeling awkward, Em hesitated to say anything. An awkward silence ensued.

"What can I get you, detective?" Sophie stepped in to ask.

"An iced tea and a *mahi* sandwich."

"Fries?"

"Sure, why not?"

As soon as Sophie left to take the order into the kitchen, Roland turned to Em.

"I hope you were listening. That speech was meant for you, too."

"I figured," she said.

"Do you know how serious I am?"

"I think so." The *koa* wood bar was all that separated them, but she felt as if an ocean had come between them in the last couple of days.

He glanced over his shoulder at the Maidens. Kiki was on the phone, and the rest were leaning into the center of the table talking in hushed undertones, clearly discussing his ultimatum.

"You know, I'm not fired up just because that bunch is a menace to North Shore tranquility and each other, Em."

Thankfully, his expression wasn't as closed off and angry as it had been during the standoff. *If he was really so furious, would he have stayed for lunch?* she wondered.

"Do you want to know why I'm so upset?" he asked.

"Why?"

His stare made her nervous. She brushed her hair back behind her ear. He leaned forward and lowered his voice.

"I'm afraid one day you'll get in over your head, and I won't be there to save you."

She was so stunned by his honest expression of concern that she didn't know what to say.

"You don't want to know what I was thinking on way up here after the call went out that shots had been fired on the Princeville golf course, and I knew that you were somehow involved."

She shook her head. "But I wasn't. I didn't even know what Kiki was up to at that point."

"But if you had known before hand, you would have gotten dragged along on their little escapade even sooner. I know you're somehow under the impression that you tag along just to keep them out of trouble." He shook his head. "Let me tell you, that's impossible. Trouble finds that bunch faster than Flora can suck a Gatorade bottle dry. You're not invincible, Em."

She sighed. There wasn't any way she could argue with the truth.

Sophie shot Em an apologetic look for interrupting, set Roland's order, silverware, and a napkin on the bar in front of him then moved a bottle of ketchup closer. She walked away without a word.

"I'm sorry," Em said. "Really."

He hadn't picked up his *mahi* sandwich yet. She almost wished he'd break his stare, because she certainly couldn't look away from those dark eyes.

"How about we go out for dinner on Friday night?" His invitation startled her. "Maybe a movie if there's anything worth seeing. Or we can do anything else you'd like. Maybe go hear some Hawaiian music at Shutters."

"Seriously?"

He nodded. "A nice dinner. A real official date. The kind you go on with your neighbor. We will not discuss any police business, any murders, any clues, any suspects. Those subjects are off limits from now on."

Em knew she was grinning like an idiot, but she couldn't help it.

Finally Roland smiled, too.

"So? Is it a date?"

"It's a date."

"Good." He picked up his sandwich, nodded and said, "Good. Friday night then."

Across the room Kiki jumped to her feet and waved her cell phone over her head.

"Attention everyone! I just got a call from the Keep Kauai Mongoose Free organization. They've invited us to appear on their float in the King Kamehameha Day parade in June."

A cheer went up from the Maidens still seated around the table.

Kiki raised her hand for silence. "It gets even better! Someone from the county called and asked if we could 'possibly fit in some time' to appear in Puhi at the dedication of the new bus bench shelter!"

More screams and cheering. Little Estelle laid on the Gadabout horn.

Kiki shouted them down.

"The *mayor* is going to be there. You know that means a great photo op."

"Can you believe it?" Suzi joyfully waved jazz hands in the air.

"We're on our way!" Big Estelle shot her fist.

Lars lifted his head off the table and mumbled, "Ya! Ya!"

Kimo walked out of the kitchen and stood at the end of the bar smiling at Kiki. Then he winked at Em and Sophie.

"Congratulations, Hula Maidens," he called out. "Have another round on me."

"Really, Kimo?" Em envisioned a parking lot full of comatose Maidens sleeping it off in their cars.

"Water 'em down, eh?"

"You got it." Sophie started mixing Sour Notes in a tall plastic pitcher.

"I'd better get to work," Em told Roland. "Needless to say, things have been piling up around here. I've got a ton of potential catering job inquiries to return."

"No worries." He polished off his sandwich in four bites and had started on the fries. "Don't forget to put Friday on your calendar."

"For sure." She would rather stay and watch him dip fries into a puddle of ketchup than anything else in the world, but duty called.

Before she knew it she was in Louie's office. She must have floated in because her feet didn't seem to be touching the ground yet. She sat down in Louie's old office chair that squeaked when it swiveled and was sorting and stacking important messages when her uncle walked in the back door.

"What's all the screaming? I could hear them over at the house." He sat on the corner of the desk.

"Kiki just got some calls asking the Maidens to dance at two different venues. They're stoked. By the way, your new Sour Note cocktail is a hit."

"Hopefully the new creation for the Shake Off will be as well received."

"We sure have a lot of potential work here." Em indicated the desk. "I guess we can thank *Trouble in Paradise* for that if nothing else."

Louie sighed. "Speaking of the show, I just got a phone call from Randy Rich."

*Here it comes*, Em thought. "Don't tell me."

"The head of the network saw the standoff on national news last night, and they want back in. They're willing to negotiate a whole new contract for another season of *Trouble in Paradise*.

She stared at the file of receipts and phone messages on the desk. There were bills to pay, food and beverage distributors to meet. Em sighed and rubbed her temples, then smiled up at Louie. This was, after all, his bar and his business. She was only the manager.

"That's great," she said.

"You don't sound like you mean it."

She shrugged.

"I turned them down," he said.

"Really?" She was stunned. "Why?"

He stood up and looked around at the walls filled with photos of Irene and him over the years, photos of the two of them alone and others with celebrities and friends from all over the world.

"The Goddess is already famous. We're in every Hawaii guide book and Internet travel website," he said. "The production company will be running as many episodes as they can put together from the film they've already shot, so when it airs, we'll be riding the crest of that wave for months to come. How much is too much?" He obviously didn't need an answer, for he didn't wait for one. "Fame brought out the worst in all of us. I think we can live without it."

Beyond the office door, another cheer went up from the Maidens' table in the bar.

"Are you going to tell them Randy called?" Em asked.

Louie shook his head no. "Not today. Probably not ever."

"Thanks, Uncle Louie. I think that's for the best." No more cameras in her face, no more disruptions other than the norm. "Are you all packed for tomorrow?"

"Got everything ready. I'm looking forward to it. When I get back I'm going to focus on finding somebody who wants to publish the Booze Bible."

"Sounds great."

"You have any plans while I'm gone this weekend? I don't want to think about you sitting here behind this pile of work or alone watching TV with Letterman while I'm gallivanting around Honolulu."

She pictured Roland and smiled.

"Actually, I have a date on Friday night, and it's not with Letterman."

"Anybody I know?"

"Let's just say that with any luck, my evening might turn out to be as explosive as one of your Flaming Infernos."

# Drink Recipes

## Even More Tropical Libations from
## Uncle Louie's Booze Bible

### Final Cut

*Dedicated to the memory of Bobby Quinn, a young cameraman stabbed to death while filming Trouble in Paradise, the reality TV show based on the Tiki Goddess Bar and all the antics that go on there. Unfortunately the murder weapon, Chef Kimo's special sashimi knife, must remain in the Kauai Police Department's evidence files.*

Per cocktail you will need:
1/2 Fresh Squeezed Orange
2 oz Gin
Splash of Grenadine
Club Soda.

Glass: Uncle Louie uses a tall glass.

Mix first three ingredients in a tall glass over ice and pour in club soda.

### Pink Lilies

*Created by Sophie Chin, the Tiki Goddess' young bartender, in honor of a visit from Hula Maiden Lillian Smith's Official Fan Club from Iowa. Lillian's devoted fans dye their hair pink and wear it bouffant style just like Lillian. No fan of Lil's would be seen dead without her black "cat's eye" style rhinestone encrusted glasses.*

Per cocktail you will need:
Chilled Pink lemonade
Caribbean Lime or Coconut Flavored Rum.

Glass: Champagne Flute

Pour 2 oz. of your favorite flavored rum in a champagne flute
Fill with Chilled Pink Lemonade

## Frothy Fang

*Uncle Louie created this specialty to commemorate the day he lost the tip of his index finger, but Louie can't remember if he lost it to a pit bull on the Okolehau Trail above Hanalei, or if it was bitten off by an eel when he was snorkeling at Anini Beach! Either way, enjoy!*

Per Cocktail You Will Need:
3/4 oz. of Lemon Juice
1 oz. of Simple Syrup
1-1/2 oz. of Pineapple Juice
1-1/2 oz. of Whiskey

Glass: Tall Glass

Shake with ice in a cocktail shaker and strain into a tall glass full of crushed ice.


## Sour Note

*Who knew the Hula Maidens would save the day with their off-key renditions of* hapa-haole *melodies and "Ninety-nine Bottles of Beer on the Wall"? Uncle Louie created this one to celebrate their heroic action during the Princeville Standoff and Hostage Crisis for which the Maidens received special commendation from the KPD.*

Per Cocktail You Will Need:
2 oz. Sweet and Sour
1-1/2 oz. Tequila
1 oz. Cointreau

Glass: Cocktail or Margarita Glass

Shake all ingredients in a cocktail shaker rimmed with Li Hing Mui Salt, then drop a Li Hing Mui seed into the glass (To make Li Hing Mui Salt mix Li Hing powder with sea salt and sugar. If you can't find Li Hing Mui powder or seeds in grocery stores, you can order them on line. If you are too befuddled to try to find some, you can always use plain old margarita salt.)

# About Jill Marie Landis

JILL MARIE LANDIS has written over twenty-five novels which have earned distinguished awards and slots on such national bestseller lists as the USA TODAY Top 50 and the New York Times Best Sellers Plus. She is a seven-time finalist for Romance Writers of America's RITA Award in both Single Title and Contemporary Romance as well as a Golden Heart and RITA Award winner. She's written historical and contemporary romance, inspirational historical romance and she is now penning The Tiki Goddess Series which begins with MAI TAI ONE ON and TWO TO MANGO.

Visit her at thetikigoddess.com.

Made in the USA
Lexington, KY
29 July 2019